RELEVER

THE IRONSIDE SERIES

BOOK FOUR

JANE WASHINGTON

Washington, Jane
Relever

www.janewashington.com

ISBN: 979-8326778321

CONTENTS

Also by Jane Washington

Ironside Academy

Book 1: Plier

Book 2: Tourner

Book 3: Sauter

Book 4: Relever

Book 5: Glisser

A Tempest of Shadows

Book 1: A Tempest of Shadows

Book 2: A City of Whispers

Book 3: Dream of Embers

Book 4: A Castle of Ash

Book 5: A World of Lost Words

Bastan Hollow

Standalone: Charming

Standalone: Disobedience

Standalone Books

I Am Grey

Curse of the Gods

Book 1: Trickery

Book 2: Persuasion

Book 3: Seduction

Book 4: Strength

Novella: Neutral

Book 5: Pain

Seraph Black

Book 1: Charcoal Tears

Book 2: Watercolour Smile

Book 3: Lead Heart

Book 4: A Portrait of Pain

Beatrice Harrow

Book 1: Hereditary

Book 2: The Soulstoy Inheritance

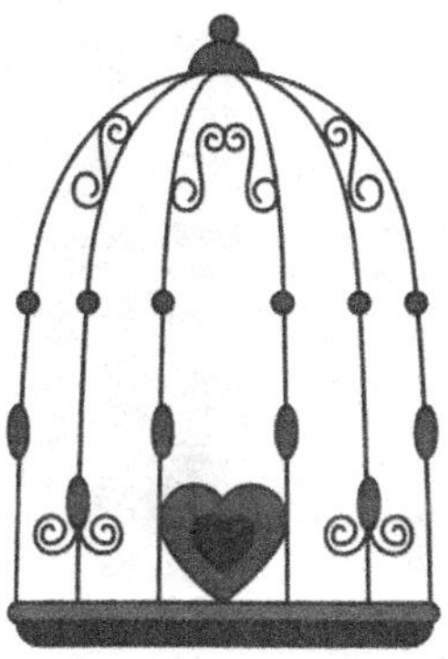

Oh, the horror of this nightmare scene,
Where broken wings twist and teem,
These little birds sing as they fly upstream,
While little men wait to bottle their screams.

TRIGGER WARNINGS

explicit (non-gory) physical and emotional torture

torture resulting in death *(not within main group)*

If you or anyone you know needs support, please visit lifeline.org.au.

CONTENT WARNING

This book will feature intense and explicit scenes involving the exploration of boundaries and power dynamics within intimate, consenting, adult relationships.

While all intimate scenes written in this book are considered—by the characters—to be consensual, please be aware that there may be scenes where consent has not been expressly given in a clear verbal manner.

These scenes are intended for adult readers, and they may be triggering or uncomfortable for some individuals.

Reader discretion is advised.

DISCLAIMER

Not any ol' balls will do.

This will make sense later.

Ironside Academy Map

To view the map of Ironside, please scan the QR code below.

IRONSIDE ACADEMY PLAYLIST

To listen to the playlist for the Ironside series, please scan the QR code below.

Ironside Academy Cheat Sheet

To view the character cheat sheet for the Ironside series, please scan the QR code below.

I

THIS KIND OF SHITSHOW

"Up!"

The command was a sudden boom of bitten sound. An order from a master to their well-trained dog. It was accompanied by a pounding sound that hammered through Isobel's head and jolted her into consciousness.

Her heart vaulted into her throat and her legs darted out from beneath the covers that weighed her down as she tried to roll off her mat of blankets on the floor.

Instead, she found herself *falling* ... from a real bed.

The ground rushed up to meet her face and she sprawled with a painful thud, a husky groan slipping from her lips as she placed her cheek on the cool wood and stared toward the other side of the room—where the pounding noise was coming from.

What the hell was going on?

Where *was* she?

The floor was polished, patterned parquetry. There was a familiar divot by her knee, reminding her of when her father had thrown a phone at her. It had missed, perhaps deliberately, chipping the surface instead.

"Get out here, Isobel!" The voice behind the door shouldn't have been a shock—not with the familiar floor of her childhood bedroom staring back at her—but she flinched at her father's impatient bark all the same, curling into a ball, cradling her bruised knees, and staring at the door the way a cornered, wild animal tracks their aggressor through waving thatches of forest undergrowth.

She knew the look of a cornered animal. She knew it from those nature documentaries, and she knew it from her reflection in the mirror. It was the way she had stared at that same door, in that same way, a million times before. Her brain was still catching up, but her muscles remembered exactly what to do. She watched and waited, barely breathing, her chest barely moving.

He didn't force his way inside. Not yet.

What had she done now?

Did she deny him?

Defy him?

Disappoint him?

His heavy, lumbering footsteps retreated, and only then did she glance around the room.

Her room.

Her room in her father's penthouse in Nevada.

Her hands shot to her pockets, shaking and fumbling at the unfamiliar material. She glanced down. The jacket she wore was Mikel's. She had seen him in it several times. She began to yank down the zipper.

Why was she wearing Mikel's—

She froze, her eyes widening on her bloodstained dress. No. Her blood-*drenched* dress.

And her fingers, now freed from the overly long sleeves.

They were caked with cracked, dried blood.

The trembling grew worse, and she tried to stand, but her legs collapsed, her head spinning dizzily. There was another—more polite—knock against the door.

"Carter? Can I come in?"

For a moment, her mind went blank, and then it kicked back into gear, spinning overtime.

Bellamy?

Adam Bellamy?

"W-what the h-hell?" she croaked, her thoughts still tripping and tumbling over each other in an attempt to catch up to what was happening.

Her father wanted a movie deal.

He had made a deal with Bellamy's father.

Bellamy would be her surrogate.

Mikel had intervened.

She had ... stood up for herself. *Against her father*. For the first time in her life.

Where was Mikel now?

Even without Mikel there to protect her, she wasn't sure she could go back to cowering before Braun Carter. She had stepped over the line he had worked her entire life to bully her behind, and there was no going back.

The door cracked open, and Bellamy stepped inside, his eyes widening on her, snapping from her stricken face to her blood-stained fingers as they clutched her knees.

She was already cowering.

Her mind refused to be afraid, but her body hadn't yet received the message.

"What the fuck?" Bellamy took two hasty steps forward, and she scooted back along the side of her bed, holding her hands up sharply. "J-just stay where you are!"

He halted, his mossy gaze darting between her hands. "Your dad didn't say you were injured in the shooting."

The shooting.

That was what happened after she stood up to her father.

She had been so happy. Deliriously happy, after dancing with Gabriel and Elijah. It was the lightest she had felt in years, certainly since being separated from her mother. It had felt like she belonged somewhere. Like she had people she cared about, who might just care about her in return. Until the sound of *pop pop popping* brought her fragile hope crashing down hard enough to shake her foundation.

And then the screaming started, and her foundation cracked.

Then there was the look of fear in Cian's eyes as he fought to get to her, and the crushing weight of the crowd as they shoved her further away.

The crack turned into a chasm.

And then ...

And then ...

All of a sudden, she found it hard to breathe. The air lodged into a tight ball halfway up her throat, threatening to choke her.

Bellamy glanced around nervously, like something might jump out at him as useful—a tool to calm her down, or a clue to understand the situation—before he spun on his heel. "I'll get your dad."

"No!" she hissed, suddenly reaching out to him instead of warding him away with bloodstained palms.

He paused, his back to her, and when he turned again, there was more than a little caution in his eyes. If she was prey in the woods, then he was the entitled hunter who had just realised he was trespassing on someone else's grounds and had encountered someone else's prey. She wrapped her arms around herself.

"Carter, you have to tell me what the hell is going on," he said, closing the door.

For a moment, she wondered if she had just traded one monster for another.

Crowe had brought a gun to Ironside. Crowe had tried to kill her.

Crowe was Bellamy's friend.

"I'm not hurt," she mumbled distractedly, staring him down.

But other people were.

People were killed.

Crowe had been killed.

By ... her?

Meaty fists pounded against her delicate skull, rattling her foggy memories around and making them hard to examine.

Bellamy kept his distance, his hand rubbing agitatedly along the back of his neck. "Whose blood is that?" he finally asked, waving at her dress.

"Nobody's." She quickly zipped up Mikel's jacket. "How long has it been since ..." Her mouth went dry, the words dying off on a choked sound. She couldn't say it.

"The shooting? Yesterday?" He finally decided to sit on the ground a few paces away from her. "Are you sure you're not hurt?"

"I'm sure. Don't pretend we're friends." She searched the pockets of Mikel's jacket. "Where's my phone?"

"Your dad said you lost it. I tried texting you a few times to let you know my dad wasn't letting me pull out.

I thought maybe something happened to you, you know … so I asked my dad to call yours."

"You should have tried harder," she spat.

"I should have succeeded where you failed, you mean?" he bit back, his cheeks blushing with a thin wash of pink. "That's a bit rich."

He was right, and she hated it.

"Did you actually try to get out of this?" She peered at him, lowering her walls slightly to taste his emotion.

Confusion. Apprehension. Pity.

"I did," he sighed. "I figured it was the least I owed you. I swear I didn't know about Crowe dragging you behind Dorm A. I mean … I had my suspicions. We've been fighting about it since I found some really creepy pictures in his room. But I didn't *know*. I would never encourage anything like what he did."

"He's—" Her voice cracked, and she had to clear it. "—done a lot. You're going to have to be more specific."

Bellamy glanced up, sorrow flitting across his expression, and she realised her walls were still cracked when his grief washed up against her.

And his guilt.

"I had *no* idea he had a gun." Bellamy's voice was hoarse. "But I should have paid more attention. I thought icing him out of the group would solve the whole situation … but anyway, he's dead now."

Her eyes snapped to his, and he frowned, misreading

the torment that was digging into her features with hot, bloody claws.

"You didn't know?" Bellamy shook his head. "He barricaded himself in the chapel when he heard the sirens. The place burned down. We still don't know what exactly happened. Some people are saying he did it deliberately, and some are saying it was an accident. Apparently there was no evidence of anyone else having been in there. So either someone killed him and then covered their tracks really well—which is impossible with how quickly everything happened. Unless there was a whole team of people there to make sure there was no evidence left behind, but this is Ironside we're talking about, not a spy movie. So I guess he just wanted to burn himself to death. Maybe he thought that was better than getting caught by the—" He glanced at the door. "Better than getting caught."

She dropped her attention to her folded legs, jolting when a door slammed elsewhere in the apartment, her entire body curling in on itself.

Bellamy watched her, his light green gaze flitting across her cowering body, the silver Beta ring making his eyes appear almost frosty. "Your dad said he had to get to a meeting."

Her father was gone. Nobody else would have dared to storm out of his apartment that way.

She rose to her feet, catching herself against the edge of the bed as a dizzy spell overtook her. Bellamy also stood, shoving his hands into his pockets instead of reaching out to help her.

Smart of him.

"I have to find my phone," she croaked, moving to the door.

"Guess I'll help." He followed, pausing when she did.

She had turned to stare at him, her mouth pursing, her brows pinching in.

He pushed elegant brows up, his posh accent deepening into something that might have been an insulted tone. "I'm just as stuck here as you are, Carter. Give it a damn rest."

"Fine," she bit out. "But don't touch me."

"Why the hell would I touch you?"

"Just making sure you didn't have the wrong idea about this surrogate thing." She flung the door wide, inviting him to come with her, and stalked down the hall.

"Seriously?" He trailed her lazily. "I think you have enough of those and last time someone tried to touch you, Golden Boy Kane burst into Dorm B and broke like five of his bones and landed him in hospital."

She couldn't think about Crowe—or even Theodore—so she just swallowed past the bile that tried to rise in her throat and peered into the rooms branching off from the hallway. They were all unoccupied, but she could hear a male voice speaking faintly from the direction of the breakfast room. She put a finger to her lips, glancing at Bellamy, who gave her a confused nod in acknowledgement, and then she moved quietly toward the kitchen.

There was a delicate, frosted glass sliding door leading from the kitchen into the breakfast room. She leaned gently against the wall beside the door, inching it open to peer through.

Cesar Cooper, the manager her father had forced her to sign with, sat at the marbled bar, looking down at the city skyline, distracted by a call, headphones plugged into his ears as he glared at his phone resting on the surface before him. He had a coffee and a scotch, one in each hand, and he kept diverting his attention from his screen to consider his options, attempting to decide which one to drink. There was nobody else in the room. She eased back, closed the door again, and backtracked to her parents' room.

No ... her *father's* room.

She opened the door and stepped inside, the familiar sight making her throat tighten in sorrow.

Wrong again.

It was still her parents' room.

Still the bedsheets her mother had picked out.

Still her hand cream and lip balm on the nightstand.

Still a dog-eared book she likely never had the chance to finish, waiting patiently to be thumbed through.

Isobel crept around the side of the bed, sucking in a breath. The silk slippers were there, *right there*, waiting for her mother to drift out of the sheets and slide her feet in with practiced ease.

"Where is your mom, anyway?" Bellamy asked, surveying the room from the doorway.

Isobel swallowed. "Gone." She filtered the fresh outpouring of grief away, right on top of the horror of what she had done to Crowe, and the panic that threatened to overwhelm her at being separated from her mate—her Alph—no, not *her* anything.

The Alphas.

Or her friends? Her group?

Fuck it.

She locked it all up tight, labels and all.

It didn't feel like it would hold for long, but it would do for now.

"I'm sorry," Bellamy offered quietly.

She nodded without looking at him and began searching the room, barely noticing when he joined in, hesitantly opening a drawer here and there. When they had searched everything, she went back to her own room, just in case she had missed it, but it quickly became obvious that she hadn't. Frustration threatened to explode inside her, and she dragged her hands through her hair before pausing, the red stain on her skin sending her over the edge.

"Gonna ... gonna be sick." She pushed into her bathroom, tumbling to the toilet and shoving the seat up, her stomach heaving violently.

"Bloody hell." Bellamy stood in her bedroom, shifting uncomfortably as she vomited. "Maybe you do need a surrogate."

She dragged herself back to the door and kicked it closed in his face before crawling back to the toilet, tears now tracking unheeded down her cheeks.

"Was it ... one of the Alphas?" Bellamy's voice carried through the door. "I know you were close to some of them. Is that why you're covered in blood?"

"N-no!" The word was almost a scream, and she fell back against the wall, sweat gathering to mix with her tears as she began to panic. "No ..." It was a whimper this time. "They're fine." *Please be fine.*

She dragged her knees up, her head hanging between them as she tried to think clearly.

"Oh. Okay." Bellamy shifted against the door. "You can borrow my phone if you want?"

Her head snapped up, and she forced herself to her feet, shoving down her emotion once again as she flushed the toilet. She quickly rinsed her mouth and wobbled back to the door, wrenching it open. Bellamy was already holding out his phone, but he frowned as she tried to reach for it with blood-caked fingers. She flexed her fingers into fists, shoved up the sleeves of Mikel's jacket, and spun back to the sink, scrubbing at her arms until her skin was pink for a different reason.

She dried her hands and Bellamy unlocked his phone for her, but then she was just holding it and staring at it.

She didn't have any of their numbers memorised.

They didn't even have individual social media accounts, only a group one, called Dorm A. It made sense, now that she knew their plan to win the Ironside game as a group.

She frowned, chewing on her lip before opening one of Bellamy's social media accounts and searching for Dorm A. Bellamy peered over her shoulder, and they both waited for it to load.

It was taking too long.

She cursed, flicking out of it, and opening another.

That one wouldn't load either.

"No service," Bellamy noted, a frown in his voice as he pointed to the top of his phone. Then he straightened, his eyes widening, a strangled sound catching in the back of his throat. "He wouldn't."

"He who?" She whirled on him, panic making her skin itch. "Wouldn't what? Why won't your phone work?"

"My dad." His throat worked, a lump moving up and down beneath smooth, pale skin. "I think ..." He snatched his phone off her, tapping away at it furiously before groaning, his hands falling to his sides helplessly. "He cancelled my service."

"Why would he do that?" Her voice had risen to a shrill level.

"At Carter's request." The voice came from the doorway to her bedroom, and they both whipped to face

Cooper, who leaned in the open frame, small brown eyes flicking between her and Bellamy. "Good to see you're finally awake, Isobel."

"It's Carter," she corrected thinly.

"No." He chuckled, low and slow. Condescending and indulgent. Like he thought she was awfully small and cute. "That would be your father, young lady. I'm afraid you just missed him. He couldn't wait around any longer."

"He didn't wait that long." Bellamy sounded confused, already tucking his frustration away as he glanced at a gleaming silver watch with a sapphire face. It seemed to be a deliberate reminder. Bellamy wasn't a settlement kid, he was an Icon kid, riches and all.

Cooper levelled him with a flat, unimpressed look, before digging into the pocket of his vest. He held out a little pill bottle, shaking it at Isobel like she was a dog and he had some treaties for her.

"He left these for you. You won't be getting extra surrogates this time. You need to take one of these every day."

"I need a phone." She ignored the pill bottle, keeping her attention steadfast on his face. "It's urgent."

"Sorry, sweetheart." He smacked his lips together. "That's in the safe. You have everything you need right here. And if there's anything else you require." He spread his thin arms, his mouth stretching wide beneath a moustache he had started to grow over the past few months. "I'm at your service."

Black spots flashed before her vision and she stumbled, catching herself against the solid, wrought iron end of her bed frame.

"Carter?" Bellamy appeared at her side, his hand reaching for her elbow, but he stopped short of touching her. "You good? Do *not* do that teleporting thing and leave me here alone please." He shot Cooper a quick look. "No offense, dude."

Cooper let out a jovial laugh, waving his hand. "Oh, no need to worry about that. This new version of the surrogate pill takes care of all those nasty side effects. We already gave her a double dose through an IV when she arrived."

Panic. So much panic. She was *dizzy* with it. There didn't seem to be any way to hold it all inside her body.

"How?" she croaked, unable to focus on anything. Her trepidation was a maelstrom, filling her head with a too-fast swirl of white noise and blurred, worst-case scenarios.

How long could she survive without them? Were the pills enough?

"We had a nurse drop by." Cooper's tone suggested she should have guessed as much already. "You were covered in blood. Carter was concerned you might be injured."

"Then why didn't he check me himself?" she gritted between clenched teeth.

Cooper ignored her question, tugging his phone from another vest pocket and tapping away at the screen.

She stared at the device in his hand, wondering if she could overpower him and wrestle it out of his grip. Likely not, in her current state.

"You've got the rest of the day to help your new surrogate settle in," Cooper told her, unaware of the desperate way she sized up his phone. "But we've got a full schedule tomorrow. You need to refresh your birth control—can't have you barefoot and pregnant before you win the game." He glanced up at her, his moustache twitching. "Can we?"

She just stared at him.

Bellamy shifted his weight to his other foot, looking uncomfortable again.

Finally, Cooper returned his attention to his phone. "We also need to visit the stylist to take new measurements for the assistants to plan your wardrobe for your third year." He glanced at her again, his eyes trailing her body. He breathed in deeply, rolling his lips together and making an appreciative sound. "Yes, that's a must. Then you have a laser maintenance appointment. The rest of the evening, your father expects you to record videos for social media."

"She's going to need a phone for that," Bellamy noted calmly, and for the first time, she felt a spark of gratitude for him, because she hadn't been thinking clearly enough about what Cooper was saying.

"There's already a camera set up. One of my assistants will handle the recordings and post them for you. This week we also have you booked in for a haircut, a teeth-whitening appointment, your first injection of Botox, and an initial consultation with a plastic surgeon." He seemed to flick to a different list on his phone before peering at her again. "How attached are you to those freckles? Skin bleaching is an option."

Bellamy whistled low beneath his breath.

Isobel was at a complete loss for words, but she shouldn't have been. She knew how her father operated. He always won. Always got his way. He bullied and twisted the rules until everyone was crushed beneath the weight of his influence.

He was an Icon, after all.

This was what she got for standing up to him. He would be sure to whittle away at her until she was nothing more than the puppet he had intended—cut, polished, lasered, primed, and laced up in designer clothes, ready to represent the Carter name. Someone worthy to be called his daughter, despite her inferior Sigma rank.

"Right." Cooper sniffed, absorbing her shell-shocked expression. "You can think about it later. I think the first order of business is a bath—"

"Get out." She pointed behind him, over his shoulder, her finger trembling.

"You're weak." His mouth tightened into a thin line. "Your father left you in my care and the nurse has already been sent—"

"OUT!" she screamed, her voice breaking off at the end, her entire body beginning to tremble.

"I'll help her." Bellamy quickly stepped in front of her and then walked toward the door, somehow shepherding Cooper backward, though he managed to do it in a casual sort of way. "I need to start surrogating at some point," he said with a jovial tone. "Might as well crack on with it." And then he shut the door in Cooper's annoyed face.

He leaned back against it, his head shaking slowly back and forth. It sounded like he was cursing under his breath. He turned, put his ear to the door, and then seemed to relax, his shoulders inching down. He pushed both hands through his wavy chocolate hair, the skin around his eyes tight.

"The hell kind of shitshow did that asshole drop me into?" he grumbled.

She had no idea if he was talking about her father or his own.

"We can't stay here. *I* can't stay here." She darted her attention around the room, the tremble in her limbs only abating somewhat, her gaze wide and lost. She didn't know what to do with herself.

"Sure you can." Bellamy shrugged, but his mouth was pulled down at the corners. "You have a surrogate." He waved at his own chest. "And those pills that stop your side effects—why haven't I heard of those, by the way? Cooper said they were new, I think? Shouldn't that be all over the news? Is that why I had to sign a nondisclosure? But anyway, I mean Cooper is a creep and all, but I just won't leave you alone with him and everything will be fine, right?"

She was going to have a complete breakdown.

"S-sure," she managed, trying to shove it all away.

She shoved and shoved, and it just kept rolling back over her, tumbling down onto her head like an overfull closet stuffed with one shoebox too many. She pushed the mess in, and it collapsed outward until she was buried, fatigued, and drowning in the piles of her own panic.

"You don't understand," she croaked. "I need ..."

What could she possibly say?

Technically, he was *right*.

The whole world thought she had survived on surrogates this long, and there was no reason she couldn't continue to survive on surrogates.

And then there were the pills.

"I know I'm not an Alpha." His expression pinched inward. "But Betas are powerful too."

What aren't you telling me? His voice pushed into her

head, echoing around like a silky whisper, attempting to illustrate his power.

She flinched back, scowling at him. "Nothing. You're right. It's not like I don't think I'll survive or anything." *Lie.* "This is about letting my father poke me and prod me and cut me and *bleach* me until there is no 'me' left. It's about how he has abused me my entire life, and when he's not abusing me, he's neglecting me and handing me off to be abused by someone else." She pointed accusingly at the door, her vision clearing with the outburst of emotion. "And stay the fuck out of my head, Bellamy."

"Fine." He raised his hands in supplication.

Damn. That felt good.

"I'm not *doing* this anymore!" She wanted to scream. To rage. To hurl things about the room until someone *listened* to her and *did* something about it.

"You don't have to." Bellamy's lips twitched like he was considering giving her a wan smile—it was there in his cool eyes, but it didn't quite make it to his mouth. "Your father can make all the appointments he wants, but no surgeon is going to operate without *your* permission. We can make it through this, Carter. I promise. It's just for the summer break."

She fell back, sitting on the edge of her bed as she stared at him. "Why would you help me?" she demanded flatly. "You hate me, remember?"

He rolled his eyes. "Grow up. I certainly did."

"You're not even going to apologise?" she pressed. "You're just going to blame the way you treated me on immaturity and hope I forget about it?"

His expression fell into something stern and droll, his tone lightly cutting. "Your father didn't try to make you ruthless? Imagine how hard he would have tried if he thought you were actually *capable* of it. I didn't grow up in the settlements holding hands with everyone and singing camp songs. I grew up thinking I was the most important kid in the world, and everyone was beneath me. It took me a couple of years at Ironside to learn that I wasn't, but I did learn."

She felt her mouth tugging up a little, wry humour flashing in her eyes despite how she wanted to pull it back behind a curtain of disdain. "I suppose that's as good an apology as I'm going to get."

"I'm sorry, Carter." He frowned, a wince racing across his face as he brushed both hands through his hair again. "I'm not good at apologies. I'm much better at plans and scheming, so just accept the help."

"In exchange for what?" she asked plainly.

"Damn." He chuckled. "Ironside's done a number on you too, eh? I'm well aware that I have no chance at being the winning Icon. Not with the way things stand at the moment. Eight Alphas and you, with your mysterious mate. Unless I discover a mate of my own or the Alphas decide to drop out, I might as well accept my fate. There's nothing you can give me right now."

"So you want a favour, for later?"

He shook his head. "Sure. Why not?"

"All right." She nodded. Those were terms she could live with. "If you really want to help me, then help me get a phone. I ... you're right. I have grown close to some of the Alphas, and I have no idea what happened to them after the shooting. I have to make sure they're all right."

"I can help with that," he said, angling his head to give her a serious look. "But are you sure they aren't using you?" He displayed his palms in supplication at her murderous look. "I'm just saying, if this whole 'Sigma and the Alphas' thing is a publicity stunt, I wouldn't be surprised to find out your dad arranged it somehow."

"If my father arranged it, then why are *you* here?" she groused.

"He could be double dipping." Bellamy shrugged. "I've seen all the clips, read all the debates online about you guys. I just ... I'm not buying it, that's all. Not with—what? Three of them?—acting interested in you. Alphas don't share. Everyone knows that."

"Which three?" she asked.

He stared at her, frowning, and then he burst into laughter. "You're serious, aren't you?"

"I try not to read the comments anymore."

He rolled his eyes, apparently finding her aversion to being in the spotlight weary. "I'm talking about Kane, Sato, and Ashford."

Theodore, Oscar, and Cian?

"Oh." She picked at her nails. "Interesting."

"Is it?" He smirked at her.

"Not really."

"You're kind of ... unemotional," he noted, pinching his chin as he looked down at her. "Can Sigmas do the emotion-sucking thing on themselves?"

"No." She sighed, dropping onto her bed. "Only dickheads like you."

"I prefer the trembly, stuttering Carter from first year," he declared, sitting at her desk. "Bring her back, will you?"

"I would say that I prefer when you were punchable, but I guess not much has changed."

"Oh, a sense of humour. Delightful. Where've you been hiding that?"

She shook her head, but her lips almost twitched. "Shut up, Bellamy."

"No. Let's get to know each other, since we'll be ... living together—where am I sleeping, by the way? Your dad said I'd be staying in here with you, but there's only one bed."

"The floor," she said immediately. "The hallway. The bathtub, I don't care."

"More humour. Less delightful."

"I was being serious."

"I don't get it," he suddenly declared, looking like he wanted to laugh. "The appeal. I don't get why you have three Alphas chasing after you, Carter. You're dry as a bone."

"Not around—" She paused, pressing her fist to her mouth, her eyes wide on the ceiling.

"Oh my god." Bellamy's feet, which had stretched out to notch against the chaise along the end of her bed, dropped, and he leaned forward. "You were about to say not around them, weren't you?"

She made a choking sound behind her fist. Despite the panic. Despite the dizziness. Despite the potentially *dire* situation. She was trying not to *laugh*.

Maybe Bellamy wasn't so bad after all.

"Okay," he said, kicking his feet back up again. "I get it now. You're just a ... how do I put this politely? A sexually prolific Alpha fangirl like all the rest of them?"

"A slut for Alphas?" She deadpanned. "Seriously?"

"Your words, not mine." He grinned at her.

She picked up one of her pillows and tossed it at his head.

2

DE-ESCALATING PRIVILEGES

"Overkill, don't you think?" Bellamy asked as a black van pulled up to the front of the building. He was casting his eyes over the group of people Isobel's father had stuck them with for the day. "Your dad still hasn't come to see you himself, but you need three stylists, a manager, a manager's assistant, and—what are you?" He aimed the question at a man Isobel didn't recognise.

"Driver," the man grunted, rounding the van.

"More like parole officer." Bellamy sniffed, yanking open the van door and motioning Isobel inside.

They had spoken the night before as Bellamy stretched out on the long chaise they had moved up against the window, as far away from the bed as they could shove it, heaping it with blankets to make it more comfortable. As it turned out, Bellamy was *quite* the spoiled little rich boy and he complained endlessly about his new arrangement, though he refused to take her bed and displace her to the chaise.

As they had whispered to each other in the darkness, they had decided that the best plan would be to wait until they were rushing between appointments to try and get their hands on a new phone.

Easier said than done, apparently.

Cooper's team watched them like circling hawks, never leaving them alone or allowing Bellamy to sneak off while she was busy with her appointments. One of Cooper's assistants even stood inside the room with Isobel for her laser hair removal session.

The next day was the same, with Isobel shuffled from appointment to appointment, both of them monitored constantly.

The days dragged into weeks, with Isobel's strength decreasing at an alarming rate. She was unable to explain why she was suddenly so weak, why she seemed to need more than the pills, more than a single surrogate, more than the combination her father kept declaring to be overkill.

She couldn't explain why none of it was working, and if Teak was trying to contact her through her father, she wasn't hearing about it.

Isobel slumped down on her stool, her throat coated in acid and her stomach roiling, even though she had already thrown up that morning.

"Everyone is always talking about how strong your mate must be." Bellamy was hunched over at the breakfast bar, flicking through his phone with a severe frown—he liked to make sure it still wasn't connected every morning. "They say that's how you survived after the Vermont attack, and it's why you need so many Alpha surrogates. I always thought it was stupid. I thought you didn't *need* them, you were just taking advantage—and they were too." He pushed his phone away in disgust, leaning back and cutting her a sideways look. "Seemed like such a brilliant stunt. Too insane to be true. Television gold."

Neither of them had touched the breakfast Cooper had ordered up to the apartment.

"You should eat," Bellamy prompted when she didn't respond to him. His voice was almost gentle, though the severe frown still twisted his lips.

"Not hungry." Isobel stared down at her plate with a sniffle, which quickly turned into a sneeze, and then another, and then another.

She swiped a tissue—she had taken to carrying boxes of them around—and blew her swollen nose. Her throat tickled with the action, causing her to descend into a coughing fit, which then set her head pounding in a vicious staccato. Shoving her food away, she slumped forward onto folded arms with a pained groan.

She was so *tired.*

ADAM BELLAMY WAS AT A LOSS.

The Sigma wasn't in a good way, and he was growing increasingly uncomfortable in the penthouse apartment. Her father had slammed her up against the wall and almost choked her when she refused to go to her breast augmentation appointment. They had been fighting about surgery *often*, and it always ended in a bruised Sigma with murder flashing in those weird eyes of hers as she flounced off to her room, refusing to let her massive Alpha father stamp the fight out of her.

Except for the rare occasion when she seemed too weak, too sick, and the fire in her was extinguished.

Those nights broke his heart because he could see how it must have been for her before Ironside taught her to fight back. He thought of the Sigma he met in their first year, the one who could barely meet his eyes, and something sickening clenched inside his chest.

He never considered himself very soft or emotional, but it was hard to hear her crying into her pillow, rasping and gasping for breath because her throat was already swollen, and Braun had made it worse by grabbing her too tightly.

And then there was that Sigma power.

At first, Adam didn't understand what was happening when she would stumble and groan without Braun ever laying a hand on her. He didn't understand why he had to carry her back to her room after Braun stalked away, leaving her depleted and crumpled on the ground without so much as touching her, like their argument had emotionally drained her to the point of collapsing.

He didn't understand why it took so long for her to open her eyes again, and why she sometimes shook so hard he could see her blankets trembling.

Until one night, when she began to suck away all of his confusion and concern, still bleary-eyed and groaning in pain, hugging her arms around her chest as he laid her down. She didn't even seem to be aware of what she was doing; she was so out of it.

He finally understood that night.

Her father was drowning her in his negative emotional shit, somehow forcing it on her.

Adam had thought Sigmas were powerless—or else useless—because they never seemed to help anyone out. He didn't realise it affected them so badly. He probably should have.

"Shut up," she groaned, swatting her hand out behind her.

"What?" He swallowed, pulled from his thoughts. He glanced behind them at the empty dining table. "I didn't say anything."

"*Notttyou*," she slurred, closing her eyes. "Talking to Grandpa. Just need a little ... nap ..."

Adam straightened in his stool, his eyes sweeping the room properly.

Grandpa?

Shit.

Was she losing it now?

The sliding door swooped open, the delicate mottled glass shivering in its frame as Braun stepped into the room.

Adam slipped off his seat, looping an arm around Isobel and quickly picking her up, just so that Braun wouldn't touch her. It wasn't that he liked the girl or anything—he enjoyed having his balls attached to his body. He just didn't particularly enjoy giant Alphas tossing around tiny Sigmas.

Adam's father was an asshole, *sure*, but he didn't beat Adam's little brother or sister just because he was three times their size. His father believed in fair fights.

Adam also believed in fair fights. That was why he had left her alone after realising she wasn't going to stand up for herself or fight back. He had assumed, with her being the only other Icon kid, that she would be competing directly with him.

But she never gave a shit about him.

"She's sick," Adam explained as Braun just stood there with thick arms crossed and a brow twitching up in silent question. "I was going to take her back to her room."

Isobel's head lolled on his shoulder, a small noise slipping out of her lips. "Shut," she mumbled, probably still trying to tell her imaginary grandpa to shut up.

Braun fell to the side a step, almost giving Adam room to pass him and escape ... but not quite.

"Your father wants me to send him more footage for your content team to post." Braun sounded annoyed. "Apparently, several hours a day isn't enough. He needs *variety*."

"If you hadn't made it a condition that he deactivate my phone plan, I'd be able to post endless content," Adam returned dryly. "It would be *quite* varied."

Braun didn't seem amused, his expression remaining unchanged, his arms still tightly crossed. Eventually, he reached for his phone, holding it up to start recording without a word of warning. Adam's posture stiffened, but he worked to smooth the frown from his features, schooling his expression into a careful, blank mask.

"Carter is sick," he explained to the camera, holding the Sigma just a little further away from his body. She was light as air. He was pretty sure she had lost weight.

Fuck. The fucking Alphas were probably going to see this video.

He *really* liked his balls attached to his body.

Usually, the content they uploaded was just Adam

singing while Carter danced. Sometimes, she attempted to teach him her dance routines, and sometimes, he convinced her to sing with him. They got along, and that surprised him, but still ... they trained hard all night in the dining room so that they wouldn't have to interact in front of the camera.

It was too difficult to force a smile and a good attitude with Cooper and his assistants checking on them every five minutes. It was much easier to be panting from exertion, frowning in concentration, or wincing from overextending.

But this ... this was different.

"She's, ah, not doing great," he continued, summoning a drawn expression to his features and drooping his shoulders with an exhausted sigh. "She's used to more than one surrogate. We've been trying to hide how tired she is from you guys, but ..."

Please let those crazy assholes see this.

He couldn't say too much in front of Braun, or the giant Alpha would just turn around and take out all his anger on Carter.

Braun circled his finger in the air, annoyance in his brown eyes, telling Adam to wrap up the sob story and move on to a different topic.

"Anyway." Adam swallowed, forcing a tremulous smile. "We've been having some trouble connecting—" He paused there deliberately, pretending to adjust Carter in his arms. "—with the latest song we've been practicing. I don't think it's for us. She's probably faking this to get out of it. I should go put her to bed. I don't think her vitamins are working."

Please be watching. Please read between the lines.

He didn't know why the Alphas magically worked for her unformed bond, but it was clear they did. They did, and *he* didn't, but Braun acted like the side-effects were something he dealt with every day, something he had seen a million times before, and he was utterly unconcerned.

Carter had been concerned since the very first day of the break. She had known this would happen. She had tried to hide it, tried to brush off her own strange behaviour and explain away her own inexplicable panic, but he had seen it. And now he knew it was justified. She had known the pills wouldn't work for her. She had known that *Adam* wouldn't work for her.

If he could just get the attention of the Alphas, somehow, maybe Carter could go back to being normal.

Braun rolled his eyes at Adam's explanation for the camera, but he moved out of the way, following to capture what appeared to be a tender moment as Adam lowered Carter into her bed. He didn't feel particularly tender, but he still pulled the covers up to her chin and stood there staring down at her in fake contemplation until Braun left.

. . .

CIAN PULLED HIS PHONE FROM HIS POCKET HALF A SECOND before it vibrated, already tapping his brother's shoulder to silence the TV in the living room.

He knew what the notification was.

He always knew when it was her. Isobel. Or *him*. Bellamy. He never thought he would *ever* spend so much mental energy keeping tabs on Adam fucking Bellamy, but there he was, with social media alerts set up and every psychic bone in his body attached to the thought of them.

Every single day, he pulled the *Eight of Swords*, which depicted a kneeling, blindfolded woman with a ring of swords piercing the dirt around her. No matter which deck he used, it was always the same card, and while sometimes the illustration was different, he always felt the same cold sensation when he touched the silky surface of the cards.

Logan hit the Mute button, startling their dad and stepmother, but all three of them stayed silent as Cian clicked on the new notification. Elijah had somehow managed to set up alerts to all their phones whenever Bellamy or Isobel—or whoever was controlling their accounts—posted. They were even getting google alerts for any news articles mentioning them.

"What the fuck?" Cian spluttered, unfurling from the couch in a sharp twitch of movement, both hands gripping his phone tightly as he turned it sideways, enlarging the video to take up the whole screen.

The Beta boy clearly had a death wish, because he was *touching* Isobel. Even when they danced together, they were very careful not to touch. Cian had seen all the comments on their videos asking if Bellamy was a "real" surrogate or a publicity stunt, because he didn't seem very close to Isobel.

Perhaps one of their fathers had forced this little scene on them to quell the rumours.

"Carter is sick." Bellamy's posh accent filled Cian's tiny family living room. Logan jumped up, peering at Cian's phone. Cian could see his parents trading a guarded look from his periphery.

They were all careful not to ask about Isobel, especially after Cian spent the first two weeks back in his settlement exercising excessively, snapping at every unfortunate soul who looked his way and snarling "do *something*" at anyone who would answer his calls. He watched as Bellamy's eyes flicked over the camera to whoever was holding it, suddenly switching topics.

Cian's teeth pressed together as the Beta adjusted Isobel in his arms, and then began carrying her down a hallway. He laid her in a bed, and Cian drank in every minute detail, because it was the first look he had gotten of anything other than the same room they always streamed from every night.

He didn't even realise there was a low rumbling sound emitting from his chest until Logan took a furtive step away from him.

"I have to go work out," he gritted, feeling the rage, frustration, and agony swirl up inside him as it did every night.

"Cian." Hanale Ashford edged toward him, catching his arm.

Cian quickly jerked away from the older man, shocking both of them.

His father held up rough, golden-skinned palms, his expression twitching to cover up the hurt that had briefly flashed over his handsome features. "I think you need to tell us what's going on," he urged quietly, in that accented voice that had always calmed Cian when he was little. It was deep, musical, and relaxed, some words pronounced longer and softer.

Hanale reached out again, and this time Cian allowed his father's hand to cup his shoulder. The smaller man had to reach up while Cian stared down, fury vibrating through muscles that seemed to have grown and hardened in the month he had been home. It was hardly surprising since all he had done was work out, act like a brute, and slink off to get a new tattoo whenever he could.

There was no flicker of fear in his father's bright blue eyes, only concern. "Talk to me, son. I may not be Kalen West or Mikel Easton, but I'm still your father. We would do anything for you."

Hanna Ashford rose from the couch, regathering her

long, white-blonde ponytail before slipping to his side and wrapping her slender arms around his waist.

She wasn't his biological mother, but she was … everything. They were his family. They meant *everything* to him.

But he couldn't tell them this.

They still thought Ironside had some good in it—that it was a shining beacon of hope for people in the settlements. They didn't know it was a rotten seed sprouting corrupt roots that dug deep and poisoned the very foundation of their society, sucking the nutrients from the soil, turning it into a husk of dust to feed the visage of vibrant leaves and gilded fruit that flourished on the surface. They didn't know that all the glittering little stars on camera were just glittering little lambs being herded right into a factory to be sliced, diced, and packaged up real nice.

Ironside wasn't a guiding light in the darkness of poverty, as they had all been taught to believe.

It was their singular downfall.

His parents had sent him there to get him away from the seedy officials who were hunting down rare Alphas for their child trafficking ring. He wasn't about to tell them they had handed him over to seedy officials hunting down rare Alphas to inject into their adult trafficking ring.

Though he supposed the Stone Dahlia was more than that, perhaps that wasn't a point in its favour.

"It's Iso—Carter," he managed to get out, still staring into his father's eyes.

To their credit, they didn't react. Even Logan, who was perched up on the couch, blinking widened sapphire eyes like a stunned bird.

They obviously knew this was about Isobel.

Cian froze whenever an Ironside rerun came on and Isobel appeared on the screen. He shushed them, turned up the volume, paused at critical moments to furiously text the other Alphas about how Ironside was twisting a narrative on Isobel—something he hadn't cared so much about when she was there within grabbing distance because that was just what Ironside did. Now, he became irrationally furious about it. He also irrationally barked at anyone who tried to change the channel while he was clearly busy on his phone.

He had entirely commandeered the ancient family laptop to search every gossip site for sightings of her zipping between appointments and ducking into high-end fashion boutiques, or briskly walking down the street with one of those reusable, takeaway coffee cups approximately the size of her head cradled protectively in her grip. Cooper and an entire team of assistants were usually hurrying behind her, Bellamy walking a little off to the side like he was considering jumping into a passing car—or in front of one.

They didn't paint a particularly happy pair, but there had been a few sneaky videos taken of what appeared to be Bellamy standing close and comforting her while she spoke lowly and rapidly to him, his hand half-raised like he might squeeze her arm or something. In those videos, she was looking at him like she trusted him, as though she could actually *stand* him.

It made Cian want to pull out the Beta's intestines and use them to spell out *Look at her and die* in the dirt.

"Did something happen?" his father prompted, appearing a little alarmed.

They had apparently been waiting for him to continue, and instead, he had gone off on an internal rant about Bellamy.

That ... also happened often.

"She almost died." Cian decided to tell them part of the truth. "The shooter had her cornered."

His parents shared a quick, heavy look. There was no surprise in it. Only dread.

"Did you have something to do with the shooter ..." Logan was the one with the guts to ask the question, though it took him two attempts. "Were you there when the shooter died?"

Nobody said Crowe's name anymore. He was *the shooter* now.

"Not exactly." Cian could feel his phone vibrating in his pocket. One of the Alphas was likely calling to discuss Bellamy's latest post. He searched for something to say that would explain away his insane personality shift. "We've grown close," he settled on. "She's a good friend. That asshole was going to hurt her, and it's not her fault that he's gone, but I'm worried it'll be twisted that way."

"We're worried about *you*," Hanna said gently, stepping back from him and dropping her arms to her sides. "Did you have something to do with it, Cian? You can trust us. We'll do everything in our power to protect you."

"Just like I've always done," his father added, squeezing Cian's shoulder and lowering his brows, reminding him ...

Hanale *had* always protected him—as far as *he* knew, anyway.

Now it was Cian's turn to protect them.

"I didn't kill Crowe," he reassured them with a sigh. "I promise. This isn't about him, it's about Isobel. I just feel like I should be with her, protecting her. That's what surrogates do—that's what friends do."

Logan pushed between their father and stepmother, pulling Cian into a rough hug. "He's in *loooveeee*," the idiot crooned, lightening the mood instantly and drawing a snort from Cian as the hug turned into a brief scuffle before Cian pushed his little brother back onto the couch.

"You're an idiot," Cian muttered, turning his attention back to his parents. "Everything is fine. I promise. I'm fine. I need to go work out, though. I'll be back in a few hours."

. . .

Hanale Ashford sucked in a heavy breath of air that filled his chest, shoving his hands into his pockets and spinning on his heel as soon as the door to the house closed. He fixed his attention on his younger son, cocking a brow.

"Well?" he asked. "Anything?"

"Just these," Logan muttered, tilting his head, dirty blond hair brushing into his eyes as he turned the little case of contacts over in his fingers. "Why were these in Cian's pocket?"

Hanna stumbled, catching herself against the side of Logan's chair. She plucked the case from his grip, swallowing dryly, and then swallowing again.

Hanale was numb with shock.

There was no way.

Impossible.

"And you're sure you searched everywhere else?" Hanale pressed, his attention boring into Logan's nonplussed eyes.

"Sure I'm sure." Logan shrugged, glancing between them. "We share a room—there's only so much he can hide. What's the big deal? Even Alphas need glasses sometimes."

"Because he doesn't need glasses," Hanna whispered.

"That you know of," Logan quipped.

Hanale shook his head, falling into an armchair, the

shock beginning to settle with a heavy finality into his bones. His son had a mate.

His son was *hiding* a mate.

There was something else going on here, and it wasn't anything good. He could feel it in his bones.

"How is she still alive?" he husked, his wide eyes crawling to the muted television, expecting to see the Sigma herself. Perhaps in an old episode, perhaps with Cian. "So far away from him?"

"It *is* her, isn't it?" Hanna's attention tracked his, also settling on the screen, which was still playing the movie they had been watching earlier. "He's suddenly ... obsessed. Aggressive. Loses control over anything to do with her."

Hanale nodded but then frowned, switching his attention down to the contact case in his lap. "Their eyes don't match."

"You think *Cian* is mated to—" Logan began to splutter, but Hanna quickly wrapped her hand around his mouth, silencing him.

It didn't feel like a safe topic to talk about in such certain terms. Not out loud.

"She could be wearing contacts?" Hanna whispered, pulling Logan against her chest for a quick, reassuring hug. Almost as soon as the words were out of her mouth, she was shaking her head. "No, I remember, they tested her."

"We need to keep this between us," Hanale decided,

slipping the case into his pocket. He was talking to Logan, who took a moment to think about it before pulling in a deep breath and nodding.

"Okay."

Elijah was still waiting for Cian to pick up the damn phone. He leaned back, lifting his gaze from the screen for a moment to stretch out his neck. The other Alphas were all silent, waiting on the call.

Likely seething quietly.

Or some, not so quietly.

Oscar's breath was sawing in and out, muted thuds echoing through Elijah's laptop speakers. With no other way to channel his aggression in the settlement, Mikel had sent him a punching bag.

And then another.

And then another.

Theodore and Moses were also pulling in air a little too heavily, each inhale and exhale too deep and measured, like they were practising breathing exercises as they jogged somewhere—probably wherever they could find a bit of privacy, or just away from the watchful eyes of their father.

"Cian's calling back." Elijah's attention snapped down as his phone vibrated. He routed the call to his laptop and added Cian to the group.

"Everyone here?" Cian asked immediately. He also

sounded out of breath.

"Everyone's here," Kalen answered. "You somewhere private, Cian?"

"Private as it gets," Cian muttered. "There's an abandoned house at the end of the row. Damn roof caved in."

"Good," Kalen said. "Go ahead, Elijah."

"Everyone put headphones in or turn me on speaker. I'm going to share my screen." Elijah stretched out his stiff fingers, his vision turning momentarily blurry before he skimmed the video to the first point of interest. "I think the first thing we should know is that Bellamy wasn't expecting to be recorded."

Elijah circled his curser around the brief, perplexed widening of Bellamy's eyes, the subtle shift in his posture as he held Isobel a little further away from his body. It was all done in the blink of an eye. "His father must not be happy with the level of attention Bellamy is —or isn't—getting from this gig."

Not one of the Alphas spoke.

Even Elijah could feel the slight vibration in the back of his throat when he spoke. The curl of fire through his body at the image of someone else's hands on Isobel.

He pushed it all down, dismissing it as an inconvenient side effect of the bond.

And then he wound the video back a few seconds, pausing it in the brief flash of footage before Bellamy rearranged himself and Isobel.

Oscar let out a deep, rattling sound and Theodore snarled out a curse.

"Protective," Gabriel noted, his voice breaking as though the word had been too bitter to speak.

"Yes," Elijah said.

Bellamy was holding Isobel against his chest, his posture tight and wary.

He was protecting her from—

"Braun Carter has a reckoning coming," Mikel spoke lowly, the words utterly calm and unbothered, making the threat he had issued all the more sinister.

"Wait," Theodore snapped, still breathing heavily, just as Elijah was about to skip to the next part of the video. "Is that a bruise on her neck?"

"Could be shadow." Moses didn't even sound like he believed himself.

"It's not enough to use as proof," Elijah said, skimming ahead in the video. "Teak said we would need *irrefutable* evidence of abuse. Without it, the other officials are blocking her from interfering. Now ... here." He pressed Play on the video.

"Anyway ..." Bellamy visibly swallowed in the recording, a tremulous smile hooking his lips. *"We've been having some trouble connecting—"* Bellamy paused to adjust Isobel, and Elijah punched a key to stop the video again.

"That was for us," he said. "I'm sure of it. Nobody can get an answer from Isobel or Bellamy, and it's obvious someone is controlling their social media. You've seen how many people are shadowing her to her appointments. They haven't just cut her off from contacting anyone. They've cut him off too."

Kalen grunted a sound of agreement. "That much is pretty obvious. Why go to the trouble of trying to mention it, and so subtly?"

"Because of the next part." Elijah shifted the video marker ahead and hit Play again.

"I should go put her to bed," Bellamy was saying. *"I don't think her vitamins are working."*

"See the way he looks over the camera?" Elijah asked.

"And the weird emphasis on 'vitamins'," Gabriel added.

"Didn't hear any emphasis," Kilian said.

"He stared really hard at the camera when he said it." Niko seemed to be pacing, if the soft shuffling sound in the background of his call was anything to go by.

"You think he's trying to say she needs more surrogates?" Kilian asked.

"No." Kalen's voice rumbled with alarm. "The surrogate pills."

"That's what I think," Elijah confirmed. "I think Braun has been feeding her the pills to sustain her with Bellamy as surrogate, and I think Bellamy is trying to say they aren't working."

"So she's not just *sleeping*. She's not sick, and she's

not even unconscious because of something her father has done." Oscar sounded very still all of a sudden.

"It's because she's away from us." Theodore's tone was rough.

"I'll try Teak again," Elijah promised.

"No, I will," Gabriel groused. "You need to come out of there and eat at some point. Or sleep. Or shower."

"Can't," Elijah murmured, glancing toward Gabriel's icon on the call. "Almost in."

He had already turned off his screen sharing, exited out of the video, and returning to his previous task. Everyone stayed on the line, and they would remain that way until they hung up themselves. He was busy now.

"You've been saying that for three days," Gabriel pointed out.

"This shit doesn't happen overni—*finally*!" Elijah straightened his posture, a bead of sweat forming on his brow as he loomed closer to one of his screens. He had stolen as much equipment from Ironside as he could fit into his luggage—opting to leave behind most of his belongings to make room for it all.

The human driver had attempted to lift Elijah's suitcase from the storage area of the bus, but he wasn't even able to drag it an inch from the spot Elijah had slid it into. He had given Elijah an absolutely filthy look as the Alpha picked up the suitcase like it was nothing and stacked it onto the sidewalk, seams threatening to burst and unravel.

"You're in?" Kalen asked sharply.

"I've got my opening," Elijah said, adrenaline flooding his system, staving off the exhaustion that had been threatening to pull him under. He had barely left his desk since they arrived back at the Piney Woods Settlement.

He spent the first week butchering all the hardware he had stolen to set up a customised hacker suite in the second room of his and Gabriel's minuscule house. They had both shifted Elijah's bed into Gabriel's room, but he had barely used it, and by the third week, he had begun to neglect it completely in favour of short naps on the floor by his desk.

"Where was the weak spot?" Oscar asked, shifting closer to the phone until his gravelled voice rang out clearly.

"The first was Cooper," Elijah muttered distractedly. "It was easy to hack into his emails and figure out which building they were in. From there, I narrowed down the building's on-site manager and the off-site security they had on file. I targeted the manager in a phishing attack using the security company's details. Then I used his credentials to gain access to the building's security system."

"So you can view their CCTV?" Oscar asked. "How does that help?"

"That was last week," Gabriel sounded tired as he chimed in.

Elijah wanted to roll his eyes, but he resisted. It would be a waste of energy.

“And since then?” Mikel asked, sounding apprehensive.

What he had done “since then” was exactly why Elijah hadn’t been keeping them informed. Everything he was doing was illegal ... but necessary. Isobel was part of the group now, and they protected each other. That was how it had always been.

“Since then, I’ve been inching my way into the system of the parent security company.” Elijah spoke steadily, refusing to pause for argument. “I’ve been exploiting vulnerabilities and escalating privileges to gain more control. But I’ve had to do it slowly, and I’ve had to clean up after myself. I have an established backdoor now and they haven’t noticed anything. I’ve just gained full access. What do you want to do with it?”

“I want to get the irrefutable evidence Teak asked for,” Kalen said before anyone else could respond. “Access any security cameras inside that apartment, and any devices with recording capabilities. Get eyes everywhere.”

“Done and done.”

3

An Impressive Display of Vitality

The fire alarm suddenly blared to life, interrupting Braun's rampage.

He had thrown Isobel against the wall after she refused—*again*—to do the breast augmentation surgery. She sagged there, her arms wrapped around her ribs, glad for the distraction. There was a sharp pain in her torso, making it hard to draw breath.

Bellamy was holding his shirt over the lower half of his face, catching the blood that spilled from his broken nose. Isobel had no idea if her father had intended the vicious elbow he threw into the Beta's face when Bellamy attempted to intervene, or if it had been an accident.

"I'll be making that appointment again," Braun threatened, grabbing his soft briefcase and filling it with his keys, two phones, and his wallet, before stalking for the door.

"Make as many as you want," she wheezed, watching him go. "I'll never give my consent."

Bellamy was at her side as soon as Braun was out of sight, helping her to her feet as Cooper and his assistants flooded out of the apartment. One of the assistants paused to help Isobel, but her father barked from the hallway for the others to hurry up, and the assistant rushed out without looking back.

"Wait," Isobel croaked when Bellamy tried to walk her to the door. "Go back to where Cooper was working. I think they left their laptops."

He didn't even pause, switching direction to help her into the breakfast room, where they found a line of laptops and tablets strewn across the table and the bar. Bellamy gently lowered her into a dining chair, and she pulled one of the tablets across the table, doing her best to ignore the pain in her ribs. She opened the first social media app and signed into her own account, searching for Dorm A.

There were no results.

"Didn't that reporter the other day ask you why Dorm A deleted their account?" Bellamy asked. "Remember, they wanted to know if it had anything to do with the rumours that Ironside was working on something big for the next season? Cooper told them to back off before I could ask them anything."

Isobel swore, trying to focus through the permanent, dizzy haze that had settled into her mind over the past few days. She typed each of their names individually, but still only found fan accounts.

Bellamy reached for the tablet. “Maybe I could—”

She slapped his hand away, tapping out one more name.

Lily Sato.

There were only about a hundred options, but one of the account names caught her eye.

LilySquirt.

She tapped on the profile and saw dozens of fan-made videos of ...

Herself.

Bellamy snorted. “Got a fan, you think?”

Isobel shushed him and saw the button asking her to respond to *LilySquirt's* friend request. She clicked confirm, and then immediately tried to video call the account, holding the tablet up to her own face.

“Ohmygod *Oskie!*” The excitable screech was almost enough to rival the wailing fire alarm, though Lily's voice was cracked and husky. “C-Car—C-Carter, hello it's me, Lily.” The image on the camera shifted from black to a blur of colour, and then back to black, accompanied by a thump, and the scrape of nails as the blurry view was knocked around a little. “*I dropped it!*” Lily wailed before finally recovering her tablet and holding it up before her face with both hands.

The image was shaking.

Lily's dark eyes were wide and sparkling, but the warm mahogany blush of her skin had grown sickly with a greyish pallor. Her breath was coming in short little gasps. "H-hello."

"Hi, Lily." Isobel smiled, working to keep all the pain from her own voice. It was hard to speak. "How are you?"

"I'm good." Lily was suddenly whispering. "I-is there a fire?"

"No, it's just a drill. I ... like your page. Did you make all those videos yourself?"

"Seriously?" Bellamy plopped down into the seat beside hers. "*This* is your one emergency call?"

"I did!" Lily squeaked, the colour rising in her cheeks. She had gone from ghostly pale to feverish very quickly. "I share everything you post! You're such a good dancer. I really wanna be a dancer too—"

"Who the hell are you talking to?" a deep voice grumbled, and the room behind Lily was suddenly flooded with light.

"It's C-Carter!" Lily said, waving her tablet so that the image of her on screen blurred.

"I told you not to watch those videos all night." Oscar sounded tired. He fell into the single bed beside Lily and reached for the tablet. "What did they post this time?"

He froze, his eyes connecting with Isobel's.

"No, it's really her." Lily tried to wrestle the tablet off him, but he held it away from her. "She called *me*!"

"Just a minute, Squirt. Can I talk to Carter?"

Isobel stared at Oscar, her voice sticking in her throat. Bellamy suddenly sat up straight, his eyes flicking between her and the screen.

"Oskie." Lily sounded like she was crying.

"Just a few minutes," Oscar promised. "Just give me a few minutes."

"She called *me*," Lily repeated petulantly, and a door suddenly slammed.

"Is that the fire alarm?" Oscar demanded, his attention flitting to Bellamy before fixing on Isobel again. At the same time, he pulled out his phone and began tapping on the screen.

"Yes," Bellamy confirmed, when the only sound that came out of her mouth was a short, devastated puff of air.

She wasn't even sure what her relationship with Oscar was. They had been intimate, and yet there was nothing *intimate* about them. Other than the small detail of him being tied to her soul.

He was right there. *Right there.* And too far away. And she didn't know what to say.

Suddenly, it all felt hopeless.

She was too tired. Even now, her eyelids were drooping. The adrenaline of her fight with her father, and then the alarm, was wearing off.

"Braun hurt you again," Oscar said, his tone rough, but calm. Frighteningly so.

“Ye—” Bellamy started, but Oscar cut across him.

“Wasn’t a question. The recording is being sent to Teak. This is what we’ve been waiting for—though we weren’t expecting him to throw you halfway across the fucking room. She needed hard proof of abuse to go against your father’s wishes. I need you to hang up this call and erase the history on the device you’re using. We don’t want anything to send Braun over the edge before Teak gets there, okay?”

Isobel nodded dumbly.

“Say something,” Oscar demanded.

“Okay,” she croaked.

His firm lips flinched, pressing together tightly as a rumbling sound built up in his throat. His dark eyes were sharp, and ... *insane*. They seemed to promise endless, bloody violence.

“Okay,” he echoed, the word a scrape of gravel. “We weren’t expecting you to find a way to contact us. I’m glad you did.” He glanced down at his phone and his words turned cutting. “The fire alarm will turn off in a few minutes. You need to get out of there.”

“Let’s get you back to bed,” Bellamy sighed, standing up and moving closer to Isobel.

Oscar snarled out an aggressive sound of warning. “Get your fucking hands off her, Beta.”

“She can’t walk on her own.” Bellamy avoided eye contact with the tablet.

Oscar flipped the camera down, and they listened to

the tense silence for a moment before he brought it back up again, an erratic muscle ticking in his jaw. His eyes flickered with heat—the dangerous kind that hinted at an imminent explosion.

"Hurry," he finally gritted out. "I'll see you soon, Isobel. Stay out of your father's way until Teak gets there. Pretend to be unconscious if you have to."

"Thank you," she managed to choke out. "Even if it doesn't work, thank you for trying."

"It'll fucking work. I need you to hang up."

She nodded, her finger shaking as she tapped the button to end the call, trying to memorise his face, etched in deep lines of fury, the shadows beneath his eyes darkening into bruises, his eyes still burning in that familiar, spine-tingling way.

"Seriously? Him?" Bellamy asked, snatching the tablet off her and quickly erasing the history before helping her to her feet. "There's something wrong with that guy."

"Sounds like we're a good match, then." Isobel sniffed, finally giving in to the pain in her ribs as her limbs began to shudder, almost like shock was settling in.

"Are you?" Bellamy pressed. "A match? A ... couple? I just didn't really think those rumours were true. Figured at the very least you wouldn't be his type, or that you'd be staying faithful to your mate."

"What do you imagine his type to be?" She felt a

sneer building up behind the question, but bit it back. Barely.

"I don't know." He huffed. "Someone older. Someone crazy. Covered in tatts, maybe. A few piercings. Possibly a settlement engineer. Not the spoiled little princess of Ironside Academy."

"You're a dick," Isobel huffed.

"I'm the dick who carries you to bed every night."

"You're all right, as far as dicks go."

"High praise."

"You're welcome."

He set her on the edge of her bed, and she groaned, falling back slowly as her dizziness fought with the sharp, throbbing pain in her ribcage. The combination blackened her vision.

The alarm shut off, and Bellamy dragged a chair over, leaning forward to rest his head in his hands. Isobel flung out an arm, swiping the tissue box by her bed and handing it to him.

He licked the end of a tissue and began cleaning the blood from his face, before realising just how much he had bled. With a huff, he launched from his chair, and she listened to her bathroom tap run before he returned, sinking back into his seat with bits of tissue stuck up each of his nostrils.

"I can hear them I think." He turned to the door, tilting his head. "Pretend you're asleep. Your dad always acts guilty after, you know ... I think he'll leave us alone."

She closed her eyes to block out the spinning room. "I'll just rest for a bit ..."

"A BOMBSHELL WAS DROPPED THIS MORNING IN COORDINATED posts across all Ironside social media accounts, creating a shockwave that quickly took over the internet. In the posts, it was revealed that there has been a joint decision by the Official Gifted Governing Body and the Ironside Board of Directors to split the show—and the Academy itself, in half! In a surprising turn of events, it appears that the upcoming season of the Ironside Show *will be divided between two locations. A strategic move which has secretly been many years in the works.*

"The first and second-year students will remain at the original location and will comprise a new, online-only segment: Ironside: Rising Stars. This new segment promises to be a complete digital experience with more opportunities for fan interaction than ever before."

Isobel tried to force her eyes open as the broadcaster's voice echoed sharply around her skull. She blinked blearily, squinting at the IV in her arm and the slow *drip drip* of the fluid bag hanging beside her bed.

She reached for the metal bed railing, a low groan catching in the back of her throat as she searched the empty hospital room. She was alone—the only sound coming from the TV—but there was a half-finished coffee on the bedside table, a chair pulled up beside it. There was also a vase of pretty yellow tulips by the window and a leather duffle beside the chair.

She turned her attention back to the TV, squinting at the headline that scrolled across the bottom of the screen.

Top secret location unveiled for the new Ironside Academy - The Icon race begins again!

"*The third, fourth, and fifth-year students will be attending the new Ironside location ...*" The newscaster pulled at Isobel's attention as she struggled to sit up. "*This elite group of stars-in-training will now be the sole focus of the* Ironside Show, *raising the stakes of each episode—*"

The door swung open, Bellamy striding inside, a croissant half hanging from his mouth. "Wor wake," he garbled around the pastry, before tearing it with his teeth and quickly swallowing. He dropped into the chair beside the bed, placing the croissant on the table beside the half-finished coffee and motioning the TV. "Heard the news, eh?"

She swallowed dryly, glancing back to the screen, where a new headline had replaced the last.

Countdown to premiere: how long until first look at new Ironside location?

"*The stage is set,*" the broadcaster announced, "*and the Gifted are primed to redefine the boundaries of reality television once again, proving that the Ironside team truly are without equal when it comes to entertainment-making."*

"We're—" She cleared her husky throat, trying again. "We're moving to a new location? Where are we going?"

"France, I guess." Bellamy shrugged, tugging open the duffle she had noticed and pulling out two envelopes. "We have tickets to Paris, at least. I overheard Teak telling your dad that he won't be permitted on campus this time. There won't be family days, anymore. They won't allow settlement people to travel to Europe, just Ironside people. Not that your dad is a settlement person, but yeah, family days are now through video chat only."

She fiddled with the sealed envelope he dropped into her lap, her eyes darting over his shoulder. "Teak?"

"Uh, yeah. You're ... in hospital. Teak brought us here."

"I know I'm in a hospital," she said dryly.

"Okay, but you haven't even asked why you're here." He picked up his croissant again. "You're far too relaxed about this."

"I guess I'm used to it." She winced, slowly stretching out her limbs. "At least this time I'm not covered in blood or—" She darted a quick glance to her scarred arms. "—stitches. It could be worse."

"Hate to break it to you, Carter, but it *is* worse. They think you're too sick to re-join Ironside."

She froze, her inhalation sharp, which triggered a coughing fit so violent it had tears springing to her eyes.

"I'm ... fin—" She stared at the back of her hand, which she had raised to her face.

It was spotted with blood.

What the fuck?

"Not fine," Bellamy corrected her, also staring at her hand. "You have pneumonia."

"How long have I been here?" she asked, her voice breaking.

"A few days now," a cheerful voice declared as Teak's face popped through the door. "So happy to hear your voice! How are you feeling?"

Confused.

She remembered fighting with her father, and the fire alarm going off. She remembered speaking to Oscar, and then Bellamy was carrying her to bed. After that, there was only blank space.

Bellamy swiped a tissue from the box on the table beside her bed, turning his back to Isobel and surreptitiously dropping the tissue beside her leg.

She stared at it as he shielded her from Teak with his body. Her stomach twisted sharply, and she quickly swiped up the tissue and scrubbed away the spots of blood from the back of her hand.

"I'm feeling so much better!" She forced a dose of energy into her tone—though it likely sounded a little manic—and shoved the tissue back into Bellamy's hand, which he was holding conveniently open behind his back.

"Amazing!" Teak perched herself on the edge of Isobel's bed as Bellamy stepped away, swiping up his coffee cup and croissant, and tossing everything into the bin.

"Going for a walk, I'll give you guys some privacy," he announced, before slipping outside and closing the door behind him.

Teak gripped Isobel's hand, her soft brown eyes bleeding with sympathy. "I'm so sorry I couldn't get you out of there sooner. I saw that video of Bellamy carrying you to bed—is that when the sickness started?"

"Ah, I guess?" Isobel attempted a reassuring smile as Teak squeezed her surprisingly sore fingers. "I had the flu, and I just fell asleep after training. It wasn't bad or anything. I think the stress made it worse."

"Well ..." Teak laughed hollowly, a brief flash of frustration tightening her features. "I don't think it was just the stress. It seems the new surrogate pill wasn't as effective as the previous version—you were the trial for this version, as it turns out. They want you to answer some questions about your experiences"—her jaw flexed—"when you're up to it."

Isobel flinched, the movement sending pain shooting down her stiff neck and into her spine. The effort to simply hold her head up was immense. She just wanted to go back to *sleep*. "I feel up to it," she lied.

Teak surveyed her before blowing out a breath and pulling out some paperwork. She licked her finger, flicking past the first page before settling the tip of her pen to the page.

The questions were invasive and extensive.

Detail several instances where the surrogate pill dampened specific emotional responses to thoughts of your mate.

Describe any unusually vivid nightmares experienced while taking the surrogate pills. Please go into detail.

Describe any sexual dreams experienced while taking the surrogate pills. Please go into detail.

Describe any vivid hallucinations experienced while taking the surrogate pills.

Have you become significantly less able to perform social interactions?

Have you felt any intense sensations of loneliness or a strong pull toward suicidal ideation?

Did your time on the surrogate pills change your sense of self or force a re-evaluation of your personal values?

Did the surrogate pills trigger any unexplained physical sensations, such as sudden tingling, euphoria, or violent outbursts?

By the time Teak had finished with the first page of questions, Bellamy was back, and Isobel was struggling to speak. She shot him a desperate glance, and he perched on the other side of her bed, shooting off answers to half the questions before Isobel even had a chance. *No, she hadn't experienced any side effects of prolonging her unformed bond. Yes, that included teleportation. Yes, that included dreams. Yes, that included halos, red strings, flower crowns, and golden chains.*

Her chin had tipped up at that question, suspicion winding through her mind as she examined Teak, who was writing each of Bellamy's answers down.

Did they know about the string?

"So what happens now?" she croaked as Teak wrapped up the final page of questions and began to tuck the pages into her document case. "Can I go back to Ironside?"

Teak pursed her mauve-painted lips, making a sound of hesitation. "We'll need to keep you for a little longer, I think, just to make sure your symptoms continue to improve." She peered between Isobel and Bellamy like she knew very well that Bellamy was trying to cover for her. "You were in and out of consciousness when we brought you here, and you were pretty drugged up, so you may not remember it, but the doctor said you likely have pneumonia. You've been getting antibiotics through the IV, but we were growing increasingly concerned when you didn't wake up again."

"I probably just needed the sleep." Isobel tried to joke. "Bellamy snores."

She chanced a quick glance to the Beta—he had moved away from the bed again and was now busy on his phone, but there was a slight smirk hooking up the corner of his mouth.

Teak didn't look convinced, but she didn't press the issue. "They've agreed to take you off the surrogate pills for now, but if you teleport back to Arizona, then you'll be back on them faster than you can blink. They don't want to waste resources flying you back and forth between America and France all the time."

Isobel nodded that she understood, and Teak stayed for another half an hour, explaining that the European Gifted laws were more restrictive than the American Gifted laws and that most of Isobel's luggage had been sent ahead to the new Ironside location—just in case. When Teak stood to leave, she seemed to waver, pulling another envelope from her pocket.

"Your father hasn't come to visit since you were brought here, but one of his assistants dropped this off." The bond specialist appeared unsure, worrying the envelope between her pinched fingers. "Do you want me to—"

Isobel held out her hand. "It's okay. I'll read it. He's probably apologising. He does that sometimes."

Teak handed over the note and moved to the door but paused again as she held it open, her hand gripping the frame, her gaze flitting between Isobel and Bellamy. "I won't be far," she promised quietly. "And ... if they don't let you go back to Ironside, I'll stay here." She closed the door just as Isobel opened her mouth to argue.

"That bond specialist is Gifted," Bellamy noted thoughtfully, staring at the closed door. "And hot. Have you seen her mate?"

"You only just realised?" Isobel felt her attention drawing back to the envelope in her lap.

"No." Bellamy fell into the chair beside her bed again, also staring at the envelope. "I was prompting you to explain to me why there's a Gifted official because nobody else seems to be able to explain it."

"How can the officials claim to be specialists in something they can never experience?" She carefully tore open the envelope, sucking in deep, husky breaths as she contemplated unfolding the note that slipped out.

"Never stopped them before," Bellamy grumbled. "So —her mate? He punching or what?"

"*She* isn't punching. They're well matched."

"Think there's any room for me in there?"

Her eye roll was not to be contained, despite how much the effort made her head ache. She flattened out the note, her fingers trembling violently as she tried to bring the words into focus.

To my daughter,

You don't know where I came from. Not truly.

My home was brutal, stark, and full of suffering. I know my methods seem cruel, but I tried to give you everything I didn't have. I climbed and worked and fought my way to the top of this world, just like I did inside Ironside, for you and your mother.

Because of me, you never wanted for anything—but of all the gifts I gave you, you can consider my harsh mentorship the most important.

You will need to climb and work and fight your way to the top just like I did, just to stay free of that place.

Don't forget where you came from, Isobel, and don't ever forget where I came from.

I paid for our ticket out of there with my blood, sweat, and soul. I won't let you drag my bloodline back there. Not in my lifetime.

Regards,

Your father.

"So?" Bellamy asked, growing impatient. "What does he have to say?"

"The usual." She dropped the paper onto her bedside table with the information packet on the new Ironside location, flopping back down with an exhausted groan. "It's for my own good. I need to toughen up or I'm going to end up poor and pathetic like all the other Gifted."

Bellamy snorted. "It's like our dads took the same masterclass in being pretentious tyrants."

She cut him a look, quirking up her brow—or at least she tried. In reality, she suspected it barely twitched. Bellamy didn't talk about his father much. He returned her inquisitive look with a challenging stare, daring her to inquire further. She didn't.

"So ..." Bellamy leaned back in his chair, spreading his legs and stretching his arms above his head with a heavy yawn. "Why is it that *I* know you need to go back to Ironside and be surrounded by big-dick-Alpha-energy to get better, but the bond specialist doesn't?"

"Because I'm guessing you didn't tell her that I've been sick from the first day of summer break," Isobel returned.

"Me?" He blinked at her, his arms falling back into his lap. "Sigma, they didn't even *ask* me." He laughed, shaking his head. "There was some other official who turned up with Teak—he had a private meeting with your dad, then he came out and gave Teak permission to call an ambulance." He rolled back to his feet and reached over the end of her bed, swiping up a duffle. "Your dad packed this for you, by the way."

He dropped it into her lap.

She wanted to shove it off the bed since it likely contained a designer outfit—which she would rather poke her eyes out than squeeze into at that moment—and a makeup kit, on the off-chance a camera crew managed to sneak into the hospital. She reached out to do just that, but instead found herself feeling for the zip, fumbling weakly to open it.

"That was not a convincing show of vitality, Carter." Bellamy huffed out a sigh, leaning over and yanking the bag open for her. He helped her to sit up straighter, bundling the pillows behind her back so that she was propped up. She thanked him distractedly as she rooted around the contents, pulling out the predicted folds of clothing and the canvas makeup bag.

"What are you looking for?" He lifted his chin, peering into the duffle.

"I don't know ..." What *was* she looking for? She stilled, her fingers tangling around the strap of a smaller, cross-body handbag. She pulled it out, swallowing hard.

She had been wearing it the day of the shooting.

She tore it open and emptied it onto her blanket-wrapped lap, her heart jumping into her throat. Her phone tumbled out, along with a tube of lip balm, and a tangle of red string.

She tried to turn on the phone, but it was dead.

"Here." Bellamy grabbed the device. "I've got a charger." He knelt by the wall below the television, swiping up a cord that dangled to the ground. "Do you need to use mine?" He pulled his phone from his pocket as he walked back to her. "I'm back online and the Dorm A account is back too. Someone has been messaging me from it to check up on you." He paused, his blond brows dipping together in consternation. "I know this sounds insane, but ... I think they have access to the cameras in the hallway. I left the room the other day and the Dorm A account messaged me to go back immediately because someone else was in the room with you. It was just your doctor, for fuck's sake."

She winced. "Yeah."

"Yeah?" His brow smoothed out, his head dipping down to fix her with a piercing look. "What do you mean *yeah*, Carter?"

"Yeah, someone is probably watching the hallway cameras."

Considering the Alphas had managed to gain control of the Ironside cameras and the cameras inside her father's apartment, *and* the fire alarm in his apartment building, believing they would also get eyes inside the hospital was not a stretch for her. She ignored the phone Bellamy was holding out to her as she turned her attention back to the string tangling between her fingers.

She wanted to call one of them. To hear Theodore's smooth, deep voice, or Kilian's silky tones. Or even Gabriel's calm, steady reassurances.

She would kill to video call Cian. To see the intent look in his aquamarine eyes, to watch his tattooed hands brushing his hair from his face.

Or Kalen—

But no, not with Bellamy in the room. Not when she felt like she couldn't even lift her head more than a few inches from the pillow. She just needed to sleep, just a little more ...

"Whoa, Carter." Bellamy caught her as she began to fall sideways, flattening the pillows out again and laying her down.

Her eyes fluttered, sweet darkness blacking out her

vision as the weight of the bag lifted away from her lap and the blanket was pulled up to her face.

"Wake me up before anyone comes in," she mumbled, turning on her side, her hands curling beneath her chin, the string bundled up tight in her grip.

4

29,000 CUBIC YARDS OF DIRT

WHEN SHE WOKE UP AGAIN, THE FIRST THING SHE NOTICED WAS that the soft bundle of string pressed between her palms was gone—replaced by some sort of stone sharp enough to cut into her skin if the sting at the base of her palm was anything to go by.

Her eyes flew wide, registering Bellamy's hand shaking her shoulder and the door opening behind him, a team of bustling nurses spilling inside, headed by a doctor with a clipboard.

She forced herself to sit up, staring into Bellamy's eyes to keep herself from swaying with the intense bout of dizziness that tried to topple her from the side of the bed. He quickly dropped onto the bed beside her, winding his arm around her shoulders, his grip on her tight.

“It’s a surrogate thing,” he explained, when it seemed like one of the nurses was about to ask him to move.

Isobel slipped her hands beneath her thighs, hiding the stone that still dug into her skin.

“I see you’re awake, Miss Carter.” The doctor introduced herself as one of the nurses began to check her blood pressure. “How are you feeling?”

She dug deep into her lungs, suppressing the urge to cough. “I feel so much better, thank you.”

The doctor muttered something and checked her chart. “Any chest pain?”

Holy fuck, yes.

“No.”

“Sore throat?”

Like coughing up razor blades.

“Not really.” She cleared her raw throat, her face almost red from the effort not to cough. “I am a bit thirsty, though.”

Bellamy poured her some water and pushed it into her hand, buying her another minute as the doctor finished with her chart and nodded at them both.

“Well, we’ll keep you a little longer, but if you keep improving, I don’t see any reason why you can’t be released. We’re really not qualified to deal with Gifted issues.” She swept from the room without waiting for a response, her team following behind her.

Bellamy switched back to his chair, his posture

slumping a little, the stress of their situation beginning to show on his face.

"Thanks," she said with a wince, pulling her fist out from beneath her thigh and stretching out her fingers.

What ... the fuck?

There was a large, blood-red gem in her palm, dipped in blood at the sharp tip, from where she had apparently gripped it too tightly, digging it into her skin.

"Um." Bellamy stared at the gem. "What ... the fuck?"

"Yeah," she croaked.

"Yeah?" His gaze snapped to her face. "Not the 'yeah' again, Carter. *Actually* what the fuck?"

She turned the gem around, tumbling it from one palm to the other, catching sight of the slightly golden light that twinkled out of it at different angles.

"I think ... it's the artefact," she said, dropping it to her lap and shoving off her blanket.

"What artefact? What are you looking for?"

"The red string," she said, realising it had, indeed, disappeared.

Or ... turned into a gem?

"What?" Bellamy said. "You're doing the crazy thing again."

"I don't do a crazy thing."

"Tell that to your imaginary grandpa," he shot back.

"Grandpa?" she asked, her brow furrowing.

"Yes?" a voice answered. A voice that *wasn't* Bellamy's. A voice that was, in fact, her grandpa's.

"Oh, dear god," she groaned, flicking her attention to the man now standing at the end of her bed, staring at her with a sarcastic look on his face.

"Well?" Buddy Carter prompted. "Grandpa is here, so what are you going to do with him, kid?"

She swallowed, looking back to Bellamy, who appeared even more confused. He blinked at the spot she had turned to stare at for a moment before raising his brows at her.

"Tell me you can't see him right now," he begged. "I'm not equipped to deal with hallucinations."

"Don't be ridiculous," she scolded before her body locked up. Her eyes darted to the door.

The last two times her grandpa had appeared, it had been in the presence of her father. She waited, her chest pinching, but Braun Carter didn't barrel into the room.

"You expecting someone else?" Buddy Carter drawled. "If you wanted your mama, you should have asked for her instead."

"Ground control to Major Carter." Bellamy leaned forward and plucked the jewel from her hand, before hissing and dropping it again, staring at his fingers in horror, as though he expected the skin to be melting off or something.

"Fucking *ow*?" He stared at her in accusation.

"Sorry." She scooped it up again. "I told you it was the artefact."

"How does that explain how it just *burned* me?" he complained loudly.

"It's a *soul* artefact." She gently turned it before her eyes, enjoying the way it glittered in the light streaming through the window. "There's no way you missed the one on my chest, so you already know I have one."

"Yeah, hi, I'm Adam Bellamy," he drawled sarcastically. "*Icon* kid who didn't grow up in the settlements. I have no bloody idea what a *soul* artefact is, you nutter."

She felt her mouth twitching up a little at the tone of frustration in his words. "Sorry." She tugged down the top of her hospital gown, just enough to reveal the first few links of her chain. "You saw this at some point, right?"

He nodded.

"It first appeared as a chain, then one day it turned into this." She released the gown, holding up the jewel. "Just like this appeared as red string before transforming."

"Why did the chain fuse to your skin and this didn't?" he asked, frowning.

She shrugged, before flexing out her hand and staring at the small injury the stone had caused. "They both drew blood, though."

"None of the others got those," Buddy Carter stated, looming closer.

She willed him and his riddled rambling to go away.

"Why don't I know about this?" Bellamy asked quietly. "Surely they would have shown a magical chain fusing to your chest on camera. I remember seeing the piercing and reading an article about it—but there was nothing in there to suggest it was any sort of magical bond item. The article was about what that type of piercing was called, and whether it was the cool new thing to do."

"Niko Hart was standing in front of me, blocking the cameras when it happened, and then we went into a bathroom. The officials don't know it's an artefact."

"You sure about that?" He rubbed at his chin, a thoughtful look in his mossy gaze. "Teak got a good look when they first brought you in. I remember thinking at the time it was a little weird how long she stared at it."

Isobel swallowed and then shrugged. Oddly, it seemed that she actually *was* beginning to feel a little better. She could sit up at least, and her eyelids didn't feel like they were being weighed impossibly down. She was also desperate to pee. She swung her legs over the side of the bed and turned to face Bellamy.

Her grandpa seemed to have disappeared again.

"I'm not an anti-loyalist, but I don't feel like being a science experiment," she said plainly. "So can we keep this between us?"

She didn't dare try to use her Sigma ability on him, not when she was so weak that she wasn't even sure if she could stand without assistance.

Bellamy considered her for a moment. “You know, this summer break has been the worst of my life. When it started, I felt like I owed you for allowing things with Crowe to go too far. Now, I don’t feel quite so indebted.”

“I thought we were friends,” she said blandly.

He grinned. “You’re an emotionally expensive friend. You settled our debt in a matter of weeks.”

“Then make it uneven again,” she demanded. “This time I’ll owe you.”

“You got yourself a deal, nutter.” He stood up and held out his hand. “Want some help?”

After struggling through the world’s longest and most laborious shower, Isobel felt stronger than she had in a week—but it was still a pathetic show of strength. She wasn’t coughing up blood and struggling to move her limbs, but she was still weak and exhausted. It had taken her almost half an hour to wash her hair with all the breaks she had to give her failing arms.

Still, these were symptoms she could easily lie about.

After putting in a fresh contact, she settled into bed, heaving out a sigh as she finally turned her phone back on. Since she began sharing a room with Bellamy at the start of summer break, she had taken to walking around with her contacts case in her pocket, so they were still there in the clothes she had been brought to the hospital in. She also had several sets stashed in her toiletries bag, which her father had tossed into her duffle.

After dinner, Bellamy had disappeared to go for a run, giving her some much-needed space as the phone in her hand began to vibrate. She sat there, waiting for the notifications to stop, but they continued for a good minute after her screen switched on. She watched the messages and missed calls stack up, worrying her lip as anxiety churned in the pit of her stomach. As soon as the deluge stopped, she navigated to the group chat with the Alphas.

Isobel: Hi—

She backspaced, her fingers trembling.

Isobel: I'm sorry—

She shook her head, deleting the words.

Isobel: I got my phone back—

"No shit," she grumbled, backspacing.

Gabriel: Hey, puppy.

She dropped her phone, heat flooding into her cheeks. Gabriel had seen her typing and deleting.

Moses: What?

Theodore: ??

Cian: Did she say something?

Gabriel: She was working her way up to it.

Kilian: Illy?

Isobel: Hey

Niko: Hey

Theodore: OH MY GOD.

Theodore: ARE YOU OKAY?

Elijah: According to her chart, she's fine.

Isobel: Do you have cameras inside my room?

Elijah: Unfortunately, no. Also, hey.

Isobel: Hey.

Moses: Jesus Christ with the heys.

Mikel (admin): Send a picture please, Isobel.

Isobel: Of what?

Moses: Yeah, Mikki, of what?

Mikel (admin): Of your face. Shut up, Moses.

Isobel: Why?

Mikel (admin): I don't trust you to answer honestly if I ask how you're doing.

Mikel (admin): Picture.

Kalen (admin): He means now.

She frowned, pulling the phone up and snapping a quick picture of her face, punching the Send button.

Kilian: Oh my godddddd, the little pout.

Theodore: Aww, you guys should have asked nicely.

Kalen (admin): We'll be nice once this shitshow is sorted and the group is back together.

Mikel (admin): Thank you. When did you eat last? It looks like you showered. Did you have help?

Oscar: Maybe don't answer that question right now.

Isobel: No.

Isobel: I mean yes.

Oscar: Careful.

Isobel: I mean yes, I showered. No, I didn't have help. And

I just ate like an hour ago. And also, you don't own me, Oscar. I can have help if I want to have help.

Oscar: As your owner, I say otherwise.

Kilian: He's joking. Ignore him.

Oscar: I'm really not.

Theodore: You really are.

Oscar: You need fingers to text.

Mikel (admin): Next person to issue a threat is getting muted.

Cian: Hey, Illy.

Isobel: Hey, Cian.

Cian: I've missed that adorable pout.

Her fingers stilled, emotion climbing up her throat.

Isobel: I've missed you too.

Isobel: Something happened.

Oscar: What?

Elijah: When?

Gabriel: Just now?

Isobel: I found the red string in my bag and fell asleep holding it. Then ... I guess it transformed? Like how the chain transformed.

She snapped a picture of the red jewel, which she hadn't let out of her sight. Even in the shower, she had kept it as close as possible.

Elijah: Did you bleed?

She blinked at her screen.

Isobel: Yes. It cut my palm. How did you know?

Elijah: I've been doing some research, and an anonymous

email address sent me some old religious texts concerning soul artefacts. They claimed that the gods gifted their bonded pairs with soul artefacts—but the real gift could only be revealed with a sacrifice, often a blood sacrifice. They aren't supposed to be able to force people to bond, so this is their way of encouraging people to hurt themselves and possibly permanently mark themselves and accidentally form the bond in the process of trying to access their gifts.

Isobel sat back, digesting the information as she examined the jewel. Was the value of it the true gift? Didn't the gods know who her father was? She didn't exactly need gems.

Finally, she responded.

Isobel: An anonymous email?

Elijah: Well, she tried to remain anonymous. It was Maya Rosales, the Guardian.

Isobel: Why did she send it to you instead of me? You aren't even registered as one of my surrogates.

Elijah: I stopped by the chapel before break and asked to see some of her religious texts.

Niko: Does the stone do anything?

Isobel: I think it made me a little stronger, but maybe I'm stronger just by having it near me. I don't know. The chain healed my skin right after it cut me, so maybe this healed my sickness a little?

Kilian: You'll be here soon, and we can figure it out together.

Isobel: You're already at Ironside?

Theodore: Half of us are. They're flying the different settlements in on different days. The European branch of officials are uptight as fuck about not letting us "disturb" the human population.

Kalen (admin): We're waiting on Gabriel, Elijah, Oscar, Niko, and you.

Isobel: Why the change of location? Why split the show up?

Mikel (admin): They've outgrown the Stone Dahlia in Arizona. They needed something bigger and better. Nobody knew about it because they purchased and developed the land in secret.

Gabriel: Probably so that nobody would question why they were digging out a small town underground and meticulously reconstructing neoclassical chateaus back on top as though they never moved them in the first place.

Isobel: What's it like?

She turned the TV on as soon as she typed the question and flicked through the channels until she found one covering Ironside. She almost dropped her phone as a drone flew over the new academy. Gone were the beautiful, rocky mountains and vibrant desert flowers set against the red dirt. The new location was flat and sprawling. The layout was meticulous—as though each perfectly square lawn, pristine row of hedges, and symmetrical white building facade had been pencilled in by the greatest—or cleanest—architects in the world.

Theodore: It's ... more.

Kilian: A lot more.

“No kidding,” she scoffed, her eyes widening on the TV screen as the drone flew across the middle of a large rectangular lake. It was set between two cobbled pathways, with perfectly tall fir trees lining the other sides of the paths. The dark green foliage was striking and lush, each tree shaped and trimmed to appear beautifully symmetrical. The centrepiece of the lake was a towering, white marble obelisk topped by an intricate finial, which was, in turn, topped by a brass equatorial sundial. The lake ended in a pillared white building, a smaller copy of the multi-storied structures she had caught a glimpse of toward the front of the property.

It was ... *stunning*. And absolutely immaculate.

Isobel: I’m watching it on TV right now.

Isobel: Gabriel is going to love it there.

Gabriel: Bad puppy.

Isobel felt a low laugh trying to bubble in the back of her throat. She pulled her phone up again and snapped a picture of her patting herself on the head.

Isobel: Good puppy.

Kilian: Dies from cuteness.

Cian: Gah.

Niko: GOOD PUPPY.

Elijah: You’re in a good mood.

Isobel: I’m happy to have my phone back.

Theodore: You’re happy to talk to us again, admit it.

Isobel: I will not.

Oscar: You will.

Theodore: Soon, too. Like now.

Isobel: It's becoming less likely by the second.

Mikel (admin): Don't wind them up, Isobel. They're being painful enough as it is.

Isobel: Fine, I missed you ... all?

Kilian: The question mark?

Moses: RIP

Moses: Here lies all you thirsty bitches. Namely Cian.

Cian: Fuck off, namely Moses.

Kilian: Who are you so unsure about, Illy?

Isobel: Um, anybody who doesn't want to be missed, I guess.

Kilian: So Niko and Moses, then.

Niko: Hey.

Isobel: I guess?

Niko: Hey!

Isobel: No?

Niko: No would be correct.

Isobel: Aww, miss you too, Niko!

She yawned, the adrenaline of speaking to the Alphas again finally seeping out of her body. Wiggling further down in the bed, she placed the phone where she could still see it and tucked the gemstone inside the shirt she had changed into, preferring to feel it against her skin.

Bellamy returned to the room, talking to someone on his phone. He dropped a small cup of ice cream onto the bedside table and nudged it toward her before sinking into his chair and retrieving a laptop from his duffle. He pulled over a high table on wheels, set up his laptop, and proceeded to ignore her as he tapped away on the keyboard, still chatting away to whoever was on the other side of his call.

They mostly seemed to be gossiping about the new academy. She listened for a little while, learning that half of the new Beta and Delta dorms were underground, but her attention slipped the more she tried to follow the conversation, and eventually, she felt her eyelids weighing down again. Bellamy claimed the ice cream she was too tired to eat, and she turned the other way, holding her phone close as some of the dread finally lifted from her shoulders.

Isobel was sure that having the soul artefact close was helping, but the difference was minimal, and the extra week away from the Alphas didn't help. Still, she was cleared from the hospital, and the only thing left to do was to actually *walk* out. And to walk onto the plane—and then all the walking she would have to do once the plane landed. Bellamy stepped out the day before their departure to buy them both hoodies, caps, and facemasks. He kept his arm securely looped through hers all the way out of the hospital, and then all the way onto the plane. By the time he deposited her into the first-class seat the officials had arranged, he had been taking almost all of her weight. She was asleep in minutes, waking only when Bellamy decided to force her to eat something.

She fell asleep again on his shoulder in the shuttle bus to the academy and shoved him off when he tried to make her stand to leave.

"We're here, Carter." He shook her shoulder again, and she forced her eyes to blink open and narrow on the window. Everything was blurry.

"M'kay." She wobbled to her feet and he helped her off the bus, both of them stumbling several steps as he tried to shoulder their bags.

They had barely made it a few steps before there was a hand on her other arm and a low warning sound that went right over her head. She swayed toward the familiar, gravelled sound as Bellamy stepped away from her.

Emotion swamped her from two different directions, briefly crashing down on her before the wave was pulled back, becoming oddly muted.

"We've got it from here." Theodore's beautiful voice was like music to her ears. "Thanks, Bellamy."

"Yeah, no problem." Bellamy sounded uncomfortable. "Um, she's going to be okay, right? All the walking really took it out of her. And she still needs to make it through registration. Plus this place is huge—"

"We've got it," Theodore repeated, a little sharper, before he pulled in what sounded like an unsteady breath. "We've dealt with her bond sickness before. It's okay. I'll text you later to update you, if you want."

"Yeah, I mean, I guess that's cool. You good, Carter?"

Isobel peeled back her eyelids, blearily bringing Bellamy into focus. He had handed her bag off to Theodore and was shifting from foot to foot, glancing toward the curved driveway that dipped into a huge, gated entrance.

"Y-yeah." She tried to wave him off. "I'll be okay. I'll text you later."

He nodded, rolling back his shoulders. "Well then, catch you later."

He strode off, and Kilian suddenly stepped in front of her, cupping her cheeks, his eyes drilling into hers. The bergamot and amber swirl of scent that wrapped warmly around her told her that it was just him and Theodore. She breathed deeply, and Kilian's grip on her face softened, his forehead lowering to hers, their skin touching in the briefest press before he was drawing her tightly into his arms, pulling her feet from the ground.

"Hey," he mumbled against her neck. "I'm so fucking relieved you're finally here."

He was wearing a short-sleeved, pale blue linen shirt with light grey, khaki chino shorts, and she didn't realise until he was wrapped around her just how *hot* it was. She could feel the warmth against the backs of her hands, but she still felt cold in her hoodie and tights, her bones refusing to thaw.

Theodore wrestled her out of Kilian's arms, pulling her into another hug that lifted her feet from the ground. He was also wearing chino shorts, his linen shirt hanging open around the collar where he had popped a few buttons. That was where she pressed her cheek as he hugged her, breathing in against his hot skin.

"Do you think you can make it through registration?" he rumbled, setting her down again far too quickly.

She shrugged and then immediately winced at the painful muscle spasm in her neck. "Don't have much of a choice."

"It'll just be ten minutes," Kilian promised, grabbing her hand, his strong fingers pushing between hers. It made her hands ache—because *everything* made her ache—but it was worth it. "And then we'll hitch a ride on one of the golf carts—this place is so big, we have carts now."

"They'll have cameras on you the second you step in there," Theodore warned. "They're probably filming you from inside right now. They've been waiting for you guys to arrive."

Isobel scoffed. "My first time at Ironside, I was in every cameraperson's way. Now they're *waiting* for me."

"My advice?" Kilian pulled up the facemask she had tucked beneath her chin, arranging it to cover her features again. "Be stingy. Don't give them too much.

You don't have to fight for airtime anymore. Make them work for it a little." He tugged her cap even lower and then pulled her hood up for good measure, his lush lips twisting into a beautiful smile, which immediately crumbled. "There's something else. We only just found out—he arrived a few hours before you did, but since he's an official now, he's supposed to stay off camera and not interrupt your airtime."

"He? What?" She looked between Theodore and Kilian. "What official?"

"Cooper." Kilian winced. "He's the new Dorm A manager. Kalen's been chipping away at him all break, trying to figure out what he'll give up his contract with you for. Apparently, this was it."

"Fuck," she groused. "Seriously?"

"Kalen will tell you the rest—we were down to our last option. We blackmailed your dad with the footage we captured over the break, but he was willing to risk his reputation to keep some control over you—and Cooper is that control."

She winced. "Sounds like my dad. So Kalen is my manager now?"

"We might have to go over this later," Kilian interjected. "If we linger out here, they'll send a crew, and we don't want you fainting on camera. Not until you're safe in your bed and they can assume you just needed a nap."

She nodded, already dreading the walk to the gate.

"Don't worry about Cooper," Theodore said. "Moses and Oscar started a bet on who can drive him to quit first. I don't think he'll last long."

"You're underestimating him." She sighed. "He works with my father every day. He just rolls with the punches and comes back with a slimy little spring in his step."

"It's no fun if it isn't a challenge," Kilian teased lightly, before adding, "You're going to have to hold onto me, I'm afraid."

"I guess things are still going well with Wallis then?" Isobel dug her sunglasses from her pocket, slipping them onto her nose as she glanced at Theodore.

The golden muscles in his arms twitched as he shoved his hands into his pockets, levelling her with an unamused look. The storm in his grey eyes was subdued, though there was a tightness about his features.

"It would appear so," he drawled, his eyes flicking down to her shoes before crawling back up again. "You're not hot?"

She didn't have the effort to lie. "No. Have you gotten bigger?"

He grinned at her, his teeth a flash of brilliant white. "Probably. Have you gotten smaller?"

"Probably," she grumbled, but she couldn't take her eyes off him.

He had definitely grown.

His hair was a little longer, threatening to cover his eyes as it waved forward, the sides shorn short the way he liked. He brushed it carelessly back, and it settled into a relaxed tousle, a few strands falling down again to caress his dark, winged brow.

"The parking courtyards and helipad are all back there," Theodore gestured behind them before he strode ahead of her and Kilian. "And these are off-limits, official spaces." He flung his arms to either side, pointing out the buildings to the left and right, just before the gates, mostly hidden behind hedge rows and fir trees.

She ignored everything he pointed at, instead choosing to trace the broad, strong lines of his back, swallowing hard as she remembered their last night together. The night the red string appeared. Her heart was suddenly thundering in her chest, her eyes wide, her steps a little quicker, spurned by the butterflies in her stomach.

She had all but told him she had feelings for him—*sort of*—and they hadn't spoken about it since. Not that there was much time between the shooting, her blackout period with her father, and the time she spent in the hospital—most of which she had been unconscious for.

Kilian must have sensed the nervous turn of her scent because he squeezed her reassuringly, releasing her only to tuck her hand into the crook of his arm, allowing her to lean on him as they approached the new entrance to Ironside. Theodore led them through the huge, wrought iron gates and into a beautiful courtyard, the paved road narrowing and continuing through the centre, and then on and on, as far as she could see.

"This whole area will be restricted," Theodore explained. "But they've had it set up for registration all week." He led them past buildings obscured by hedging and greenery, and to the end of the split garden, where the road sprouted off in several directions. They stepped into a building with a Registration sign hanging above the door. The cool air-conditioned breeze stirring beneath her hood yanked her right back to her first day of Ironside and how it had felt to walk into that giant building, knowing that privacy would be a thing of her past.

This time, the woman with the tablet didn't ask for her name.

"Miss Carter, welcome." The official up from behind her antique desk, bringing her tablet with her. "I trust you had a comfortable journey?"

"It was great," Isobel said, feeling stiff.

Her first summer break at Ironside, she had stayed at the academy, wondering why her mother wasn't answering any of her messages. The past couple of months had been the longest she had been away from Ironside in years. The longest she had been away from the cameras.

She suddenly felt nervous and awkward, unsure how to act.

Because, unlike last time, her every word now mattered.

This time, her aim wasn't to be left alone and to fly under the radar. She wanted—no, *needed*—to be popular. Adored. Supported.

They were on a one-way track to either stardom or complete disaster, and even though their plan was insane and impossible, she had chosen it because failing with her friends seemed preferable to winning alone. Or failing alone, if the new version of the surrogate pills were anything to go by.

"Congratulations on your new private room in Dorm A," the woman exclaimed, her eyes bright, her slight accent deepening as she beamed at Isobel. "I'm biased, of course." She pressed a hand to her chest, her red fingernails tapered into arrow-shaped tips. "But I think the Dorm A here is just ... *magnifique*." She sighed dramatically, before flicking up her tablet again and tapping a few times on the screen. "Sign here to register that you arrived. Would you like me to organise a private tour of the new grounds?"

Isobel's knee-jerk reaction was to say no, but she faltered, wondering if it might be a good opportunity for exposure. Her first "official" sighting at the new Ironside, out of her baggy disguise, on her own terms.

"What's the time now?" she asked, glancing up at Kilian.

"Around seven," he said. "Still have the whole day ahead of us."

She turned back to the woman. "How's this afternoon? Around five?" One of her father's assistants had said that sunset was the best time to film outside ... and this was the kind of nonsense that took up space in her brain, now.

"Perfect!" the woman exclaimed, tapping furiously at her tablet. "A golden hour tour! Will you be bringing any guests? We'll arrange champagne and macarons." She directed her adoring expression toward Kilian, before peeking out at Theodore beneath long, dark lashes.

"Uh, yes," Isobel said, fighting the sudden urge to snatch the tablet off the woman and use it to smack her across the face for daring to—

To what?

To notice *the alphas?*

"The golf carts can fit three in the back," the woman said with a wink.

"Then I'll be bringing two guests." Isobel was starting to waver on her feet again, but she didn't need to figure out a quick escape from the office.

Theodore shuffled her bag on his shoulder. "We should get going, Illy. All your stuff arrived and ... it's a lot. You're going to be unpacking all day."

"Do let me know if you need to make use of our interior design services or wardrobe organisers," the woman—

who Isobel assumed was either an official or a human hire, due to her lack of a rank ring—called after them as Kilian steered her to the door. "All the services cost popularity points, but you already have a few of those banked up."

Theodore thanked the woman, and they spilled back into the sun. Isobel was grateful for her sunglasses as she spotted a camera crew making their way over, headed by a producer who was barking something angrily over her shoulder.

"Let's make this getaway quick," Theodore mumbled, leading them to one of the golf carts parked outside the office, the keys waiting inside.

Isobel pretended not to notice the crew as they sped past, turning her head to talk to Kilian, giving the frantic group her back.

"It's so difficult to spot the cameras," she whispered.

Kilian ducked forward, his lips by her ear. "They're in here too. Top corners of the windscreen. I've found cameras *everywhere* in this place except the bathrooms and changing rooms."

"Everywhere?" She pulled back, her brows shooting up.

He nodded, his full lips pressed together, letting his expression serve as a silent warning, and then he began pointing out various locations as they rolled down the paved road, through sprawling gardens and past stunning buildings, all in the same white, neoclassical French style of architecture. She didn't pay attention to any of it, and eventually, her head lolled onto his shoulder, her eyes fluttering shut.

"We're here!" Kilian announced loudly, jolting her awake as the two Alphas slid out of the golf cart.

They were elevated above the rest of the academy, it seemed. High enough that she could see the surrounding township beyond the academy walls. She could only assume the hill was man-made since the landscape was so flat in every direction.

"Another Alpha Hill?" she asked, stumbling as she tried to exit the cart. *How much dirt had they hauled in for that?*

Theodore stepped in front of her, catching her elbow before tucking her under his arm and holding onto her tightly.

"You guessed it," he said. "They recreated all the popular landmarks—although Jasmine Field is now Jasmine Court. And instead of Alpha Lake, we have Alpha Terrace." He swept his arm out over the gardens that had been built into the side of the hill below them. Adorable, winding stone walkways trickled down to a lush oasis with a long, limestone pool. An elaborate, tiered fountain rose from the centre of the pool, erupting in dancing patterns of water that spilled from the limestone basin in a short waterfall.

There was enough space on the vivid green lawn for all the parties and events Dorm A was known for hosting. On one side was a natural stone retaining wall overgrown with ivy, looking like a remnant of a grand battlement as it curved around one side of the garden and merged seamlessly with the walls of Dorm A high above the terrace. The other side of the terrace was hugged by a wrought iron railing that circled the sprawling lawn, creating a magnificent lookout over the academy and the surrounding suburbs. It showed a hint of the wide river that bordered the academy on one side and the deep parkland that bordered it on another side.

Isobel was struck still with awe—and a feeling of strange *wrongness*. Ironside had always felt so isolated to her. Separated from the humans, from society and the outside world. Now she could *see* them. She could look out and know that they were watching her right back, on their TV screens.

It was an uncomfortable sensation, but not entirely an unwelcome one. It might help to humanise them, and they would eventually get to a point where they would need the people to see them as more *human* than *creatures of the settlements.*

Now that she really paid attention, she could see the cameras. Hidden amongst the greenery. On poles or stuck to the sides of buildings. Camouflaged in the hedges and winking from the stone retaining wall.

They *were* everywhere.

Her breath turned shaky with panic, but she bit back the sensation, following Theodore and Kilian to the front of the dorm. They had parked in a spot close to the pathways leading down to Alpha Terrace, and they walked back along the paved road now, which looped around another fountain at the top of the hill.

The dorm itself spanned three stories with a polished limestone facade boasting thin, marbled gold accents. Every part of the structure—save the doors and wrought iron railings—seemed to be constructed of the same gorgeous white stone. A grand, wide entrance with detailed Corinthian columns framed the short limestone staircase up to the double-wide doors. A pediment above the entryway sported a sculpted constellation, some of the details stamped with gold. She spotted small, wrought iron balconies along the sides of the building, framed by high, square-paned windows.

"All of the dorms now have an official manager," Theodore said, stepping ahead to grab the door as Kilian drew her hand through his arm again. "Ours was finalised while you were flying, but you're familiar with him."

Right. Cooper.

She frowned at the sudden souring of Theodore and Kilian's scents. Kilian's free hand landed over hers, squeezing gently. It almost felt like a warning.

"Are you ready?" Theodore asked, now turning the brass door handle.

Hell *no*, she wasn't.

"Ready as I'll ever be," she said, forcing her voice to sound excited.

5
BELLAMY REALLY IS A WET NOODLE

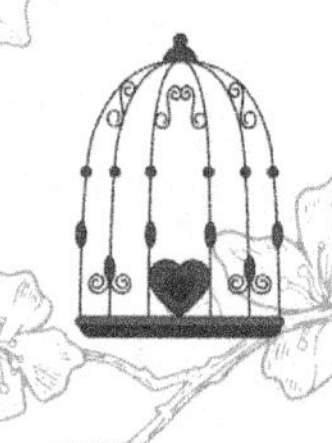

THEODORE SHOVED OPEN THE DOORS, STEPPING INTO THE foyer.

She followed cautiously, staring up at the soaring ceiling stretching two stories above. There was a grand stone staircase branching off to either side of the mezzanine above, a balcony wrapping around the sides of the room, and a wrought iron and crystal chandelier commanding attention as it hung centre stage.

They stopped beneath the huge chandelier, and she craned her neck further, trying to take it all in. The layered drips of crystal reflected sunlight from the large circular skylight several floors above, filtering it between delicate iron chains and twisted iron filigree, sending those fractured beams all over the room, where they shimmered off the gold accents in the polished limestone.

The sight had her catching her breath.

"Isobel!"

She snapped her parted lips shut, her attention darting to one of the arches along the left side of the room, where a man had appeared.

"Cooper," she said, sounding numb but feeling *sick*.

"I doubt you've had time to check your emails, so ... surprise!" His jovial tone made her want to punch him. "Please don't be upset with me ending our arrangement, but this was something I just *couldn't* pass up, and I'm so excited to continue working with you, my love." He had reached her and was reaching *for* her. Theodore smoothly stepped in front of her, clapping Cooper on the shoulder hard enough to make the man wince and cut his eyes up to the Alpha now looming over him.

"Aren't you supposed to be staying off-camera?" Theodore asked, sounding good-natured. Teasing. "I'm so confused about these fancy new dorm manager rules."

"Yes, well." Cooper shrugged off Theodore's hand and stepped away, straightening his button-down shirt. "I suppose I can slip into your room later—" He settled his eyes back on Isobel, letting her know that he was talking to her ... talking about going into *her* room. "—while you're unpacking, and give you a run-down then."

"Now is fine." She ripped off her sunglasses, shoving them into her hoodie pocket. "They aren't going to want footage of me looking like this anyway." She indicated her cap and facemask. "What ... exactly is going on?"

"I resigned as your manager," Cooper announced, his moustache twitching like he was holding back a grin. "I was offered the position of dorm manager for Dorm A. It's a three-year contract, so you could say I'll still be managing you in a sense."

"I don't understand." She forced a smile. "Why do we need a dorm manager?"

"Oh, all the dorms have them now." He waved a dismissive hand. "We coordinate events and liaise with the housekeeping, catering, and maintenance teams. I'll be facilitating every Dorm A party and live event from now on, and I promise you—we have some exciting stuff planned."

"Already?" she asked, the shock causing her brain to stall until she could think of nothing else to say. "You were still working for my father a week ago?"

"The officials have been pre-planning," he said, like it should have been obvious. "I'll be in charge of booking time at Ironside Row for you and distributing your popularity points onto debit cards for use at Market Street, so you make sure you stay on my good side." He pointed at her, his smile finally breaking free, his moustache curving up, his beady eyes narrowing to slits.

"Well, good to see you." The words tasted like acid on her tongue, and she glanced over his shoulder to the two men filling two of the four archways behind him.

"Professors," she greeted, her tongue feeling thick.

Kalen and Mikel didn't look like they were about to move from their framed spots, but both of them nodded at her silently. Their stares were guarded, their bodies just relaxed enough to make her think they weren't relaxed at all.

Mikel carried his tension in a more obvious way—it seemed to line the severe planes of his face, and it emanated from his body in an impossible aura. Kalen was much better at hiding it. In his impeccable dark blue suit, with his fierce expression and unbothered air, he could have been on his way to a meeting with the director of Ironside, or he could have been staring down a waning Sigma who just happened to be his half-bonded mate. He gave nothing away.

"Is everyone here?" she asked as Cooper checked his phone, frowned, and made a hurried exit—through a door built into the wall at the back of the staircase. It was protected by a keypad and was practically invisible after Cooper vanished through it, the door sliding seamlessly back into place along the wall.

"Everyone is here," Mikel affirmed, his slightly mismatched eyes fixed to her face. "I just messaged them on the dorm tablet—they should be down in a moment. They're quite worked up over the fancy new dorm, so you may get an enthusiastic greeting. Brace yourself."

"Illy!" The bellow came from the top of the stairs—her only warning before Cian was barrelling toward her in a blur of tattoo-patterned skin and golden hair unravelling in a silky flow from the bun it had been tied into.

He landed before her and swept her into a tight hug, his nose pressing to her neck, a small, almost imperceptible sound grating from his throat. His arms wrapped so far around her that his fingers dug into her stomach. He made her feel *tiny*.

"Have you all grown?" she managed to choke out as soon as he set her down, holding her back at arms-length, his fingers curling around her shoulders.

He had several new tattoos, including a very complex and complicated weave of designs that climbed up his neck. He also now had a thin black piercing in his left brow, and a black ring hooked into the side of his lower lip.

"Probably." He shrugged, his grin coy. "You look terrible, doll."

"Thanks." She tried to elbow him, but he dodged out of the way and slid behind her, grabbing her up again and sticking her arms to her sides.

"It's giving sibling energy," Moses said dryly, his expression deadpan as he descended the stairs, his stormy eyes dark with scepticism as he eyed Cian and Isobel.

"You shut your mouth," Cian snapped at the other Alpha, though his tone was light. "You can't be the official surrogate of your sibling."

"I'm pretty sure Bellamy is her *official* surrogate, isn't that right, Carter?" Moses reached the bottom of the staircase and leaned back against the marble post at the end of the handrail, crossing his arms and arching a brow at her.

She couldn't help the grin that tugged at her, a sense of strange relief spreading through her at the casual, sarcastic way Moses had greeted her. It was just so ... *him*. And ... she supposed she had missed him.

His lips twitched in response to her wobbly smile. He pushed off the post and stalked towards her. Cian released her, moving to whisper something to Theodore.

Moses pulled her into a quick, almost gruff hug, before stepping back and flicking off her hood. "Ah," he said, tugging the bill of her cap. "Another layer."

She brushed his hand away and he moved to join Theodore and Cian's conversation, leaving her to face the three men who were descending the stairs after him.

Elijah and Gabriel took each step in unison, Niko a step ahead of them. They were all wearing workout shorts and active shirts, sneakers on their feet. She felt a slow flush descending over her features and nervously tugged at her face mask to make sure her reaction was concealed. Usually, Elijah and Gabriel liked to dance in loose-fitting clothing, like sweats and overlarge shirts, so they must have been preparing for a different kind of physical activity. She was finding it hard to look into any of their faces with so many muscles on show, and the way they were taking the stairs two at a time had *a lot* of those muscles twitching and bunching. The workout pants were just tight enough to show off perfectly sculpted thighs, and Niko's shirt bounced as he leapt down the last two steps, flashing her a few inches of a delicious stack of abdominal muscle.

She swallowed, flicking her gaze between them.

"Puppy." Gabriel yanked her facemask down, tucking it beneath her chin. "Morning."

"Morning," she squeaked. She had grown so much in confidence since befriending the Alphas, but suddenly, after so long away from them, she was devolving into the timid Sigma of her first year.

She blamed the workout clothes. Bellamy often wore them when he visited the gym in her father's building, but he never looked like *that*. Bellamy just looked like a normal guy, not like the kind of guy who made normal guys cry themselves to sleep every night.

"How was your flight?" Niko came to stand beside Gabriel, the beautiful meld of his greenish-brown eyes striking as he grinned at her. "Need some help unpacking? These two hate it when I work out with them anyway. Makes them feel so inferior."

"She needs time with a real surrogate," Elijah stated calmly, his frosty eyes categorising her features with an almost calculating glint flashing in the cold depths before he blinked it away, his fingers lighting beneath her chin, tilting her face up further for his inspection.

"After all that time with Bellamy, you must be suffering," he murmured. "You're used to being surrounded by our energy. You basically went decaf for summer break."

She shuddered. "I could never."

His lips curled into a half-smile, his hand dropping back to his side. "No ... so you should organise to spend some time with one of your surrogates before you unpack."

He wasn't telling her—he was giving her an opening to do what she needed and explaining it for the cameras at the same time. Minimising it. Making it no big deal.

"She already has," a gravelled voice declared—not from the stairs, this time, but from behind her.

She began to turn. "Hey—"

Oscar had reached her before she had even managed to turn fully, and he swooped down and tossed her over his shoulder before she could even get a good look at his face.

"Hey!" She thumped his back, but she was so weak he likely didn't even feel it.

"Hey back at you, rabbit." He was taking the steps two at a time, making her head spin dizzily. He turned when he was at the half landing where the steps branched off to either side, spinning around to face the others. "I'm on Sigma surrogate duty."

"Well, that's that sorted." Elijah's dry reply held the tiniest inflection of humour and relief—just enough to tell her that he was acting because if he had responded naturally, it would have been without inflection whatsoever.

"Did you draw the short straw?" she teased, keeping her voice light and casual—like she was *friends* with the most terrifying Alpha on academy grounds, instead of half-bonded to him and more relieved than she had ever been in her life to see him. She was trying and failing to prop herself up as Oscar strode across the mezzanine and into one of the rooms lining the balcony.

"You guessed it," he said, just as light and casual as her, even though he was kicking the door to the room closed behind him.

Cameras in here, too, then.

He slid her down his body but didn't set her on her feet, instead spinning to sit her on the surface of a dresser. She jolted with the shock of it, throwing out her hands against the polished wooden surface to steady herself as he wavered a few inches from her knees, his fingers trailing down the thin material covering her thighs, drifting away as he reached her knees, his hands clenching before he shoved them into his pockets.

"You want to shower before you nap?" He took half a step away from her, the dark pools of his eyes heating as they swept down over her, before turning away.

He seemed on edge. Evasive, almost.

The increased level of surveillance must be making him uncomfortable.

"Y-yeah," she croaked, clearing her throat. "Wow ...

this room is nice." She could have been sitting in a broom closet for all she noticed.

Too awkward.

She tried again, casting her eyes around and taking in *no* details. "How ... um ... how was your break?"

"It was a lot more interesting than yours," he returned, his expression twitching. "Bellamy really is a wet noodle, isn't he?"

Oscar turned and strode across the room before she could reply, pushing open a heavy door and revealing a glimpse of a marble-coated bathroom, stacked with boxes. "You can't shower until we've unpacked this shit."

He stalked back to her, and she quickly held out her hand when she saw the intent in his eyes. "You don't have to carry me everywhere. I'm jetlagged and I need a nap. I'm not *dying*."

She ended the false statement with a light laugh, but her breath caught at the end and his head shook, just barely. Just an inch to either side.

"Surrogates are supposed to spoil their ... people," he said gruffly, gathering her into his arms. "I'm worried about how you survived with the wet noodle. You're supposed to be one of us, a Sigma-Alpha, so you need to be *strong*."

He carried her into the bathroom, set her on the marble counter, kicked the door shut and was suddenly pushing her legs apart and tugging her right up against his body.

No cameras in here, then.

"Let's play some music while we unpack," he said, yanking his phone out of his pocket and stabbing his thumb at the screen a few times before tossing it onto one of the boxes by the door.

And then he was pressing tightly against her again, whipping off her facemask. He gripped the neck of her hoodie and ripped it apart, his strength sending a tendril of fear down her spine, which in turn made her stomach burn with desire. The sunglasses tumbled from her pocket and into the sink with all his rough handling.

It was something Oscar seemed to be particularly skilled in—simultaneously scaring and arousing her.

"Sorry," he rasped, tearing the hoodie the rest of the way off and tossing it to the ground. His hands pushed beneath her loose shirt, settling around her naked waist, his fingers digging in, his forehead dropping to hers.

He had his eyes closed, his body vibrating with tension.

"Are you ok—" she started to ask, but his eyes suddenly flew open, and his mouth crashed down on hers.

He pulled back almost instantly, licking his lips, staring at her mouth. "I should have asked." His words were the lowest growl.

"You have my permission not to ask," she reassured him.

He tilted his head, a dark curl falling into his eyes, the

pupils blown out. "You don't want me to be gentle with you? Aren't you sick? Weak?"

"Desperate," she countered, heat flooding into her cheeks. She didn't have the luxury of feeling shy. She *was* desperate. Her entire body arched toward him, a sob building up in her throat at how close he was, how much his scent dug into her pores, and how much he *wasn't* touching her.

His chest rumbled, his head lowering again to hover his mouth over hers. "Desperate girls beg."

Lust was making her stupid, convincing her that the darkness in him was everything she needed.

"Good Alphas make me." The words were almost a whine, her hands tangling in his shirt. She knew what she was asking for, but she didn't really *know*. She just wanted to push him, to get as much from him as she could. There was some incredibly fucked-up part of her that recognised the man between her thighs as an Alpha and sensed, on an instinctual level, that only his Alpha aggression would temper the need bubbling in her blood.

A definite growl reverberated through his body this time. He expelled a harsh breath, his lips moving to her ear. "I swore to them I could do this without tearing into you."

"No," she whimpered, trying to move against him. "Tear into me."

"*Carter*." Her name was a sharp warning, his hand

flashing to her neck, peeling her off his body and pressing her back to the mirror. “I really need you to not talk like that while I’m this close to the edge.”

She tried to pull his hand away, but his eyes darkened, his grip tightening. Her stomach swooped low, her thighs pressing against his hips. His nostrils flared, like he could smell how damp she was growing.

“I’m supposed to be rubbing your fucking temples and telling you about how this place is recording every goddamn breath we take.”

“I’m not stupid,” she huffed. “I noticed.”

“I’m supposed to be checking if you’re okay with Cooper.”

She immediately released his wrist, but instead of backing off her, his stare only grew more intense, his jaw flexing.

“Scrap that,” he grunted. “You don’t get to think about that corpse when I have my hands on you.” His palm slid to the back of her neck, and he hauled her mouth back to his.

His kiss was hungry, impatient, and angry. He didn’t touch her like she was fading away and might crumble at the slightest pressure from his fingertips. He touched her like she was a clay silhouette, tough enough to withstand his firm pressing, kneading, and moulding. His tongue was a vicious thrust into her mouth, both of his hands gripping her head, forcing her into the angle he needed.

As soon as his punishing kiss had her squirming

again, he pulled back, breathing ragged. He hauled her off the counter with one arm, his free hand tearing her tights and panties down her legs, and then he was setting her back onto the counter, gathering the hem of her shirt and pushing it up to bare her stomach.

"First of all," his voice was a low, grating sound, "there are cameras everywhere except the closets, the bathrooms, Kalen's office and room, and Mikel's office and room. And when I say cameras, I mean cameras *and* microphones. They're capturing every angle, every conversation." He tugged at his fly and suddenly she was staring at his cock. A dark caramel colour, smooth and long, with a wide mushroom head. He fisted it, and it throbbed, the veins growing thick. "I need it wet, baby."

The sudden switch of topics had her head spinning.

His fingers were at her chin, coaxing her forward, pulling her into a trance. She had gone *months* feeling empty and disconnected, sapped of colour and life, and part of that had been a side effect of being parted from her incomplete bonds, but part of it was just ... *them,* and who she was when she was with them.

With Oscar, she could be reckless. She could explore her boundaries and play with the darkly bubbling desire that she barely dared to think about in her more sensible moments. Amongst the Alphas, there always seemed to be someone she could trust, someone who would support her, someone who would protect her, someone who was thinking about her best interests, and someone who was challenging her to do better and to be a better version of herself. They formed a safety net around her that allowed her to explore herself and the world around her in a way she never had before.

Being away from them, she hadn't changed or reverted to that shy, timid, terrified version of herself, but she had become hollow, deprived of feeling or sensation.

Perhaps that was the bond magic at work, dulling her senses when her mates weren't around, or perhaps it was simple Alpha magnetism. Maybe it was just them. Or maybe it was the way they mixed with her.

Whatever it was, having *it* again was making her dizzy and heady, her skin tingling all over. Oscar was barely even brushing her chin with his fingertips, but she followed the suggestion of his touch as he pulled her head down like a magnet, until she was bent at the waist and his dick was anointed with her shaky breaths. He brushed her lips with his thumbs, and she opened them, allowing him to push in, the thick head of his erection making her mouth stretch.

If they keep growing ...

Fucking hell.

She was going to die a virgin or die in the process of losing it.

Oscar groaned softly and pushed himself in further. "Get it as wet as you can, Sigma."

She wiggled her tongue until it was flat along the

underside of his steely flesh, turning her eyes up to blink at him as tears gathered in the corners of her lashes from the strain of opening her throat to him.

His thumbs stroked along the corners of her eyes, catching her tears, and he throbbed inside her mouth, his eyes growing impossibly dark, transforming him into that severe, cold, wrathful visage that stalked through the shadows of the *Ironside Show*, terrorising people with the suggestion of his presence alone.

He brought his thumb to his mouth, licking the tear he had captured and pushing suddenly to the back of her throat, making her choke on him as he stared down at her calmly.

She blinked a stream of tears free, and he tried to force himself deeper, strangely fixated by the salty droplets racing down her cheeks, and then suddenly he pulled out, lifting her up and pressing her back to the mirror with a hand on her chest. He pulled her legs up, cinching her thighs together and holding them locked with one of his hands, the span of his grip managing to capture her legs together just above her knees.

"Don't try to tease me again, and I'll make sure I leave this bathroom with your claim all over me. Nod for me, baby."

She bobbed her head up and down, still locked in her overwhelmed feelings, drowned out by an ocean of sensations. She could feel the crackle of energy in the air, enough to raise the hairs on her arms. She could *smell* him. His aroused scent was a sweet, subtle poison. It hung in the air like a cloud of nectar, reminding her of honeysuckle and warm sugar melting on the tongue. It threatened to lull her into a daze, to lay her down and close her eyes, and do wicked things to her as she dreamed.

There was nothing comforting about it.

"We're supposed to be treating you like a little dorm sister that we protect and love in a platonic way," Oscar snarled, feeding his cock between her tightly pressed thighs, right against where she was damp and throbbing and wishing to be filled—but he only thrust against her, enjoying the slide of her slickened flesh. "We wanted to wait until you were better and could stay awake long enough to discuss everything, but with the increased surveillance—" He grunted, squeezing her thigh. "Are you paying attention, Carter?"

She was staring at the head of his cock as it pushed between her thighs, pressing into the soft skin of her stomach. He rolled back and dug into her skin again, leaving a drop of stickiness against her stomach.

"Uh," she managed. "Ye—" The word choked off on a whine, which had his jaw clenching. She tried again, recalling Moses' joke from earlier, now realising how deliberate it was. "Uh, sibling energy?"

"Yeah, something like that." Oscar sounded distracted now, one hand still cinching her legs together above her knee, the other gripping her thigh so tightly she was sure he was forming bruises.

"Like this?" she asked, a small giggle falling out of her throat.

"Not like this." He slapped the side of her thigh lightly. "Fuck ... if they find out this is how I settled your bond, there's going to be a fight."

"Y-you love ... fighting." Her hips rolled up, seeking more friction as she neared orgasm.

"Do I sound disappointed?" He reached for her shirt, using it to haul her off the mirror.

She steadied herself against the counter, and he pulled the shirt over her head, his eyes lingering on her bra. She wanted to be confident and sure of herself, to whip it off and watch him lose control, but she was unsure. He was just placating the bond, wasn't he? This wasn't the passionate collision of two lovers coming together after months apart, desperate to taste and feel each other again.

This was ... a type of claiming.

This wasn't normal.

"Stop overthinking it." He hooked a finger into her bra and drew her closer before switching his grip to her chin and lifting her face to his. He tasted her shaky exhale as the new angle dug the head of his cock right against where she needed it most.

He kissed her sweetly, keeping her anchored there, his hard flesh grinding, grinding, until her head was spinning and her body was spiralling, hooked into a trembling release that had a sob building in the back of her throat.

His grip on her leg wavered and her thighs broke apart, hooking around his hips. He took hold of his erection, stroking it as she fell back, her eyes dragging down to his hand.

"You're covering me," his tone was husky, wavering at the point of control. "Is this enough?"

She bit her lip, watching as his dusky skin was covered with her glistening essence. Something inside her purred, pleased with the sight, her lungs expanding as she deliberately drank deep of their combined perfume—something she could only experience when her scent mixed closely with one or more of theirs.

Her head bobbed, her eyes wide, her blood singing. *Yes*, that was enough. That was what she wanted to see.

He licked his lower lip, a distinctly male satisfaction briefly burning in his eyes before he began to tuck himself away. Despite the pleased rumble emanating from his throat, she could also feel the slightest spark of emotion spiking against her chest, too subtle for her to label.

She caught his wrist. "Is it enough for you?" She hadn't asked any of them how the separation had affected them—not because she didn't care, but because until the moment she felt Kilian and Theodore surrounding her, it had felt like she was treading water, every molecule in her body focussed unwaveringly on just being *okay* and making her way back to them.

"This isn't about me," Oscar said, gently removing her grip on him and securing himself back into his pants.

"The bond is about all of us," she countered, slipping to the edge of the counter, strength flooding into her body and brightening her vision. She wanted to reach out to him, but his body language was suddenly closed off, a shutter falling over his expression, his jaw clenched so tightly it made her wince.

"I can't ..." He considered her, a dark spiral of emotion twisting in the shadows of his eyes. "I don't want to hurt you. Not when you're so desperate from the bond that I can't tell if you'll regret this later or not."

She nodded, chewing on her lip. "Okay." She would have preferred to continue *now*, with the heady feeling of being attention-lavished by one of her mates making her usual sensibilities and hang-ups flee the room, but not if it made him uncomfortable.

His lips twitched like he might smirk at her. "Okay. Let's unpack some of this shit and get you in the shower. Kalen wants to have a group meeting as soon as you're strong enough."

She hopped off the counter on wobbly legs, shooting out a hand to steady herself. Oscar shook his head, gripping her hips and hoisting her back up again, sitting her right on the edge.

"You just tell me where to put things," he ordered, lingering like he didn't know how to step away again.

She frowned. "Sorry, I thought ... I felt better. It was just a head rush."

"Last time you deprived the bond and then overloaded it with affection, you passed out. We need to get you into bed. You should feel better in a bit."

"Oscar?"

"Mm?" he grunted, lifting his fingertips from her bare hips, one at a time, like he was forcibly removing each one.

"Er, I kind of need my clothes back."

"My instinct is to say no." He pressed those retreating fingertips back down again, digging them in stubbornly. "I'm not cut out for this delicate nonsense." His head lowered, his sharp teeth nipping at her bottom lip. "They're testing me."

"Did you pass?" she whispered.

He groaned, pushing back from her. "For now," he spat, spinning and fishing her clothes from the floor. He pushed them into her lap and then fell back against the wall, cupping himself through his pants, a look of pain on his face as he stared at her.

"Hurry." He delivered the word like a warning. "Do you need help? For the love of god, just say no."

She didn't answer him at all, instead slipping off the counter again to rapidly dress. Her hoodie was ruined, but she fished out the jewel from the pocket, curling her fist protectively around it, shivering slightly at the warmth it shot up her arm.

"Sit," Oscar ordered, pointing to the counter again.

She slid back onto it, glancing down at her jewel and freezing, opening her fingers from their protective clasp. It was no longer red, but a pale, rose-tinged gold.

"It changed," she muttered as Oscar drew close again, realising what she was holding.

He touched the warm, smooth surface, blunt fingertips tracing the faceted sides. "When did it change?"

"I don't know ... sometime after I landed in Paris, I guess?"

"Better take a picture and send it to the others."

She fished her phone from the pocket of her tights and took a picture of the blushing jewel in her palm, sending it to the group chat.

Isobel: It changed colour. I think it's a little warmer too.

She tilted her head, watching Oscar tear open a box and begin piling things into the cupboard beneath the sink. It was awkward to carry on after what they had just done—especially with the thickness still outlined in his pants, making him grimace as he knelt to stack products on the lower shelf.

"The hell kind of shampoo is this?" he grumbled. "Damn jars are tiny and there are a hundred of them. What happened to putting shampoo in bottles?" He squinted at one of the labels. "Russian amber?" One of his dark brows inched up, and he speared a look at her.

She held up her hands in supplication, keeping the gem anchored to her palm with her thumb. "I didn't pack any of this stuff. I didn't choose that."

His stare dug into her before lowering again. He flicked the jar over, his other brow twitching up at the price sticker on the bottom. "A hundred and sixty?" He held the jar between his thumb and pointer finger, pinching it to make it look minuscule. He tossed it into the cupboard and then started on the second row of jars. These ones were gold.

"Imperial gold masque?" he asked. "Is this still for your hair?"

She fiddled with the jewel in her lap, a laugh threatening to form no matter how hard she bit her lip.

Oscar was *rambling*.

"Oh, this one has literal gold dust in it," he said, now openly scowling at the new batch of product he had uncovered. "*Elixir* of *Opulence*," he drawled sarcastically. "Radiant diamond infusion face mask. With cactus extract and powdered diamond." He snorted. "Just when I think I've seen it all. What's next? A crystal dildo?"

He glanced up from the box, catching her eye, his expression uncomfortably blank, terrifyingly without any hint as to whether that was supposed to be a dig or not. She was sure he had gone through her bag the year before and had seen—or more accurately *smelt*—the crystal Cian and Moses had used ... with her? On her? *In* her?

"That's ... absurd," she said, when he just continued to stare at her, waiting for a response.

He narrowed his eyes. "Right." Spinning, he opened the door to the bathroom and threw a few of the emptied boxes into the other room, giving the cameras a brief glimpse of him surrounded by boxes and crouched before her bathroom cabinet before he slammed the door again.

"Did you guys get any side effects from the bond?" she asked, holding out her hands when he opened a box full of makeup and skincare products.

He passed the smaller box into her hands. "Extreme restlessness, an increase in aggression and aggressive behaviour, and general moodiness." He said it all in a robotic, droning voice before poking his dark head out from the cupboard and giving her a bored look. "At least that's what Elijah and Gabriel put in their report."

"They wrote a report?" She fought back another chuckle but ultimately failed, and the sound of amusement spilled free.

"They sure fucking did, and they'll be writing one on your experience over the summer as soon as they get the details out of you," Oscar groused, shoving back from the cabinet as he finished with the products.

He began piling a small selection of them into the shower, and Isobel let her eyes wander for the first time since entering the bathroom. The floor was the same polished limestone as the rest of the dorm, but there were several thick, white circular rugs edged in cotton filigree, creating beautiful patterns against the stone. The sink was a delicate porcelain bowl, the faucet curved into the shape of a swan's neck, brushed in gold, the taps made of glass. Small porcelain vases were set into the wall on either side of the mirror, housing delicate crystal flowers.

There was a claw-foot porcelain tub resting beneath a window—which thankfully had etched glass, impossible to see anything more than mottled colour through. She really should have checked that earlier, preferably before Oscar began to strip her.

There seemed to be a large shower alcove, but she couldn't really see into it, since it was mostly tucked away behind marble walls, with only the entrance visible, where alcove shelving housed rows of fluffy, terracotta-coloured bath linen.

"Everything's ready," Oscar announced, striding to the door and snatching up his phone. "We'll discuss this in the group meeting, but ... we think it's best if you keep the same public surrogates. Me, Cian, and Kilian. For now."

"And later?" she asked, wondering at the inflection in his tone.

"We'll claim that our schedules were so busy we

were forced to add more surrogates into the mix to ease up the pressure on the current surrogates."

"Why do it that way?"

Oscar shrugged like he didn't care either way. "Public approval. We need everyone to love you, not want to tear your hair out."

Or her light out.

"Right. That makes sense."

"So ..." His fist tightened on the crystal doorknob. "Cian or Kilian?"

"Huh?" she blinked at him.

"After you shower. You need someone to nap with you. On camera."

"Oh." She felt fire flaming up her neck and into her cheeks. "Ah ..."

A small shudder travelled over his body like he was visibly shedding a violent feeling—odd, because she hadn't felt anything from him. "Forget I asked." He bared his teeth. Maybe he was trying to smile. "I'll let them fight over it. I'm going to leave now."

He looked like he was about to crush that door handle into crystal dust. Another tremor seemed to ripple over him.

"As soon as you say goodbye," he tacked on, a demand suddenly blooming in his eyes.

She approached him hesitantly, her fingers shaking as she reached for his shirt. When he didn't move or even so much as twitch, she flattened her palm to his hard stomach, using his body to anchor herself.

"Thank you for helping me," she whispered, pressing her cheek to his chest, his oleander scent so strong that she released a ragged breath of relief, her eyes fluttering closed. His fingers threaded in her hair, flexing against the back of her head.

"Welcome," he grunted, back to his monosyllabic self. "Shower, rabbit." He peeled away from her, turning off the music on his phone and slipping from the bathroom.

6
STRESS BALLS AND RAZOR BLADES

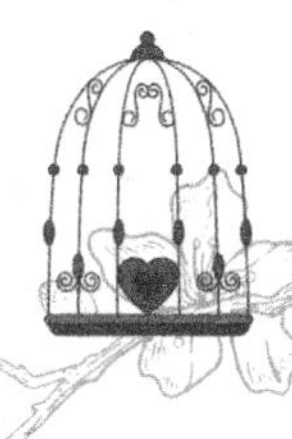

It wasn't until she was tucked into the shower alcove, her head turned up to the gentle stream that drifted like rainwater over her skin, that she came to terms with what she had just done.

Her last sexual encounter had been with Theodore, where she had admitted to having *feelings* for him, and here she was, letting his *friend* fuck her thighs. She hadn't even thought about what confessing her feelings for Theodore would mean with the other surrogates. Did it make it wrong if she continued allowing them to ease her bond in the same way? Was she leading Theodore on and then betraying him?

She stumbled to the bench cut into one of the shower walls—the shower seemed to be designed around a spa experience, with massage jets set into the walls and a small bench to rest on as steam choked the alcove. The stone of the seat was lined with amethyst gems, sprigs of dried flowers hanging from hooks above her, their cloying perfume wrapping her up in a comforting embrace.

But she couldn't relax.

She was getting *very* involved with more than one man at once, and none of them subscribed to the idea that "fate" could determine who belonged to whom. They wouldn't simply accept her taking her pick of the Alpha group just because she happened to be half-bonded to them all—the bond meant nothing to them, and it meant nothing to her. It was simply a problem they had decided to tackle as a group, a *problem* they had decided to share responsibility for. It had no great, magical power to decide their personal and sexual relationships for them.

They still had to decide for themselves.

And what Alpha in their right mind would decide to share the woman they were interested in with nine of their closest friends?

Oscar may have only been appeasing the bond for both himself and her, but the way he had refused to push further for fear of hurting her when she wasn't thinking straight made her uneasy. She wasn't experienced with relationships or harbouring feelings for anyone, but now suddenly it felt like she was growing emotionally attached to more than one of her bond mates. Theodore, certainly. Oscar, surprisingly. Kilian—because how could anyone *not?*

And Cian ... who concerned her even more than the others.

Cian had more charisma in his little finger than most people had in their wildest dreams, and he rarely ever deviated from his playful, easy-going personality. It made him seem utterly unreachable, and that intimidated her. It made her unsure how to approach him or talk to him. She mostly waited for him to come to her, but she couldn't keep doing that, not if he, Oscar, and Kilian were acting as her surrogates for the cameras. She would need to get comfortable telling him when she needed him—or they would likely all suffer the consequences of her ignoring the bond.

Her phone lit up in the towel recess, so she stood and fetched it, along with the jewelled artefact. She sat back on the bench, pulling in deep breaths to fill her lungs with the aroma of the dried flowers as the steam seemed to activate their scents.

She rested the jewel on her thigh and sleepily tapped at her messages.

Theodore: What were you doing when it changed colour?

Oscar: Not me.

Niko: What kind of joke is that?

Oscar: The kind that's a statement, not a joke.

Kilian: Isobel?

Oscar: She's in the shower.

Elijah: And you are...?

Oscar: Not a fucking idiot. You told me to rub her temples and use a soothing voice and to not make any sort of suspicious scenes.

Elijah: And you...?

Oscar: I rubbed, but I missed the temples. I used a voice, but it wasn't soothing. I didn't make any suspicious scenes.

Oscar: Gold star for me.

Moses: Regular saint, over here.

Niko: This is fucking awkward.

Cian: How is she?

Oscar: Dizzy, a bit confused. Her reflexes are slow and she's lost a lot of weight. But $10,000 worth of beauty products say she'll be a brand-new person in no time, thanks to all the cactus juice and diamond shavings her father could spare.

Theodore: What?

Cian: Rich girl shit.

Kilian: Who's going in there next?

Mikel (admin): Kilian, you go in. You and her in bed together probably won't cause a riot.

Elijah: Probably.

Mikel (admin): Cian, bring her some food and coffee at 4.

Cian: Will do.

Kalen (admin): Everyone be ready for a group meeting at 4:30 in my office. We have a lot to discuss

before classes start tomorrow and this brand-new shitshow really takes off.

Since everyone else had reacted to Kalen's message with a thumbs-up, she did the same, and then propped her head back on the wall behind her, deciding to close her eyes for just a minute ...

Tap tap tap.

"Illy? You all good in there?"

She blearily blinked her eyes open, the world around her swimming dizzily as she tried to orient herself.

"Illy?" Kilian called out from the other side of the door.

"Y-yes," she croaked, before raising her voice in a wobbly imitation of a shout. "Yes! Be right out!"

She stood up too fast, almost pitching into the stone wall, but she tossed out an arm at the last moment and caught herself. After waiting for her equilibrium to return, she turned off the shower and dried herself in record time.

There was a door to the right of the shower alcove, which she assumed was a dressing room, but Kilian interrupted her deliberations over whether she should chance peeking into the room to see if it was camera-free.

"I have some clothes for you," he said through the door.

She propped it open, standing clear of the cameras, and

he slipped the bundle into her hand. Sandwiched between the layers was her small contacts case, which he must have fished from her bag. She switched out her contact and dressed quickly, combing out her hair, brushing her teeth and slipping the stone into the waistband of her boy shorts.

She paused before pulling open the door, realising that the shirt was one of Kilian's—not one from her bag, but one from *him*. A breathy sigh of relief escaped her throat as she tugged the neckline up to her nose, inhaling deeply, a well of gratitude almost choking her.

She pushed into the room, blinking in surprise at how dark it was.

"Blackout curtains," Kilian explained, waving a tablet at her—as though that explained anything—before dropping it to one of the bedside tables.

Before she closed the bathroom door, she swept her eyes across the room while she still had light to see by, her heart squeezing at the beautiful, thoughtfully decorated space. She didn't have the highest opinion of the Ironside officials, but they sure knew how to make people feel like they had been transported to a whole new world.

The gleaming marble floor was cut into sections by silk rugs decorated in geometric patterns and floral motifs, in pale greens and creams. A king-sized bed dominated the centre of the room, the rich walnut of the frame contrasting deeply with the pale mauve and buttery gold bedding. She blinked at the bed, realising that twisting vines and floral motifs—which echoed the patterns on the rugs—were carved into the footboard, the sides, and the headboard. There was a canopy over the bed, a smooth fall of cream silk tied to either side of the headboard and footboard.

She cast a brief glance to the sitting area behind the bed, currently shrouded in shadow, though she could make out velvet armchairs and a chaise beneath the window, and what looked like a very ornate fireplace opposite the sitting area.

The officials had steeped her new home in luxury, the vastness of the wealth underfoot and overhead making her feel tiny, light as air, like she could glide across the gold-veined marble and tangle seamlessly with the airy silk canopy of her towering bed. It reminded her of how large, heavy, and cumbersome she had felt, stuffed into a closet with a blanket on the floor and a lock on the door as effective as glass against the power of the sun.

They truly wanted people to feel the difference. To *feel* their poverty being lifted from their shoulders, turning them so buoyant they could almost float.

It was the prettiest of gilded cages.

But it *was* a cage, and they could only float so far before colliding headfirst with the solid gold bars.

Kilian had dragged back the plush duvet as she took in the room, and he was sitting up against the pillows now, fiddling with the tablet again.

"You like it cold, right?" he asked.

It took her a moment to realise he was adjusting the temperature of the room. "Oh, yeah."

She closed the bathroom door and padded over to the bed, her head beginning to pound—her entire body protesting that she had been woken up in the shower. She slipped into bed beside Kilian, rolling onto her side to prop her phone onto the bedside table.

It was so dark, but there was the faintest hint of a daytime glow emanating from behind the blackout curtains and peeking beneath the door to her room. Still, when she lowered herself back to the mattress, it could have easily been night for all she could tell.

"Kalen installed the curtains," Kilian explained, rolling from the bed and untying the canopy. "He got here early and decided all the rooms needed them. We're going to have insane schedules this year, so he wants us to get sleep when we can." He pulled the canopy all the way around the bed, and she watched as his shadowed form ducked back through the fluttering silk, settling beside her again.

"White noise?" he asked, picking up the tablet again. He pressed a button and the fireplace suddenly flickered to life, making them both jump. "Oops, not that one." He tapped at the tablet and the flames turned off immediately—apparently, it was only an aesthetic fireplace. Which made sense, considering the climate.

"There we go," Kilian muttered as a soft wave of

subtle sound suddenly emanated from the ceiling. "This room system takes a minute to get used to."

He tugged the duvet up over both of them, shifting close to her. As tired as she was, she was also jittery and nervous. She had no idea *where* the cameras—or microphones—were. She had known almost everything about the previous Ironside location, having watched more episodes of the show than she could ever hope to count, but other than a few news articles as she had struggled to stay awake in the hospital, drifting in and out of consciousness, she knew next to nothing about where they were now.

"This is the longest I've been awake in a week," she whispered, barely louder than a breath.

Kilian crept closer, probably to hear her better. "Turn over," he muttered, also as quiet as a whisper. His hand gripped her hip beneath the cover, pushing her gently to face the other direction.

He slid one muscled arm beneath her head, tugging her right back into his body, his mouth against her hair. He pulled in a breath so deep his chest expanded against her back, forcing a shiver to travel through her body. His hand slipped into her shirt, flattening against her stomach. He pressed there, eliminating any space that might have remained between their bodies.

He didn't say anything else, and after a few moments, her exhaustion won against all the other sensations in her body, quieting the thoughts that zipped restlessly around her mind. She closed her eyes, soothed by his sweet bergamot scent and the warmth of his solid muscles surrounding her, even his possessive grip against her stomach, his hand spanning one side of her waist to the other. It might have kept her awake with nerves had she been less exhausted, but the protective, almost dominating touch calmed her, and she melted back against him, slipping into sleep.

KILIAN WAS IN THE COSIEST HELL ON EARTH.

His Alpha instincts were raging at him to turn the Sigma around, to part her pale thighs and force her to take his weight. To drag her eyes open and wear her out until those lids were heavy again, weighed down in satisfaction.

But their relationship wasn't like that, and he could smell Oscar on her. She hadn't washed him off her well enough. It was making his blood boil with the painful need to *erase* him from her skin, and then to go deeper, and erase the memory of him from her mind.

He tried to talk some sense into himself as she slept in his arms. As he pretended to sleep with her. As he kept his hand on her stomach. As he refused to twitch it an inch in any direction. He tried to tell himself that she was his friend, and in any case, he needed to get used to other people's scents on her, because she had never been *his*, not even for a minute.

It just ... wasn't working.

Whenever he thought he had talked some sense into his rioting thoughts, she let out a distressed puff of air against his bicep, and his hips jerked the barest inch against her soft flesh. He was aggressively hard, desperate for friction, but his frustration at their lack of privacy soared above his other emotions because most of all, he just wanted to talk to her.

He wanted her eyes wide and bright, those puffy cheeks bunching as she tried to hold back laughter. He wanted her healthy, not this wilted Sigma who had stumbled off the bus. He wanted her warming his lap as her lovely voice recounted all the reasons why they needed to set up her father for some sort of high-collar financial crime and get him locked up for life.

He wanted her head tipping back, her mismatched eyes catching on his, his hand drawing up to her neck, catching beneath her jaw and drawing her up, closer to his mouth ...

He throbbed against her and buried his face deeper into her hair.

So fine, maybe he wanted to do more than talk.

The door cracked open, the room flashing with light briefly before the door clicked and it grew dark again.

"Time already up?" His voice cracked.

"Yeah," Cian answered. He pushed through the silken canopy, holding what looked like a tray. He set it on the bedside table before crouching by the bed, his face placed before Isobel's. "Wake up, Sigma." He tapped her on the nose.

Kilian eased back from her, spreading out on his back and closing his eyes, willing his persistent erection to just fuck off and give him a break.

"Illy." Cian tried again, slipping his hand beneath the duvet.

Isobel twitched, and then rolled back and forth, like she was shaking off a bug, before settling again. She had her face half turned toward Kilian, and he watched as Cian's hand crawled up from beneath the blanket, only the tips of his tattooed fingers appearing as he rested them along her collarbone. He leaned over, planting his mouth by her ear, and whatever he said had her eyes flying open, immediately connecting with Kilian's.

Her lush lips parted on a silent sound, her tongue sneaking between them, wetting her lower lip, the slightest whine catching in the back of her throat. Kilian was seconds away from deciding that their whole plan could go jump off a cliff because he was going to kiss her, taste her, grab her, force his tongue past those parted lips —but then Cian inserted his hands beneath her arms and hauled her up, falling into her spot on the bed and bundling her into his arms.

Asshole.

Kilian scowled at him, sitting up. "Hand her over. You can get the food."

Cian shot him a narrow-eyed glare. "Wake up grumpy much? I even brought you chocolate."

Kilian's vision washed red, a growl snapping from his lips. "*Now.*" Alpha voice.

Cian tried to fight it, Isobel's widened eyes flicking between them in alarm, but Kilian won.

Just because he didn't use his influence, didn't mean he was without it.

The only people who outranked him were Oscar, Mikel, and Kalen. After forcibly swallowing down his own reaction, Cian plastered a smile onto his face that was all teeth and temper. He passed Isobel gently into Kilian's arms before flicking a switch on the wall beside the bed, turning on the halo of soft light set into the cornices of the ceiling.

Isobel placed a small hand against Kilian's chest, rubbing back and forth, so subtle. He let out a rattling breath, calming somewhat, before forcing a wry, empty grin onto his face. "I'm not a good napper. I always wake up crabby."

"You think?" Cian rolled his eyes, pulling the tray onto his lap.

Isobel strained out of Kilian's arms, snatching a steamy mug of coffee from the tray before Cian could even offer her anything. She sucked down several mouthfuls that were likely scalding her, if the wince in her forehead was anything to go by, but she didn't seem to care. She released a deep groan that went straight to his cock, followed by a full-body shudder as the caffeine seemed to hit her system. She did some sort of wriggle, like she was trying to shake some movement back into her body or like she was just *that* happy about the coffee. He hissed out a warning breath, pinching her thigh.

She froze, and it took her a moment to realise she was pressing his dick right up against her ass, nestling his hardness in the layer of soft cotton wrapping her body, but then her face was blooming with a soft, rosy flush—an adorably stunned expression arresting her features. She hid her face behind her mug and refused to lower it again, taking small, measured sips to maintain her disguise.

Isobel was embarrassed, but not nearly enough to move until she had finished her coffee. Especially since Kilian had looped a strong arm around her hips—a deterrent to her going anywhere, though she wasn't sure if he had done it consciously or not.

"How was your sleep?" Cian asked her, leaning back and folding his arms above his head, his cotton shirt sleeves slipping down to show a delectable swell of golden muscle.

"Good," she answered.

There was a knowing look in his stunning aquamarine eyes, so she uncurled a leg and kicked him in the thigh. He caught her leg, draping it casually over his lap, pushing the tray further down his thigh so that she wouldn't knock over the other coffee balanced there. Cian picked up the cup and handed it to Kilian, who grunted out a thanks that sounded a little forced.

"How long was that nap?" She squinted at the curtains, unable to tell how light it was outside. Kilian leaned back, switching out his coffee for the tablet and holding it in her lap, his chin notched onto her shoulder.

"Around seven hours," he said. "No wonder."

"No wonder what?" she asked, watching as he tapped on a house icon, and then a black curtain icon, and then the word *open*. The curtains slowly parted, filling the room with soft afternoon light.

Kilian didn't answer her, instead deciding to give her a mostly silent tour of the tablet, showing her how to order food from the dining hall—only available outside of general mealtimes—how to control the aesthetic fireplace, the lights, the speakers, and the projection screen that rolled down from the ceiling opposite the seating area. There was a popularity bank app, showing how many popularity points she had accumulated, and a rewards program to order things from Market Street.

"They rebuilt Market Street and Ironside Row?" she asked, absently eating the bowl of fruit and yogurt that Cian had handed to her.

"Bigger and better," Cian confirmed as Kilian flicked to an interactive map of the academy, zooming in on a huge slab of the grounds labelled *Ironside Row*. "They separated them, though. They needed more room for Ironside Row. They'll be holding games there every Friday night, and we're going to have to compete."

"For what?"

"Special privileges?" Cian guessed. "Popularity points? We don't actually know. I guess we'll find out."

She finished her food and coffee, and they all tumbled from the bed when Cian said it was time to meet with the others. She padded after them as they left the room, surreptitiously patting the waistband of her shorts to make sure the artefact was still there.

Cian and Kilian led her back downstairs, where they ran into Oscar, Elijah, and Gabriel—all of them carting around heavy book bags that were almost overflowing with cords and laptops. Gabriel and Elijah had changed out of their exercise clothes, donning linen shorts and loose shirts.

"How was your nap?" Elijah asked, nodding slightly in the direction of the archways Cian and Kilian were already heading toward, indicating that they should head that way.

He moved to follow them, and so did she. Oscar and Gabriel trailed them silently, so close that she could feel the heat of their bodies.

"I feel amazing," she answered, cutting Elijah a small, unsure smile.

He nodded, a flash of relief in his cold eyes. They had

entered a passage with a kitchen area on one side and a lounge on the other, the furnishings and fixtures as luxurious as she had come to expect. They passed into a closed-in hallway with a single door on either side, a plaque above each. Cian rapped his knuckles against the heavy walnut door with *Professor Kalen West* on the bronze plaque above it. He opened the door before anyone could answer his knock, and the rest of them filed in after him.

The office was much like her bedroom—open and sprawling with towering, squared-paned windows and plush, velvet-lined furnishings, hints of rich, honeyed walnut features scattered about. There were sheer silk curtains mottling the view outside the windows, and Kalen was leaning against a heavy wooden desk, his arms crossed over his chest, his yellow-amber eyes fixed on her face. The unwavering way he stared at her was enough to tell her that there were no cameras in the room.

"Isobel," he grunted, his gruff tenor enough to tell her that there were no microphones either. Oscar had told her earlier ... but she had been a little distracted.

She relaxed instantly, her shoulders slumping slightly. "Thank fuck for private offices."

Cian smirked, stopping at the bar, and bending to fish something from the small fridge set beneath. "Iced coffee, anyone?"

"Yes," she answered, quick as a snap. "Please."

Gabriel smirked at her quick add-on, nodding at Elijah before sinking into the velvet couch.

The door to the study opened again and the rest of the Alphas filed in, Mikel appearing last.

Isobel felt herself drifting toward Theodore—for what, she wasn't sure—but Kalen cleared his throat, pulling her up short.

"Will you oblige me?" he asked, holding out a large hand.

What?

She stared at his hand, and then peered up into his face, trying to figure out what he wanted.

The stone? She flicked up the hem of her shirt, pulling it from her shorts—the sudden stillness in the room wasn't lost on her, but the narrowing of Kalen's eyes had her attention caught.

"No," he rumbled, giving the artefact a rapid flicker of his attention before his eyes were boring into hers again. "You, Carter."

Oh.

Oh.

There are two sides to the bond, asshole, she admonished herself. While Oscar's dominant claiming and seven hours of sleeping baked in Kilian's scent and wrapped securely in his arms had settled things for *her*, it apparently didn't work that way for the rest of them.

She walked on light feet over to Kalen, placing her hand in his. His rough fingers wrapped around hers, dwarfing her hand as he tugged her a step closer and then turned her so that she was standing between his legs, facing the rest of the room. But that's all he did. He held her hand and had her stand there, so close but not touching other than their hands.

Elijah handed her a cold can, his cool attention flicking up to Kalen in brief question before he moved to the couch, passing another can to Gabriel before falling down beside him.

Moses and Theodore dragged the armchairs away from the heavy wooden coffee table, forming a semi-circle around Kalen and Isobel instead, as the others found seats. Mikel leaned against the wall by the window, his eyes narrowing on the way Kalen's hand enveloped hers for a moment before a mask of indifference fell over his face.

"Well," Mikel started, lips thinning, voice tight. "What a summer."

Isobel choked on an unwilling laugh as the others rolled their eyes.

"I think it goes without saying ... but that can never happen again." Elijah sighed. "It was a severe miscalculation on my part—you'll have to forgive me." He turned his heavy stare on Isobel. "Before you came along—and after you came along, to be honest—all of my plans have centred around covering for Theo and Moses and hiding their ferality. You were standing in that chapel, having a panic attack, and I knew you needed to get out of there before you could watch us burn Crowe's body, but I couldn't spare anyone to go with you because when Theo and Moses turn feral at the same time, it's a shit fight for our lives and we need all eight of us on task."

Isobel blinked at him, surprised at the grim expressions everyone else was throwing Elijah's way.

"I don't blame you," she said, frowning at him. "You told me to go next door. We're talking fifteen feet. You told me to go straight there, straight to Sophia and her family—who had literally just saved my life, so of course that made sense. I'm the one who fucked up. I should never have answered the phone. He—my father used Alpha voice on me."

"We figured." Gabriel's hands dug into his hair, his body language tense. He didn't fix his hair afterwards, which spoke volumes, and she examined them a little more thoroughly.

They all seemed to have grown, except for Mikel and Kalen, who must have already reached the end of the mysterious Alpha growth cycle that she still didn't understand. But other than that obvious sign of vitality, they looked ... almost haggard. Dark circles were smudged beneath their eyes. Elijah's pointed, streamlined features were more pronounced, as though he hadn't been eating properly, despite his swelling size. Gabriel's hair was more than just messy from the ministrations of his hands—he had outgrown his cut, the strands uneven as they brushed his neck and ears. Cian had fierce frown dimples digging into his cheeks, his brows drawn low, weighed down by his thoughts. Theodore and Moses were twitchy, fidgety, both of their eyes darkening until they began to look more like the twins they were pretending to be.

Oscar was rubbing his knuckles, which seemed to be bruised.

Kilian looked like he had seen a ghost.

Niko had an actual *stress ball* in his grip, his fingers flexing around it reflexively. Gripping, releasing, gripping ... *pop*.

He frowned, looking at the deflated thing in his palm.

Not a stress ball, a tennis ball.

He sighed, tossing the fuzzy green remnant to the coffee table before folding his arms and leaning up against the wall perpendicular to Mikel—almost matching the other man's pose. She was ashamed that she had been so out of it that morning she hadn't noticed how much the summer had affected them.

Elijah, who had taken a moment to mull over her words, finally shook his head. "No, this is on me. You were out of your mind with panic, utterly traumatised, and the group relies on me to come up with a plan in situations where everyone has lost their head. I failed everyone. I'm sorry."

"Is that why you won't fucking sleep?" Gabriel

snapped, surprising everyone, except for Elijah, who only clenched his jaw tightly, ignoring the other Alpha.

"What?" Mikel asked, fixing his stare on Gabriel. "You said he calmed down after we got Isobel out of that apartment."

"I lied," Gabriel said, without inflection, before turning back to Elijah. He downed the rest of his iced coffee, setting the can on the coffee table, his fingers shaking slightly. "He kept working, right up until the day we left. And in case none of you have noticed, he's sneaking out every night to work in the library."

"You're with me half the time," Elijah growled back, pale eyes flashing in a dangerous warning.

Kalen squeezed her hand before releasing her ... and she was moving before she could even think it through, passing the room to the couch where Gabriel and Elijah sat, plopping herself between them and setting her drink on the coffee table. They both shifted closer—the movement more of a reflex than anything—while glaring at each other over her head. Unsure how to proceed, she placed her hands on her thighs, her pinkies stretching out nervously to brush against their hard legs, which were already pressing up against hers.

Elijah was intimidating and cold, and she didn't know how to approach him on the best of days, let alone a day when he was tense and glaring holes through everyone. And Gabriel was no easier, being so particular about hygiene and personal space. She was almost trembling with nerves as she hesitantly moved her hands from her own legs to theirs.

It was awkward and clumsy, but at least they had stopped snapping at each other. Elijah grabbed her hand, drawing it over his lap and lacing his fingers with hers.

"Smart girl," he muttered, relaxing into the back of the couch, drawing her eye as his posture changed in an instant, morphing from tense, to exhausted.

His cool gaze simmered to a calm, icy ocean, lids lowering to half-mast.

Gabriel's thigh nudged hers, and she turned her attention to the coffee table, waiting for him to take her hand. He didn't, but he also didn't brush her off.

"Well, on the subject of what Gabriel, Elijah, and Oscar have been working on," Kalen said, "who wants to explain the app to Isobel?"

"We've infiltrated the Ironside network and set up a few precautions," Gabriel said, glancing down at Isobel. "Do you have your phone?"

"It's here." Cian dug Isobel's phone out of his pocket and handed it to Gabriel.

Gabriel began tapping away at her phone, and after a few moments of silence, he explained, "As soon as you get into bed at night, you need to hit the sleep icon in the Eleven app I'm installing," he said. "After exactly thirty seconds, it will start recording, preparing a loop of overnight activity. That's why Kalen had the blackout curtains installed—so that the officials won't realise they aren't monitoring a live feed. In the case of any accidental teleportations or ferality outbursts, this should cover us. As soon as one person hits the sleep icon, the entire dorm will start looping, erasing and replacing the last three minutes of footage. That should be enough of a buffer if anything happens suddenly, but don't fuck around—as soon as shit starts to go down, hit that button. We can only replace the last three minutes of footage. All the cameras will reset at four in the morning—before the sun rises. If something happens during the day, there's another button to scramble the cameras. They already think that having so many Alphas in one place fucks with their networks, but we want to use that option sparingly.

"We've added an AI proponent to the program that can cut together frames of you sleeping in different positions. It will insert transition footage at the end of the loop so that it looks seamless when the cameras reset. Try to toss and turn as much as you can for the next few nights. Move your bedding around. Give the algorithm a few options. There's too much room for error to implement this for daytime use, so all group meetings will have to happen at night. We tested the AI on scenes from movies where there were two people in the frame, and it was buggy as hell, so we're not going to risk that."

"Which means no bed sharing while the cameras are live," Niko explained, catching the struck look on her face. "When you need to settle the bond, we'll start the cameras looping and everyone will need to be back in their beds before four."

"O-okay," she croaked, still overwhelmed at the scope of what Elijah, Gabriel, and Oscar had created.

No wonder Elijah had been working non-stop.

"There's also a live recording sensor," Theodore spoke up, drilling his fingers agitatedly against his knee, his stormy gaze flicking to the Alphas on either side of her before he tore his attention back to her face, masking whatever emotion he was feeling. "So you can check the app at any time to know if the cameras around you are recording or turned off. Some of our training and tutoring sessions are supposed to be off-camera so that we can develop projects for the show without spoiling them. With the beefed-up surveillance, we weren't confident that they wouldn't try to spy on us—especially on you."

"We all have watches with the app installed." Mikel pushed off the wall, stopping before her and holding out a smartwatch with a plain, threaded white band. "It will vibrate when cameras around you are switching back on —both on the Dorm A loop and anywhere else if you're having a private session."

She took the watch and slipped it immediately onto

her wrist, biting her tongue at the question that almost spilled to her lips—of how they had afforded eleven smartwatches. They all seemed to be wearing one, all with the same simple white band.

She shook her head in bemusement. "That's amazing. Thank you."

Mikel nodded, shifting back to the wall. "About Cooper—we're sorry for the unpleasant shock. Theodore said they filled you in."

She grimaced. "He's supposed to stay out of our way, right?"

Mikel nodded, his nose twitching briefly as he quickly shut down whatever expression had briefly arrested his severe features. "Both a good thing and a bad thing, because that means he'll call you into his office more than seeking you out where there are cameras. You aren't to meet with him alone under any circumstances."

She blinked, glancing from tense, angry face to tense, angry face.

"How long were you watching us, back in Nevada?" she asked.

"Long enough," Moses grunted.

"Right." She sniffed, suddenly uncomfortable, though she wasn't sure what she had to be embarrassed about. All she had done was sleep, train, and drag her feet to appointments. "And what if nobody is around to go with me? What if he catches me alone? I'm not saying I can't hold my own. I'm just trying to manage expectations here. I'm new to being ... one of your ... one of ..." She trailed off, looking away from Mikel, her face flaming. "Last year I very much did my own thing. And it's pretty clear there's a hierarchy here, and orders to follow."

"Yes, mine," Mikel stated calmly. "Occasionally Kalen's and Elijah's."

"Only you three?" she asked, glancing to Kalen, who was standing as imposing and impassive as when she had walked into the room. "Just want to be clear."

"We all have a role." Niko surprised her by speaking up before anyone else. "Naturally, as a group of Alphas, we've formed a hierarchy amongst ourselves—it's one of the side effects of cohabitating as a large group, along with the surging. Our hierarchy naturally fell in order of age, starting with Moses, then Theodore, Elijah, Gabriel, me, Cian, Kilian, Oscar, Mikel, and finally, Kalen. So, when someone of a higher rank uses Alpha voice on someone of a lower rank, that person is generally compelled to obey. But as you will have noticed, not everyone flexes their dominance, and we don't let rank decide who listens to who."

"That's why everyone listens to Elijah and Gabriel and not one of these dickheads listens to me," Oscar said, flashing his teeth in a smile that could have been a snarl, one of his dark brows inching up, almost in challenge.

"But as the baby of the group, you'll have to answer to all of us."

She cocked her head to the side, a wry smile threatening to curl at her lips. "Not because I'm a Sigma?" She continued before anyone had a chance to answer. "Speaking of which ... are you all masking your emotions? I can't feel anything."

"We don't want to overload you," Kilian answered. "You've been through hell, and you've only had *hours* to recover."

She shook her head. "Don't bother, you'll just tire yourselves out. I can handle it."

"Can you?" Moses shot back quickly, though his tone wasn't combative.

"Can I carry on living exactly as I have for all of my life so far?" she returned dryly. "I think so."

He held up his hands, displaying his palms in supplication. "You asked for it, Sigma."

She wanted to roll her eyes, but she was suddenly struck. Bowled over by worry, frustration, and *need*. As far as she knew, "need" wasn't a negative emotion, but it was pinching into her skin from every angle, sharp and acerbic. She turned toward where she could feel it was a little more muted, not stabbing into her skin quite so insistently, and found Elijah still slumped against the couch, except this time, his eyes were closed and his chest rose and fell in a gentle rhythm.

Gabriel's hand crept over her thigh, his fingers

gripping tightly, drawing her attention back to him. "So yes, to be clear, you will take orders from Mikki first and foremost, as the rest of us do. It's his role to manage us. Elijah has the authority to direct or redirect us, and Kalen's word supersedes everyone else. If you were any other Sigma, we would be asserting our dominance over you until your rank as the youngest was observed, and then we would back off unless you challenged us. As our …" He trailed off, swallowing, unable to say the word.

"Mate," Niko said, surprising her again—except this time, he seemed to also surprise everyone else.

Gabriel's hand twitched on her thigh, his jaw clenching, his discomfort rolling over her in waves, along with tinges of guilt. "That dominance may be redirected," he continued as though he hadn't stumbled at all. "We may challenge each other instead, trying to assert a claim over you. Please try not to take it personally. We'll do our best to control our aggression."

"Is surging like going feral?" she blurted before she could think through the question.

It was rare that they openly spoke about ferality, so she was going to take advantage of the conversation while she could.

"A little." Theodore considered her. "The feeling of not being in control of your body is similar. I suppose you've experienced that now, haven't you?"

A shudder travelled through her, and she bobbed her head in a short nod. "It was … horrific."

Theodore and Moses both lowered their eyes, their emotions immediately cutting off from the steady wave that had been buffeting against her. She frowned, realising she had probably insulted them.

She carefully slid her hand from Elijah's and began to stand. Gabriel gripped her like he would deny her the movement, but then released her leg, his fingers trailing over the hem of her shorts, making heat curl in the pit of her stomach—a sensation she worked to smother.

She walked around the coffee table and approached the brothers sitting in armchairs beside each other. Theodore didn't let her have even a moment of indecision over who to choose or how to approach them. He stood, scooped her into his arms, and sat again with her bundled in his lap, her legs hooked over the velvet arm of the chair. His hand gripped her hip securely, his other arm wrapped tightly around her back, supporting her in a comfortable position. She rested her hand against his stomach, feeling the muscles bunch and jump beneath her touch. His head lowered into the crook of her neck and he inhaled deeply, a rough sound tearing from his throat.

Kalen cleared his throat. "There's a plan for this year. A delicate balance we need to maintain. We need the audience *devoted* to Eleven."

Her eyes snapped open—surprising her because she hadn't realised she had closed them—and she turned her head at the sound of the group name she had come up with the previous academy year. Gabriel had said it earlier, but she had been too preoccupied thinking about the app they had created to register that they had named it after the group.

"At the moment, the fans love to pair you with different Alphas," Kalen continued, addressing her directly. She suspected they had already discussed most of these points with each other. "But that's only because you aren't confirmed to be dating any of them and there hasn't been any damning footage to point the fans in one direction or another. We need to keep it in that sweet spot.

"We want all evidence to point to you being the protected princess of Ironside, building on all the PR work your father's team has already done, with one notable difference. We don't want the focus to be on your mate. For several reasons." Kalen nodded to Mikel, who picked up where Kalen had left off.

"Firstly, it's going to bite us all in the ass if it leaks that one of us is your mate. So we're just not going to address it at all. That way, we're not doing major damage control and trying to take back lies we've publicly spoken if that ever does happen. When people ask about your mate, just deflect, or say that you're not willing to talk about that subject."

Isobel nodded. "That's easier than acting."

"The other reason is purely a safety issue." Kalen shifted, crossing one of his leather shoes over the other, uncrossing his arms to grip the edge of the desk behind him. It seemed like "safety" might have been his area of concern, whereas Mikel was more focused on the PR side of things. "The more you advertise that you're searching for your mate, the more you open yourself up to creeps and stalkers trying to prove that they're your mate. We can't control the way the show twists their narrative, but if we give them *nothing*, they'll do one of two things: they'll latch onto the next best story if it's good enough, or they'll force the story they want out of you."

"So we need to give them something better to focus on than my missing mate?" she asked.

Mikel's hard lips twitched. "Precisely. We're going to give them Eleven. As a group. You and eight Alphas: all of them fighting to be your favourite, but none of them succeeding. A fun game for the fans to gamble and gossip and fight over. Endless material for the officials to twist and frame however they like—except they won't succeed in framing any of the guys as your favourite because the Eleven social media accounts are going to tell the *real* fake story."

She opened her mouth to ask *how*, but Gabriel had anticipated the question and was already counting items off his fingers. "Lives, reels, photos, behind-the-scenes videos, sneak peeks, and posts. I'll be handling the social media, so you all just need to capture as much as you can and send it all to me. I'll make sure it doesn't violate our Ironside contracts."

"There's one more piece to the puzzle," Oscar said, leaning forward in his chair. Prickles of unease skittered over her skin—not her own unease, but theirs. "You're going to need to get a fake boyfriend."

She stared at him, already shifting uncomfortably in Theodore's lap at the sudden influx of possessive fury threatening to hammer her into the floor, though all their faces remained impressively blank. Something they were clearly well-practised with.

"What?" she choked. "But I thought ... I mean Kalen and Mikel said ..." She swallowed, and then gave up trying to find the least offensive way of phrasing her question. "Could you all handle that? Not that you're *into* me, I know that. I just mean, with the bond, with the surging and everything."

"We have no choice." Oscar sounded like he was aiming for a reasonable tone, but the words jumbled out on a snarled breath instead. He tried to clear his throat, but it ended on a growl, and then he gave up masking his rage altogether, leaning forward and fixing her with a dark look. "Just don't let him touch you, or look at you, or go any-fucking-where near you."

"Fuck's sake." Gabriel sighed, his head falling back. He pinched his nose. "The Beta is going to have to talk to her and stand near her, Oscar."

"The Beta?" She whipped to face Gabriel. "You've already picked someone?"

"A third-year," Niko answered, pulling another

tennis ball from his pocket and resuming his flexing. "Someone Oscar had dirt on. Mateus Silva—one of Wallis' friends. You know him. Is he acceptable to you?"

"I suppose." She chewed on her lip, spurred to shift off Theodore's lap by Niko's agitation. Theodore lifted his head from her neck, blinking his eyes in a confused way as she slipped out of his arms—had he almost fallen asleep too? He seemed to shake himself, shoving his hands into his pockets, his darkening eyes tracking her as she hesitated by Moses' chair.

"Well?" The combative Alpha shifted his hips forward, apparently getting more comfortable. "You can't skip me, not after you did Kalen. Now *everybody* is on the table."

"You're the worst," she said, staring at him.

"Stop teasing her," Mikel ordered.

Moses beckoned to her—definitely still teasing her. "Just pretend I'm my brother."

"Stop it," Theodore snapped. Judging by the amount of tension radiating off him, she hadn't helped him overly much.

She sucked up her courage and perched on the arm of Moses' chair, wringing her hands in her lap as she tried to decide where to put them. He rolled his eyes at her, dragging her down to his lap and turning her to face the rest of the room, his arms wrapped around her waist. Despite his teasing, he held onto her tightly, his nose brushing the back of her head.

“Goddamn,” he groaned, inhaling deeply. “Have you always smelled this good?”

“Have you always spoken your intrusive thoughts out loud?” Theodore demanded.

“Pretty much, yeah,” Moses drawled, squeezing Isobel.

7
KALEN IS TOO BIG

"MAYBE YOU SHOULD ASK *WHY* SILVA BEFORE YOU AGREE." Theodore's voice was harsh, but he didn't look angry at her.

He didn't look anything except tense and frustrated.

"Okay. Why did you guys pick Silva?" she relented, not that she really cared. If Theodore could put up with Wallis for so long, then she could put up with the most popular male dancer in her previous lyrical ballet class.

"He sent you a package." Kilian spoke calmly, but there was a dark undertone to his voice that had her head snapping around to look at him. "He obviously didn't know that you were arriving late, because he gave it to me when I said you were sleeping and that I'd deliver it to your room."

"What was the package?" Unease slithered down her spine at the looks on their faces.

"A prayer card, two dolls, and a whole lot of razor blades tucked into the packaging," Kilian gritted.

"What?" She jumped to her feet, tearing out of Moses' hold. "Are you okay?"

"I tipped it out onto the table," Kilian reassured her. "I didn't stick my hand in there."

The fight drained out of her body, quickly replaced with confusion. "Wait—a prayer card? Dolls?"

"A silly settlement superstition," Cian explained. "He had already bled on one of the dolls and the prayer card. Some people back in the settlements believe you can bleed onto voodoo dolls and bury them with a prayer card, and the gods will bond the souls of the dolls together."

"He was trying to *bond* me?" she screeched, the blood draining from her face. "And you want him to be my fake boyfriend?"

"We have his life in our hands." Oscar spoke like his own words were leaving a bad taste in his mouth. "You know how serious the officials are about people messing with bond magic and trying to force bonds. There's nobody in this academy we can control as completely as him right now. And he's already been warned about fucking with you. I've already told him that if we catch him doing any more voodoo shit, he's dead."

"Dead how?" she asked, cutting Oscar a suspicious look.

"Dead like a corpse." He didn't even hesitate.

She winced. “Oscar.”

“Isobel.”

She sighed, glancing around the room, hoping for someone to step in. They just stared impassively back at her.

“You can’t go around threatening to *kill* people,” she hissed.

“Threats are for people who don’t intend to follow through,” he snarled.

Niko’s second stress ball popped, making her jump. He sighed, tossing it to the coffee table. She approached him cautiously, holding out her hand. “I am not a tennis ball,” she warned him, hesitant to put her ligaments into his flexing grip.

He snorted, taking her other hand—the one she hadn’t offered—and spinning her back to the wall beside him so that he could tuck her beneath his arm, their linked hands hanging across her chest.

“To be clear,” Mikel spoke up, “Silva will not be permitted alone time with you unsupervised, and he will not be added as a surrogate. Since your surrogates were established before he came into the picture and you won’t be sleeping with any of them on camera—and especially with you putting on such a platonic display with Bellamy over the summer—we’re confident that people won’t question the morality of you having a boyfriend and maintaining your surrogates on the side. If anyone questions you, you can just say that you'd like to keep the bond separate from your romantic life. This will help to minimise the bond even more."

"Won't people get angry that I'm being unfaithful to my mate?" she asked.

"The mate who hasn't materialised despite you touring the settlements to find them and broadcasting your odd eye colour all over the world?" Gabriel arched a perfect brow at her. "I don't think so, not anymore."

She shrugged. "I suppose that's a fair point."

He nodded, crossing his ankle over his knee. "You've waited long enough. You did your best to find them. It should be acceptable for you to move on with your life now."

"Next item on the agenda." Kalen checked his watch. "Is the group itself. With Cooper out of the way, you can sign a contract appointing myself and Mikel as your co-managers. The others have already signed. The term is for ten years, and it grants us the full rights to every song produced by Eleven."

"We insisted," Kilian explained before she could even question it. "It makes Kalen and Mikel indispensable. The laws governing Ironside are different to the settlement laws. Anyone here can sign with a manager or a public relations team, for any length of time. The stipulations are that if those people don't win, the contracts are void. So if we win as a group, our contracts are valid. They apparently didn't account for the absurd notion of anyone wanting to hire *Gifted* representation instead of a human team."

"The Track Team will put up a fight," Kalen allowed. "They control the Icon track and every Icon past and present, we know that. But if we time our moves right, we can reveal to the public that Eleven is signed to myself and Mikel, and lean on the popularity for some protection."

"Because if we make it really big, they can't just disappear us," Isobel surmised, drifting unconsciously closer to Niko, sipping on his heady whiskey scent as she sought the heat of his solid body.

"Everything we do from this moment on," Mikel said, "we do for Eleven. Every drop of sweat, every hour in the practice rooms, every class you take, every picture you upload. Gabriel is in full control of social media, so when he tells you to do something, you do it." Mikel seemed to be lecturing everyone at once, fixing each of them with a slow, careful, calculating look. "When Elijah tells you to switch things up, you don't ask questions. You switch things the fuck up. When I tell you to train harder, you train hard enough to bleed. When Kalen tells you to take extra lessons, you don't think for a second that you don't need them. From tomorrow, this show is ours. We direct it. We take it where we want it to go. And it's going on the journey of our group forming."

"There's a way this is all supposed to play out." Elijah's husky voice had them all turning to look at him.

He was hunched over his knees, looking haggard, as though the short nap had only made him sick. She knew the feeling—it was exactly how she had felt in the shower. She almost broke away from Niko to go back to him, but Mikel shook his head, catching something on her face.

He mouthed, "Keep it even," at her while everyone was still focussed on Elijah.

"We've already started pushing the hashtag *#eleven* across social media, getting everyone interested without explaining what it could possibly mean," Elijah went on to explain, acting like he hadn't just slept through half of their discussion. "And we're going to go live with one of our group sessions every week, where we will start to publicly form the group, getting everyone curious and invested as we choose who is going to be assigned to certain roles in the group and test each other's skills. Kalen and Mikel will be directing those sessions, so it gets them in front of the camera too. We won't announce anything, so the officials will just think we're preparing a group project and will let it play out for the ratings. By the time they figure out we're intending for this to be permanent, it needs to be too late. We need the fans backing us completely. We need them threatening a riot at the idea of the group being broken up. Let me see the artefact." That last bit had been tacked on so suddenly, it took Isobel a moment to realise Elijah was talking to her.

He had his hand held out.

She wiggled out of Niko's hold, dug into the waistband of her shorts and was about to drop it into Elijah's palm when the colour caught her attention. "It's changed again," she said, shocked.

The colour was still rosy, but it had thicker gold tendrils weaving through, making it appear veiny.

"Yes, I know," Elijah said, plucking it out of her hand before turning his attention to Theodore and suddenly changing the topic again. "When are you going to have sex with Wallis?"

Theodore stared back at him steadily, one dark, winged brow popping up in question.

Isobel's stomach swooped low, acid rushing to the back of her throat.

Was this part of the plan?

What the fuck?

Elijah hummed in triumph, turning the jewel before his eyes. It was changing again, bleeding more red than gold.

"Well, that confirms that," he said.

"What?" Isobel snapped, sharper than she intended.

"This monitors the health of the bond," Elijah explained, still staring at the jewel. "Red is bad. Gold is good." His eyes lifted from the artefact, quickly categorising her pinched expression before a flash of understanding chased away the distracted look on his face. "Theo isn't actually going to sleep with Wallis. Sorry for that."

"Wait," Theodore groused. "Illy, you *believed* that?"

"I don't know!" She tossed up her arms. "I've never been *half bonded* before."

"Sex is off the table at this point." Mikel announced it like he was reading out their schedule for the afternoon, his face never so much as flinching. "For all of us."

"What?" She swallowed, guilt surging up into her chest.

She had almost had sex several times now. She would have, too. In the storage room with Moses. In bed with Theodore. Maybe even in the bathroom that morning with Oscar. She would have without hesitation—but each of the Alphas steered it in a different direction.

"I felt that," Elijah said, all of the exhaustion wiped from his features. He held his hand over his chest.

"Felt wh—"

"Guilt," he answered before she could ask the question.

"I think we all felt it," Mikel said, dark brows drawing together as he surveyed the room, before settling on Isobel again. "I wasn't talking about ... within the group. I meant sex with people outside the bond is no longer possible."

"Why?" She swallowed again, praying that them feeling her emotion was just a random once-off, that she might have accidentally pushed it out at them through the bond the way Kalen had taught her. "Was it possible at some point?"

"When we were more or less strangers to each other?" Kalen shrugged. "It could have been accomplished with minimal to no damage to the bond. But now? I don't think so. With you taking most of the side effects, it's not something we're going to risk."

"Then ..." She glanced around the room, realising she was standing in the middle of them all, having not yet moved to the next person. "What ... Who ..." She gulped, facing off against ten utterly impassive expressions. Bond magic was such a mysterious, taboo topic, steeped in superstition and paranoia. She knew as much as the humans did—from watching Ironside. The only time either of her parents truly spoke about their relationship or the bond was when her father revealed that Caran wasn't even his mate, but the Tether of his deceased brother.

He made their relationship sound like a cold, emotionless transaction ... but it couldn't have been *that* emotionless or cold. Not if Isobel existed.

Still, none of that could have prepared her for the realisation that she was now the reason that ten aggressive *and* energetic Alphas could never have sex again, for as long as she lived.

Unless they had sex with her.

She swallowed again, her breaths coming faster, her chest beginning to rise and fall rapidly.

Would they expect that of her?

Theodore?

Kilian?

Oscar?

Cian ... *oh god, Cian will never survive.*

Elijah? Gabriel? *Niko?*

Mik—

Oh god.

Kalen was too big.

He would destroy her.

"This may not be the best time ..." Kilian hesitated, a wince in his voice. "But we can more than feel what you're feeling right now."

"W-what do you m-mean?" She was hunched over, her hands on her knees, about to have a full-blown panic attack.

"We can hear your thoughts, Illy." Theodore was by her side, a hand on her back, rubbing back and forth in a light skitter of strong fingers.

Fuck.

FUCK.

What had she thought? Something about Kalen's size, certainly ... and now that she was thinking about it, she was *thinking about it*. Because she had seen *it*. When she slipped into his head while he had a woman hanging suspended before him.

"Isobel," Kalen rumbled. "Just calm down. Take a few deep breaths. I—"

"Oh my god, *you* can't be the one to try and calm me

down right now," she wailed, pressing the heels of her palms into her eyes.

"You can't tell me what to do," he rumbled back, sounding closer than before. His hands were on her arms, drawing her hands away from her face. "Come here," he muttered, walking backward and drawing her with him.

She obeyed because that was exactly what he had trained her to do. Their hours spent in the climbing gym—rarely interacting outside of it—had conditioned her to listen for the sound of his voice and to obey him as though a forty-foot drop depended on it.

He caught her eyes, holding her captive as he drew her back to his desk with small steps, before he turned, picked her up and sat her on the edge, his hands fleeing her waist as soon as she was settled. He took a step away, still close, but not crowding her.

"Nobody is asking you to have sex with them and nobody is expecting it," he rumbled.

When she just stared at him, still trying to batter away the panic they all *knew* she was feeling, a gravelled sound rumbled out of his chest.

"Acknowledge, Sigma."

"A-acknowledged," she squeaked.

"Your body is your own, and you choose what to do with it at all times—including when you choose to give that power away to someone else. I know you've experimented with a few things to ease the bond, but do not *ever* forget your safe words. They're for you now and always."

"What about the others?" She voiced the first question that popped into her head, still a little too overwhelmed to digest the situation.

"They'll use the same words you're familiar with, princess." Kalen was using that low, soothing timbre that the Alphas used when they were trying to appease the bond.

But it wasn't going to work, because her thoughts were finally starting to catch up. Surely, they would begin to resent her when they couldn't have sex with their girlfriends.

How would they maintain relationships?

The harder she spiralled, the more she seemed to lose her grip on the wall she usually kept her emotions locked behind, and they started to spill over her exactly as they had when she woke up in her father's apartment after the shooting.

There was panic, jealousy, discomfort, and guilt. Her stomach clenched, saliva pooling in her mouth.

She was going to be sick.

"I need to—" Mikel sounded like he was in pain as he pushed off the wall.

"All yours," Kalen interrupted, voice tight.

He stepped away, and Mikel took his place, tilting her chin up until his mottled blue-black eyes were an inch from hers.

"This is causing me physical pain," he said, probably hoping to appeal to the Sigma inside her—which was smart, because it worked almost immediately, and she tried to halt her spiral so that he wouldn't be affected.

She hadn't had a chance to go to him yet, to settle the bond for him, and now she was pushing a boatload of panic onto him.

"Stop," he groused, his hands cupping the sides of her face, his forehead falling to hers. "You didn't do this to us, Isobel. This happened *to* you. Just breathe, pet." His rough thumbs stroked along her cheekbones, making her blood hum in fizzling realisation because *Mikel Easton* was touching her.

He was touching her a lot.

"Yes, I am." He let out a gruff sound that might have almost been a laugh. "Focus on that and focus on breathing."

His steadfast, abrasive demeanour was easy for her to latch onto, his roughened voice easily commanding her attention, his mismatched eyes disconcerting and arresting, pulling all of her focus until she was matching his breaths with her own. He pulled air through his firm lips, and she copied, both of their chests expanding, his gaze flickering down to the way she pursed her lips. He held his breath, and she held hers.

His eyes darkened, his breath rushed out, his face inching closer before he suddenly released her head, his hands falling to the desk either side of her thighs. "Good girl."

The words were a heavy vibration that shivered down her spine and landed low in her belly, unfurling warmth through her body. His eyes flashed with realisation, his pupils expanding to darken his gaze further.

Realisation of ...

How he had just made her feel.

"S-sorry," she stumbled over her apology, already mortified. "It's the bond—"

"No," Mikel interrupted calmly. "It's not. Don't apologise. Do you find everyone here attractive, Carter?"

She opened her mouth, but Kalen spoke before she could answer.

"Don't lie again." His voice was deep silk, his broad features arranged into severe, harsh lines.

She wanted to curl up into a ball and die, just a little bit. But these Alphas, they were her people, now. They were her people forever. Whatever that meant.

She *had* to assert herself within the circle of their influence. Had to make her voice heard and not shrivel away beneath their testosterone.

"Yes," she forced out, attitude leaking into her tone. "W-what of it?"

Kalen and Mikel both smiled like sharks, like her sassiness was adorable.

"It's not news," she immediately defended. "Everyone thinks you're all attractive."

"Correction," Oscar drawled, his scratchy voice making her throat tighten up. "They think everyone but myself and Mikel are attractive."

"That's bullshit," she spat, anger coursing through her. "Don't believe everything you read online. I ... like your scars." She was blushing so hard she could feel the heat emanating from her skin as she flickered her gaze to Mikel for the briefest second to include him in the statement before she was staring hard at her own lap.

She hadn't ever tried to think about why she found the more savage beauty of Mikel and Oscar appealing, but she also didn't care to analyse it further. Not with them *listening to her thoughts.*

"So it could be worse," Kalen reasoned with her, tugging at her with that smooth, persuasive tone. "You're stuck with people you find attractive, at least. Moses, Theo, Gabriel, Cian, Kilian, and Oscar have all offered to ease your bond in any way you need—and they were well aware of what that could entail. If you end up having regular sex with all six of them, that's between you and them, and any of you could back out of that arrangement at any point, for any reason. The existence of the bond doesn't erase consent."

"What about the rest of you?" she mumbled, still staring at her lap.

"I won't touch you," Kalen announced, forcing her head to jerk up.

She had calmed down enough to slam a wall down on *whatever* emotion threatened to bubble up at that statement.

"I won't be assisting you either," Mikel said.

KALEN COULD SEE IT IN HER FACE.

The Sigma was *insulted*. He happened to like that spoiled little rich girl side of her, but only because it made his hand itch to punish it out of her until that little pout had a matching stream of tears.

"We're in a position of authority over you," he explained. "Quite an intense one too. We'll be treating you like one of our Alphas, which means telling you what to eat, when to exercise, how hard to push yourself, and more or less everything else. We can't complicate that position."

"But what about your *lives*," she insisted, that flush burning brighter in her cheeks. "Your girlfriend." She said it almost accusingly, her mismatched eyes searching his face. "And um, your sex life," she tossed at Mikel.

Kalen's girlfriend really was becoming a problem. Most of the year before, she had been content with her bragging rights, and with the few visits back to the settlement he made. But over the summer, things had begun to fracture. He couldn't fuck her, and he was stumbling over the practised words of adoration that he had been feeding her for years now.

She was his cover—and that wasn't something he could let go of easily. Josette was his plant in the settlement. The loyal whisperer who flattened out all the wrinkles he caused, all while he was absent and doing whatever he wanted at Ironside. She didn't expect monogamy—he had made it clear that wasn't an option from the beginning—but she did expect her perfect little world to keep running without any incorrect brush strokes in the portrait of them she liked to wave under people's noses.

She wanted to tell people she was dating *the* Professor West of Ironside Academy—not fielding questions on where *the* Professor West was, and whether *the* Professor West had forgotten all about her.

Why was he never with her, even after he came home for the break?

Why were they still not living together?

Why did she never sleep at his place?

The other professors all brought expensive gifts home for their partners—where were her expensive gifts?

She wasn't going to stand for the questions much longer. That wasn't part of their arrangement. She hadn't done anything about it yet—other than pushing and prodding him for more. But that wouldn't last.

"My sex life is not your concern," Mikel said, folding

his arms. He had taken too long to answer, but his voice was stern and brooked no argument.

Isobel nodded at him, chewing her lip.

Kalen knew he had to say something, but he was stuck between a rock and a hard place.

The Sigma was about to see a *very* sexual side of him. Their first night in the Stone Dahlia was looming, and there would be no shielding her from what he did inside his room.

He couldn't touch her.

He couldn't touch anyone else.

He couldn't break up with his girlfriend. Not when her ire could turn the tide for him within the settlement.

"There are people relying on me in the Mojave Settlement—and many of the other settlements," he said, thinking over his words carefully. "Just like all of these guys relied on me or my grandmother at some point." He tilted his head, nodding briefly to the rest of the room, though he kept her gaze. "My relationship with Josette was never about romance. She offered me the influence I needed in the settlement, and I offered her the status she needed to get in with the officials—because they wouldn't even blink at her before she became involved with me, but I was able to put her into contact with important people. She's a fierce loyalist, and without her, some of my actions might start to look ... a little less loyal. I need to find a way to keep her on board for a little longer."

Isobel was chewing her full bottom lip, her fingers twisting together. It was her usual nervous tell. It seemed she wasn't projecting her thoughts or emotions anymore, and he immediately wanted to dive back into her mind and rummage around until he could lay out the future—*all of their futures*—into a neat timeline. Because he had no idea how to make this work.

None of them knew how to make this work.

There were fucking *ten* of them and one of her.

Not to mention Theodore and Moses were the two most likely to fight over her, and they were the two they really could not afford fighting or losing their tempers.

Did he really think he could go the rest of his life without having sex?

He didn't know how to answer that question.

Or he did, but he didn't want to admit it to himself, because whenever he tried to think about it, the question changed to whether he really thought he could go without sex with *her* around.

He didn't want those thoughts in his head.

"I ..." Isobel was trying to vocalise something, but it must have been difficult to say because her brow wrinkled and her teeth dug deeply into her lip as she cut herself off.

He was transfixed for a moment, his instinct screaming at him to order her to bite deeper, and deeper ... until she drew blood and offered for him to taste it. But she wasn't a pretty little toy for him to play with. She was his mate, and they were balancing on a very fragile ledge.

"This summer was too much," she finally said. "I can't live like that. And what Eve did to me? If that's what a bond infraction feels like, I can't live with that either." She lifted her stunning eyes, ignoring everyone else to stare at Kalen because *he* was the one she had identified as most likely to hurt her. "You can't sleep with her."

Don't tell me what to do, little girl. The Dom in him roared to the surface, and he shoved it down with a wince. *Don't make her beg for it. This is her right.*

"I won't be," he promised.

"Or anyone else."

"I won't be, Carter."

She sucked in an unsteady breath, addressing the room without actually looking at anyone.

"Nobody can defile the bond like that. If anyone plans to do that, I'm out of the group."

She was rubbing her arms, trying to calm her goosebumps. This was taking a lot for her to make such demands of them, and he felt a swell of pride that he had no right to feel. He didn't make her this way.

She was incredibly adaptable.

Surprisingly so, for a girl who had everything handed to her—except freedom, of course. She was very unlike an Icon child in that regard.

"We hear you," Theodore said. "Loud and clear."

None of the others answered, and Kalen knew why. They had already discussed this issue over the break, and everyone had agreed that anything resulting in a soul infraction was unacceptable, but Isobel wasn't just addressing a room of men, or a room of Alphas, or even a room of her own friends.

She was addressing her *mates*.

Cutting them off from all the avenues of sexual gratification they weren't even slightly interested in, and not addressing the one avenue they *were* interested in—or at least some of them.

Probably most of them.

Elijah wasn't about to admit it, but he stared at her like every flutter of her long, dark brown lashes was the most fascinating thing he had ever seen—which was a dangerous thing for her, but she didn't seem to realise it. Gabriel looked at her like she was one of his precious notebooks and he was barely controlling the urge to stack her onto his desk where she belonged, erecting a ten-foot wall around her so that nobody else could contaminate her.

He hadn't known Kilian to show interest in anyone other than his ex, but Isobel had him wrapped entirely around her finger. She could tell him to burn down the entire academy and he wouldn't even hesitate.

Cian was harder to read. He wanted to fuck her, that much was clear. Kalen suspected the younger Alpha had become obsessed with Isobel, but could never find any actual signs of it. Cian was too good at putting on a mask.

A mask Theodore and Oscar didn't even bother with and hadn't bothered with since the Sigma waltzed into their lives. Both of them would tear apart anyone who so much as blinked wrong at Isobel, including the members of their own group.

Niko was, thankfully, displaying far more self-control in Isobel's presence than the others, but it didn't change the fact that he wasn't acting the way he would act if he was disinterested in someone. Niko was warm on the surface, but cold underneath to everyone except those closest with him. If he wasn't interested in Isobel, he wouldn't even be standing inside the room right now. He certainly wouldn't be standing there silent at her demand they cut off all sexual activity with anyone outside the group.

He was holding his tongue for the exact same reason everyone else was holding their tongue.

Because the urge to ask her if she was also off limits was too strong.

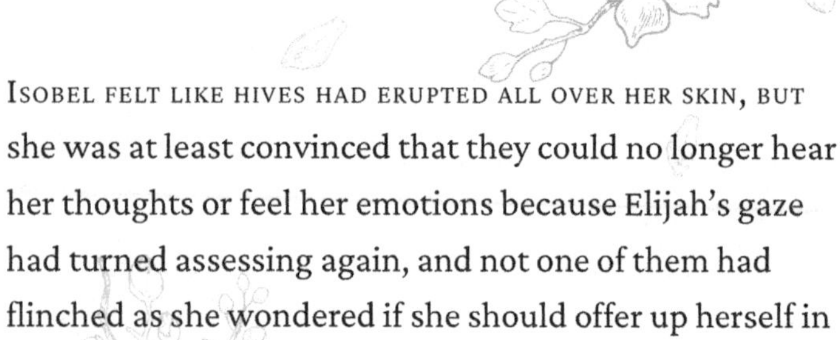

8

IF ANYONE CAN, A SIGMA CAN

Isobel felt like hives had erupted all over her skin, but she was at least convinced that they could no longer hear her thoughts or feel her emotions because Elijah's gaze had turned assessing again, and not one of them had flinched as she wondered if she should offer up herself in place of any outside options.

That would have been an insane thing to say.

"We need to address the obvious," Elijah sighed out. "What if Isobel wants to develop sexual relationships with several of us at the same time?"

Okay, maybe it wasn't so insane.

"To appease the bond?" she asked, just to be clear.

Elijah cut her a flat look. "No."

"No?" She froze, the word almost getting stuck in her throat.

"Because you want to be fucked, Isobel." Those

words delivered in Elijah's calm, almost cutting tone, were doing strange and confusing things to her insides. "That's why you would fuck someone."

"Oh." She relaxed somewhat, her colour rising again. "Yeah, sorry. I don't really know how all this works."

"Nobody is trying to force you into marriage so they can turn you into your moth—" Moses cut himself off, but it was too late.

"I wouldn't marry you anyway," she snarled at him.

"But you'd fuck me," he snapped right back, rising from his chair. "Just as long as it doesn't have to mean anything."

"What else would it mean!" Her words were shrill, and Mikel cut her and Moses a quelling look, making her want to shrivel up.

"It would mean that touching you lights me on fire," Moses growled, advancing on her, his eyes flashing black. "It would mean I would crawl out of my own skin to get inside you. Hypothetically," he tacked on, pausing his strides and holding up his hands, turning partially toward where he must have sensed Theodore leaping out of his chair. "Just as an example. Anyway, we're done with this meeting, right? I have shit to do."

"Not yet." Kalen's expression had become blank and terrifying again. "There's still the issue of the teleporting side effect. If Isobel teleports to one of us, there's no chance of sneaking her onto the fire trail. We'll be completely exposed."

"One of us has to be glued to her at all times and the bond must be kept satisfied," Elijah said, flashing the jewel to the room. "Our first priority needs to be keeping this shining pure gold."

"Give it to me," Mikel demanded, striding over to the couch. Elijah handed over the artefact and Mikel slipped it into his pocket. "I'll keep an eye on it and pull everyone up if there's a problem. It's absolutely essential that Isobel has one of us by her side—preferably touching her in some way—throughout the day. After a few days of letting the AI system record us, there should always be someone in her bed, unless she needs some alone time. If that's okay with everyone?"

The Alphas nodded, and Isobel bobbed her head along with them, but then cleared her throat nervously. "Actually ... I was wondering if it might be a good idea to talk to Maya."

"The Guardian?" Gabriel asked.

"It's risky." Elijah sighed. "But so is the bond. It could expose us at any second. I think the Guardian can be trusted. She tested the first soul artefact—risking her position and safety to keep the results of her test hidden—and she didn't tell the officials about what actually happened in the chapel. She was questioned quite extensively too."

At Isobel's confused look, he tacked on: "I hid a camera in their cottage."

"Of course you did," she muttered. "So? Can I talk to her?"

Mikel and Kalen shared a look, both of them frowning.

"Take Niko with you," Kalen finally said. "He'll be able to tell if the Guardian is lying about anything. Don't tell her the whole story, but you can tell her that you're bonded to more than one person, and that those people are here with you. She's going to assume it's some of us, but don't give her any names."

"Understood," Isobel said.

"All right, then we're done," Kalen answered. "Isobel, Moses, and Theo, hang back."

Cian made a beeline for Isobel, tugging her from the desk and into a hug. It was fast, but it made her head spin and her breath catch as she was briefly doused in his sun-baked ocean scent.

"We can talk later," he promised, and immediately, her chest pinched.

She more than wanted that. She needed that.

"Okay," she croaked as he left the room.

"You two should go on this tour with Isobel," Mikel said, somehow knowing exactly why Kalen had asked Moses and Theodore to stay back. "You're the most agitated right now. Use this time to stay close to her and try to settle the fuck down before you lose your shit on camera."

"I feel like I'm going to tear out of my fucking skin."

Theodore spoke roughly. "I don't know if I can play it up for a whole tour."

"You're going to manage it," Mikel responded calmly. "And you aren't going to go for each other's throats. Learn to play nice in this situation and learn it fast. We want to see the Kane brothers doting on the Princess of Ironside. We want half the population dreaming about being in Isobel's place and the other half dreaming of being one of the Alphas. Sell the dream and sell it well."

Isobel straightened her shoulders. "I can do that."

"You can be doted on, can you, rich girl?" Moses drawled.

Theodore twitched, but then shed his agitation in the blink of an eye, brushing back his unruly dark hair with a peaceful, unaffected expression arranged on his stunning features.

It was borderline terrifying.

Isobel stepped toward Moses, trying her best to shed her agitation the way Theodore had, though she was sure she wasn't anywhere near as good as him. She tugged on the front of Moses' shirt, knowing that despite all of his blustering, he always clutched at her in some way when she put her body within his reach.

"I can be," she said, blinking up at him. "You don't want to dote on me?"

His dark eyes narrowed into slits, his hands lifting like he was about to grab hold of her before he blinked and stepped back, his eyes widening on her face. "You're a little too good at that. Theo is rubbing off on you."

"That's my girl." Theodore tucked her under his arm, steering her toward the door. "Ready for your tour?" It seemed that as soon as he had donned his mask, he was back in character, ready to perform before they were even in front of the cameras. Maybe it was the only way he could hold it together.

THE TOUR WAS OVER THE TOP. TWO OFFICIALS TURNED UP WITH an entire film crew who followed them around in a separate golf cart, despite cameras already filming them from every angle. She was pressed between Moses and Theodore in the back of the first golf cart, clutching a crystal champagne flute in one hand and a chocolate macaron in the other, her stomach too full of butterflies to consume either. Moses downed his own glass and then hers, and when he realised she wasn't going to eat the macaron, he took that too. Theodore waved away the offer of more refreshments and pulled up the map of Ironside onto one of the dorm tablets, dropping it onto Isobel's lap.

"Where to first?" he asked.

She chewed on her lip, tracing the roads and pathways, reading all the labels and quickly orienting herself with the layout. "Could we finish up here?" she asked, pointing to a small building marked *The Chapel.* "It would be nice to visit it and then walk home from there."

"Absolutely," one of the officials answered. "We'll start at Ironside Row and go from there."

They didn't go into any of the buildings on Ironside Row—since they were still closed until the official start of the semester, but they cruised past the pillared, grand facades, reading the polished brass plaques over each of the entrances.

The Den.

Pixel Play.

The Hunt.

The Teller.

Trend or Die.

Reputation Race.

"What do all those signs mean?" Isobel asked, leaning over Theodore in an attempt to peer through the windows.

Theodore leaned back slightly, his hand falling to the base of her spine, hot and heavy, making her stomach squirm.

"You'll have to wait and find out!" the official in the passenger seat exclaimed gleefully.

Isobel exchanged a look with Theodore, and they fell into companionable silence as they rolled all the way to the end of Ironside Row and then turned, heading back toward the main lake. They made a left, passing a long line of tall hedges.

"The Delta Maze," one of the officials said. "Dorm D is surrounded by a maze, with most of the dorm underground and only the common areas above ground. There were height restrictions in this area, so we couldn't build any high rises. And that's still part of Jasmine Quarter." The official pointed to the right, where an elaborate garden extended from the main lake. They looped Jasmine Quarter, moving to the other side, passing the dining hall and Market Street, the restricted areas by the entrance of the academy, and then they hugged the other side of Jasmine Quarter before branching off to the left and driving for a little while until they hit the fitness complex, which sprawled an impressive distance of interconnected buildings and outdoor areas.

"We have extensive spa and recovery facilities," the official boasted. "As well as private climbing rooms, private training studios, a fake beach with a wave rider, a vertical wind tunnel for skydiving, a bouldering canyon with natural rock formations, biometric sleep pods, VR adventure rooms, and a vertical dance studio with hoops, poles, and silks."

"No antigravity chambers?" Moses joked.

The officials laughed, the driver remarking, "Quite impressive, isn't it?"

They did another loop, passing another maze on

their way back to Jasmine Quarter. "The Beta Maze," the officials explained, prattling on about all the engineering marvels that had been performed to build most of Dorms B and D underground. They travelled to the eastern point of the campus, passing Dorm O, which was not ensconced in a maze, and the library, which was a sprawling, four-level building hugged by a thick forest.

"And that brings us to the end of the tour!" the official announced, after cutting through a tree-lined road to end up at the chapel, not far from the library.

The chapel was a simple building, unlike every other structure they had seen. It had plain, whitewashed sandstone walls and a gently sloping roof of weathered tiles. The simple, white-painted entrance door was flanked by large, stained glass windows, impossible to see through. A narrow stone pathway stepped up to the front door from the cobbled road, forking off to wind through the cute, manicured garden to a second building attached to the side of the chapel. The gardens and the ivy climbing up the white stone produced a calming, tranquil air that had Isobel's tense shoulders inching down slightly.

The film crew departed after dropping them at the chapel, surprising Isobel. She had expected everyone to follow them inside while she struggled to find a way to talk to Maya or Sophia privately. Moses caught her wrist before she stepped up to the door, allowing Theodore to go first. Moses stepped up close behind her, sandwiching her between him and his brother as they entered the cosy space. The scent of wood polish and beeswax was strong in the air as sunlight filtered through the stained glass to lighten up the small, semi-private prayer niches along the sides of the room.

There were five of them on each side, a small altar in each space, a candle set atop with matches beside it. Each little booth had a tall banner above it, depicting what Isobel could only guess was one of the Gifted gods.

"Carter," Maya's voice called out, and the woman appeared from behind a cupboard door. "Oh. Gods. It's nice to see you." She closed the cupboard with a snap and hurried over before pausing and holding up a finger. "Sophia will want to see you. Come next door, won't you?"

Isobel nodded, nonplussed. *Were there no cameras in the chapel?* She couldn't spot any.

Maya smiled, hurrying the rest of the way over and capturing Isobel's hands. She squeezed them and then dropped one of them, using the other to pull Isobel toward a door at the back of the chapel.

"Hello to you both, of course," she tossed over her shoulder, apparently talking to Theodore and Moses.

Moses scoffed quietly, half in amusement and half in surprise. Theodore stepped between Maya and Isobel before they could move more than a few steps, taking hold of both their arms and gently separating Maya's grip from Isobel's wrist. He dropped Maya's arm immediately.

"Sorry," he said plainly, looking about as apologetic as a stone.

"Oh." Maya waved him off. "Not a problem. I'm sorry. Come on."

She led them into the attached residence, which was small and cluttered, boxes overflowing with books and other objects.

"I apologise for the mess." She spoke over her shoulder. "We only arrived today. They almost replaced me. I heard Professor West pulled some strings to keep me here. I'll have to thank him later."

"He'd prefer if you didn't," Theodore said, still in that emotionless voice.

"Well." Maya eyed him, and then Moses. "Pass on the message, won't you?"

"Will do," Moses grunted.

"Isobel!" Sophia dropped a box onto the small dining table as they walked into the kitchen. She raced across the room and pulled Isobel into a hug that Theodore and Moses seemed to bear with gritted teeth. "You're okay! We were so worried! I couldn't text you all summer because the officials took our devices. They said they'd mail them here after we were cleared from questioning and everything, but so far nothing—"

Maya pulled her daughter back, watching Moses and Theodore over Sophia's head, her mahogany eyes weary.

"Put the kettle on." She gave Sophia a push toward the kitchen.

"It's good to see you," Isobel said as Sophia rolled her eyes at the looks on the Alphas' faces. "I'm also happy you guys are okay."

"Hello to you guys too," Sophia said pointedly, flouncing past Theodore and Moses. Their eyes had already snapped back to Maya—presumably because she was standing closest to Isobel.

"Is there anything we can do to make you both more comfortable?" Maya asked them, picking up on their stony expressions and tense bodies.

"Yes, stop him." Theodore pointed to the door, to where Luis had appeared, dropping a box and launching himself toward Isobel.

Maya deftly intercepted, picking him up and swinging him into her arms. He gripped her, unfazed, his huge eyes flicking between Isobel and the Alphas.

"Carter," he squeaked, his glasses threatening to tip right off the end of his little nose. He still hadn't grown into them. "You came to visit. I told them you'd come to visit today."

"Yes, you did, *mi Cielito*." Maya pinched his chin. "You're very smart."

Luis beamed. "I said the scary demons too—"

Maya slapped a hand over Luis' mouth, plopping him into one of the dining chairs without so much as an eye twitch.

"Did he just...," Moses muttered, trailing off.

"Sure did, demon boy." Isobel winked at Moses, who narrowed his eyes on her, catching her arm before she could skip away from him to sit at the table with Maya and Luis. "No cameras?" He directed the question to Maya over her head.

"No, not here or in the chapel. I convinced them it was against the Gifted religion."

"Elijah said you were smart." Moses tugged Isobel to the table, pulling out a chair for her and settling his arms on her shoulders when she sank down.

Theodore pulled a chair beside hers, sitting close and laying a large, possessive hand over her thigh. They were acting just as surrogates should—from Isobel's understanding, anyway—but Maya observed it all with a keen eye.

"Tea, everyone?" Sophia called over her shoulder.

"Carter likes coffee," Luis chirped, a smug look on his face. "You'd know that if you watched Ironside like I do."

"And you two?" Sophie ignored her little brother, directing the question to Moses and Theodore. Although she added as an afterthought, "I watch the highlights."

"Coffee for us," Theodore answered, flashing Sophia one of his camera-ready, superstar smiles. She must have won some points with him for basically saving Isobel's life in the chapel.

She blinked at him, seeming stunned for a moment,

before shaking her head and gathering what she needed to fix their drinks.

"So, let's cut to the chase." Maya folded her arms over her chest. "You aren't just here to check on us."

"What makes you think that?" Moses challenged.

Maya sat back, tapping her bicep with a neatly manicured finger. She considered the three of them silently, and just when it seemed like she was about to say something, there was a knock on the door leading from the kitchen. Sophia moved to answer it, revealing a tidy little porch and a very tall Alpha.

"Hi," Niko said. "I'm here for Carter."

Maya's lips curved. "Of course you are." She stood, indicating a free chair, and Niko strode into the now-crowded room, dragging the chair to Isobel's other side. He pushed his big thigh immediately against hers, jiggling it unconsciously, his arm stretching out across the back of her chair. Moses shoved his arm off, and he let his hand fall to her thigh instead.

Isobel cast him a concerned glance.

It wasn't like Niko to insist on touching her, and this wasn't a show of surrogacy for Maya, because Niko wasn't supposed to be one of her surrogates and she doubted Maya could even see where his hand was resting beneath the table. Isobel subtly slipped her hand from her lap to cover his, and he immediately turned his palm, twisting their fingers together tightly. So tightly it was almost painful.

"Is this everyone now?" Maya asked, hiding her smile behind her cup of tea. Sophia set a cup of coffee in front of each of them, some of the lively energy dropping out of her as she nervously stood behind her brother's chair and divided her attention between Moses—who was likely glowering over Isobel's head—to Theodore—whose body felt far too tense to her right—to Niko, who was shifting and fidgeting in his chair.

"Unless you're expecting anyone," Moses answered.

His tone was far too combative, so Isobel leaned forward, clearing her throat. "You're right. We did have another reason for visiting—but I would have visited anyway. I've been ... compromised this summer. I didn't have access to my phone and then I was too sick—"

"Bond sick?" Maya inserted, her back straightening in alarm.

Instead of answering, Isobel sucked in a breath. "We think we can trust you." She glanced at Sophia.
"Can we?"

Maya exchanged a loaded look with her daughter, who nodded slightly. The Guardian heaved in a steadying breath, setting down her tea. "Let me take the leap first. My Alpha ability is seeing auras. The officials think it's some wishy-washy nonsense, but it's far more than that. I can see when people are linked—similar in nature, like you and Sophia, or like Kane and Hart." She gestured between Theodore and Niko. "But I can also see when people are tied together, like the four of you." She paused, making sure they were properly absorbing the weight of her statement before adding, “And when those ties are incomplete, as they are now.”

“Christ,” Isobel spluttered, at the cool, calm, and collected way Maya had just revealed that she *already knew everything*.

“I’ve told nobody,” Maya assured them. “Not even the bond specialist—though that woman has pure intentions, if you were wondering. I can’t give you specifics—this isn’t a mind-reading ability—but her soul is pure and well-meaning.”

“Tell us exactly what you think you know.” Niko’s demand was soft and polite, but it was still a demand.

“I know that Carter is half-bonded to you three,” Maya announced. “Plus Kalen West and Elijah Reed. I suspect Oscar Sato, Kilian Grey, and Cian Ashford as well—not because I’ve seen it, but because I do know *some* of the Ironside rumours, and your friends would be dead if they weren’t included in this bond, from how close they are to her. Alphas more than the other ranks cannot abide people touching their mates.”

“Why haven’t you told anybody?” Isobel asked. “Your life, your career, your position at Ironside, it would all be over if they found out you kept something like this from them. You could be imprisoned, or worse, for anti-loyalist behaviour.”

“Because I am a Guardian,” Maya returned calmly, watching Isobel with a steady expression. “The half-bonded and fully-bonded are the most coveted, most protected people of our religion. They are chosen by the gods."

"Chosen for what?" Theodore sounded dubious.

"To serve the gods in whatever way the gods decide." Maya shrugged. "That's not for us to know. And it's not something we have a choice in. But it's believed that those who try to harm the bonded people will suffer the gods' wrath—and they can be quite wrathful."

"If they're so wrathful, why are their people stuffed into settlements?" Moses asked casually, his fingers tapping agitatedly against Isobel's collarbones.

"The gods do not exist to serve us." Maya surveyed the four of them with a hint of exasperation. "We are talking about ancient, cognizant beings who haven't been seen or heard of since ancient times—and even during ancient times, their goal was never to *help* us. All we have to go on are statues, carvings, paintings, and translated texts, and our main goal is just to not piss them off. The bonded were always thought to be their chosen, but if you want my *honest* opinion? Whoever decided Carter would be bonded to so many Alphas was *fucking* with us—excuse the language."

"Well now this is a theory I can get behind." Theodore sounded amused.

Isobel frowned. "Fucking with like ... all Gifted people?"

"They do these things." Maya waved a hand. "Always

have. When they aren't worshipped enough, they cause chaos, hoping to terrify us into compliance. We used to be their favourites, the *bonded people—*"

"We?" Isobel interrupted, frowning. "You're bonded? But your eyes ..."

Maya smiled kindly as Isobel trailed off. "All Gifted are bonded people, Carter. The gods decided, one day, that they would bless a section of the human population, giving them abilities and soulmates, and then blessing them with gifts when they found their soulmates. The bonded were supposed to be their temple servants, but ..." She lifted her shoulders in a delicate shrug. "Humans have always been greedy and lazy, and jealous more than anything else. They started hunting the bonded in the 16th century, and this is the result of that." She waved a hand at the table, not really indicating anything in particular. "So now I suspect the bonds are punishments more than anything, though it's impossible to tell one way or another. Aphelina is just as likely to bless a couple with a bond to see love blossom as Moros is, just to see the couple fail to be together at the moment of the Tether's death. The only thing I'm sure of is that disrespecting their chosen people will make them even angrier."

"The gods are cruel and mean," Sophia suddenly interrupted. "What's new there? Can we go back to this clusterfuck of a bond? Are there more? Is Spade in on this too?"

"All the Alphas of Dorm A, including both professors," Isobel informed them, seeing no point in lying. All Maya needed to do was catch sight of her standing near Mikel or Gabriel and she would know, and this fragile trust they had established between them would be broken.

Luis was counting slowly on his fingers, his brow furrowed in deep confusion. Sophia's elegant brows had shot up to brush her fringe. Maya didn't look surprised, but she did seem perplexed.

"I don't see how this is going to work," Maya said frankly. "Not with ten Alphas. To be completely honest, I don't even see it working with ten Omegas, but *especially* with Alphas. We're known to be more aggressive than the other ranks—and I've heard things about what happens when more than a few Alphas start to live together in groups."

"Well ..." Niko shifted, his fingers flexing in Isobel's grip. "That's unfortunate because we really need your help. If Isobel teleports to one of us at this academy, with cameras in the fucking *bushes*, we're all done."

Maya sighed, nodding her understanding. "Yes, that particular bond side effect might just be your downfall. Have you considered completing the bond?"

"With who?" Theodore gritted out.

"Anyone." Maya's eyes flashed at him, a subtle warning not to get too aggressive in her kitchen—likely for the sake of her children. "Maybe just one of you?"

"Would that even do anything?" Isobel asked.

"There was a case, actually ..." Maya rose from the table suddenly, her attention distracted as she began to rummage through the boxes piled against the wall.

"Looking for your diary?" Sophia guessed, pointing to a box on the kitchen counter.

Maya crossed to the box and fished out a green notebook, flipping through the pages. "So I did a bit of research, trying to find examples of where a Tether might have attached to several Anchors, and I found this old newspaper article in the archives of the Ironside library. Yes, here." She tapped a page in her notebook, her finger scrolling across her own handwriting as she sat back down.

"There was a man in the 1930s—they called him John—who was experiencing severe side effects from resisting a bond to one of his childhood friends—they called her Jane—because he was secretly in love with a man he was exchanging letters with from another settlement. It was all quite scandalous, as you might expect." She briefly glanced at them over the top of her diary. "So John eventually bonded Jane, hoping to ease the side effects for both of them. They had a cutting ceremony where a doctor was called in to make small, surgical incisions to scar them. It was all the rage back then. He ignored all letters from the man he was truly in love with—who they called Dave in the article—in an attempt to be loyal to his new wife, but the bonding didn't work. The side effects grew worse. People assumed it was because he was being disloyal to his wife, that he was committing some sort of soul infraction. But, you see, what happened ..." She trailed down her notes. "Was that six months earlier, John and Jane had been visiting a family member in another settlement. That visit was when John and Dave met.

"On their last night, there was some sort of incident which Jane narrowly escaped from, and shortly after, Dave had a cardiac event and entered his Death Phase, Tethering himself to John and Jane. All of their eyes changed, but because of Jane's incident, and because John and Dave were so in love, they resisted telling each other about their half-bonded status. None of them realised that there was a third person in their bond. And since Dave was the Tether, he unfortunately passed away before it was figured out."

"Are you saying that we should mark up Isobel instead of each other?" Moses asked dryly. "Because I believe those instructions were already clear."

Maya snapped her diary closed, placing it onto the table. "I'm saying that their side effects drastically changed when they did *something* with the bond. There's a good chance that Isobel's side effects will change if she completes the bond with someone. They might lessen."

"That's your only suggestion?" Niko asked, his frustration leaking through, though it was easy to tell from his tone that he was frustrated more at the situation than at the Guardian.

Maya picked up her tea again, sipping it delicately. "I'm afraid so. Bonding magic is incredibly complicated, but in some ways, it's also very simple. If you want it to back off, you need to give it what it wants."

"I'm sorry but—" Sophia sucked her lips together, apparently embarrassed by the way the words had just exploded out of her, before she continued in a more measured tone. "What's the big deal? Just complete the bond with everyone. It's not like any of you are free to go off and live your lives the way you want anymore. And if you complete the bond and one of you wins the *Ironside Show*, isn't there some sort of rule that the person's mate is considered an extension of their household?"

"We have other plans to stay together that don't involve us irrevocably tying our souls together," Moses shot back calmly.

"And because there's one of Carter and ten of us," Theodore added. "Not even the gods can make that math work."

"Gods?" Sophia clucked her tongue. "No. But Sigmas? If anyone can anticipate and counteract the needs of ten aggro dudes, it's a Sigma."

Isobel snorted, and Sophia sent her a wink, flipping her shiny black bob in a flourish. "Far as I'm concerned, one Sigma is absolutely equal to ten Alphas."

For the first time since entering the room, Moses's

grip on Isobel's shoulders relaxed, and Theodore's hold on her thigh eased, both of them seeming to deflate with a single breath. Even Niko flexed out his fingers, allowing hers a short break.

"I see we don't have any arguments there," Sophia preened, far too pleased with herself.

Luis grinned at her, like he was proud that she was proud, but didn't fully understand what battle she had just won.

"You know we need to be more popular before we try anything like that." Theodore shook his head. "Right now, it would be too easy for the officials to make us disappear without consequence while they experiment on this bond phenomenon."

There wasn't much for them to say after that. They needed to think about their options and discuss it as a group, so they thanked Maya and returned to the chapel. Sophia promised to text Isobel as soon as she had her phone back, and the four of them began walking back through the trees. They all pulled out their phones as Niko began sending a barrage of texts to the group chat, filling everyone in on what had happened.

After several minutes of walking in silence, a reply finally came through.

Kalen (admin): First of all, is this something you would consider, Isobel?

Her heart immediately jumped into her throat, everything within her screaming at her to say no, but she couldn't allow her trauma with her father to inform all of her adult decisions, so instead, she forced herself to think about it logically. As they passed out of the thicker forest and headed toward the dining hall, which was welcoming scattered groups of students, Isobel finally responded.

Isobel: I would prefer to have a full bond than to be subject to questioning by the officials, but only if the person I am bonded to is willing and won't resent me for it.

Kalen (admin): Is this something anyone else would consider?

Theodore was already tapping away at his screen.

Theodore: I have no issue with it.

Kilian: I'm okay with it.

Cian: I would also rather be bonded than the alternative.

Oscar: Same.

Moses: Same.

Niko: Same.

Gabriel: I won't refuse.

Elijah: I won't be refusing either.

Isobel almost tripped over her own feet, but managed to keep her shock under control, tucking her phone against her stomach as they passed a group of students. As they rounded the main lake, she pulled up her phone again.

Isobel: I know we agreed to tackle this as a group ... but I'm finally starting to realise what that means. I'm grateful. Thank you.

Mikel (admin): That was the easy part, Carter.

Mikel (admin): Now we narrow it down, assuming you aren't going to pick your favourite Alpha.

Isobel: I'd rather impale myself on one of the thousand pillars or iron gates around here.

Kilian: Why don't we just draw a damn name out of a hat or something?

Cian: Yeah, a friendly game should settle this. What's a little competition between Alphas?

Moses: Very funny.

Moses: Actually ...

Cian: Now you want to compete for it, don't you?

Elijah: Alphas are nothing if not predictable.

Kalen (admin): Nothing violent.

Gabriel: You never answered your own question of whether you would consider this, and neither did Mikel.

Kalen (admin): Everyone is aware.

Gabriel: Well now we're all VERY aware.

Mikel (admin): Yes, thank you for that.

Isobel: It's okay, I understand. Can I compete too?

Theodore: We're rubbing off on you.

Kilian: Well, someone is, anyway.

Moses: Come again?

Kilian: I'm sure she will.

Isobel: Huh?

Oscar: Don't be jealous, Kiljoy. The hunt hasn't even started yet.

Mikel (admin): A hunt sounds like an exceptionally bad idea.

Oscar: Who wants to hunt?

Kilian: You only want to hunt because you think you'll win.

Oscar: ... My question stands.

Kilian: I might.

Theodore: Ugh. Yes. What does that say about me?

Niko: You don't want to know. I'm in for a hunt. Sorry, Isobel.

Isobel: What is going on? What kind of hunt?

Elijah: A very literal one. You hide somewhere, and whoever finds you first wins.

Isobel: Last year nobody wanted a bond and now it's a prize?

Elijah: If you had made it a competition earlier, it would have been a prize earlier.

Gabriel: Unlikely.

Gabriel: But not entirely untrue.

Isobel: You guys are insane.

Cian: You don't want to play anymore?

Isobel: I never said that. What do I get if I win?

Niko: If none of us find you? That won't happen.

Isobel: It might.

"It won't." Niko had spoken the answer out loud, his gaze clouded over with an emotion she couldn't quite read as he watched her. "Not a chance."

9
THE LITTLE SIGMA IS PLAYING

AS SOON AS THEY ARRIVED BACK AT THE DORM, THE OTHERS were gathered in the marbled foyer, dressed in dark workout clothes like they were about to go for a run and then break into one of the Market Street shops. Kalen and Mikel were still in their suits, obviously not about to participate in whatever they had set up. They hadn't discussed over text *when* the bonding would occur, but she supposed if they were all willing to take this step to keep their secret, then it made sense to do it as soon as possible instead of risking a teleportation incident.

Especially with the strain on the bond still visibly bothering everyone.

"What's happening here?" Niko asked as they took in the serious expressions of the gathered Alphas.

Elijah and Gabriel were stretching. Oscar was bouncing lightly on his feet. Kilian was sitting on the last few steps of the staircase, his chin resting in his palm. Cian was leaning back against one of the pillars at the end of the staircase, playing distractedly with a deck of cards.

"We're going to play a game," Mikel announced. "Call it a group bonding activity, since it's our first night all here together and the last night before classes start tomorrow. You guys may want to change. There will be running involved."

He glanced at Isobel, arching a brow, a subtle warning in his splotchy eyes.

There will be hunting involved.

His anxiety over the situation was stabbing at her chest, and she gave him a subtle nod, letting him know she was consenting to ... whatever the hell this was. He nodded, releasing a breath, and caught her arm as she moved past him.

"Wear black. Cover yourself as much as you can."

She trailed up the stairs, not having the same restless energy as the others as they bounded off to their rooms to change.

For the first time since her father had snatched her from the academy, she felt settled, and that felt like *nothing*. Like there was no towering pile of emotion hanging over her, raining down on her, flattening her to the floor. Like there was no bubbling pit of rage choking up her oesophagus and spitting from her lips.

She was completely exhausted, and she eyed the bed

as she passed it to get to her closet, but as soon as she began flicking through her clothes, a strange sort of change overcame her. Maybe it was competitiveness, or stubbornness, or that insane urge to be *claimed* that she felt around the Alphas, but her calm was invaded by a slow trickle of frantic energy that worked its way through her system. She forgot about the ordeal of the past months. She forgot about her need to sink back into the soft-as-sin bed in the other room, burrowed beneath layers of blankets with the air conditioner turned up high and several of Kilian's shirts stuffed beneath her nose.

The idea of a hunt, which had been so ridiculous only half an hour ago, was now decidedly more appealing. Who had suggested it? Oscar? Had he known that this would be what she needed, or was it just what he needed?

Was it what they all needed? No, that didn't check out. It wasn't healthy for *eight* close friends to compete over a single girl, in any form, ever.

Except ... from what she knew of Alphas, it would be extremely appealing to prove their worth to their mate against other Alphas, even if they didn't exactly want to be bonded.

She pulled on a tight black shirt with long sleeves that hooked over her thumbs and dark jeans—designer, of course. The weather had cooled on their walk back to the dorm, growing balmy with an evening breeze and allowing her to cover up. That rioting feeling inside her was refusing to make this easy for the Alphas. She added socks and soft-soled leather boots that zipped up to her knees and a tight black coverup that she often tossed over her leotards. It was thin and stretchy, fluttering loosely just below her breasts, with a high neckline and a loose hood, the sleeves hanging over her hands.

She tied her hair into a high braid, securing all the wisps and loose strands, and then hunted through her bathroom cabinets for perfume. She found an unfamiliar bottle that she had never tried before and spritzed herself with it. Not enough for them to follow the trace of it all the way to her hiding place, but enough that it might muddle her natural scent for a little while.

Declaring herself ready, she skipped back to the foyer, realising she had taken longer than the others, as all ten Alphas were gathered at the base of the stairs. She paused halfway down the stairs at the looks they gave her. Emotion spiked against her chest, whipping out in a lashing of dark energy before it was yanked back, too rapidly for her to get a proper reading on it.

Most of them had worn the same severe expression, but as she kicked herself back into motion, they suddenly appeared more amused than anything, making her wonder if she had imagined those flashes of grim intensity.

Kalen and Mikel were the only two who hadn't managed to replace severity with amusement, and they both stared her down like they could somehow make her go back upstairs and reverse what she had done—whatever that was. Mikel muttered something to Kilian, who nodded and disappeared upstairs.

"Right." Mikel stared at her for a few seconds longer, a muscle in his neck pulsing. "We've planned a hunt, which should play to all of your individual strengths. Carter, as a Sigma, you should have a heightened awareness of the people around you, so I expect you to hide successfully and evade Alpha capture, and I expect you to do it well. Can you do that?"

She nodded, and he immediately moved on to the others as Kilian came back downstairs, dropping a handful of what looked like Isobel's colourful silk scrunchies into Mikel's palm.

"As Alphas, your senses are heightened, and this should put you all to the test. Carter will get a thirty-minute head start and will hide within either the Beta Maze or the Delta Maze. Once hidden, she will be free to move around and change her position within her chosen maze to evade capture." Mikel handed a scrunchie to each of the guys, giving Isobel the last one. "Everyone put these on your wrist. If it's snatched off you, you're out of the game. You've lost. You can capture Carter by stealing her scrunchie and you can wipe out your competition using the same method. Use of academy vehicles is prohibited. Let's try to keep this game clean. No bloodshed."

Isobel quirked a brow, arranging her scrunchie on her wrist, but none of the others seemed surprised about the warning.

"Everyone understood?" Mikel barked.

"Understood," they chorused back.

"U-understood," Isobel tacked on, a second too late.

"Good." Kalen stepped up to the door, pushing it wide, his eyes landing on her. "Best of luck, Carter."

Don't smile. Don't smile. Don't smile.

A small giggle burst out of her lips, and she clapped a hand over her mouth. *Why was she enjoying this so much?* There was something wrong with her.

"We are *definitely* rubbing off on you," Moses muttered low.

Isobel skipped past them, almost bouncing on the tips of her toes. There was so much energy swirling around inside her body, she worried it would explode out of her.

"I'm not the one who needs luck," she goaded, passing Kalen, and pausing in the doorway, issuing a challenging stare to each of the tensed, twitching bodies gathered in the foyer. "Just out of curiosity, what will I win, when I ... you know, win?"

Mikel's hard mouth twitched, his eyes crinkling in the corners. The stony-faced professor was *definitely* thinking about smiling. "You get to pick the theme of the first Dorm A party for the year. Better run, Carter, your timer has already started."

She spun on her heel without a word, jogging away from the dorm. She raced down the paved road that wound up Alpha Hill, the tickle of energy that had been steadily building inside her now thrumming deep within her core. Her arms and legs itched as she raced to the dining hall, ignoring the way students scattered out of her way, surprised at her all-black ensemble and the frantic way she grabbed a takeaway container and began to stalk around the circular food bar.

In true Ironside fashion, there seemed to be some sort of food theme, overflowing with decorations and sparkling under the light of crystal chandeliers. She found the dessert section and began picking cherries from a fruit display. When she realised she was taking too long, she started grabbing handfuls of berries and shoving them into the container, staining her hands as some of them burst in her grip.

THEODORE HAD HALF AN HOUR TO FORMULATE A PLAN AND HE was going to use every minute of it, because nobody in that room was about to win the game based on speed alone.

Kalen stalked out of the room, leaving Mikel to eye them all and guard the exit as the heavy doors fell closed. Not that they would have left early. It was clear that the hunt appealed to Isobel in some way, and they couldn't deny her a little fun after the summer she had endured.

Even if her fun ended in complete, bloody chaos—which was highly likely.

The eight of them split up, scattering around the room and looking at their phones, refusing to talk to each other, despite Kilian's feeble attempts to make light conversation for the cameras. Theodore first examined the official interactive map of Ironside on his phone before abandoning it in favour of the map in the Eleven app that Elijah, Gabriel, and Oscar had created. He zoomed in on Beta Maze, and then Delta Maze, tracing the hedged corridors. There were no camera icons inside the maze, though they surrounded the above-ground sections of the dorms and the maze entrances and exits. That didn't mean they had privacy—not this early in the night. The mazes would be littered with people making their way back from dinner.

But maybe it would be enough for a little foul play.

Isobel escaped the dining hall as soon as she had what she needed. She ran to Delta Maze, crushing berries in her palms and letting the juice drip as she passed between the towering hedges. Students were filtering into the passages, and she skirted around them, refusing to stop even when someone called out her name. She did Beta Maze next, dripping cherry juice along the path at random, and then she stripped off her ballet wrap and wiped her hands clean. She tied the wrap around one of the columns gracing the entrance to Dorm B, and then raced back out of the maze, her heart in her throat.

THEODORE CHECKED HIS PHONE, GROWING RESTLESS.

Their thirty minutes were almost up. He had formulated a plan based on the few blind spots that Ironside had to offer, and he had ranked the other Alphas in order of who he most wanted to eliminate, to who he least wanted to eliminate. Mikel shifted, checking the time.

Theodore stood and stalked to the door, staring straight ahead, focussed.

The others did the same, the room growing heavy with silence.

ISOBEL WAS *DESPERATE* TO WIN, AND SHE NO LONGER EVEN understood why. It just ... wouldn't be right if she let them win. She couldn't just hand it to them.

Maybe it was the fact that none of them wanted her as a mate, even though she didn't want to be bonded to anyone either. Maybe the part of her soul that was tied to theirs was demanding them to not just *accept* this, but to fight for it.

It was a dangerous thought, because if she wanted them to *want* the bond, then ... *didn't that mean she wanted it too?*

She shook her head to dislodge the dangerous epiphany, shoving it far, far away where it couldn't taint the buzz of energy and excitement leading her back to Alpha Hill. She checked her phone as she reached the base of the hill, realising she only had a few minutes to spare. Not long enough to make it up to the dorm—where she had planned to hide—without running into any of them.

She circled around to the right, following the paved road until she found a garden she could disappear into, and then she checked her phone again, bringing up an aerial view of her location. She couldn't leave the academy, of course. She had received an extensive email about all the laws governing the presence of the Gifted in Europe while she was in hospital—she had fallen asleep trying to read the first paragraph, but the warning was clear enough. There would be no excursions outside of the academy unless they wanted to be detained, expelled, and either arrested or sent home. Still, there were options.

Like the section of woodland beside a large lake bordering the northern point of the academy. She paused, listening out for male voices in the distance, and when she heard nothing, she took off running in the opposite direction.

• • •

Eve Indie lifted her head as someone dressed in black rushed past—too caught up in their phone to realise Eve had been tucked into the shadowed gazebo in the back corner of the garden. The familiar figure was small and slight, with a long, thick blonde braid bouncing against her back.

Eve waited for one of the Alphas to come after Carter, but when it didn't happen, she raised a brow. *Interesting.* She glanced back down at her phone to re-read the email that had prompted her to come and loiter around the base of Alpha Hill.

From: sponsor-noreply@TSD.com

Subject: Try again, Omega.

Message: This time, don't forget the evidence. You have until midnight.

She looked up from the phone, and then back down, and then back up.

No way did this just fall right into her lap.

Theodore wanted out.

Now.

"It's time," he growled impatiently.

"Keep it clean," Mikel reminded them, voice low, a subtle Alpha command riding his tone.

He pushed open the door and only Kilian and Niko stepped forward, both of them turning back to eye the rest of the group as they stood there, frozen.

Fighting off Mikel's command.

Because *hell no they would not be fighting clean.*

Kilian rolled his eyes and took off running. Niko snorted, jogging after Kilian. Oscar broke away next, and then Cian. Theodore fought off Mikel's command before Moses did, but he pretended to continue struggling so that he was behind his brother when Moses bound down the road to Alpha Hill.

The first camera blind spot.

He didn't bother looking behind him to figure out why Elijah or Gabriel hadn't left yet. He was focussed, and he had a very narrow window before the next camera. He pounced on Moses, sending them both tumbling across the pavers, snarls tearing out of their throats.

"Just *wait*," Moses shoved him off, holding his arm behind his back. "What the fuck, Theo? You know you'll lose your band attacking me head-on like this. You're seriously willing to put yourself out of the race just to keep me out?"

"Obviously," Theodore mocked, feeling cold rage wash up inside his stomach. He waited a moment, tempering it before he spoke again.

Don't lose control.

"I'm everyone's first target," he said. "If you don't take my band, someone else will."

"You know that's not what I'm asking," Moses growled, eyes darkening as he stared down Theodore.

"You're my *brother*." That temper inside Theodore was surging, bubbling, threatening to spill over and explode. He needed more of Isobel to calm down the bond ... but that wasn't going to solve everything. That was just a Band-Aid, and the bond wasn't his only problem. He was a whole problem in itself.

"And?" Moses challenged, raising a brow. "I swear to god, Theo, if you start with the 'I saw her first' bullshit again I am going to lose it."

"But I did," he said, just to be an asshole. He knew he was being unreasonable, but nothing was more unreasonable than *sharing* the girl he was falling in love with.

"No." Moses sighed, some of the fight draining out of him. "Elijah did. He noticed her before any of us. He's just smart enough not to mention it. And Oscar saved her first. And I kissed her first. And Kilian was her gay best friend first. You made her come first but Cian's cock was in her mouth first. And Niko has taught her to stand up for herself, to fight back, and to carve out a safe space for herself between all of us before any of us could even think about the need for it. You really want me to go on? Because I can. You never had her, you never owned her. You never will."

"I know." Theodore pounced on Moses as soon as his hand dropped back to his side, losing his own scrunchie in the tussle that followed, both of them breaking apart and breathing heavily.

"The real question is where does your loyalty lie." Theodore lowered his voice to something that crumbled and trembled with equal parts rage and insecurity. "Your brother or your best friend? Because I'm taking out Oscar next."

Moses eyed him carefully. "I'm with you."

"Good." Theodore dropped the rage and anger from his face, something calmer taking its place.

Moses watched the manipulation of Theodore's features, shaking his head in exasperation.

MIKEL HAD INTENDED TO GO FOR A RUN, TO WORK OFF SOME OF his frenetic energy. That was why he had taken the narrow staff path—just big enough for one of the small service carts to climb—back to the base of the hill, on the opposite side to the main entrance. He pulled up short when Eve Indie cut across his sight like a bullet, only thirty feet away.

Chasing something.

He stared ahead, making out the small figure in black that was just turning a corner, quickly disappearing out of sight.

Of course Carter hadn't played by the rules.

He swore roughly, catching up to the Omega and intersecting her, his hands burning to grab and *tear* and *destroy*, while the rest of his body wanted to turn and chase ... because he knew where his mate was ... and she was far away from the others.

Tempting him.

But no, he had to be the responsible one.

"Miss Indie," he said, as the girl pulled up short, her breath catching in fright. She stumbled back several steps, her gaze darting past him.

Don't remind me, he wanted to snap, but he kept his tone even and polite, with only the slightest burr of command. "Myself and Professor West would like a word."

"W-with me?" She stumbled back another step and cast another despairing glance behind him, before she seemed to release the idea of chasing after Carter and switched her focus to Mikel instead. Her blue eyes widened in false innocence, her shaking fingers tucking loose strands of hazel hair behind her ears.

"I was j-just—"

"Now is good." Mikel cut her off, turning on his heel and stalking back toward the main road, allowing the faint tenor of Alpha voice he had trickled into the words to have their effect.

Eve scurried behind him, unable to help herself.

THEODORE FELL BEHIND MOSES, TRUSTING HIS BROTHER'S sharp nose as they headed toward Beta Maze.

"You can't manipulate your way through this entire

situation," Moses warned. He spoke low, the words expelled between rough exhales as they sprinted to catch up.

"We all have to play to our strengths," Theodore shot back. Students were gathered at the entrance, whispering lowly to each other and peering into the start of the maze, too afraid to enter.

"He's definitely in there," Theodore muttered. "We need to be fast."

Moses nodded, and they barrelled into the maze. Theodore had been so focussed on trying to pick up on Oscar's scent that he had completely missed the hint of cherry juice until it was filling his nostrils. They both paused, looking down at the deep burgundy drops littering the path.

"Is she bleeding?" Theodore demanded, bending down to get a better look.

"No." Moses barked out a sharp laugh. "That's actual cherry juice. She's playing."

The little Sigma is playing.

Theodore's dick twitched and something roared to life inside his blood. Even though he wasn't going to win this race, he felt a deep sense of satisfaction that they had given her this chance to play, to give in to her nature and to let out her mischievous, teasing side.

It meant that she felt safe with them, that she trusted them.

Knowing that they were making her feel this way

settled something inside him. Some of his rage quietened, becoming less tempestuous.

"He's coming toward us," Moses grunted, pulling Theodore up by his shirt and dragging him into a run. "Get ready."

Oscar rounded the corner ahead, his stance switching into one of readiness without a second of hesitation. He had likely been intending to take them out as soon as he saw them, but he quickly realised he was about to be teamed up on and decided he could outrun them.

He spun and took off, and they took chase, the rage boiling back to life inside Theodore as he realised that Oscar would rather run away from a fight than lose the hunt.

MIKEL'S BREATHS WERE COMING IN SHORT, HARD PANTS, HIS mind clouded with anger, the edges of his vision wavering with the effort it was taking to keep his stride normal and the tension out of his face.

He was torn in two directions, between two very different needs. One was angry and violent, the other ... violent still, but in a different way. Carter ran, and it made him want to chase.

She disobeyed their rules, and that made his hand itch and his stomach burn with the need to see pretty tears in her eyes and even prettier words on her lips like *I'm sorry* and *Sir*.

He let some of his tension leak into the air, thickening the humidity just as he stepped into the dorm, the Omega still trailing him. Thunder rumbled outside, the first pattering of rain sounding against marble as the door fell closed behind them. Mikel led the girl to Kalen's office. He knocked, and then pushed the door open, standing aside.

"After you, Miss Indie."

Kalen's head snapped up, his eyes connecting with Mikel's before he turned away from the window he had been standing at, grinding his jaw as the curtain fell back into place.

"Miss Indie," he drawled, as the door closed. There was a thinly veiled threat in his tone, but he said nothing else, waiting for Mikel to explain why the Omega was there.

Mikel just ... didn't feel like it.

"Phone," he demanded, holding out his hand, all pretences dropped.

His face was now, he was sure, displaying nothing but feral rage.

Indie backed up a step, colliding with the door, and Mikel could see her pulse jumping in her neck as she felt for the handle.

"Stay put," he lashed out in Alpha voice, forcing her

muscles to lock up. "You can move your hand to retrieve your phone. Do it now."

Her hand was moving, her eyes widening in panic, and she whipped out her ability, a flash of darkness and dizziness shooting into Mikel's head, making him clench his fist. Kalen stepped around him, whipping out a hand.

The *crack* echoed through the room and through Mikel's frazzled mind, which cleared as quickly as it had become muddled.

Indie was flattened against the door, her hand covering one side of her face, staring at Kalen with a mixture of horror and realisation.

"Don't mistake me," Kalen snarled, his tone dripping with ice. "You aren't looking at a gentleman. If you attack one of my Alphas or my Sigma, I *will* strike back. I'll crush you like a fucking bug, wipe the blood off on my resignation letter, and walk away without a single fucking regret, are we clear?"

Indie deflated, her hand falling, her back straightening as she pulled away from the door. "Yes, Professor."

There was no fear, no snark in her voice. It was the response of a well-trained soldier. Someone used to being bullied. Which made sense. She had to learn it from *somewhere*.

"Sit," Mikel demanded, yanking out a chair opposite Kalen's desk. "And hand the phone over."

She perched in the armchair, crossed her legs, and

dug into the pocket of her skirt, producing a phone that she dropped into Mikel's waiting palm.

"You won't like what you're going to find," she warned, sounding tired. "But you already know that. You must be deeply involved with the Stone Dahlia if you can walk around like you're freaking untouchable."

Kalen regarded her with a cold, bored stare, a scowl hovering along the corner of his mouth.

Mikel ignored her completely, pretending to search her phone. Instead, he downloaded one of Elijah's apps, gave it full permissions, and then clicked the image of the mask in the app, triggering it to adapt its name and icon to something innocuous based on the other applications Indie had downloaded. He hadn't the slightest clue how Elijah's programs did what they did, but Elijah had made sure to instruct them all on how to install them after they arrived at the new Ironside location. Mikel handed the phone back and Indie frowned, giving him a disbelieving look.

"Why ask for it if you aren't going to search it properly?" she asked, jutting her sharp chin out.

"I changed my mind." Mikel rounded the desk, standing beside Kalen. "How did the Stone Dahlia recruit you?"

"The same way they recruit everyone, I'm assuming." She crossed her arms and legs after returning her phone to her pocket. Her foot hung above the ground, juggling agitatedly. "They got dirt on me and asked me to do something small—something that wasn't exactly *ethical*, but they filmed it, and they used that footage to blackmail me into doing more. And more. And more. The collateral piled up until they owned me completely."

"Did they tell you to attack Carter?"

"Why so invested in Carter?" Indie shot back, eyeing Mikel with a wild look in her eye. "You mated to her or something?"

"Cut the shit," Kalen ordered coldly. "You know her secret, and we know that there's no way you would have thought to tear apart her bond in that way without very specific information from people far more important than you. So, who told you to do it and what did they say, exactly?"

"You really don't know?" Indie scoffed. "You aren't as well connected as I thought. You're no better off than I am."

"Are you saying you don't know who your sponsor is?" Mikel asked, his patience thinning into a tenuous, frayed thread.

"She communicates through an email I can't even reply to," Indie replied. "I've met her—in one of the holding rooms at the Stone Dahlia, well, the *old* Stone Dahlia—but she was wearing a mask like how some of the other humans and officials do down there."

"So she isn't Gifted." Kalen tapped his fingers against his desk. "What does she look like?"

"Above average height, I guess. Long, straight blonde

hair. She has thicker lips, I think, but she could just be overlining them. I've never seen her without lipstick. Her eyes are grey? Or blue? Maybe green? They keep the lights so low, and she hates when we stare at her so I don't really know. She seems pretty fit. Always has her nails done. Wears designer clothes. Even without the mask, you can tell she's hot."

"You said 'we'." Mikel frowned. "You said 'she hates it when *we* stare'."

"Alaric?" Indie arched her neck forward, raising both of her brows at them, her face showing a mix of surprise and confusion, as though they really should have figured it all out by now. "Alaric Crowe? She sponsored us both. And Kikki Rayne."

"Rayne?" Kalen asked, trading a quick look with Mikel, who nodded.

Kikki Rayne was on their list.

Outside, the windows flashed bright with lightning, absorbing the temper Mikel was slowly leaking into the atmosphere.

"And what exactly did this woman tell you to do to Carter?" Kalen asked, his voice silky. It sounded like he was contemplating bodily harm—more than he had already indulged in.

"To your *mate*, you mean?" Indie shot back, trying to display a backbone even though her lips were quivering and she had goosebumps. "She told me what to say to Carter. She said something would appear, and I was supposed to steal it. She said it might be *inside* or attached to Carter, and in that case, I would have to cut it out or cut it off. She also said it might be a chain or a thread or a crown or a cloak or golden light."

"But you didn't steal the light you cut out of her," Mikel stated.

Indie shuddered, her eyes growing dark with an unpleasant memory. "I thought Oscar Sato was about to break down the fucking door, and I panicked. I just wanted to get out of there. The settlement guards caught me and then they tossed Aron in the same holding room as me, and then suddenly they were questioning Aron instead of me and I knew my sponsor was working her magic because that's what she does. She plays with you until you're useless to her, and this entire fucking world seems to be her playground. But I'm smart. I lean into it. I don't resist it like Crowe did. I tell her 'use me more, use me harder', and I *learn* from her. Like how I managed to find out Dorm A's big dirty secret and I'm keeping it locked up nice and safe." She tapped the side of her head. "Unless something happens to me, of course. I was going to tell Carter this, but since I'm here ..." She uncrossed her arms and stopped jiggling her foot, clutching the sides of her chair as she drilled them both with a stubborn, almost manic stare. "All of my secrets are on a timer to be released. If I don't reset that timer at the same time every day ..." She held out her hands, palms up, and shrugged. "Then they become your problem."

"Well," Kalen rumbled, eyes narrow and hard, "that answers the question of why we shouldn't make sure you go to sleep all safe and sound tonight and never wake up again tomorrow."

"It's good to know how far you'll go for your little mate," Indie remarked. "Then you understand me when I say there is *nothing* I won't do to get on the Icon track."

"What's the point?" Kalen asked, as Mikel's thoughts twisted into spirals.

They had already assumed the Omega was holding onto the information as some sort of insurance policy, since the officials hadn't come after them, and they were prepared to deal with her in whatever way was necessary ... but the frantic, almost hysterical way her attention was flicking between them, and the stubborn set of her jaw made him uneasy.

This girl was not a victim of the Track Team.

She was practically vibrating with the need to get onto the Icon track, and it was clear there wasn't much she wouldn't do to make it happen.

"What's the point?" Her eyes bugged. "Don't act like you don't know what the Stone Dahlia can offer. Just because I haven't been offered a job down there yet doesn't mean that I don't know that you're both heavily involved in the Dahlia. My sponsor told me you're both *big* stars down there."

"I ask because you're in your third year," Kalen said calmly, growing more in control of himself, just as steadily as Mikel was losing control. "Even if you get onto the Icon track, you'll never win. Not even the Track Team can pull that off. You're going back to your settlement no matter what."

Indie threw her head back and laughed, the sound hollow. "Oh, you don't know, do you? There are *plenty* of us who won't go back to the settlements. We've been promised full-time positions in the Stone Dahlia with Ironside employment contracts. The more popularity points we amass, the more comfortable our lives will be."

Mikel froze, glancing at Kalen, whose jaw tightened.

This was new.

"Let's cut to the chase," Kalen demanded, standing, and leaning his weight against the heavy, walnut desktop. "You want us to not make you disappear and we want you to keep your fucking mouth shut about Carter's bonds ... so it would seem we're both safe for now."

"Almost," Indie crooned, her breath coming faster. "Actually ... I think I may be a little safer than you."

"I wouldn't," Mikel warned, his tone gravel and dust.

She flinched away from him, keeping her attention on Kalen, even though he was the one who had slapped her. It was probably Mikel's face. It terrified people even when he was smiling at them.

"I've decided I would like a little extra insurance," Indie said boldly. "I want Carter to publicly acknowledge me. A coffee date on Market Street would be nice—"

"Not happening," Kalen cut in. "Not a chance."

Indie pouted, the expression theatrical. "Fine. I guess I'll settle for Gray, then."

Kilian? Mikel hid his wince, but before they could refuse again, Indie jumped to her feet. "Anyway, I'll be going now." She plucked a pen from Kalen's desk and dragged one of his notebooks toward her, scribbling her number onto a blank page. "Give Gray my number, have him organise that date, and I'll make sure Carter's little secret remains a secret."

CIAN KICKED OPEN THE DOOR TO HIS ROOM, STALKING OVER TO his bedside table and staring down at the card he had pulled before the hunt.

The Five of Wands.

He had run to the Beta Maze, but he hadn't been able to enter. He fell back and waited, watching as Kilian disappeared inside, and then he drew back further, witnessing Oscar storm inside like he would rip the hedges apart if he had to. And then Theodore and Moses ran after him, both of them with bare wrists.

He had *wanted* to go in, but the card wouldn't stop appearing in his mind, flashing up like a persistent bad memory.

Competition and compromise.

A time to stand back and wait.

A time to withhold action.

He didn't want to accept it, so now there he was, standing in his room and shuffling it back into the deck, assuming it was a mistake even though he didn't make mistakes.

He pulled a card at random, and the *Five of Wands* stared back at him yet again. He drew it three more times before tossing the pack at the wall and releasing a snarl from his throat. His door opened a few seconds later and Gabriel appeared in the opening, looking entirely too calm.

"What are you doing here?" Cian demanded, glancing at the scrunchie still secured around Gabriel's wrist. "Is the game over?"

"No." Gabriel glanced at the pack of cards lying on the floor, and then at the single card Cian still held in his hand, a brief flash of pity racing across his features before he locked his expression down. "You haven't figured it out yet?"

Cian rolled his eyes. "Figured what out?"

"Who the winner will be," Gabriel stated calmly. "Theodore and Moses would take each other out first, of course. Theodore knows he's everyone's main target, being ... the strongest runner." Gabriel raised his brows. "So he knew he had lost before he even started. His aim was to rig the game, not win it. And who is Theodore most competitive with?"

"Moses," Cian grunted, sitting on the edge of his bed, and staring at the card in his hand.

"And who would they agree to take out, once they had eliminated each other?"

"Oscar, and then me." Cian flopped back, bringing the card up before his face and turning it over. "That's all very obvious ... but why are you still here? Who's going to take you out?"

"Elijah will." Gabriel leaned against Cian's dresser, crossing his arms and kicking one ankle to rest over the other, his posture relaxed. "This game was made for him. He's very good at tracking ..." He trailed off, and Cian focussed on him, trying to read between the lines.

Elijah was tracking Isobel? *Duh*, that was the game.

Unless ... Elijah was *tracking* Isobel. He raised a brow as Gabriel tapped the side of his pocket, where his phone was.

Well damn, Elijah had won the game.

"Let's go work out," Gabriel suggested, though there was a note of hardness in his voice. "I have energy to burn."

"I'm in." Cian rose from his bed but paused to glare at the card he had tossed onto his duvet.

"Seriously?" he growled at it after Gabriel left the room. "Every *damn* day it's moon card this, moon card that, and *now* you want me to pump the fucking brakes?"

NIKO HAD DELIBERATELY FALLEN BEHIND THE OTHERS WHEN they sprinted away from Alpha Hill, falling back, and climbing up the steep cliffside of the hill that was, most definitely not made to be hiked upon. He hoisted himself onto the terrace and hid around the side of Dorm A, waiting for Elijah to appear.

When the tall blond had stepped from the building, calmly walking down the road, Niko followed him at a distance.

He suspected Elijah or Gabriel had already put a tracker on Isobel's phone, though he wasn't entirely sure how or when they had managed to pull it off. Still, he knew those two better than anyone else did—though not quite as well as they knew each other. There was no way they were allowing Isobel out of their sight without knowing exactly where she would be at all times. Never again.

He was surprised Elijah had waited so long before he left the dorm, but it seemed the other Alpha was in no hurry. He strolled, and Niko stalked, their direction leading them away from the mazes, toward the northern point of the academy, where it was less populated. There were more arboretums, more gardens, more ponds and isolated gazebos, the road narrowing to a pathway, the cameras growing scarce.

Eventually, they grew closer to the sound of a river, and Elijah stopped walking, his eyes fixed ahead.

Niko took a deep breath, analysing the tense lines of Elijah's shoulders. Up until that moment, Niko had been caught up in the chase, but now, just like Elijah, he was pausing.

Was this what he wanted?

There were so many questions to consider, so many moving pieces and players, but he put all of that aside. The idea of sharing, he managed—with great effort—to put aside, so that he could consider the only question that really mattered.

Did he want Isobel?

10

Some Stars Fall, Some Are Plucked

Isobel spent a good hour simply canvassing the riverbank for cameras, and then when she didn't find any, she decided to cross the river itself, holding her phone above her head as she did. She wasn't sure if their little game would be of enough interest to the officials to send out a camera crew to cover the blind spot, but she doubted they would be able to follow her across the water with all of their equipment.

She was dripping as she hiked along the other side of the wide riverbank, picking her way between thick tree roots, scattered rocks, and crumbling earth. She had found a shallow part of the river to cross, but the cool water had still been deep enough to sway up to her chin. It now rushed beside her in a pleasant wash of noise, birds tangling in the leaves of the canopy above, unbothered by the rain. The scene might have been relaxing, if her blood wasn't boiling and her skin itching with a strange mixture of anxiety and anticipation. She didn't doubt that one of them would find her—hard as she had tried—but now that she had reached her hiding spot, she had no option but to face exactly what was about to happen.

She had agreed to *fully bond* one of her mates.

And she didn't even know how they were going to do it. There would be no formal tattoo ceremonies with family and friends in quiet attendance and flower crowns perfuming their hair. There would be no Guardian helping them to choose from the ancient symbols, or each other's names or initials.

There was just them, a storm, and the longest day of her life turning dark and deep with night.

When a twig snapped behind her, she flinched, pulling up short, but there was no time to turn around before a thick, tawny arm wrapped around her waist, the heady scent of whiskey washing over her.

She glanced down, spotting the two scrunchies around Niko's wrist, and all of the tension she had been holding so tightly inside her body suddenly loosened, flooding out of her in an immense wave.

It was Niko.

Niko was safe.

Her composure broke, and she burst into tears. He spun her around, his eyes tracing her face, her tears, her heaving breaths, reading her like a book and filing away the relief etched into her features.

"You're glad it's me," he said, his hand settling on her hip. His hair hung over his eyes, rainwater trembling from one of the strands. "It's because you don't have feelings for me. I'm uncomplicated." There was a small, understanding smile tight on his lips. "It's okay."

She sucked in a shuddering breath, wiping her tears with the backs of her hands. "I'm s-s-sorry."

She was awful. Horrible.

Niko wanted to be bonded to her less than the others, but here she was feeling selfishly relieved it was him because it would cause less trouble with the others.

"Isobel." He caught her hands, pulling them away from her face, and then he cupped her cheeks, gently brushing at the droplets that wobbled and spilled from the line of her lower lashes. "They let me win for a reason. It's okay."

"Can I have a hug?" she asked stupidly, raising her arms.

He was already pulling her into his body. "Yeah, babe." His thick arms enveloped her, the heat of his body and the way his muscles dug into the softness of her stomach and chest through their soaked clothing an immediate balm. Her rioting emotions calmed with the physical contact, and she hid her face in his neck, breathing him deeply as she clung to his shoulders. Her legs were dangling above the ground, her mind dizzy with his robust, multifaceted scent. She had been this close to him before—mostly when he was handing her ass to her on the mat—but this was different. He was ... letting go of something.

Accepting something.

It was there in his deep, unsteady breaths, in the indulgent lining to his tone, like suddenly he would give her anything and all she had to do was ask for it. She could easily imagine that he would use that voice with his family, or his girlfriend, and it made her ache.

The longer he held her, the tighter both of their grips became. He shifted her closer to a tree, angling his body so that the rain washed against his back instead of hers. She traced her nose along his neck, unfolding the layers of his perfume, growing intoxicated. It was sweet and indulgent butterscotch dancing playfully with the lightest touch of caramel, everything wrapped in toasted oak and earthy vanilla, lingering in smoky, peaty wisps.

"Isobel," he rumbled, his breath a rasp. "I need to ask you something."

"Mhm." She snuggled closer, lost to the pleasurable hum singing through her veins.

She was sure that some of it was the bond buzzing happily at one of her mates lavishing attention on her, but mostly, it was *her*. Her heavy feelings of relief and security were breaking like a dam and flooding over every inch of fear and anxiety she had harboured for the past few months.

It surprised her that of all the Alphas, Niko was the one who could make her feel like that, but then the more she considered it, the less shocking it became. Niko was steadfast, not volatile. He had never pushed to change their friendship. He was always giving her the same version of himself, even when the other Alphas pulled away to maintain their images for the cameras. After she was released from the hospital following Eve's attack, Niko was the only one who didn't draw away from her, their relationship growing slowly but surely, with a consistency that soothed her. Just like her climbing lessons with Kalen, the regular, dependable sessions with Niko had taught her to trust and rely on him.

"Could you ever want more from me?" he asked.

She drew back, shaking off the haze that had begun to drag her under. Niko's face appeared before hers, their noses inches apart, his mottled green and brown eyes drifting over her face with a heavy sort of acceptance, like he already knew the answer to his question.

"What?" she asked, her voice small.

"I want more." He spoke calmly. "I want you." And then, before she could even respond, he added, "I just need to know if you feel what I feel because if you don't, this is going to go in a different direction."

"W-what direction?"

"If you don't feel this"—he captured her hand, pressing it over the erratic beat of his heart, the only part of him betraying his calm exterior—"I'm taking you back to Dorm A and giving this opportunity to someone else. I don't know what's going to happen when we bond, but some people say they feel each other's feelings and hear each other's thoughts and if I have to *feel* that your heart doesn't speed up for me the way mine does for you, I don't think I'll handle it well."

"How do you know when it's the bond and when it's ... normal?" she asked, her voice almost a whisper now.

A person would have to be *blind* to not be attracted to Niko. His touches always made her stomach swoop ... and his tongue on her skin when her chain appeared had completely short-circuited her brain, but how could she suddenly crack herself open and reveal all of that? After she had admitted to Theodore that she had feelings for him? After she had let Oscar do what he did to her in the bathroom that morning?

How could she naturally develop so many feelings for so many different people all at once? How could that *not* be attributed to the bond?

"Sigma." He nuzzled her cheek. "Don't look so guilty. Just tell me, and we can go home."

"That's not why I feel guilty," she rushed out, horrified at the wave of pain he tried to hold back from her.

It washed against her gently, despite the acrid sting she could sense hovering just above the skin of her chest. He reined it in, still holding her so tightly, still comforting her with the brush of his bristled cheek against her smooth skin, but then her words seemed to register, and he stilled.

"You like me." He sounded shocked—astounded almost.

"How could I not?" she whispered close to his ear, scared to say the words out loud, losing her nerve before she could utter the rest. *You're every girl's dream.*

"That's all I need to know," he said, his damp skin now pulsing with heat. "It doesn't have to mean anything right now. But why do you look so guilty? What happened?" He drew back again, peering into her eyes as he set her gently back onto her feet, his hands anchored to her hips.

He walked her backwards, almost distracted, like he couldn't help himself as he pressed her closer to the deeply furrowed bark of the tree they stood beneath.

"I don't want to tear the group apart," she said, hoping he would read between the lines, before sucking her bottom lip between her teeth and shaking her head. There would be plenty of time for cowardice later—omitting her feelings before completing a bond with one of her mates after he had confessed his feelings for her was *not* that time. "If we keep going the way we are—and I don't mean me and you, I mean the whole group—then I will develop relationships with several people at once. I already am."

"We know." He released her hips, planting his hands against the wide trunk of the tree either side of her head.

He didn't seem to be boxing her in intentionally, more like looking for something to lean against as he hung his head, his eyes dropping from hers, though his attention didn't wander far, catching on her chest, where her wet shirt was clinging to her skin, the material puckering around her chain. He dragged his eyes back to hers, his tongue peeking out absently to lick a drop of rain from his lower lip.

"This isn't something we can plan. The relationships you have with each of us are up to you and those individual people you're involved with, not all of us as a group. But we're very aware of the connections you're forming. I grew up with Eli and Gabe. Moses and Theo grew up together. Kalen and Mikki have known each other for a long time. Theo and Kilian are best friends. Moses and Oscar are best friends. And all ten of us have been living in the same dorm for two years now. We *know* each other and we *know* what's going on. I'm not saying we're happy about the situation, but we're not going to sit around complaining about it either. We'll make it work. We'll make sure there's happiness and space for ourselves because that's what Gifted people do, right? Give us coal and we'll give your economy diamonds."

Isobel snorted out a soft laugh and he lifted his head at the sound. Since he was already leaning over, propped against the tree, his movement brought his face close to hers, affording her a rare, up-close glimpse of his eyes.

They were actually predominantly hazel, she noticed. A deep mahogany with subtle emerald flecks like scattered leaves on a forest floor. He blinked, a droplet falling from his lashes and sliding down his cheek. She reached up, touching it, tracing the glittering path of water as he loomed closer.

"We can't be out here all night," he rumbled, his big chest heaving as his gaze dropped to her mouth. "I need to mark you before they send a camera crew ... or a rescue crew."

She began to nod, before wincing. "I should have asked this back in Kalen's office, but there was so much—"

"Tattoo pen." Niko anticipated her question, pulling a Ziplock bag from his pocket and unwrapping plastic from a device. He also pulled out two small sachets and two small gauze patches, waving them at her before dropping them back into the bag. "Alcohol wipes and tiny bandages—so I suppose we need to keep this small. You just have to decide what you want me to draw and where you want it."

She swallowed past her relief. "I don't know what I was expecting, but I'm glad it's a tattoo. Who—"

"Elijah." He anticipated her question again. "Although all this packaging would suggest it was actually Gabriel who got the pen, but it was Elijah who gave the package to me. He tracked you here and stood back, waiting for me to approach him with everything I needed to complete the bond in his pocket, like the psychopath he is."

She let out a nervous laugh, glancing at the tattoo pen. "You know how to use that?"

He grinned. "Can't be too hard."

She groaned low. "Right." Looking down at herself, she couldn't think of where to place the tattoo *or* what she wanted. She had avoided all thoughts of forming a bond, and now she was paying for it.

"Want me to choose?" Niko asked, surveying her.

"Depends." She bit back a smile. "Where would you choose?"

He reached out immediately, touching the soft spot behind her ear, his eyes darkening. "Here. When we're fighting, I love it when you tie up your hair and I can see your neck. Your smell is so strong right here." His thumb brushed back and forth over her skin, sending shivers down her spine.

This was a different Niko. She almost didn't know what to do with him. He had always been focussed, but he rarely turned that focus on her with such unrelenting intensity. He never stared deep into her eyes, and he definitely didn't allow his touches to linger.

"What if I had said I didn't like you?" she blurted. "You would have taken me back to the dorm and that would have been the end of it?"

His smile was slow and sad. "No. It would have been the end of tonight. I was going to change your mind, but

I wasn't going to put you on the spot and do it tonight, not with this hanging over you. I was going to let you bond with someone else and then make sure you felt it. And then I was going to demand you bond me too." His grip slid down her neck, his body looming closer, his thumb tilting up her chin. "I can be very very—" His lips brushed hers, both of them inhaling deeply. "—*very* stubborn, Illy."

At the sound of her name on his lips, growled out so lowly, she finally gave in and grabbed handfuls of his wet shirt, dragging him back down to her mouth.

He kissed her deeply, a savage edge to the hard press of his lips and the way his tongue pushed against hers, demanding immediate submission, but then he pulled back with a hiss, holding the tattoo pen between them, the bag dangling from two of his fingers.

He didn't say anything, and he was still staring at her mouth, his breathing ragged. She wanted to pull him back in and see how far she could push him—the fire in her stomach was *demanding* it—but he was right. They were out there for a reason, and it wasn't to make out under a tree, or even to confess their feelings.

They needed to complete the bond.

"Okay," she whispered hoarsely, pulling her high plait over one shoulder and turning to give him her back. "Just draw a small heart," she said quietly, picturing what a line of hearts crawling down her neck would look like. She could add more later at a tattoo place on Market

Street—maybe do a line of hearts on either side, like etched black earrings hanging from her ears. Or maybe ...

Maybe someone else would add to the line of hearts.

She wasn't sure how she felt about that, but her *body* definitely knew how it felt. Heat flooded her stomach at the fantasy of ten pairs of hands holding her neck and etching dark little hearts into her flushed skin.

Niko didn't mess around. He cleaned the spot he had chosen with one of the alcohol wipes and then turned the pen on, his big hands twisting her head just the way he needed it.

The first sharp bite of the tattoo gun was all it took to convince her that *something* was happening, and by the time he finished, covering what he had done with the tiny piece of gauze, the shift inside her was so tangible, she could almost *see* it.

It felt like a deep and dark void opening up inside her, filling with a power that shook her to the core. It felt like waking up. Like coming back to life after years of sleep. From somewhere deep inside that void, she felt pieces of herself being pulled up from where they had fallen, thrown into a war with the dark hands of fate that tried to drag them back down. Those pieces were golden and bright, and they reached higher and higher until they were burning inside her chest, yanked from the pit of her stomach.

Niko spun her around, staring at the golden light she now realised wasn't simply imaginary as it burst from her chest in tendrils and burrowed into Niko's skin beneath the wet fabric of his shirt. He grunted, dragging his eyes to hers, swearing and jerking away from her.

"Jesus *fuck*," he yelled, clawing at one of his eyes. He pulled his hand away, a *melting* contact burning into his palm. He swore again, shaking out his hand, and then stepped back further, tilting his face up to the rain to wash out his eye. "Take out your contact," he told her. "Quickly."

Isobel removed it with shaking hands and then stood there, stuck, throat dry and eyes wide, because she could feel ... everything. Niko was inside her body, inside her mind. His pain was her pain—as keenly as if her own eye were burning.

She blinked away tears, finally breaking out of her shock and hurrying over to him, one of her eyes too blurry to see out of. "Are you okay? Did it do any damage?"

"I don't think so," he groaned, holding his eyelid open as rain washed over his face.

"Let me see," she demanded, tugging on his arms.

He tilted his chin back down, crouching to her eye level, and she caught his chin, furrowing her brow as she assessed the damage. "It's all red and swollen, but it's not bleeding or anything."

"Good." His voice turned quiet. "I can feel you. You're worried."

She nodded, wetting her bottom lip as she realised

she was seeing Niko without his contact for the first time. The honeyed brown of his iris was more familiar to her than the contact she wore every day. It was more *her*. But the longer she looked at it, the less familiar it became. It was *changing*. It grew cloudy, grey washing in behind the honey-gold specks. Some of the grey paled, turning icy and shrinking to pinpoints like the scattering of stars. And then there was a shimmering arc of deeper brown, almost red, which faded into a thin curtain, layering over emerald green. Splotches of black exploded, and threads of gold wove through, interacting with pale green and brighter sapphire.

It was her multicoloured eye.

Speckled and splotched and ... special. Because she finally realised it was all of their colours.

He took her breath away.

“It’s your turn,” Niko rumbled, backing her up until her spine brushed the trunk of the tree and they were marginally protected from the rain again. He passed the tattoo gun into her hands, and then the bag. “It needs to be somewhere the cameras won’t see. We can’t both suddenly have new tattoos.”

“What should I draw?” she asked, touching the small patch of gauze on her neck.

His eyes followed her unconscious movement. “A heart is fine.”

“Should we really be matching?” she asked, distracted as he lifted his shirt, pushing the hem of it between his teeth to hold it up as he shifted the waistband of his pants down, revealing more sharply muscled skin than she really knew what to do with.

"No." Niko's voice was tight, the word spoken between his teeth. He tucked his shirt beneath his chin instead, allowing him to speak clearly again. "Now ask if I care."

"Okay." She smiled at him, unaffected by his cold tone because she could *feel* that he was amused with her and impatient to get her mark on his skin. "But don't you want something a little more 'Alpha?'"

She lowered to her knees, ripping open the second alcohol wipe and cleaning his skin.

"Like what?" he rasped, eyes darkening.

Hurry up before I ruin you in the middle of a fucking forest.

"L-like a dumbbell o-or a b-burger," she squeaked, her cheeks burning with colour. "Did you mean to talk in my head just now?"

"No." His confusion sparked inside her. "You heard me? What did I say?"

"Never mind," she rushed out, pinking further. "So ... a can of beer?"

"Make it a heart, mate." This time it was a growled order, and she fell back to her heels, staring up at him.

He blinked, wincing. "I mean ... please?" His voice was strangled now.

"You can call me that," she whispered, her skin tingling.

He took a moment, probably to catalogue the butterflies in her stomach and her hitched breath before he slowly nodded. He knelt, putting his face by hers, his fingers soft on her chin.

"Then, mate—" He kissed her gently, both of them groaning at the soft, fleeting contact. "—please draw a heart and please draw it now."

He stood again, taking her breath with him, and she forced herself to focus, turning on the pen. "How do I do this?"

"Just press down—not too hard. It should feel like drawing on paper and the pen should glide smoothly."

She let out a grounding breath and outlined a small heart below his hip bone, drifting closer, her breath on his skin as she tried to concentrate. She could feel the flare of lust that burned through him, and a hardness pressing insistently to the inside of her left wrist as she steadied herself against his thigh. It throbbed as she coloured in the heart, and one of Niko's hands drifted to the side of her face, tracing the wet tendrils of her hair as they spiralled over her cheek.

He let out a deep, heavy breath as she finished, leaning back to observe her work. Satisfied, she covered it with the gauze patch but blinked as Niko's awe and shock suddenly tunnelled through their bond. She whipped her head up, and found him staring at her with wide eyes, his hand trembling as it drifted along her hairline.

"Stunning," he whispered, capturing her plait, and drawing it forward into her eyeline.

Her hair was *shining.* Glimmering and glinting with the soft colours of an aurora, speckles of light like scattered stars blinked out at her in a soft glow, reminding her of the pattern of her eyes.

"W-what the hell." She gripped Niko's forearms as he pulled her up, but it wasn't Niko who answered her.

It was someone else.

Someone who made her blood run cold.

"*Finally,*" Eve spat, stepping out from behind a tree. "Thought it was never going to happen. Time to go night-night, lovebirds."

Niko had begun to advance on Eve, but her power rolled over him in a wave so strong it had him stumbling and falling. He tripped over one of the gnarled tree roots as Isobel was knocked backwards into the tree, the wave of power hitting them both at the same time.

She tried to call out to Niko, whose eyes were rolling into the back of his head as he fell back, and back ... tumbling down the steep bank and disappearing with a loud splash into the river.

He can't swim.

Isobel fought the haze that had blackness flashing over her vision, but failed, and when she blinked again

Eve was already in front of her and she was sprawled on the sodden ground.

You're going to die for this. The Alphas will kill you. Isobel fought to say the words, but they wouldn't come, so she tried to say it with her eyes instead.

Eve laughed, pulling a pocket knife from her jacket. "I'm *protected*, bitch. Your Alphas can't do shit to me."

Isobel fought to get away, straining with every muscle, frantic and agonized, willing her body to crawl, to fall, to get to Niko any way she could.

He was going to drown.

Their relationship had changed in the blink of an eye and already, she was losing him.

"Don't worry," Eve said, examining the blade. "He's just awake enough to hold his head up, to breathe, to cling on. I wanted you awake for this."

And then she began sawing away at Isobel's hair, and that horrible, all-consuming pain that Isobel had hoped to never feel again was *there*.

Again.

11
SOME STARS BURN OUT

THE BEAUTIFUL, SOUL-ILLUMINATING LIGHT THAT HAD tethered her so securely to the world was unravelling. She had felt those threads of light keenly enough to imagine she could see them, and as they were ripped and torn away from her, she felt them even more vividly.

She felt the absence of them as they drew further and further away, leaving her sobbing in the leaves, strands of sunlight hair scattered all around her like she was only the bare trunk of a fallen tree, her foliage scattered in dying ruins, the light blinking out.

Eve was gone. Her light was gone.

She crawled, agonising inch by agonising inch, toward the unsteady bank of the river, allowing the earth to crumble beneath her weight and send her tumbling down. Niko hung from a half-submerged log, hooked by his arms, looking like he was a moment away from becoming dislodged and floating away with the current.

His unfocussed eyes drifted to her as water lapped at his chin, spilling into his mouth, and it was as though he was seeing a ghost.

And she could feel it.

The deep, dark void between them. Sucked of power. Drained of light.

Poisoned.

Broken.

Grief washed through her, tearing and ripping at the walls of her soul.

Don't feel it. Not right now.

She clawed the rest of the way down the bank, reaching out an arm to Niko, but her arm sagged and trembled like a twig about to break off in the wind.

He only stared at her, slipping further.

"Niko!" she attempted to scream, but the word was a broken rasp as she slipped, her body catching against a mud-covered rock as she tried to edge closer.

She heaved herself to the side and fell against the trunk he was hooked onto, jostling him and loosening his grip, but it didn't seem to be the jolting of his perch that sent him into the water.

It seemed that he lifted his fingers and simply ... let go.

Deliberately.

He drifted away, his eyes still locked on her, the deep

darkness between them flexing and stretching and swallowing her mind.

The water rushed over his head, and he didn't fight it.

She dove in after him without a thought, her limbs weak and uncoordinated as she continued fighting off Eve's power. The current tugged at her, pulling her through the water and folding over her head as she desperately tried to beat her limbs and break the surface again.

But it was too hard, and black spots exploded over her eyes, her lungs straining as a bubble-filled scream erupted from her mouth. She wasn't expecting a body to shoot through the surface of the water above her, or the face that appeared before her own, blurry and cut with shadow, like some sort of wraith of the lake.

Mikel?

He hauled her toward the surface of the water, where they both clung to the bank, Isobel gasping desperately for breath.

"Ni-iko," she wheezed.

"We've got him," Mikel said stiffly as hands appeared from above.

She reached up, but her limbs failed as her wrists passed her shoulder, falling back down again. A male voice swore above her, and Mikel raised her at the same time as the arms above dipped, gripping her arms and pulling her from the water.

"Illy." Cian was touching her face, his eyes wide with horror, his hands trembling against her scalp as the pads of his fingers threaded through her shorn-off strands. "What the fuck, Illy?"

"Eve," she wheezed. "Is the ... is the light gone?"

"What light?" Cian's tone sharpened to a vicious edge.

Her tears spilled over again, because that was the only answer she needed.

"The light in her hair." Niko's voice floated over to her, sounding oddly detached. He was supported by Gabriel and Elijah, limping, his hair plastered to his face. It was too dark to make out his expression until the three of them shuffled closer, and then she was rearing back, shock lodged in her throat.

"Why the fuck didn't you just let me *drown?"* He was a wild, snarling animal, shoving away from Gabriel and Elijah and stumbling for a few steps on his own.

"Ni—" she started, but he cut her a dark look, and that void inside her cracked.

"Don't," he snarled. "Everyone just leave me the fuck alone."

"Niko, stop," Kalen barked, Alpha voice riding his tone. "Your eye."

"I'll keep my eyes down." Niko's voice was full of a poison Isobel had never heard from him before—a poison she could never even *fathom* resided inside him.

He was a completely different person.

The cracked void opened further, fissuring and splintering until she was gasping for breath, but Niko only stared down at her with a kind of absent pity before he turned on his heel and stalked off.

With every step, another crack appeared. Tiny little hairline fractures that spread and spread and spread until the void inside her collapsed, sending her spiralling down as pain flowed freely through her body.

It was more pain than she had ever felt before.

It was too much, too soon, too overwhelming.

And she just *knew* it was going to claim her, this time.

She could sense Kalen's vanilla scent all around her, his rough hands holding her face, his warm power nipping up against her skin, but it didn't make a difference.

Her soul was a shredded, bloody mess, the viscera painting the walls of her mind in a vicious, horrifying wallpaper. She was living inside a nightmare, wasting away in a cage of her own greatest fear.

"Her hair is growing back," a voice noted.

"But she's still fading," another added, panicked. "Fuck, *fuck!* What do we do?"

"Do you have another pen?" Kalen demanded of someone, but she didn't hear their answer.

"I'm sorry, Isobel." Elijah's voice floated through to her, piercing her pain. "It's either this, or we lose you." His hands were on her neck, peeling away the gauze Niko had pressed there. "Is this the mark you want?" He seemed to be asking himself, more than her.

There was a prick of something in her neck that might have been pain, at some point in the past. She barely felt it, this time.

What was pain?

Pain was breathing. Pain was hearing. Pain was remembering.

She was too busy falling through endless darkness, wondering where her light had gone and if her sight would ever return—because that seemed to have disappeared too.

Maybe her hearing would be next.

She hoped it would take her memory before she succumbed.

She didn't know if her eyes were open or closed, but there was only black. Endless black. Elijah sounded like he was in pain, and then there was a strange pressure against her eye, mumblings about contacts burning floating around her.

There was another tickle in her neck, a voice that sounded like Gabriel's brushing an apology against her temple. And then another, and another.

"Do I keep going down?" Theodore's voice asked, strained and broken. "These reach the bottom of her neck."

"Try the other side," someone suggested.

There was another tickle of something against her

skin. This one seemed to take longer, and she felt more pressure. By the time it stopped, there was the faintest little spark of light below her, and the fall felt less terrifying, but she was still falling, still lost. The hands against her neck dropped away, replaced by another set, another apology muttered above her. After two more—each longer and slightly more painful than the last—her fall halted. She floated, on the precipice of terror, unsure if she were about to drop again or if this might be it. The place where it ended.

"It's not enough," Elijah stated calmly.

This was followed by another apology, and another trickle of pain shooting down her neck, pulling at her tender skin. The ground suddenly rushed up to meet her, and she was able to blink her eyes open in time to watch Mikel pull away from her, his eyes darting away as he stood and handed something to Kalen, who knelt beside her.

He was holding the tattoo pen. Moving it to her neck. He was *drawing*. She felt a small tug, a tiny thread of light—shy and wounded—peek out from some corner of her consciousness. It slithered along in the dark, fraying in places, crooked and kinked. It reached up and up until she could feel it in her chest, wiggling to be free.

She didn't want to let it go.

Not after what happened last time.

Please stay, she begged, gathering the broken mess of

her soul about her like a cloak. *We can't take anymore. Please stay.*

But the broken little sprig of light didn't *care* what Isobel wanted. It burst out of her chest in an explosion so bright several of the Alphas shielded their eyes as tendrils of light arced toward their chests, hooking in with greedy claws and wrapping around them so tightly that Isobel could feel the delicate tug pulling her body in nine different directions.

"Will it help if she marks us in return?" Mikel asked.

"Not necessary." Elijah was watching her—they were all watching her.

They gathered in a circle around her, some of them crouched, some of them standing, the rain soaking their clothes and hair, dripping down fierce expressions and curling around hardened mouths ... but she could feel that they were terrified and confused. She didn't know who, specifically, was feeling what, as it poured inside her in an overwhelming, confusing tangle.

Their contacts must have burned away because they were each showing her a single, multi-hued iris, speckled with their combined colours. It might have made her heart ache, if her heart wasn't broken.

For several minutes, they all just stared at each other, drinking each other in and coming to terms with the change they had rushed into to save her.

They were bonded.

All of them.

They had tethered themselves to her extinguished soul, to the hungry depth of pain that yawned below her, seeming wide and willing enough to swallow them all.

They had bonded a corpse.

As if hearing her thought, a rippled reaction scattered, like a breeze, across their faces. Kilian's eyes filled with tears, his chest heaving. Theodore's jaw clenched, his eyes also shimmering with unshed tears. Oscar's tanned skin had taken on an impossible pallor. Moses was shaking his head, denying what was in her head. Elijah looked like he was in pain, and Gabriel's face twitched, showing her a flash of agony. Cian's chest was rising and falling rapidly like he was finding it hard to breathe. Kalen and Mikel both seemed to brace themselves against competing fear and sorrow.

"Don't look so glum, you lot," she rasped, clasping for a fraying thread of humour. "This is ... this is ... supposed to be romantic."

The joke didn't land. Probably because she had struggled to breathe in the middle of it.

She remembered bonding to Niko, and how all his pain had felt like hers.

Fuck. They were feeling everything. She was *torturing* them.

"We have to go and make sure this also fixed Niko." Gabriel's usually steady voice wobbled, the skin around his eyes tight.

"Go," she said weakly, after feeling hesitancy through

the bond. "Both of you, it's fine." She had no idea who the hesitancy belonged to.

It was difficult to sort out all the thoughts and feelings being vaulted into her, so she simply pushed them all away, hiding behind the crumbling remnants of the wall she was accustomed to building. Several of the Alphas flinched like she had struck them.

"Eve has my light," she said, trying to stand.

Mikel grabbed her immediately, and she clung to him, rising on wobbly legs. She felt the strangest hint of bittersweet euphoria peeking through the cracks of her wounded heart, but it was as though she was feeling it from far, far away.

Something was terribly wrong.

"What happened?" Oscar's gritty voice cracked as he tugged her coverup, which she had left in the maze, over her arms.

"My hair glowed after we formed the bond. Eve cut it off." She glanced down as Oscar tugged her hair forward over her shoulders, the mass heavy and familiar, just the same length it had been before Eve cut it off. He arranged it to cover her neck, his fingers lingering, his eyes dark pools of ink, his rage tasting like acid against the back of her throat.

"It grew back when Kalen took your body back in time," Oscar said, his tone dangerously low and gravelled. "But there was no light."

"Kilian, go after Eve," Kalen ordered. "Take Oscar."

"I'll fucking ki—" Oscar began to snarl, but Kalen cut him off.

"You won't do any permanent damage. She has a failsafe. If anything happens to her, we're all exposed and every single one of us is at risk, and that will likely extend to all our families back home, so she is *not* to be … incapacitated. But she clearly thought her failsafe would protect her if she went after Isobel again, and she needs to be informed, without room for misunderstanding, that she was wrong. She needs to learn a lesson. Can I trust you with this?"

Oscar stared back at him, Kilian glancing between them, the rest of the group silent.

"Be more specific," Oscar finally returned, pain lacing his tone. "Define permanent damage."

"You know what he means," Kilian snapped, his pale eyes still glittering, though they looked like angry tears now. "Just give him your word so they can get Isobel back to the dorm."

"Fine." Oscar pointed at Isobel, his eyebrows drawing together. "*You* …" He sucked in a breath, holding it like he didn't know what to say. "T-text us if you need us," he finally said. She had never heard Oscar stutter before.

Kilian stared at her, also unsure what to say. "I'll see you later," he finally whispered.

Oscar spun on his heel and Kilian grabbed his arm, making them both disappear.

She could feel grief travelling down the string that now connected them—much stronger than the muted thud against her chest—but it took a moment to realise it was Kilian's, and by the time she did, even the sounds of their footsteps had faded.

Fresh tears began to fall down her cheeks, a sob shuddering through her chest.

How did it go so badly so fast?

"I always carry spare contacts." Kalen was already covering his multihued iris. "I'll go and report that Isobel passed out at the border of the academy, but it seems to be a bond side effect and she'll address it with her bond specialist tomorrow. Cian—"

"I've got her." Cian stepped up to Isobel's other side, wrapping a strong arm around her.

Mikel slipped away from her. "I'll act like I was running and have nothing to do with any of this." He was already dressed in exercise clothes, so that made sense.

He backed away further, flicked her a last look, and then nodded at Kalen before turning and jogging off in the opposite direction to where Kilian and Oscar had disappeared.

"We can't talk about this now." Kalen briefly glanced at Theodore, Moses, and Cian to include them in the statement before settling his attention on Isobel. "Do you need the hospital? Do you think we fixed it? I can ... feel you, and you feel ... I think we stopped what was happening, but I want to be sure."

Her chin dipped in a short, hesitant nod. In truth, she wasn't sure how she felt. She was rattled ... but detached; a significant part of her mind had disengaged from what was happening around her. It helped to have her walls in place, to block out the ghostly feeling of having more than one consciousness connected with her own.

Everything inside her was shredded, and it felt like it was beyond repair ... but she was no longer falling.

"All right ..." Kalen's stern eyes dug into hers, and possibly into her mind itself—she wasn't sure that her walls were blocking them from feeling her, or just her from feeling them. "Then let's get back. Cian, stick with Isobel all night but don't sleep in her bed. We don't have enough sample footage to loop the cameras yet. Theo and Moses, reconvene in Mikel's office for a debrief. I'll meet with Niko, Elijah, and Gabriel separately in my office. Everyone keep an eye on the group chat and keep your watches on. Isobel and Cian, we'll have our meeting in the morning. Everyone clear?"

"Clear," they all muttered.

Isobel kept her head down as they walked back to the dorm, her hair covering her neck. Cian kept his arm around her, but she wasn't as weak after the bonding and didn't truly need assistance.

She felt strong ... but empty. There was a vastness inside her, and while it didn't feel fragile or vulnerable, she still sensed that it had the potential to fissure and send her spiralling down into darkness all over again.

It was there as a suggestion, a reminder.

It would always be there, now.

The thought alone had her almost retching as Cian deposited her into her room and told her to lock her door while he ducked back into his own room. He was only gone a few minutes, and Isobel spent the entire time standing exactly where he had left her, staring at the floor with a horrible numbness creeping over her body. He knocked to be let back in, his deep voice calling her name. She opened the door and saw that he had put himself through the world's fastest shower and changed into sweats and a cotton shirt. He locked her door again and gently instructed her to shower, watching her with concern creasing his brow as she shuffled silently into her bathroom.

Soul infraction.

The words echoed inside her as she put herself through a shower she could barely feel. She had suffered one before, but it didn't measure up to this feeling. Back then, she had guarded her light with everything she had. This time, she failed.

And she wasn't the same.

There was no delicate happiness, no swirling hope, no burning realisation that she had accidentally run right into the arms of everything she didn't realise she wanted. Everything she had felt while bonding to Niko was ... *stolen.*

Not exposed as an illusion of bonding magic but *stolen.*

There was nothing in its place but the dark void, and nothing to fill that horrifying space except her own poisonous emotion. She had only anger, that what was *hers* was gone. Only fear, that she would be empty forever. The emotion swirled and churned and bubbled, but that space could only ever be empty, so not even her growing rage could fill her up. It lost form, grew vaporous, and tried to escape through her veins, poisoning her entire body.

She was left to face the question of whether forming extra bonds could heal the damage of just one bond, and there was a whisper in her mind telling her that it was *all or nothing*, and that without Niko, she would be lost.

She was terrified.

Maybe her terror was the reason for what she saw when Cian turned out the lights and she crawled into bed alone, leaving him to stretch out on the chaise nearby. At first, she thought it was him—since there was no other explanation for a large shadow moving toward her bed—but then the shadow drew closer, and she could make out their features.

She froze, a scream caught in the back of her throat.

He was huge, with dark, oily hair that hung over his eyes and sunken, deep-set features.

Crowe.

He's dead, she tried to tell herself, watching as his red

mouth stretched into a smile, which morphed into a loud, hacking laugh. She squinted at the chaise—at the faint outline of Cian's long body stretched over it. Cian didn't stir at the sound of Crowe's laughter.

"Thought you got rid of me, eh?" Crowe taunted, taking another step closer before growling, glancing over to the end of her bed, where another shadow had materialised.

"You're not allowed to come here just to terrorise her." Caran Carter spoke with an edge of steel in her voice—something that had been missing when she had been alive.

"Family reunion, is it?" This had been uttered sarcastically, jerking Isobel's head to the other side of her bed, where Buddy Carter leaned against one of her bed posts. Her grandpa was looking at her mother, one bushy grey eyebrow raised. "Thought you were blocked from visiting?"

"Carttteerrrrr," Crowe sang. "Look at me, bitch!"

Isobel screwed her eyes closed, a whimper catching in her throat, her fists clenching as tears slipped down her cheeks. The slight sound must have stirred Cian, because she could smell his saltwater and sunshine scent suddenly dousing her, though she still jumped when she felt his grip on her wrists.

"Illy," he breathed. "What's wrong?"

"Cian ..." There was another voice in the room, one

that she vaguely recalled hearing once before. "Cian ... I'm so sorry."

Isobel flinched harder, pressing the base of her palms into her eyes and shaking her head.

"Oh, not this fucking girl again," a rough voice declared. "Where the fuck is my son? Where is my little wolf? Why the fuck am I constantly being dragged back to her? I don't even know her! And you're here again too!"

"Shut up," Isobel's mother snapped. "You're scaring her."

"You ...," a small female voice whispered, sounding terrified. "W-what are you doing here?"

Cian managed to pull Isobel's hands down from her eyes just as the man she now recognised as Oscar's dead father strode across the floor past the end of her bed, advancing on a small-statured woman with dark, ashy brown skin and long, curly black hair. She shook her head, displacing curls everywhere, her eyes wide and horrified as she backed away from the man.

"I see we aren't the only ones having a family reunion," Buddy remarked.

"Whose room is beside mine?" Isobel whispered, unable to focus on Cian's face before hers. Her voice trembled, breaking off at the end.

"Oscar on one side," Cian answered, his body going still as he glanced over his shoulder, realisation dawning in his eyes.

"And t-the o-other?" she whispered.

"Elijah," he answered, as another shadow materialised between Oscar's father and—Isobel assumed—his mother.

"The fuck is this?" a large man demanded, tugging at his belt, which hung unopened, his shirt hanging untucked. He had a thick moustache and stringy hair, his eyes a keen blue. "The fuck are all you people?"

Isobel lurched over the side of her bed and sprinted into the bathroom, crashing over the toilet before losing the contents of her stomach. Cian crouched behind her, pulling her hair out of her face and running his big hand soothingly up and down her back until she was finished, and then he allowed her to collapse back into him. He sat against the wall, bundling her into his lap, and whispered the same faint words against her temple until the trembling subsided.

You're safe.

I've got you.

Her bond trilled with alarm, and when she opened her eyes again, Cian was texting furiously with one hand, the other still gently soothing over her back.

"We can feel everything, now," he explained, sensing her eyes on him. He slipped his phone away. "Gabe is bringing something. I'll be back."

After he slipped out of the bathroom, she hesitantly looked around. She was alone again. Breathing out a shaky breath, she pulled herself up, flushed the toilet, and began to brush her teeth.

What the hell was happening to her?

Cian returned with a bottle of water and two pills. "Sleeping pills," he explained. "Just in case you want them."

She swallowed the pills gratefully before climbing back into bed, but every shadow on the ceiling still had her jumping and twitching.

Isobel.

The call inside her head was Cian's, his deep, husky voice forcing her whole body to turn and curl in his direction, seeking out his shadow in the dark. As her eyes adjusted, she could barely make out his face.

Can you hear me? she tried to speak inside her head.

Yeah, doll. Just focus on me, okay?

Okay.

The shape of his chest seemed to swell with a deep breath.

I've got you, Isobel.

She curled in on herself tighter, her fists notched beneath her chin. She felt so alone. Cian's voice inside her head was a balm, but it just wasn't enough.

No bandage was large enough for the wound that grew inside her.

I don't know if it was enough, she thought to him. *I don't know if you all saved me ... or if you just delayed the inevitable.*

You won't be leaving us. He sounded quiet and deadly. *No matter how many times they try. Crowe learned his lesson, and now Eve will learn hers.*

She pressed her lips together, suppressing a shudder at the sound of Crowe's name. She waited a moment, but when the hulking Beta didn't suddenly materialise by her bed, she answered.

I don't know how to fix this.

We'll find a way. We always find a way, don't we?

THE NEXT MORNING, CIAN DROPPED ISOBEL OFF AT KALEN'S door before disappearing into Mikel's office. She hadn't run into any of the other Alphas, and as soon as she saw the look on Kalen's face, she knew something was wrong.

Something *else* was wrong.

"Where's Niko?" she demanded as soon as the door had closed behind her.

"He's safe. He's here." Kalen wiped a hand over the bottom half of his face, his expression drawn. "How bad is it, Isobel?"

"I don't know," she answered honestly. "I ... really don't feel right."

He nodded, expecting her answer. "Niko isn't right, either ... but he's ... worse than you."

"Still?" Her body grew cold. "Completing the bond with everyone didn't help him at all?"

"He seems to get worse by the minute." Kalen sucked air through his teeth, shaking his head. "I'm going to give it to you straight, Carter. Niko hates you right now. He doesn't seem very fond of anyone, but he gets especially fired up whenever you're mentioned."

"What?" she croaked.

"The soul infraction twisted him. I'm worried that repeated exposure to him will only cause minor infractions and will hurt you further."

"Keeping him away from me will also hurt the bond," she reasoned calmly, despite her galloping heartbeat. "What about the light? M-my hair? Eve?"

"The boys tracked her to the northern point of the campus. There's another boathouse there at the end of a lake."

"Another entrance to the Stone Dahlia?"

"Precisely. They couldn't follow her inside because they haven't been given pass cards for the new location yet. But they waited for her to come out, and the boathouse happens to be a camera blind spot."

She waited, not daring to ask. She couldn't tell if it was good news or bad news from the stony arrangement of Kalen's features.

"She took the soul artefact to someone inside the Dahlia," Kalen eventually said, his jaw tight. "But ... Oscar and Kilian were able to question her. She needs to be able to see a person to use her magic. Even if it's for a moment and that person walks out of her range, she can infect them in the moment when she was looking at them, and she can give them just enough that it has a delayed reaction. Or she can throw the full force of her power and incapacitate a person all at once if she's standing close enough—which is what she did to you and Niko." He seemed to be watching her carefully, measuring up her reaction to something he had said or something he was about to say. "She can no longer use her power on you, on us, or on anyone." Kalen's voice lowered to a growl. "For taking your hair, we took her eyes."

Isobel stilled, trying to figure out if there was some sort of meaning to Kalen's words other than the most obvious one.

"I'm sorry," he stated, with so much calm and without looking sorry at all. "But she attacked our mate and defiled our bond *despite our warning to stay away from you*." His voice descended into a growl halfway through the measured sentence, and then he pulled back his shoulders, regaining his calm. "I cannot allow that to happen without repercussion."

Isobel wanted to scoff in disbelief or harbour some sort of righteous horror, but there was still nothing but empty numbness inside her, and as hard as she tried, she couldn't even feel a drop of sympathy.

"Good," she finally decided to say, though the satisfaction was lacking in her tone.

His jaw flexed, his eyes darkening. "You disobeyed me, Isobel."

"And you can't allow that to happen without repercussions either?" she flung back.

For just a moment, something sparked between them, burning along their connection, making the bind that tied them together look very much like a trail of gasoline with Kalen standing at one end absently flicking a lighter, but then he drew back. Not physically, as he didn't move so much as an inch, but she could *feel* his consciousness carefully pulling away from hers.

"You may be my mate," he said softly. "But you aren't *mine*. You can be grateful for that today, or you'd have most definitely received repercussions severe enough to impede your ability to walk straight for the rest of the week."

"I don't even know what that means."

"I know." He ran a hand through his hair, messing up the careful style. "Mikel will deal with your punishment this time—as is his role with the other Alphas. I seriously advise you not to push him."

She lifted a shoulder. "Fine."

He stalked toward her suddenly, looming over her, his eyes blazing—yet she could barely feel him; he had retreated so far from her mind. He seemed to want to correct her in some way. It was clear something she had just done or said had triggered him, but once again, he held himself back. He waited until all the tension had been carefully siphoned away from his expression before his finger drifted beneath her chin, tilting her face up to his.

"We're going to take this one day at a time," he said, with so much compassion that the emptiness inside her wanted to *riot*.

She realised, with a jolt, that she wanted him angry. But that didn't make sense.

"So what's the plan today, then?" she asked, hating the way her body melted at his gentle handling of her.

"Your schedule was emailed to you. You're free for the next hour, then you have Mikel's group intensive. You'll have a tutoring session with me for sixth period, and a tutoring session with Elijah for seventh period—both of them private. And then tonight, I have to sponsor your first night in the Stone Dahlia, but we're going to organise a time for you to see Teak today, so some of that may change. Are you ready for all of this, or do you need a day off?"

"No, I'm ready. What do I say if someone questions me about Eve?"

"That you have no idea what they're talking about."

"Got it."

His presence crept back into her mind, billowing up against the wall she studiously maintained, other than her brief conversation with Cian the night before. She could feel them all there, but they were only allowed to go so far. She hoarded her void all to herself.

"The stone turned red," he said, his deep voice lowering to a rasp of whispered sound. "That's how we knew something was wrong. It was washed with pink and then suddenly it was red, and then it darkened. It was a deep red, like blood."

Curiosity sparked within her, muted but present. "Oh?" She quirked a brow at him, and his eyes traced the shift in her expression.

"Mhm." He released a short rumble of sound before folding his arms across his chest. "Do you want to know what colour it is now?"

She crossed her own arms, mirroring his pose. "Yes?"

"Then check it," he ordered, expression deadpan, words inflectionless. "It's in my pocket."

"I thought Mikel had it?" she asked, ignoring his order and tucking her hands in against her body to hide the way they trembled.

"And now I do," Kalen returned smoothly. "Take it out."

He didn't use Alpha voice, but she still felt compelled to obey. She stepped toward him, but then paused, unsure which pocket to reach for. Kalen noticed her dilemma but decided not to enlighten her.

"Why?" she finally said, staring at his chest.

"Because you can't pretend you don't care, Isobel. If

you really want to know, I want you to prove it. Prove how much you care about the health of our bond."

"Why bother?" She said the words without thinking and stepped closer—still without thought. Her fingers searched for the seams of his pockets.

He stood still as a statue, without so much as a twitch of the hard muscles she brushed against. She dug both of her hands into his pockets, finding his phone in the left one and a smooth, multi-faceted object in the other.

She pulled out the stone, and Kalen stood still, watching as she came face to face with the truth.

It was still a deep, dark, blood red.

She swallowed, fighting down the well of emotion that wanted to rise up from her void and drag her back down again, but she turned her back on it, suppressing everything. She shoved the artefact back into Kalen's pocket, but before she could back away from him, he caught her wrist, halting her.

"Are you angry we made this decision for you?"

"No." She scoffed. *Why was she so angry?* "You saved my life." She hadn't even thanked them. "Ah ... thank you." Her brow furrowed, her breath rattling as she forced the words out again, this time sounding a little more grateful. "Really. Thank you."

He nodded, still examining her expression. "We'll figure this out. Just stick with us."

"Do you think I'm going to leave?" she asked, an edge to her tone.

"No, princess." He purred the words, the sudden change in his intonation pulling her up short and widening her eyes. He was appealing directly to her injured bond, and it thumped weakly in return, trying to reach out for the offered comfort. "I think you're angry and you're hurt. I think you almost fucking died again, and I think you're sick of people attacking you. What I'm saying is that we *will* deliver swift and ruthless justice to anyone who touches you, in a way that doesn't expose you, until every motherfucker out there finally gets the message that you. Are. Owned." He cut himself off on a growl, quickly releasing her. "Protected," he seemed to amend. "Untouchable. You should go."

He strode back to his desk, falling into his chair and tapping at his keyboard to wake up his monitor, effectively dismissing her. She may have blocked off any significant waves of his mood from travelling through the bond, but she was still a Sigma.

His turmoil reached her regardless, just in a different way.

It didn't travel through their bond or ripple into her mind. It swatted her body as she escaped his office, unsettling her to her core.

From that brief taste of Kalen's anguish, she knew that she wasn't the only one who could feel the damage that had been done to the bond. She wondered if the void was really *hers*, or if it belonged to all of them.

12
THE NEW IRONSIDE

CIAN WAS WAITING FOR HER WHEN SHE CAME OUT OF KALEN'S office, and they walked to the dining hall together, a tense silence stretching between them—one that she resented greatly.

She had cared about what she had with Cian, the budding friendship with moments where he would ease the bond and give her a taste of what it would be like to really *be* with someone like him without the terror of asking someone like him to be with her. But that fragility was shattered. They had been forcibly tied together with a poisoned cord, and they didn't even have the space or privacy to talk about it.

Still, he tried to put on a show of casual ease for the cameras, slinging his arm over her shoulders and muttering casual observations of the students on their way to the dining hall against her hair.

"The others should already have a table," he said as they stepped through the doors.

The hall had been remodelled to closely resemble the previous Ironside dining hall, with booths lining the sides of the room—though these had no screens for privacy. Cian gripped her hand and pulled her toward one of the booths along the right side of the hall, near the back. The same position of the previous Alpha booth. He deposited her at the table before backtracking to the food display.

She stood at the head of the table awkwardly as several of the Alphas jerked up, suddenly involved in a subtle struggle. Niko fought off Elijah and Gabriel, who snapped back with more force, sending him heavily into his seat, where he sat and glared at Isobel, his nostrils flaring.

"Just because she lives with us, doesn't mean she has to eat with us," he growled, so much venom soaking the words that Isobel fell back a step in shock.

"Shut the fuck up," Theodore snarled at him, looking like he was ready to stab Niko with his fork.

"Back off," Gabriel shot at Theodore, panic in his eyes. "We've got him."

"Get him a little *better*," Oscar said lowly. "Or find a different table."

"Don't, Oscar." Elijah sighed, his hand hard on Niko's shoulder. He turned his attention to Isobel, a tense smile twisting his lips. "Take a seat, Carter."

"Um." She swallowed, cowed by the fire in Niko's eyes. "I can—"

"Take a seat," Moses ordered, brooking no argument.

She plopped down next to Theodore, who pushed his coffee into her hands and then moved his plate of french toast before her, even going so far as to wedge his fork into her grip.

"Eat." He tried to phrase it as a suggestion, but he mostly failed, the word squeezed out through clenched teeth.

Nervously, she took a few bites, tasting nothing, and then she quietly set the fork down and took a shaky gulp of coffee. She tested her walls, prodding around the exterior to try and find a sense of Niko, but it was too complicated and muddled with so many of them right beside her, so she gave up, drinking the coffee as Elijah muttered lowly to Niko, trying to draw his dark glare away from her.

There was a stir of activity by the entrance of the dining hall as Cian returned with a laden tray. He sat opposite Isobel, his eyes lifting to the commotion as Isobel twisted around, trying to see through the crowd forming.

Ed Jones and Jack Ransom, the hosts of the *Ironside Show*, were striding through the students, a team of officials behind them. One of them seemed fairly familiar, and Isobel's memory supplied her with an image of the day she was invited to join the Stone Dahlia

—that same woman had stalked into the dining hall with the same sharp heels and had played footage of Crowe attempting to assault Isobel. There was no wheeled projector this time, but that didn't stop Isobel's breath stuttering in apprehension.

"What is it?" Theodore asked, leaning over her head. He stilled, and then drew back, exchanging a low whisper with Moses.

The entire hall fell silent as Ed and Jack took up a position in front of the food bar. One of the officials handed a microphone to Ed, and another official handed one to Jack, who spun it around with a wide grin on his face.

"Good morning, students!" Ed called, his signature drawl loud and drawn out. "Welcome to your first day at the brand-new Ironside Academy! It's so satisfying to finally see all your gorgeous faces in person!" He paused as loud, excited cheers rang through the hall.

Isobel was too shocked to clap.

"I'm standing before you and the entire world today with an announcement that will shake the very foundations our beloved *Ironside Show* was built upon. We promised bigger, we promised better, we promised more drama and higher stakes and ..." He paused, turning to Jack. "Have we delivered, Jack?"

"I do believe we have," Jack returned slyly, causing scattered laughter to ring around the room.

Cian spilled out of the booth, nudged by Kilian.

Isobel also stepped out, allowing the other Alphas to stand. They crowded around her, Theodore and Kilian standing so close she felt pressed between them. Niko stood apart from them all, his arms crossed and a frown twisting his face—though at least he was frowning at the officials instead of Isobel.

"I'm going to hand you over to the officials, who have *quite the announcement*." Ed wiggled his eyebrows at the crowd before passing his microphone to the woman that Isobel recognised.

What had been her name? Frisk?

"We have celebrated the Gifted individuals who compete in the *Ironside Show* for a long time," Frisk announced. "For generations, they have competed fiercely, giving their all to earn the ultimate prize. However—" She paused, savouring the way the excited whispers around the hall suddenly died off. "—today marks a monumental shift in that tradition. For the first time in the history of the *Ironside Show*, we will welcome humans into the competition." She barrelled on, careless of the slow realisation that sank into the hall. "Our six new contestants represent the epitome of human potential. They're coming to us from the outside world. Their spirits are unyielding, their talents unsurpassed, and I must warn you, their hunger for victory is impressive. If you thought you could manipulate this game ..." Her unwavering gaze paused on the Alphas. "This is your wake-up call, because the game is changing." She smiled out at the hall again. "The presence of these six extraordinary individuals will force you to push yourselves harder, to dig deeper, and to prove your tenacity and talent against tried and tested individuals who have already carved a space out there for themselves as young talent in the real world. Make no mistake, students, the stakes of the *Ironside Show* have never been higher. If any of these human contestants win the game, there will be *no* Gifted leaving the settlements."

She lifted her hand to quell the wave of whispering, the same benevolent smile on her face. "Our fifth-year and fourth-year students are safe, as our human contestants will be entering the academy in their third year."

Our year. Theodore's voice suddenly sounded inside her mind. *This is for us. They know something. This is damage control. They're trying to take our influence away.*

No shit, Gabriel shot back.

Isobel flinched, glancing between them, but they were still staring ahead.

You heard that? Theodore sounded confused.

You wanted us all to hear, so we all heard, Elijah responded.

Isobel eyed Niko, who hadn't reacted at all.

Niko. She projected the word, driven by a sick sense of curiosity.

He didn't so much as flinch.

He couldn't hear her.

Her breathing turned ragged with panic, but Kilian slipped his hand through hers, anchoring her as she fought to get herself back under control.

He can't hear us. She tried to send the thought out to all of them. Kilian squeezed her hand. Theodore's palm slipped to her back before he seemed to remember the cameras in the booth behind them. His touch fell away, but his pinkie brushed hers. Out of the corner of her eye, she saw Cian nod slightly.

Niko wasn't included in their connection.

"I implore you all to embrace this bold new chapter with open minds, open hearts, and a renewed sense of competition," Frisk finished off, before handing the microphone back to Ed, who stepped up with a flourish and a grin.

"And to facilitate that," he teased, waiting until the gathered students were shuffling restlessly before he continued, "we've decided to host our first game of the new season: The Mate Match! I know how much we *love* our extra special mate bonds, so this game is to match up our new human contestants with a pretend mate of their own! Isn't that just adorable?"

"So adorable." Jack rolled his eyes at Ed. "You really are easy to please, aren't you, Ed?"

"*Pish.*" Ed waved him off. "You'll see. The *rest of us* think it's adorable, don't we, Ironside? Our Gifted will accompany their fake mates everywhere and even sleep in their apartment for the rest of the week, just like real mates!"

The terrified wave of whispering shifted immediately, the entire hall seeming to realise, as one, that they were being given a gold-plated opportunity for exposure. This was their ticket to going viral and making a name for themselves.

"We're going to bring in the new contestants one at a time, and if you fancy them, raise your hand," Ed instructed. "We'll be letting our new students choose their mate for the week, so just do whatever you can to outshine our beloved Alphas, eh?" Ed winked in the direction of their group.

The dining hall doors—which an official must have closed at some point—were opened again, drawing everyone's attention.

"First up," Jack projected boisterously, "we have Naina Kahn." A young woman stepped into the hall, her long brown hair braided over her shoulder, set with pearls and small crystal butterflies. She wore a short silver dress and silver heels, the fabric of her dress scattered with crystal detail, contrasting beautifully with her brown skin and twinkling, dark eyes.

"Naina Kahn, who some of you may recognise, has captivated the world with her talent for creating sculptures made of chocolate and other edible materials."

"I've seen these sculptures," Ed interrupted. "And they are nothing short of extraordinary."

"Indeed," Jack agreed. "Naina Kahn is able to produce art that tantalises the senses and tests the boundaries of the imagination—and each piece sells for several thousand a pop, so that doesn't hurt. Her talent has attracted millions of followers, earning her a place as one of the most influential artists of her time. If you're interested in Kahn, please raise your hand."

Hands shot up all around the room, and Kahn smiled shyly at the floor, before spinning to the opposite side of the room. The food bar hid her from Isobel's eyes, but Ed announced Kahn's choice a second before the couple reappeared.

"Adam Bellamy!" he called out. "Of course, Kahn has picked the only male Icon-offspring in the room, proving her discerning taste is as sharp as ever!" He moved the microphone away from his face as he turned to arrange Kahn and Bellamy to stand behind him.

Bellamy was smiling for the cameras, offering his arm for Kahn to hold onto ... but Isobel was now well-acquainted with Bellamy's fake smile, and she was sure she was seeing it now.

Bellamy isn't happy, she told the others.

He has no choice but to dive into this, Elijah returned. *His father won't accept anything less.*

It's hard to fake a smile when you've just been told that

your chances are slimmer than you realised, Oscar added. *He's just been shoved even further down the ladder and they're making it look like they're offering a hand to help him climb higher.*

It's disgusting, Moses snarled in her head. *All of this is disgusting.*

It's Ironside hitting back, Kilian chimed in, joining the chorus of voices inside her head. *They must have guessed that we're up to something and this is them laughing in our faces, reminding us that* they *pick the Icon. They have the power.*

This is them underestimating us, Moses countered. *As usual. So they found a bunch of famous twenty-year-olds. Who gives a fuck. They aren't Gifted. If people wanted to see humans getting famous instead of Gifted, Ironside wouldn't be anywhere near as popular as it is.*

You're forgetting one thing, Gabriel suggested. *Humans may like to watch us play their game, but you give a human a choice between a Gifted and one of their own? They will always choose their own. Always.*

We'll make them choose differently, Theodore promised darkly. *The game isn't over yet.*

"Our next student is the stunning face behind the KoKo Kostas skincare brand that took the world by storm this year. Everyone, please welcome Jordan Kostas!"

A tall, willowy woman strode through the doors, dressed in high boots, a high-waisted tartan skirt, and a white-collared shirt, complete with a matching tartan tie and headband to hold back the non-existent wisps of her sleek blonde hair.

"Kostas grew her following by sharing her transitioning journey with the world on social media, generating a loyal and supportive fanbase of millions. She now has modelling deals with several luxury brands, and she just announced her global ambassadorship with not one, not two, but *three* luxury international brands!"

Isobel ran her hands through her hair, agitation crawling across her skin. *How the fuck were they going to pull this off?*

Kostas was strutting along the edge of the crowd, considering her many options as hands shot up into the air.

Deep breaths, Theodore murmured, moving close enough that their hands were obscured by their bodies and clothing ... and then he hooked his pinky into hers. *We have two years to figure this shit out. We can do it.*

She had the distinct sense that he was talking only to her. It was something in the projection of his voice. It was closer, clearer, without the echoing quality it had possessed before. More like an intimate whisper. It was as though she had been standing in the middle of a room with many doors and they had all been open, everyone able to speak, but now Theodore had stepped through his door to be in the room with her, and all the others were closed.

You sure do figure things out quickly, she thought to him. *So maybe you're right.*

I haven't closed off the bond, he said, as Kostas chose one of the fifth-year Betas, and the two of them moved to take up positions beside Bellamy and Kahn. *All this bond stuff is much more intuitive when you aren't trying to cut yourself off from it.*

Tell me how you really feel, she scoffed internally as Ed began to announce the next two students. Twins, both international chess masters, and—if Ed and Jack's sly commentary was anything to go off—they had become famous by simply being hot, playing chess outside in freezing temperatures without shirts on, and chopping firewood in front of the camera.

I don't blame you, Illy. Theodore squeezed her pinky. *I can feel how the bond is set up. We're all connected, but we're connected through you. I can only feel that there are other connections. I can't feel them the way I feel you. You ... must be feeling everyone. It must be overwhelming.*

Alexi and Anatoly Kozlov. She focused on the names of the twins as they stalked through the crowd so that she wouldn't tear up over Theodore's soft compassion.

"What's better than a set of Alpha twins?" Jack's taunt boomed around the hall, causing Theodore to stiffen beside her and Moses to scowl. "The Kozlov twins!" Ed almost screamed, whipping the hall into a frenzy. "Uh-oh, speaking of the Alpha twins ... isn't that Theodore Kane's girlfriend with her hand up?" Ed asked.

"Oh, no, never mind, she was just fixing her hair. We see you, Wallis! You cheeky thing!"

Seriously? Moses grumbled, his voice taking on the echoing quality that meant he was talking to the group. *Twins? Isn't it a little obvious at this point?*

I have a feeling it's only going to get worse, Elijah warned.

"Are you ready for this next one?" Ed asked, the question full of suspense. The students played along, shouting, "Yes," even though Isobel could spot many uneasy faces littered around the room.

"I don't think you are!" Jack countered, shaking his head, and holding up a hand. "Nope, no way are you ready for *social media royalty*. Our next new student is from *The Santoro Show*, and you all know him as the loveable goofball who has been documenting his life ever since high school! You've seen his pranks, you've bought his merch, you've turned up to hear him sing in concert even though he doesn't know how to sing! You chose his house and then dared him to donate it to someone in a Walmart parking lot! Everyone give it up for Luca Santoro himself!"

A tall boy walked into the hall, a distinct swagger in his step as he brushed heavy, burnt chestnut curls from his angular face and winked at the energetic crowd.

Isobel bit back a groan.

Anyone with a phone knows who Luca Santoro is, she said to the group. *Who the fuck is next? The pope?*

Anyone with a phone knows who you *are*, Kilian countered.

"I suppose Isobel Carter isn't looking for any more surrogates," Santoro joked, pulling Ed's microphone to his mouth.

Jack and Ed both laughed, clapping Santoro on the back, and turning him to face Isobel and the Alphas. "She looks pretty cosy," Jack muttered, his tone loudly conspiratorial. "Tucked away in a clam of Alphas like a little pearl waiting to be pried free. Ever tried your hand at pearl harvesting, Santoro?"

Her view of Santoro was suddenly cut off. Cian and Moses had both stepped in front of her, and Oscar had stepped in front of them. Instead of Santoro's face, she was faced with the disarray of golden wisps escaping Cian's haphazard bun.

"Maybe another time," Santoro joked.

"Yes, I think that would be wise," Ed consoled, seeming to draw Santoro away.

Guys, she spoke to them dryly. *Now I can't see.*

The three hulking Alphas in front of her melted away like they were never there in the first place, and she rolled her eyes.

"God forbid I ever get a boyfriend." She spoke out loud this time, knowing that their little scene would get screen time, and remembering the roles they were supposed to be playing for the camera.

They were her overbearing, big, adopted Alpha brothers.

Except for Cian ... because there was no way anyone would believe that Cian could be looked at platonically by anyone who wasn't actually related to him. She was willing to *try*, but she doubted anyone would believe it, even if they were the best actors in the world.

"God forbid you try," Oscar returned coldly. "You're not allowed to date."

That was exactly what an overbearing, adopted big brother would say *if* that overbearing adopted big brother was Oscar. So why did it sound so ... *possessive?* Isobel shook her head, returning her focus to Santoro, who was plucking a fifth-year girl from the crowd. The twins also seemed to have chosen fifth-years, though one of them—Alexi, she thought his name was—had chosen a fifth-year boy whereas Anatoly had chosen a girl.

Do you think they were told to choose fifth-years? Kilian asked. *To put the focus back on the graduating class?*

Most likely, Gabriel answered.

"And last but *certainly* not least," Ed called out, "we have the beloved podcast host who just landed a sixty-million-dollar solo deal, and who was just voted *Forbes* most influential young person of the year! She's beautiful, she's charming, she's hilarious, she's humble—and yet she's rubbed shoulders with some of the most important people in the world! Everyone absolutely adores her, and we are so excited to have her own the show! Put your hands together for the one and only Mei Ito!"

The girl who walked into the hall moved with so much grace it almost looked like she was floating. Her hair fell in ebony waves down to her narrow waist. Her eyes smiled even though her lips didn't, though a beautiful smile broke free when she reached Ed and Jack, who appeared to be completely star struck.

"Please, call me Mei," she offered, holding out her hand. "I'm so pleased to meet you."

Jack pretended to faint. Ed pounced on her hand. "You are even more beautiful in person. I must say, I'm such a big fan, Mei. Such a big fan." He was pumping her arm while she bowed her head gracefully.

"Thank you so much."

Now that she was closer, Isobel almost felt hypnotised by her. She was ... *incandescent*. Pale as a soft pink petal, her hair lustrous, her eyes sparkling. Even her jewellery seemed to shimmer, catching the light of the chandeliers above. Isobel felt a strange tug in the other girl's direction, her attention snagging on Mei's necklace again and again. Was it ... *glowing?*

Niko shifted, stepping toward the Ironside hosts and Mei, and the pieces fell into place with horrific, gut-lurching clarity ... but it was too late.

Niko had reached the hosts. He was stepping up to Mei, tilting his head down at her.

"There's no need to vote." He was calm, his forehead eased of tension. He held out his hand and Mei, appearing struck dumb by him, placed her fingers slowly in his grip while staring up at him, doe-eyed.

"Choose me," he said to her.

Isobel's heart shattered, and the ground no longer felt so solid.

There was darkness beneath her feet, a fall threatening, a void shuddering below her, gaping wide enough to swallow her.

The necklace, she pushed the words out to the group weakly. *She's ... she's wearing my hair.*

Ignore the bitch, Oscar snarled back. *Do we need to leave?*

We can't. Elijah's voice was tight. *We can't show a divide in the group. It's essential we're seen as a unit.*

It's essential I make Niko bleed for this, Oscar argued, tone cutting.

Don't blame Niko, Gabriel growled. *This isn't him and you know it. He would never hurt Isobel.*

He's hurting her right now! Theodore snapped.

Because of what Eve fucking Indie did to the bond! Gabriel insisted. *You* know *Niko. You all know him. He has a bigger heart than all of us.*

Good, Oscar snarled, *bigger heart means more blood.*

Isobel leaned into Kilian, who was taking more and more of her weight, his arm slipping around her, his grip digging into her waist.

"Isobel is getting sick again," he said out loud. "I'm going to help her get to the group intensive with Professor Mikel. I think she needs to sit down and rest. I'll call the bond specialist to meet us there."

"Good idea," Cian agreed. "I'll come too. I have the specialist's number."

We can't all leave. Theodore sounded agonised—both angry and grief-stricken, like he could feel the void rising up beneath her. Maybe it was threatening them all, shadowing all their feet and shaking the ground they stood on.

We'll take care of her, Kilian soothed. *She's safe with us. See you guys in a bit.*

They didn't walk far—Kilian steered her toward the administration buildings, where they found an empty golf cart. He deposited her in the passenger seat while Cian climbed into the back, and they drove to the new fitness complex in silence.

"The bond specialist said she'll come to the group intensive to see you," Cian said, pocketing his phone as Kilian parked the cart.

They helped her out and into the huge network of buildings, squirrelling her into a hallway lined with doors. She didn't bother searching for cameras—it was clear there weren't any when Cian bent down and swept her into his arms, holding her against his chest with his arm beneath her ass. She looped her arms around his neck, surveying the door they stopped at. There was a screen above it, with a red light beside it. The screen read *Private Session - Professor Easton. 7:00 - 8:00. Not recording.*

Kilian pushed open the door, glancing at his watch before nodding back at Cian, who stepped in after him.

"You're early—" Mikel spoke from within the room but cut himself off when he caught sight of Isobel. "What the fuck happened now?"

"Well ...," Kilian drawled, "it's safe to say our contacts in the control room have turned on us, because we were just completely blindsided, and I think they know we're up to something."

"They brought in six humans to compete in the game," Cian supplied. "And the last one was wearing Isobel's hair like a necklace."

Mikel's face turned white, his eyes scanning Isobel. "What else?"

"They offered the humans a fake mate for a week." Kilian glanced back at Isobel. "Niko chose the girl wearing Isobel's hair. He's supposed to follow her around and sleep in her apartment."

"What?" Mikel uttered in disbelief. "What the fuck? No. Absolutely not. That won't be happening."

"Did you actually call Teak?" Isobel croaked.

"Here," Mikel said before Cian answered. He dragged a weights bench against the wall, and Cian set her onto it, propping her up carefully.

She was glad for the assistance because her dizziness had become nauseating.

"I did," Cian answered her question as Mikel pushed a bottle of water into her hands. "Teak said she'll be right over."

"I want to tell her," Isobel said. "Like we told Maya."

"She's an official." Mikel frowned at her. "The Guardian is not an official. We had a camera in the Guardian's house and watched her withstand interrogation." His hand passed over her forehead, measuring her temperature before he snatched up her wrist, his finger pressing against her pulse.

"I need help," she whispered. "None of us know how to deal with this. *We* need help."

Mikel considered her, his attention heavy. He knelt in front of her, his hands on her knees. "Can you ask for her help without telling her everything? I can't trust Niko right now to make sure she's being honest with us."

Isobel worried her lip with her teeth before her shoulders slumped forward. "Okay."

"Who has the Guardian's number?" Mikel asked without taking his eyes off Isobel.

"Elijah," Cian answered, "but yesterday Theo said something about them not having their phones."

"Text Elijah," Mikel ordered. "Tell him to fetch the Guardian and bring her here. Isobel is right. We need help. It makes just as much sense for Isobel to call on the

Guardian for advice as it does for her to call on the bond specialist, so we shouldn't get any questions about it."

"Done," Cian responded.

"Thank you," Isobel managed, catching Mikel's eye.

"Mhm," he rumbled the sound of acknowledgement. "Don't thank me yet, Carter. You still have a punishment on the way."

13

THE GIRL WHO KNOWS IMPORTANT PEOPLE

TEAK ARRIVED BEFORE ANYONE ELSE. SHE WORE BLACK, HIGH-waisted pants that flared gently around her simple heels and a navy silk shirt with long sleeves. Her straight, mahogany hair had grown a few inches over the summer break—something Isobel hadn't noticed in the hospital ... though she hadn't noticed much in the hospital.

Teak's soft brown eyes were lined in subtle, natural colours, her taupe-and-rose dusted skin just flawless enough to hint at the barest coverage of makeup. Her nose ring was small and gold, matching the several gold piercings stepping up her ears. She was pristine and professional, the only thing separating her from the other officials being the black Sigma ring circling her iris.

"Good morning, Professor Easton," she said as soon as she walked into the room. She nodded to Kilian and Cian. "Gray, Ashford."

The Alphas all backed away from Isobel, giving Teak room to kneel in front of her—though not an abundance of it. The bond specialist took her hands, squeezing her fingers.

"Hey, Isobel." Teak ducked to catch Isobel's lowered eyes. "What's going on? You don't look too good."

"I don't know," Isobel lied, unable to meet Teak's gaze. She focussed on the woman's fingers, staring at her navy blue nails and the gold rings on her fingers. "Something happened last night. I think it was another soul infraction."

"You think it was?" Teak's brows scrunched together, alarm pinching her pointed features. "What did it feel like?"

"Like this huge rift opening up beneath me. Like I was falling, and like I would be falling in this horrible, terrifying, dark place forever. Like my ... like my soul had been completely shredded."

The lines of confusion along Teak's forehead straightened, her soft brown eyes widening in horror. She reared back an inch, eyeing Isobel like she didn't understand how Isobel could be sitting there in one piece. "What happened to cause that?"

"I ... don't know," Isobel repeated. She couldn't possibly say that Eve had stolen her light. Teak would never believe she had healed from that overnight without finding and forming her bonds—not if her expression now was anything to go by.

Teak made a frustrated sound, glancing over her shoulder at the hovering Alphas. “May we have a few minutes of privacy?”

“No need,” Isobel quickly rushed out, before one of them could snap out an aggravated and over-protective response. “I’m fine with them here.”

Teak frowned. “Isobel, I need to know what actually happened. What you’re describing is a soul infraction that should have you dead or close to death, and you don’t look fantastic, but you don’t look dead, either.”

“I don’t know,” Isobel persisted, a little firmer this time.

Teak’s disappointment was written all over her face, but there was a spark of understanding there too. “All right,” she muttered, releasing Isobel’s hands, and sitting on the bench beside her. She dug a tablet out of her handbag and tapped into a note-taking app, hovering an electronic pen above her screen. “Were you alone?”

“Yes,” Isobel lied.

Teak stared at her and then noted something down. “Where were you?”

“Toward the edge of the academy, right by the river.”

“Were you incapacitated?”

Isobel hesitated, staring at her hands. “Not for long. I fainted briefly, and then I called Professor West for help.”

“How long were you there for?” Teak barrelled on like she knew Isobel was lying and wasn’t even listening to what she was saying, though she still noted something down with each of Isobel's answers.

"Maybe a few hours? I'm not sure."

"That falling feeling you're describing, how long was that happening for?"

"Well ... it changed." Isobel winced, closing her eyes as she tried to recall the night before without passing out or throwing up again. "It ... at first it was just this massive *depth* inside me, with no light. And then a little later, I was falling through it. And then today I felt like I was about to trip and start falling again."

"Multiple soul infractions?" Teak snapped, gripping her pen tightly, her soft eyes hardening for a moment.

Isobel had never seen her look so fierce.

After a moment of waiting for Isobel to elaborate, Teak scribbled on her screen and took a deep breath. "Off the record, Isobel. Who did you spend the night with yesterday?"

Isobel's eyes flicked to Cian. "Um." *She couldn't lie. There was footage.*

"Ashford, then." Teak's tone brooked no argument, but she didn't write the name down.

"Are you sending that to the off—the other officials?" Isobel asked, pointing to Teak's tablet.

"A version of it." Teak set her jaw. "I'm required to report on all bond incidents. They'll need to read a report that makes sense to them."

Isobel didn't know what to make of that.

"Has Ashford left your side since the incident?" Teak asked, setting her pen down.

"Briefly, a few times," Isobel said.

"How would you describe your relationship with Ashford?"

"What do you mean?" Isobel asked. "In what way?"

Teak glanced at the other Alphas, who stood by in complete silence, hovering and not even bothering to pretend that they were affording Isobel and Teak a moment of privacy. After the night before, there was no way they were leaving her alone with anyone, and if Teak suggested it again, one of them was going to lose their cool.

Thankfully, Teak only sighed and turned back to Isobel, responding flatly, "Did you have sex with one of your surrogates last night?"

Isobel laughed. She couldn't help it. Teak was *so* far off the mark. "No," she said. "We were playing a game. Sort of like capture the flag. And then the soul infraction happened."

"Right." Teak pinched the bridge of her nose. "And today? What happened when you felt it again?"

Isobel pressed her lips together. "Nothing significant. We were at the dining hall and the officials announced the six new students. Toward the end, it just randomly happened again."

"This time, I assume you weren't alone." Teak didn't bother reaching for her pen again. "Who was in your immediate vicinity?"

"All of the Alphas."

"And what *exactly* was happening around you? Was anyone touching you?"

"Um ... I think the new girl ... Mei? Was picking her fake mate. I think Theo was touching me sort of, and Kilian was holding my hand."

"And you felt nothing?" Teak suddenly spun and fixed Kilian with a sharp look.

"Why would I feel anything?" Kilian asked plainly.

Teak shook her head, switching her focus to Mikel. "Do you know what's going on here, Professor Easton?"

"Other than what Carter just told you?" Mikel returned, just as calm and unaffected as Kilian. "No."

A flash of temper rolled across Teak's face, and she stood, facing off against Mikel. "I take my job very seriously. Carter was assigned to *me*. The health of her bond is entirely my responsibility. I do *not* like the idea that my student is in danger and another Ironside employee may be interfering with her proper care. She's been through a lot, and I worked hard to get her away from her father and back to Ironside where I could protect her properly, and I'm not going to let anyone—not even an *Alpha*, or three," she glared at the others, "or *ten*, for fuck's sake, get in the way."

Mikel stared the smaller woman down, a muscle

ticking in his jaw. "Good," he said. He gestured to Isobel. "She's all yours. Protect away."

Teak let out a small growl that, despite everything, made Isobel want to smile. The bond specialist fell back down to the bench beside Isobel, snatching up her tablet again.

"I'm sending you an official care plan. It's basically the same as the care plan I sent you last year," she said, tapping away furiously at her tablet before setting it aside. "Now, let me explain a few hypothetical scenarios. If the bond thinks you're emotionally or physically cheating on your mate with one of your surrogates, it will cause a soul infraction. The deeper the betrayal, the deeper the infraction. Of course, this doesn't apply to you," Teak's tone became flat, "since you haven't even met your mate. You need to be at least familiar with your mate for this to cause a serious infraction."

Niko.

Niko was going to keep hurting her.

"Another way a soul infraction can be caused is by defiling the magic of the bond itself, by stealing or damaging soul artefacts—though I will say that this school of thought is mostly theoretical. This method would be just as effective, if not more effective, than a direct betrayal of the bond, as it can poison completed bonds or even completely sever half-formed bonds—though in the field of bond magic, none of these things have been proven."

"And what about the artefact?" Isobel asked, playing with her fingers. "Can it be used for something else after it's stolen?"

"Used for ..." Teak looked horrified. "Used for what?"

Isobel lifted a shoulder. "These are your scenarios."

Teak swallowed, her eyes darting between Isobel's, trying to read something in Isobel's expression. "I ... really don't know, I'm sorry. Even if it could be used for something, the Tether wouldn't last long enough for the artefact to be useful for long."

"The Tether wouldn't last?" Isobel prompted, careful to keep her words free from inflection.

"If the bond is damaged, poisoned, or removed in that way, it's only a matter of time." Teak's gaze shimmered with tears, which spilled over when she tried to blink them away. She pretended they weren't there, absently flicking them from her skin with the pad of her thumb as she continued speaking in an even tone. "The Tether would need to recover the artefact as soon as possible and hope that it is willing to reintegrate with them in some way. Isobel ... please ..." She snatched up Isobel's hands again, her eyes imploring, her grip shaking slightly, her fingers wet. "I can help. I'm an official. I can *do* something."

"I know." Isobel gently extracted herself from Teak's grip. "I know you're an official."

Teak's expression shuttered immediately. "Right. Okay." She sucked in a shuddering breath, smoothing out her shirt and packing away her tablet. She stood, and then just before she walked away, she suddenly bent and wrapped her arms around Isobel's shoulders, squeezing her tightly. "I'm sorry," she whispered low. "Whatever happened ... I'm so sorry. I hope one day we can sit down and talk about it."

Isobel hugged her back hesitantly. "That would be nice," she finally said, her voice breaking as Teak lifted away.

The bond specialist sniffed as she nodded to the Alphas. "Professor Easton, Ashford, Gray."

They nodded back at her, keeping silent until Teak left the room. Shortly after, Moses, Oscar, and Theodore arrived. They all appeared tense, and they fell around Isobel, some of them sitting, some standing. Nobody seemed to know what to say.

"Gabriel and Niko?" Mikel asked, surveying the gathered bodies.

"Niko insisted on walking his new friend to class," Theodore ground out angrily. "Gabriel went with him."

Kilian swore beneath his breath, and Isobel pretended like her heart wasn't being wrapped in layer after layer of barbed wire.

"What did the bond specialist say?" Theodore drank in the look on Isobel's face with a wince.

"That we need to get the soul artefact back as soon as possible and hope it wants to reassimilate with Isobel," Mikel supplied gruffly.

"Right." Moses roughed a hand through his hair. "That should be easy. We just break into the human's ultra-secure apartment building in the *official* section of the academy—because that's where they're being housed, by the way—and rob the new queen of Ironside while she's sleeping."

"Or we get Niko to do it," Theodore countered angrily. "Since he's supposed to be living there anyway."

There was a knock at the door and Elijah stepped inside, leading Maya. She was dressed in faded jeans and a pressed linen shirt with a small pin in the collar, her short hair combed impeccably into place. She must have been spending some time in her garden outside the chapel because there was a reddish flush to her browned skin.

"Reed filled me in," she said, glancing back at Elijah before approaching the group. "How is everyone feeling?"

It was an *immense* relief to have someone around who actually knew what was happening and who wasn't involved in Isobel's shitshow of a bond.

"Ready to rip Niko's fucking head off," Oscar answered, staring down the Guardian. "You gonna say that's a bad idea?"

"A very bad one," Maya shot back confidently. "But you already know that. If any member of this bond is harmed, it will harm Carter. I assume nobody wants that."

"You assume correctly," Elijah answered when everyone else stayed silent, eyeing Maya with varying degrees of hostility.

And Isobel thought *she* had trust issues.

"What's happening to Niko?" Isobel asked.

Maya shook her head sadly. "Impossible to tell. Have you tried asking him?"

"He wasn't feeling very talkative last night," Mikel said. "He hasn't forgotten about the bond, but it's like he suddenly has more rage than he knows what to do with. It's swallowing him whole."

"And the same thing hasn't happened to you?" Maya directed the question at Isobel. "Or anyone else?"

"No more than usual," Moses muttered, as the other Alphas shook their heads.

Isobel bit down on the inside of her cheek as she once again tried to comb through the past twelve hours. "I did, a little," she finally admitted.

"I'm leaning toward Reed's theory," Maya declared, appearing troubled.

Elijah spoke up before anyone could ask him what Maya was talking about. "I was filling in the Guardian on the way here. I think previously, Isobel was taking on most of the bond side effects, but when the bond started to turn, Niko must have felt it. He must have tried to take it all to spare Isobel."

"Take *what*?" Isobel asked.

"The damage, so to speak," Maya theorised. "When

a soul artefact manifests on the outside, it's a gift from the gods. When it manifests on the inside, it's an expression of the bond itself—I wouldn't even call it a soul artefact. It *is* your bond. There's a significant difference. One can pass hands and the other absolutely cannot. You weren't robbed of a soul artefact. You were robbed of part of your bond, possibly even a part of your soul. That will cause significant emotional and physical damage. Niko couldn't have taken on your physical damage, but it's possible he took on your mental damage."

Isobel's stomach lurched, and she notched her elbows onto her knees, her head falling into her hands. "What kind of mental damage?" she groaned.

She felt so *sick*.

The door opened before Maya could answer, Gabriel entering with a thunderous expression. His lip was split, blood dribbling to his chin. Niko stalked in behind him, his left eye swollen, already darkening with a shadow of a bruise.

Gabriel bared his bloody teeth in a forced smile. "Just a little disagreement about Niko's attendance," he explained. "I insisted it was mandatory."

"Quit harping on about it," Niko snapped. "I'm here, aren't I?" He paused, his eyes narrowing on the Guardian. "The fuck is this?"

"Well," Maya muttered, "this is a delightful change."

Niko rolled his eyes, digging a pair of headphones

from his pocket. "So what's first?" He began walking toward the treadmills.

"Put the headphones away," Mikel ordered. "We're having a meeting."

"If we're not actually going to *do* the session, then I have other places to be," Niko drawled, his beautiful eyes resting on Isobel. Almost immediately, they darkened with something like hatred, but he seemed unable to look away. "What?" he finally demanded. "What the fuck are you waiting for, Carter?"

She locked down her hurt and stood, approaching him cautiously. He didn't move, but his eyes narrowed, his defined jaw clenching. She stopped before him, her eyes travelling down his chest, and then further, to where she remembered marking his skin the night before.

"Is it still there?" she asked, her eyes flashing back up to his face.

She had showered and dressed in such a trance that morning, she hadn't had a chance to look at her own marks, and since she wore her hair long and over her shoulders, nobody else had commented on them. She had almost forgotten they were there.

"Where would it have gone?" Niko sneered, his eyes dropping to her neck. He tried to look away and seemed to get stuck at her lips. Something flashed in his eyes, and he stepped back, ripping his attention away. "Why can't you just leave me alone? The bond is dead. There's nothing between us. The secret is safe with me, but I don't want to be in an eleven-way relationship, so just leave me the fuck out of that part." He fell back another step. "It happened, and now it's over."

"It's not over," she said softly, trying to see even a shadow of the Niko she was used to. "Mei is wearing our bond around her neck."

Niko scoffed, rolling his eyes. "Jealous isn't a good look on you, Carter."

"Watch it," Theodore warned lowly.

"I'm warning you," Niko snarled at Isobel, ignoring Theodore. "I know you're hurt. I know you're pissed. But don't come after *Mei*"—he jabbed a finger at the door—"just because I don't want to be with you."

Isobel followed his pointed finger, something hot and furious rising up inside her chest. "You brought her here?" she asked, portraying a calm she didn't feel.

"Of course." Niko rolled his eyes. "I'm her mate for the week. She goes wherever I go."

Isobel's hands curled into fists, but she quickly raised them and displayed her palms, stepping away from Niko so that she wouldn't do something regrettable, like send her fist *flying into his fucking face*.

It was clear that coming for Mei was only going to push Niko further away.

They needed a different angle.

And she needed to try her best not to hate this version of Niko. He was only *like* this because he had tried to spare her the mental damage of their bond being torn out.

She glanced at Mikel, projecting her words into his head.

Can we get on with the session?

He arched a brow at her, catching her eye. He seemed surprised that she had spoken to him through the bond, but after a moment, he nodded, his voice booming suddenly through the room. "Niko, Elijah, Gabriel, Oscar—on the treadmills. Everyone else, pair up in front of the mirrors for a boxing drill." He lowered his voice. "Guardian?" He caught Maya's eye. "You're welcome to stay and observe the session."

Niko was already walking away, sticking in his headphones, so he missed the tilt of Mikel's head in his direction. Maya nodded. Her mouth set into a grim line as she sat beside Isobel on the bench.

"What's going to help you get through today?" Mikel asked Isobel as the others scattered in a cloud of fiery temper and less-than-subtle, glowering looks in Niko's direction.

"Maybe some yoga?" she asked. "I checked my schedule on the way over here. I have three dance classes and I don't think they're going to go easy just because it's the first day."

"Likely not," Mikel agreed, before flicking out a mat and pointing her onto it. He never strayed far from her, always positioning himself between her and Niko, who ignored her for the first half of the session.

When Niko realised she wasn't going to do anything more than slow stretching, he began to frown at her, annoyance warring with suspicion in his eyes. When the session was over, he was so busy scowling at the back of her neck that he seemed to forget Mei waiting for him in the hallway.

"Niko!" she called out, a laugh in her voice.

He froze, flashing Isobel a rage-filled look before wiping his expression clean and turning to the other girl. "Mei." He flashed a forced smile—like a puppet trying to remember how to be happy. "Sorry. Not used to someone waiting for me."

Everyone except Mikel and Maya—who had remained in the room to talk—froze, looking between Niko and Mei.

"Everyone, this is Mei," Niko said, walking back to the girl to stand beside her, a little too close for Isobel's comfort. "My mate for the week."

Holy shit, Moses' voice spoke to the group in Isobel's mind. *I never thought I would say this, but I hope Niko dies a long and painful death, and I hope I'm there to witness it.*

Stop, Isobel chided. *He's like this because he saved me from being like this.*

That excuse is growing thinner with every passing second, Oscar drawled, before adding out loud, "That's an interesting necklace, Mei."

Mei blinked at Oscar in surprise, taken aback by his rough, threatening tone as he apparently complimented her. "Oh ... um, thank you? It was a gift from the director. You must recognise it!"

"Why would we recognise it?" Theodore asked, stepping in front of Oscar, his expression light and friendly, his stormy eyes clear, his mouth quirked up at the corner. He had turned his charm on, and Mei's cheeks were flushing with colour.

Was Theo ... could Theo be ...

Relax, Moses whispered through their connection. *He's just acting.*

"The director said it's a settlement blessing," Mei said, lifting the thin, braided rope around her neck. "You wear it until it unravels and you're blessed with luck. If you remove it before it unravels, you'll be cursed with bad luck."

Niko was frowning down at her. "That's complete bullshit," he said.

Mei fluttered her lashes in shock, her dark eyes peering up at him. "I swear that's what she said."

"I didn't mean you." He waved his hand, sure she had been telling the truth. "I mean *what* the director said. That's not a settlement charm." He frowned harder, glancing back to Isobel.

She raised her brows at him. *I told you, asshole.*

"May I see it?" Niko asked, holding out his hand.

"Um." Mei looked unsure, her hand hovering

protectively around her neck. "Well ... I'd rather not be cursed." She laughed nervously.

"With *other* settlement charms, it's always the person who removes a settlement charm who gets the bad luck," Niko lifted his hand higher, moving it toward her neck. "Allow me?"

Mei frowned, surveying the group as she stepped back. "This is beginning to feel like an ambush."

"You don't watch the show?" Moses asked blandly. "We love our little initiation tasks. If you want to hang with the Alphas, you need to play along with our rules."

"I spend at least sixty hours a week doing my best to disable the patriarchy of the *real* world with some of the most influential people alive." Mei lifted her chin stubbornly. "I'm not going to play along with your hierarchical bullshit just because you're an Alpha. We all know it's illegal for you to use Alpha voice on a human."

She pushed past them, pausing halfway down the corridor and glancing over her shoulder. "Are you coming, Niko?"

Niko was frozen, his expression drawn. He lifted his eyes, fixing Mei with an unwavering look. "Hand the necklace over or you'll lose your fake mate before first period, and it won't be a good look."

Mei rolled her eyes, gripping the braided rope.

Isobel jumped forward, her heart in her throat. "Don't rip it!" she yelled, shocking the other girl.

Mei arched a brow, switching her grip and untying

the necklace before tossing it on the ground. "Happy, freaks?"

"That's not very politically correct," Moses tittered. "You use that mouth on your fancy podcast with all your fancy guests?"

Mei ignored him, looking insistently at Niko. He began to walk toward her, but paused by Isobel, who had fallen to the floor, snatching the braided rope into her hands.

There were tears in her eyes and the taste of hope mingling with despair on her tongue. Her hair felt warm to the touch ... but something was off.

It wasn't everything. She was holding a piece, a fraction.

Where was the rest?

Niko tilted his head, examining the tears in her eyes and the way she clutched the thin rope. His attention slitted, travelling between the soft curl of her hair tumbling over her shoulder to the necklace in her hand. The colour was the same. The length was comparable.

Somewhere in that poisoned mind of his, she hoped that he was remembering the way her hair had glowed, but he only shook his head as if saying to himself *not my problem*. He stepped away from her, toward Mei.

"Let's go," Mei snapped, storming off now, her patience evaporating.

Kilian and Theodore helped Isobel up, the other

Alphas gathering to watch as she shakily attempted to tie the necklace around her wrist.

Kilian took the ends to help her secure it. “This isn’t everything, is it?”

“No,” Isobel said. “Why would Eve steal my bond and take it to the director of Ironside? And why would the director split it up and gift a piece of it to a human?”

Kilian was still fiddling with the necklace, a frown on his face. He picked at the string tying off one side of the braid, tugging it until it unravelled, something rolled and white peeking out from the twist of hair. He pulled, and the rolled white thing grew longer and longer, the hair unravelling from around it. Isobel caught the hair, frowning at the mess Kilian was making. As soon as the strands pooled into her palm, they began to glow. The hair singed and then burned, but when Isobel made to shake her hand, Cian grabbed her wrist, stopping her. The door opened behind them, Mikel likely sensing her sudden spike of alarm.

“What is it?” he asked.

Maya pushed forward, quickly assessing the situation. “Put it over her veins,” she ordered. “Hurry!”

Isobel held out her arms and Cian and Theodore both began to pick up the burning strands and lay them over her forearms as Kilian fully extracted the white thing, yanking it free of the smoking strands. Cian and Theodore were grimacing from the searing sensation of the hair touching their skin. Isobel was sucking in measured breaths, trying to brace against the pain, but a whimper still slipped free. Oscar moved behind her, his hands on her shoulders, holding her steady.

The scattered strands were now all laid out against her forearms, covering the scars Eve had caused the year before. They melted into Isobel's skin, the light escaping into her veins. It was painful but strangely exhilarating, and after absorbing into her skin, the burn lines began to heal ... but they healed more than the burns they had created. Sections of the scars Eve had created smoothed out, replaced by pale, incandescent skin.

Isobel closed her eyes, daring herself to stare into the void. There were tiny flickers of light dancing around her periphery. The relief she felt was enough to break her apart, but she held firm and kept her composure, opening her eyes and speaking calmly.

"I think it helped."

"Gods," Maya breathed, wide brown eyes taking Isobel in. "I didn't think the bond would be so willing to reassimilate."

"That's a good thing, though?" Isobel questioned.

"It's very good," Maya assured. "It must be because the existing bonds are offering a safe environment for it to return to. I imagine it would be very difficult to return a bond to a broken mind and body."

Isobel shuddered. "Right."

"Guys ..." Kilian spoke up, his voice sounding off. He had rolled out the long white thing. A note, of some kind.

He held it lengthways up to the light to read it out loud. "Within these walls, there are true Gifted and those who simply have the blood. Congratulations on being accepted into the Icon track. You have the blood. You have the guts. You've got skin in the game. And now you know what happens when you disobey us. The first rule of the Stone Dahlia is absolute obedience at all times."

"*Jesus fucking Christ,*" Isobel rushed out, her head spinning. "All of this just to scare me into following their rules?"

"They must not feel like they have enough collateral on you, yet," Elijah mused. "Which ... is actually a good thing, considering all the collateral you have available. This supports Eve's claims that she hasn't spilled the secret yet."

Maya's eyes bounced between them, wide and disbelieving.

"This is *insane,*" Isobel growled.

"Yes," Gabriel agreed, "but it's also good news. They weren't trying to kill you, so they don't understand how the bond magic works as well as we do. And if they gave that necklace out so easily, they obviously expected you to find it. I wonder if they handed one out to each of the new students. It would make sense, especially with Santoro coming so close to you and making that joke about whether you were available. He was probably supposed to be wearing the necklace and you were probably supposed to notice, and then if you raised your hand for him, that would have worked nicely for their plan to separate us."

"Which means they weren't expecting Niko to do what he did," Cian groaned. "It's possible we've just flagged Isobel and Niko's connection."

"We'll create a storyline to explain it," Mikel said. "But right now, you all need to get to first period. The rest of this, we can deal with later."

14
GOOD GIRL OR NOT?

IMMEDIATELY AFTER WALKING INTO THE LARGE AUDITORIUM, Isobel knew her first period was going to be a nightmare.

The professor for Icon Matters stood before a projected screen, his qualifications lighting up the wall behind him.

Professor Mathieu Dubois was a man with more degrees in marketing and communication than Isobel had designer dresses, but that wasn't his greatest qualification.

He was a human. An *official*.

All six of the new human students were already seated in the front row, some of them with their fake mates beside them. Niko sat on the end of the row, left leg raised, foot notched against the low wall in front of their seats. He was slumped in his chair, his face turned slightly toward Mei as though half listening to what she was saying.

Are we doing the group thing or the fake girlfriend thing? Theodore asked through the bond, likely spotting Wallis, Ellis, and James in the right wing of auditorium seats.

Isobel needs to make contact with Silva so they can start a public relationship, Elijah answered. *He's sitting with Bellamy.*

Isobel sighed, and the hall fell to silence, most of the students noticing that the Alpha group had arrived. It was rare for all of them to be in the same class, and the students were likely curious to see who would rule the academy now that the humans were there.

Isobel broke away from the group as Theodore, Elijah, and Gabriel headed to the right, the rest of the group moving to the left wing of seats.

Bellamy stood up, waving to her, and she picked her way over to him.

"Hey, nutter." He grinned, eyeing her. "You look almost healthy."

"Thanks," she said dryly. "Can I sit here?"

Silva glanced between them, confused.

"Go ahead." Bellamy gestured the seat beside him, but Isobel wedged past, claiming Bellamy's seat so that she was beside Silva. "Um, okay." Bellamy sat on her other side. "You know Silva, right?"

Isobel did her best to smile shyly at the Beta. He held

out his hand, but she pretended not to notice it because she could feel more than one set of eyes boring into her, and she felt murderous vibes emanating down through her bond.

"Why aren't you sitting with Kahn?" Isobel asked Bellamy, spotting the shiny dark hair of his fake mate in the front row.

"She told me she was *so* glad she got to go first, because she wasn't sure what kind of diseases the settlement kids could be carrying," Bellamy drawled. "So when there weren't enough seats in the front row, I was happy to sacrifice my spot."

Isobel's eyes bugged in surprise. "She didn't!"

"She sure did." Bellamy wiggled his brows. "So I never thought I would ask this, but when are the Alphas going to step up and put them in their place?"

Isobel shrugged. "When have the Alphas ever stepped up to put someone in their place?"

"They did it with you, didn't they?" Silva asked, his jaw tight as he cast a nervous glance toward the side wing, where Oscar, Moses, Cian, and Kilian were sitting. Oscar's expression was downright sociopathic—likely the reason nobody else was daring to sit on that side of the auditorium. Moses's dark, stormy eyes were crawling around the room like he was searching for someone's throat to slit. Cian's face was serious, his brows lowered, his arms crossed, his legs sprawled out in front of him, but despite his casual posture, his muscles were bunched and tight, making it look like he was ready to spring up and attack at a moment's notice. Even Kilian was glowering, his angelic features cast tight and stern.

"You mean when they accepted me into their group and made me like their precious little dorm sister?" Isobel asked Silva, crossing her arms and subconsciously mirroring Kilian's posture.

Bellamy made a choking sound.

Silva stuttered, turning red. "Y-Yeah, n-no, not really, I guess. Didn't Sato make them put you through initiation tasks last year?"

Isobel remembered she was supposed to be flirting with Silva and quickly uncrossed her arms. She bit her lip, looking up at him through her lashes. "Were you worried about me?"

Stop that, Killian ordered, barging into her mind.

She straightened, releasing her lip.

I can't get a fake boyfriend with you shouting in my head, she returned.

Do it without flirting, Cian butted into their conversation.

"I ... yeah." Silva smiled at her. "I've always had a bit of a crush on you."

"What is even happening here?" Bellamy asked, leaning over Isobel. "Their *precious little dorm sister*?"

She elbowed him. "Butt out."

"You were so much cuter when you were afraid of me," Bellamy grumbled.

"You were never cute." She smiled at him sweetly.

He gasped, pressing a hand to his chest. "The poll conducted by *Vouge Online* last week would *thoroughly* disagree with you."

Isobel rolled her eyes. "You mean *Teen* Vogue?"

"Health makes you mean," Bellamy complained, leaning over her again to fix Silva in his sights. "You should know that, if you're going to ask her out. She's a horrible bully."

"I was actually." Silva seemed annoyed at Bellamy's interference. "If you're interested—"

"Give me your phone," Isobel suggested, holding out her hand, glad that the professor was finally calling everyone to attention. "I'll text you later."

After she handed Silva's phone back, she tucked her hands into her lap and pretended to tune into the lesson.

It was nice to spend some time with Bellamy, but the rest of the day turned out to be tense and whisper-filled as the students tiptoed around the Alphas, gossiping about how Niko and the other Alphas were fighting. The students had decided, at some point, that the other Alphas wanted to make a stand against the humans, to put them in their place, but Niko had gone against the group.

It was imbecilic, but almost everyone at the academy believed it by the end of the day. She was emotionally exhausted from trying to ignore all the whispering students when she stepped into the climbing gym for her private session with Kalen, surprised that he wanted to continue with the climbing when she needed singing lessons more than anything.

Still, she was grateful, so she didn't say anything.

He locked the door and checked her harness without a word, but some of the tension eased from his body as she came down from the wall at the end of the hour, an exhausted smile spreading over her face.

Her private session with Elijah, which comprised her final hour of classes for the day, turned out to be a singing lesson. Elijah was just as intuitive and thoughtful in the way he approached that lesson as he had been with her piano lessons.

When they were finished, they walked together to one of the practice rooms, meeting up with Gabriel, who was already warming up inside. They hadn't actually planned to dance together that afternoon, but they fell into it naturally, playing around with a few different songs and choreography ideas until they found something that captured their attention. Half an hour into their practice time, they switched to speaking in Isobel's head. An hour into the practice time, they were working on group choreography and the remaining anxiety from her day had finally melted away.

She was still tense, still upset about Niko, but dancing with Elijah and Gabriel just felt so effortless and familiar. She could tell they were also shedding some of their stress, so she agreed when Gabriel suggested they train for another hour. It was almost seven thirty when all of their watches vibrated with a message.

Kalen: Isobel is due at the boathouse in an hour.

"Shit." Isobel rushed over to the seat where she had left her bag, stuffing her phone and headphones into it before pulling her shoes back on.

They jogged all the way back to Dorm A, and Gabriel stepped into her room with her, turning on her light and checking every corner as though Silva might have snuck in and planted another voodoo package.

"Are you ready for tonight?" he asked, following her into the bathroom, and then through to the dressing room.

She stared at the racks of neatly hung clothing and handbags, the rows of heels, and the boxes stacked into the corner. "Who did all this?"

"Well, it wasn't me," Gabriel said, staring distastefully at the stacked boxes. "It isn't even sorted by colour."

She realised he was entirely serious, and her lips slipped into a smirk. "What am I supposed to wear?" she asked, biting back her smile at his clear disgust over the way her wardrobe had been organised.

He pulled out his phone. "I'll ask Cian or Kilian."

"They've never been inside the Stone Dahlia." She tilted her head at him.

"Yeah ... and they'll still be more helpful." Gabriel dropped his phone back into his pocket, levelling her with a blank stare.

"I guess you're staying, though?" she asked.

"What gave me away?"

"The whole not walking out of the room thing. Dead giveaway."

"I'll try to be more subtle next time."

"You do that."

Something sparked to life in his russet eyes, causing a tug low in her stomach.

"Are you flirting with me, puppy?"

She laughed nervously. "What? No. What's flirting?"

His lips twitched. "Come here and I'll show you."

She wavered, glancing toward the open dressing room door before stepping in his direction. His eyes flared, a low vibration of sound emanating from his throat—almost a warning.

"You still haven't showered?" Cian called out, stepping into the bathroom.

Isobel froze, spinning away from Gabriel as Cian and Kilian spilled into the dressing room. Gabriel moved behind her, his hands settling onto her hips as he pressed against her back.

"Isobel doesn't know what to wear to the Dahlia," Gabriel said, releasing her hips to toy with the hem of her shirt.

Cian and Kilian both eyed Gabriel's fingers before fixing to Isobel's face, weighing her expression.

"From what I've heard, people go all out for the club," Kilian finally said, licking his lips slowly before tearing his eyes away and walking over to the racks of clothing.

Cian kicked the dressing room door closed, leaning up against it and crossing his arms. "Do you know what you're in for tonight, Illy?"

Without warning, Gabriel had pulled the hem of her shirt over her head, but he didn't free her arms. He tugged the shirt behind her and down to her wrists and then looped it around to tighten it, pulling her wrists together behind her back. Isobel stumbled, but Gabriel stepped into her body again, his hard torso radiating heat and tension.

"Are you going to ask Kalen to play with you, Sigma?" Gabriel ducked to whisper the words against her temple, twisting her shirt further and forcing her wrists into a tighter bind.

Her stomach clenched, her breath stuttering. "I'm just going to stand in a corner and stay out of the way."

"Maybe he could have pulled that off last year." Kilian extracted a dress to eye the material before dismissing it and moving on to the next. "But not anymore. There's no way he can play with another woman for hours with as much focus and intensity as he needs when you're watching on from behind him."

He chose a dress and draped it over the back of a velvet armchair in the corner, beginning to sift through a row of drawers. He seemed to know exactly where everything was, so Isobel assumed he was at least partly responsible for her organised wardrobe. Perhaps Cian had helped him, and that was why Gabriel had called them both in.

"We all know exactly how this is going to play out," Gabriel warned her lowly. "And your prince charming is now a budding supervillain, so there's nobody here to make sure the rest of us don't push you."

"I take personal offence to that statement," Kilian said calmly, eyeing some sort of satin bodysuit. "Niko isn't her only prince charming."

Cian snorted. "Right. There's nobody left except Kilian—who is happy to lie about his sexuality as long as Isobel doesn't stop showering with him."

Kilian's lips twitched, but he ignored Cian as he carried the satin thing over to Isobel. "This should do. The pale rose will look beautiful against your skin."

"I c-can't just wear that." Isobel stuttered over the words because Gabriel's free hand had slipped across her stomach and was now toying with the waistband of her tights.

Kilian seemed struck, distracted as Gabriel's thumb hooked into the waistband, pulling it down.

"You're going to wear it under a dress," he said, his

eyes travelling back to hers, the pale depths so full of heat it felt like a punch to her gut.

She didn't have that relationship with Kilian, and he seemed to realise that he was devouring her with his eyes after a moment, because he blinked, and the heat was dulled—not extinguished, but controlled.

He spun, tossing the satin garment to Cian, who watched her with a calculating expression.

"You can't go into this scared," Gabriel warned her, suddenly bending to tug her tights to her ankles. "You may need to make the first move, Isobel."

"Me?" She blanched, and then hiccupped in shock as Gabriel straightened again, cupping her between the legs, his lips whispering over her temple.

"You," he said, dragging a finger across the damp seam of her panties and making her squirm. "He doesn't want to cross that boundary, but his own stubbornness is only going to cause another soul infraction."

The heel of his palm ground against her clit, forcing a stuttered whine to trip from her throat. Cian and Kilian both stepped closer, pupils dilating.

"Say yes, puppy." Gabriel's order was a purr. "Say you'll ask him to play with you."

"Y-yes." The word was a strangled sound, and Gabriel suddenly stepped back, unwrapping her wrists, and leaving her to stand there, trembling in her underwear.

"Good girl," he praised, swiping the pad of his finger across his tongue, his eyes darkening.

Isobel's legs turned wobbly, her mouth pooling with saliva, her face burning with heat. Seeing *Gabriel* of all people doing something so *dirty* was making her insides riot. She was so wet she could feel it against the insides of her thighs, and the scents swelling around her were so heady, she was sure all three of them were feeling the same lust as her.

Cian looked like he was torn between the knowledge that she was expected somewhere else, and *soon,* and the urge to experiment with her flushed, trembling state. Kilian was controlling his expression, but she could smell how his scent had changed. It was more bergamot than bark and felt like a spray of citrus on her skin, sweet and sticky like honey. It was a scent she desperately wanted to lick off the perfect curve of his jaw, and she found herself staring at his soft, pillowy, pink lips.

"Twenty minutes," Gabriel warned, moving to the door. "Don't forget you'll be part of Kalen's performance. He'll expect you to look the part."

She jerked her head in a stiff nod, tracking Cian and Kilian as they moved to follow Gabriel. She almost grabbed Kilian's sleeve to hold him back but managed to clench her fingers into a fist and keep her hands to herself.

As soon as they left, she tossed herself into the shower, quickly lathering herself in body wash, but when her fingers slipped between her legs, she found herself still swollen and desperate, her skin slick. She stumbled back against the wall, breath ragged as her finger brushed her clit.

I'm still here. Kilian's pleasant rumble drifted through her mind, and a groan slipped unbidden from her throat.

Fuck, baby. His voice grew in volume, moving closer. *You're making the safe space feel really fucking unsafe right now.*

She jerked her hand away, pretending not to hear Kilian. His muted, husky chuckle haunted her as she rushed through the rest of her shower and stepped into the satin bodysuit—the colour and cut matched the dress he had chosen too precisely for the two items to not be a pair. The dress was pale-rose silk chiffon, hugging her curves gently, falling to a ripple mid-thigh. It dipped low in the front and the back but had delicate lace insets that made the ensemble soft and feminine, and hid the bodysuit beneath. It was plain, almost, but the way the material clung and waved over her frame made it beautiful.

She stepped into ballet flats, ignoring the heels stacked inside her wardrobe because her foray into the Stone Dahlia wasn't going to be on camera and she didn't know if she would be standing all night or not.

She teased some hair oil into the ends of her strands, trying to ignore the awful pang of pain that accompanied the slide of her fingers through the tresses. She could still hear the scraping sound of Eve's blade sawing back and forth and the rustle of her hair falling away. She swallowed past the bile collecting in her mouth, pausing to lean on the bathroom counter until the sensation had passed.

She moisturised her face and picked up a thick makeup brush to dust her skin with foundation. It was the first time she had bothered with makeup since she had last been at Ironside. There hadn't been enough time before her tour the day before to do anything except throw on a change of clothes and brush her hair.

How attached are you to those freckles? Skin bleaching is an option.

Cooper's voice floated back to her as she assessed her image, compelling her to set the foundation back down with a sound of disgust. She dusted on some blush and darkened her lashes with a pass of mascara, finishing the simple look with a wet rose tint on her lips that complimented the tone of her dress. Her freckles stood out starkly.

She slipped out of the room and found Kilian reclined on her bed, playing with his phone. His head rolled to the side, pale eyes drifting down to her toes before crawling back up.

"Where are you off to?" he asked, expression blank, pretending like he didn't know.

"Uh ... Ironside Row." She grappled for an answer

before spinning so that the hem of her skirt flared out slightly. "What do you think?"

"Hmm." His eyes became shadowed as he swung his legs over the edge of the bed, unfurling to his full height. "Who are you going to Ironside Row with?"

"Nobody," she hedged, deciding this might be a good moment to sneak in a mention of Silva. "But ... maybe I'll run into someone. I don't know."

"Someone who?" Kilian demanded, playing into his role with a little too much ease. "Who are you trying to impress, Illy?"

"Mateus Silva?" She blurted it out as a question, which seemed to make Kilian's lips twitch into an almost-smile before he smoothed it away.

"Silva?" he questioned in a grumbling voice. "The guy you were sitting next to in Icon Matters?"

"Uh, yeah?" She rubbed her neck nervously. "He's a really good dancer, and he's ... pretty hot."

"You think so?" Kilian laughed, the sound breaking free in a soft rumble. "Can't say he's my type. Too much hair gel and his shirts are too tight."

Isobel rolled her eyes, Kilian's taunt chasing her as she left the room.

"Don't have too much fun tonight!"

She hurried downstairs and was about to knock on Kalen's door when Mikel's door opened, the scarred Alpha appearing. "A word, Carter?"

He stepped back, motioning her inside.

"I already let Kalen know you'd be held up for a few minutes," he said, closing the door behind her and motioning her to his desk.

She moved to one of the armchairs facing his desk, but he caught her arm, steering her to the other side instead.

"Sit." He gestured to the thick walnut desktop.

She stared at it blankly and then blinked at Mikel.

"Sit, Sigma." His tone was gentle, this time, but it carried a hint of Alpha command, and she quickly parked her butt onto the edge of his desk.

She cleared her throat. "What's this about?"

"Your punishment." He stepped into her personal space, cocking his head as he loomed over her, his hands shoved into his pockets. He was dressed in a suit, but he had lost his tie and vest at some point, loosening the top few buttons, giving him a rumpled look that complimented his savage features. He looked reckless and stern, a combination that had her stomach flipping. "You disobeyed direct orders that were given *for your safety*, and that has repercussions around here."

There was something about him that had alarm bells ringing in her head. He had completely cut himself off from their bond so that even when she peeked hesitantly through her wall, she still felt nothing. He leaned slightly over her, washing her in his scent as he plucked a glass from the desk. She felt her chest rising as she pulled in a deep, unconscious breath of rain-soaked cedarwood, and she could have sworn he also paused, his nostrils flaring before he eased back, offering her the glass.

It was the same drink he had offered her the night he and Kalen first spoke to her about the Stone Dahlia—amber liquid garnished with a twist of orange and a single cherry. The repeated gesture seemed oddly deliberate.

"For courage," Mikel said, almost sounding as though he was warning her as he watched her carefully. "But don't drink too much."

Goosebumps peppered her skin, her chest constricting. "What's my punishment?"

"Firstly ..." Mikel fit a long finger to the base of her glass, raising it. She directed it to her lips, and he lifted it further, spilling the bitter, smoky liquid into her mouth. "I would love to treat you like one of my Alphas, but in this instance ... I can't." He eased up on the glass, allowing her to swallow and suck in a shallow breath before he stole the drink away from her, setting it onto the desk again. He stepped back, staring at her mouth as she licked whiskey from the swell of her lower lip.

"I need you to understand that I meant what I said yesterday. I won't be having sex with you."

Her posture snapped up straight, shock making her feel stupid. *What? Who said anything about sex?*

"Okay," she choked out.

"But I'm going to discipline you like you're mine because you are."

"O-okay," she repeated, a little more hesitant now.

"This is the first and last time I remind you about your safe words before touching you. From tonight onwards, I expect you to always use them when you need them. Understood?"

She stilled, her heart skipping several beats. "You're going to touch me?"

His hands dropped to her thighs, his fingers slipping between her legs and prying them apart with a suddenness and strength that had a yelp catching in the back of her throat.

He was touching her.

He forced his body between her parted legs, surveying the way her chest rose and fell too quickly, and the widening of her eyes. He gripped her chin, lifting her face to his.

"Understand, pet?"

"Yes." The word rushed out of her. "I won't forget my words. I promise."

"Good girl." He stroked his thumb beneath her lower lip before he eased back a few inches. "Your punishment is simple. No orgasms for the next twelve hours. Say 'yes, sir.'"

She didn't answer him right away, drinking in the unflinching, serious expression on his face. There was no emotion there. Nothing in his eyes. Nothing in the bond. He had separated himself from her completely while he punished her, and she wasn't sure how to feel about that.

Or how to feel about his command.

It should be easy, right?

"Why?" she finally asked.

His lips curved, satisfaction sparking in his eyes. He planted his hands either side of her on the desk, leaning down until he was at her eye level. "You just doubled the sentence, Isobel. Let's try that again. Your punishment is simple. No orgasms for the next *twenty-four* hours. Say '*yes, sir.*'"

"Yes, sir," she rushed out, her face flushing hot, her fingers tingling with shock and a little bit of fear.

It wasn't that she thought Mikel would hurt her, but she hadn't expected the rapid escalation of his punishment.

He rumbled out a sound of approval, straightening again, his fingers drifting down the front of her dress. "This is pretty." He flipped up the skirt, his fingers playing across the satin of her bodysuit, a few inches above where she was suddenly desperate for—and terrified of—pressure. She swallowed, her face flushing brighter. She was sure that there was a wet patch on the dusky pink material.

Mikel hummed in the back of his throat. "Pull this to the side and hold it there."

She opened her mouth—to say *what*, she didn't even know, but Mikel arched a challenging brow at her, his voice pushing into her mind.

Don't test me, Carter.

She chewed on her lip, hooking her fingers into the seam of the bodysuit, pulling it to the side. The sudden coolness of air-conditioned air on her damp flesh had her trembling. Mikel's gaze was lazy as he surveyed her exposed position. There was a muscle ticking in his cheek, but otherwise, he was still devoid of emotion.

"Don't move," he warned, stepping away from her and walking behind her. When he returned, he was holding a bowl of what appeared to be water, steam curling from the surface. He set the bowl down, his attention tight on her face.

"Why are you being punished?" he asked, rolling up one of his sleeves.

"Because I disobeyed an order that was for my own safety," she answered as he rolled up his other sleeve.

He smiled at her, a roguish expression that stilled her heart, because it was so unguarded, so *him*. It almost felt like a gift, like he was cracking open his carefully controlled personality for just a moment and allowing her to see the man beyond the suit and the barked orders.

"Will you do it again?" he asked, dipping his hand into the bowl. Whatever he pulled out, it was nestled into the cocoon of his closed palm as he waited for the water to run off his skin and back into the bowl.

"Probably," she said, because ... well, that was the truth.

He smiled again, but this one was terrifying. "We'll see." The words were indulgent.

His fingers unfurled, revealing two small, dark metal balls threading through a smooth, black nylon string that looped at one end. "This is going to be hot," he warned, before threading his pinkie through the loop in the thread and gripping the top ball. It was a little bigger than his thumb. He pressed it directly to the exposed flesh between her thighs, making her jump. The ball *was* hot—not scalding, but definitely warm enough to have her immediately squirming.

"Hmm ..." He loomed closer, sliding the heated metal down, probing her opening. "Good girls aren't supposed to get so wet when they're being disciplined."

She was squirming so much that he gripped her thigh, securing her to the desk.

"Maybe I'm not a good girl," she rasped.

He gave her that beautiful, crooked smile again, suddenly pushing the ball inside her. Her mouth parted, her breath hot, her belly clenching almost painfully as Mikel forced the ball up higher, his touch curling and brushing her inner wall as he slid out his finger, leaving the ball inside her.

Her eyes glazed over, her thighs trembling as he inserted the second ball. The metal seemed to get even hotter once inside her body, and Mikel pushed the punishing sphere deep, releasing her thigh to grip her neck.

"Well?" He towered over her, forcing her head back so that he could hover his lips over hers, his finger still inside her. "What's the verdict? Good girl or not?"

Her brain short-circuited. "G-good girl."

"I thought so." He stared at her mouth, something cracking in his expression. It was there and gone in a flash, but she felt the heaviness of his desire like a towering weight dropping right through her body before he pulled it back and hid it away again.

He lowered his head until his breath expelled in a choppy puff against her lips, tasting like the whiskey of the drink he had made her, and a hint of his sodden cedar scent. He usually smelled like wind whipping through trees as a storm blanketed a forest, but suddenly, that rain was hot. It was steam curling through foliage and mist creeping into her throat.

He pulled his finger from her again, forcing a whimper to her lips, and then he took her wrist, extracting her grip from her bodysuit and pressing her hand to the desk. He fixed up her clothing and then cupped her, much like Gabriel had earlier, the move possessive.

"You're mine," he growled, his grip around her neck tightening. "Nobody hurts what's mine, not even you."

Before she could answer or try to appease him—or beg him to prove it—his mouth was on hers, his tongue staking an immediate and heated claim that had her entire body shaking, a gush of honey coating his fingers through the satin, where he pressed against her insistently.

He let out a deep, satisfied growl before pulling back.

"Go, now." He jutted his chin toward the doorway. "Twenty-four hours, Isobel. Or your punishment will be much worse."

She slipped off the edge of his desk, wobbling on the spot at the strange, *full* feeling inside her, and the heat that radiated from Mikel's toy.

"How ..." Her voice broke and she tried again. "How do I get them out? What are they?"

"Ben Wa balls. And you don't," he told her, a rough timbre in his voice. "You ask for help, and you pray to the gods that you don't fucking come while you're getting it."

She stumbled on her way to the door, her body heated and weak at the suggestion that Mikel was setting her up for failure. If she couldn't remove them herself, she would have to ask one of the Alphas to touch her, which ... usually led to an orgasm.

"Good luck tonight," Mikel said before she could open the door. "I think you'll enjoy it."

She paused, her hand on the knob, turning back to look at him. "Gabriel said I would need to ask Kalen to perform on me tonight. He said Kalen won't ask me himself, but if he performs on another person in front of me, it will cause another infraction."

Mikel pulled in a deep breath, snatching up his glass

from the desk. He took a measured sip. "They're right, but they're also wrong. They don't know how the soul infraction has affected us because they aren't as ... restricted ... as we are. Kalen will need to appease his claim just as I needed to appease mine. Trust him, Sigma. Let him make his move. He won't hurt you." Mikel paused, his eyes dragging over her, fixing to her belly like he could see the weighted balls forcing her muscles to contract and sending tingles down her legs. "Well ... not emotionally, anyway."

15

SOME STARS CAN FLY

KALEN WAS WAITING OUTSIDE IN ONE OF THE GOLF CARTS.

"We're running late. Don't have time to walk," he explained as she slid into the passenger seat. "You okay?"

He cast her a few searching looks as he manoeuvred down Alpha Hill and sped toward the northern point of the campus.

Isobel only hummed in response, tilting her head to the cool breeze as she bit down on her lip and pressed her thighs together. The jostling of the cart was *not* helping her situation, and she felt out of breath when Kalen pulled up beside a small, white-painted, wooden boathouse. He helped her out of the cart but crowded her against the side of it before she could go anywhere.

His brows were narrowed, his hand hovering somewhere near her stomach. She could *feel* him pushing into her head, his consciousness brushing up against hers. He must have felt the burning, restless energy inside her body and was trying to locate the cause of it. His fingers flattened over the silk of her dress before abruptly pressing down, right over the spot where she burned the hottest. She could have sworn she felt the metal balls inside her shift as she clenched down on them, her torso muscles jumping beneath the insistent pressure of Kalen's hand.

She tried not to react, but a low whine exploded out of her, and Kalen's eyes snapped from her stomach to her face, his expression darkening.

"I see Mikel picked a highly inconvenient night to punish you," he said, backing off her.

"He's a real asshole," she returned, because she was nervous and didn't know what else to say.

Kalen grinned at her. "He was nice to you, princess. Let's go."

He strode toward the boathouse, and she hurried after him, wincing at the too-fast movement, which she suspected he had initiated deliberately.

The boathouse had a neat little keypad beside the plain white door, which Kalen entered a code into. The lock clicked, and he held the door open for her. She was shocked to come up against another door almost immediately. The space was so small that she had to step aside to let Kalen in behind her.

The door before them was heavy and black, a panel beside it blinking a red light. Kalen closed the first door and as soon as the lock clicked again, the light on the blinking panel turned green. He produced a slim black card, swiping it over the panel to open the second door, which led to a well-lit, marble staircase.

Once again, he motioned for Isobel to go ahead of him, and she clung to the curved iron banister as she descended. She was nervous and unsure, but Kalen's presence helped. His rich, heady vanilla scent dug into her pores, his presence like a tangible blanket of power that wrapped around her tightly, steeling her spine. She could also feel him in her mind, brushing up against her conscience. He didn't speak through their bond, but she felt the reassuring nudge of him with every step.

At the bottom of the stairs was another door, with another code to gain entry, and then they were in a lobby of some sort. The space was vast, with towering marble columns supporting the exposed, rough stone ceiling—which was lit up by strategic spotlights to play over the ragged edges, dips, and valleys. There were several chandeliers bolted into the stone ceiling, casting glittering light patterns across the gleaming, polished onyx underfoot. Huge bouquets of gold-brushed, ruby-red roses sprawled in large crystal vases on pillared posts along the sides of a carpeted pathway through the centre of the room, leading to a single desk at the other end, where a woman stood behind a computer.

"Welcome, Mr West, Miss Carter." She smiled politely, her eyes lingering on Kalen for a moment too long before settling on Isobel. "Welcome to the Stone Dahlia. We are happy you accepted our invitation."

Not that she had a choice.

"We just have a little bit of paperwork to get out of the way." The woman reached over her desk for a stack of paper—several booklets, it seemed, clumped together and secured by gold clips.

She set the first one in front of Isobel. "A nondisclosure," she said. "As nothing you see or hear or do after you step through that door is to be spoken about when you leave, under any circumstances, including under duress by the human government, the OGGB, or any other official or nonofficial person or governing body." She added another stack. "This is to accept full liability for your own physical, mental, and emotional health. The Track Team cannot be held liable for anything that happens within the Stone Dahlia." Another stack. "This is an agreement binding you as a limited, exclusive performer in Room 43 for a provisionary period of one month. This agreement can only be absolved by your sponsor or the Track Team. Your salary will be six hundred per room performance for the provisionary period." She dropped the last booklet onto the stack. "And this is a copy of the rules, which are quite simple, since you are contracted to a private group performance room. You are not obliged to entertain our patrons in any other room or section. You are also not permitted to accept money for private interactions with our customers without signing an additional floater contract, though I have been told—"

"She won't be floating," Kalen interrupted sternly.

"Of course," the woman continued smoothly. Isobel realised she had never introduced herself. "Well then, as for the rest of the rules, you are to wear formal attire at all times. Including footwear." She glanced down Isobel's legs. "What is your shoe size?"

"Six." Isobel glanced at Kalen, who rolled his eyes as soon as the woman turned her back, causing Isobel to smile. She had hidden away the grin by the time the woman returned with a pair of strappy black heels.

"Change, please," the woman ordered. "Formalwear at all times, though appropriate performance attire will be accepted as long as there are no bodily fluids on your costumes."

Isobel blinked at that one, but the woman barrelled on without pause.

"This is a club of the world's most powerful, influential people"—*sounds like Mei's heaven*, she thought—"so you must act accordingly. The following will result in a disciplinary strike against your membership: asking for charity; prying into private lives or asking to see identification; rude, unruly, or uncouth behaviour; flagrant disrespect of the dress code—" She paused, flicking her eyes down as Isobel hurried to change her shoes, before continuing, "Violence or aggression outside of contracted performative activities, penetrative sex with guests of the Stone Dahlia outside of contracted performative activities—"

"That's new," Kalen interrupted without emotion.

"Indeed." The woman looked at him. "Your contract was already amended. We don't need you to sign, due to the clause allowing us to make appropriate changes at any time, for any reason."

Kalen managed not to scoff, but Isobel was sure that he wanted to. Instead, he only nodded.

"And finally"—the woman tapped the top booklet—"you will get a disciplinary strike for denying private meetings or introductions."

"I thought I wasn't allowed to accept money for private interactions unless I'm a floater?" Isobel asked, growing confused with the restrictive list of rules.

"You cannot accept money for it, but if any of our esteemed guests would like to meet with you in private—accompanied by your sponsor during the provisionary period, of course—you are not permitted to refuse them the pleasure of an introduction. All of our Gifted are here to serve our guests. That is what you are here for."

Isobel pressed her lips together, choosing to deliver a simple nod, like Kalen.

"Excellent." The woman produced a pen, handing it

to Isobel. "Please sign the last page of every contract. You will not be permitted entry to the Stone Dahlia without your signature on each one. Amendments—other than those the Track Team find necessary—are not permitted. Our rules are final."

In other words, she could sign, or she could walk out and face the consequences of upsetting the Track Team.

Suddenly, their brutal warning the day before her first foray into the club didn't seem so far-fetched. They wanted nothing short of complete control, and complete obedience. Isobel's skin began to itch.

Better to just sign, Kalen whispered into her mind. *If they think they don't know enough to control you, they will look deeper. They'll do more.*

She sucked a breath in through her teeth, snatching up the pen and quickly scrawling her name onto the last page of every booklet.

"Fantastic!" the woman declared, gathering up the paperwork. "Here is your key card." She handed a slim, glittering black card to Isobel and then suddenly gripped Isobel's hair.

Kalen went tense beside her, a low warning growl rumbling through Isobel's head. The woman frowned, running her fingers through Isobel's hair, touching her like she was nothing more than a life-sized doll.

"These aren't hair extensions?" the woman asked.

"No," Isobel answered as the woman backed off, releasing her hair.

She knows my hair was cut off, Isobel sent the words to Kalen in a panic.

And she has no idea how bond magic works, he replied soothingly. *None of them do. For all they know, everyone's hair grows back after something like that is done.*

"Interesting," the woman said. "Your passcodes will be emailed to you at three minutes past midnight every three nights. There will be two. One for each door upstairs." She shifted back behind her desk, already tapping away at her keyboard. "Enjoy your night."

Kalen steered her past the desk and down another staircase. "It should be quieter tonight," he said. "That's why I chose to take you through on a Monday. The big-ticket fights are usually on a Friday and Saturday, after midnight. I also generally perform on a Friday or Saturday."

The door at the bottom of the stairs opened automatically, and she was hit with a wall of ambient sound. She hadn't realised how sterile and silent the upstairs foyer had been. The lighting was dim, bathing everything in a soft, hazy glow. The vaulted ceilings were the same rough rock, with tiny, pinpoint lights embedded into the stone to give it the appearance of a starry sky hewn with heavy, jagged clouds.

There was a stage in the middle of the room, a small orchestra corralled by a polished brass railing, their music a soft croon that crept through the open space like a mist. A fifth-year that Isobel immediately recognised was singing into a microphone, his voice twisting and winding about them in a seductive, low rhythm. The floor plan was intricate and almost chaotic, with walled-in booths, open booths, styled seating areas and strategically placed bars. There was even a long glass window on the other side of the hall where she could just barely make out several chefs lined up at their stations, plating food.

The decor was a mix of styles, with tall, twisted juniper trees in giant marble pots around the room and rich, heavy maple or cherry-wood furniture. There were polished copper and bronze brass accents, and the now-familiar marriage of marble, crystal, and wrought iron scattered about.

"I wanted to show you around properly, but we're late and I start in ten minutes," Kalen explained, leading the way around the outskirts of the hall and into a wide, echoing passageway lined with sinuous marble statues in spotlighted alcoves along the natural stone wall. "There are a few rules for Room 43," he continued as they passed into another, smaller hall. "The first is absolute silence unless you are me or my partner for the night."

The lights had dimmed further, and the second hall was divided into sections of comfortable velvet armchairs and chaises cuddling around smaller stages. Some of those stages had poles, and Isobel swallowed as she recognised another fifth-year boy performing *very* athletic stunts on his pole to the polite applause of the people strewn about in a circle around him. Another girl, a fourth-year that Isobel also recognised, was crawling across her short stage, pausing at the edge to dance seductively for one of her guests before twisting to her feet and delivering a wink over her shoulder.

They skirted the circular bar in the centre of the room, Kalen's pace swift and punishing, since each step had Isobel's insides clenching and rippling. She should have been too scared to feel any kind of desire, but the Alphas had done a good job of manipulating her mind and body before she stepped into the club, and her body had not yet forgotten.

It would take some time for her to forget the feel of a strong, unyielding grip cupping her with possession, or the image of Gabriel staring her down as he licked his finger, or Mikel's bold claim of her mouth and his gravelled sound of appreciation.

She needed a *break*. To sit down, or something. Definitely to stop moving. The metal balls weren't so hot anymore, but they were still a warm weight inside her, refusing to ease her back to a normal level of need after Gabriel and Mikel's priming.

It seemed very calculated, in hindsight.

They passed into another passageway, and Kalen began to speak again once they were alone.

"The second rule is for my partner of the night. They must obey me at all times, without question or hesitation. The use of safe words is allowed, though I don't usually observe the traffic light system. I'm not a yellow kind of man. My partner picks their safe word and unless they use it, I won't stop anything I'm doing."

They descended a short staircase into another hall that had a high mezzanine level. Here, he lowered his voice, since there were people scattered about.

"And finally, there's you. You *especially* are to obey me at all times. I want your eyes on me from the moment we walk through that door until we leave again, understood?"

"Yeah," she answered nervously. He stopped walking, turning to face her, his eyes flitting down to her stomach before snapping back up again.

"Now I know Mikel taught you better than that," he drawled, a hint of reprimand in his voice.

She swallowed, her mind racing to figure out what she had done wrong. Kalen smiled at her, and while it was kind, it was also sharp as a blade.

"Sir," he supplied. "In that room, it's only *Sir*."

She pointed out the obvious. "We're not in the room."

His grin sharpened, something she might have thought was impossible. "Indeed," he purred, his eyes growing hot, his scent smouldering, his desire crashing through her mind, knocking over the wall she had erected as though it was made of matchsticks.

Her core clenched around the metal balls, making her wince as her thighs grew uncomfortably sticky.

"Don't challenge me, Sigma." He swept from her mind as easily as he had entered, his expression settling into calm neutrality as she stood there trembling. "You won't win."

Yikes.

"Understood, Sir."

"We're not in the room yet, but that was cute." He bopped her on the nose and spun on his heel, striding toward the edge of the hall.

Asshole. She flung the word at the back of his head because she couldn't be punished for her *thoughts*, right?

Kalen's grin had turned wolfish, but it faded as he stopped before two doors. One said *Room 43 - Staff*. The other said *Room 43 - Observer*.

"Some people watch from above." He pointed to the mezzanine. "And some from the ground level. Shibari can be especially beautiful observed from above, even more so when I elevate my partner."

He pushed open the staff door and stood aside. By now, she knew the drill, and brushed past him to enter first, finding herself in a small dressing room.

"Where's your partner?" Isobel asked, glancing around the empty space.

Kalen removed his coat, hanging it in a locker before he turned to face her.

"I've been avoiding this conversation," he admitted, dragging his hands down his face before shaking his arms out. "Because the truth is ... I don't know what's right, in this situation. Either I pick someone from the crowd and possibly wound the bond, or I choose you, and push you into something you aren't prepared for."

"I watched a few videos," Isobel argued. "Last year, after you told me. I'd argue that it takes almost *no* skill to sit still while someone ties me up."

He scoffed out a short laugh. "What would you prefer, Carter?"

"What do you suggest, Sir?"

He jolted forward a step and then froze, something sparking to life in his eyes. "We should have had this conversation outside. You don't have to do what I want in this regard."

"I know." She lifted a shoulder. "But I trust you."

He stalked toward her, pinching the thin strap of her dress. "What's beneath this?"

"A satin bodysuit."

He clenched his fingers into a fist, dropping his hand. "Who planned that?"

"Kilian."

He shook his head and then gripped the hem of her dress. "Arms up."

She raised her arms and he carefully pulled off her dress, spinning on his heel to hang it in one of the lockers. He paused there, still turned away from her, and seemed to take several measured breaths before facing her again.

His amber eyes flickered over the satin that clung to

her, bunching and stretching in all the right places, and he let out a small groan. "You're going to look stunning."

"I'm nervous about the people," she said softly, trying to disregard the burning in the pit of her stomach at complete odds with the delicate butterflies fluttering from her chest to her throat.

"Ignore them," Kalen ordered. "They don't exist. You can take the heels off." He moved to another door, reaching for the handle as she removed her shoes. "If you can trust me and just let go, you might find some peace in this," he said lowly. "Most people do."

She nodded, moving close to him as he opened the door.

The room beyond was spacious but still cosy, ringed by polished brass railings on both levels, with shimmering black stone floors and the same rough stone ceiling as the first hall they had entered, with the pinprick lights that looked like stars. There were two wrought iron and crystal chandeliers, but the lights had been turned very low.

Kalen turned and held out his hand to her. She placed her hand into his much larger one, and he led her to the middle of the room where the black floors stepped up to a slightly raised platform before dropping her hand.

As soon as her eyes began to wander to the shifting shadows beyond the brass railing on the ground floor, he pinched her chin, turning her head back to his. His hands settled on her shoulders, pushing them back slightly, and then he moved behind her. She turned to keep him in her sight, and approval briefly flashed in his eyes before he stepped from the platform and drifted back to the door they had entered through, where there seemed to be a whole wall of props waiting.

He tapped away at the screen of a tablet until soft music spilled into the room, raising the hairs on her arms with the way it swelled and echoed around the otherwise silent space. He picked up a small, sturdy black table and carried it back to her, setting it into the middle of the platform, stepping back to make sure it was angled exactly how he wanted it, before he moved to her, slipping his hands under her arms and lifting her up.

Kneel, his voice whispered into her mind as he lifted her up to the table.

She did as she was told, resting on her knees as he lowered her.

We'll start off small, he added as he began to arrange her. *No suspension*. His words were short and succinct. Perhaps he didn't like to talk when he was focussing on this thing he did, so she didn't respond past a slight nod. He gently brushed her cheek—an acknowledgement of sorts—and then he stepped back to survey her the same way he had stepped back to survey the table. He picked up her wrists and laid them over her thighs before returning to his prop area to fetch a claw clip and a pile of thin, soft-looking black rope. He deftly twisted her hair up and secured it with the clip, and then pulled her shoulders back again. He tapped the back of her neck and she suspected it was a warning to not slouch again.

He looped one end of the soft rope around her neck and took half a step back, surveying the fibre against her skin before removing it and switching out the black rope for a different rope. It was a pearl colour, washed with the slightest pink. She thought it matched the dusky rose of her bodysuit, and Kalen seemed to agree. He doubled up the rope and looped it around her neck again, creating a short lead, and then he stood back, wrapping the lead around his wrist and applying some pressure. She leaned forward. He released the pressure, and she eased back.

He was avoiding her eyes, which forced her to concentrate on the rope as she tried to anticipate what his next move would be. He walked around, disappearing behind her, applying pressure on the rope again as he pressed against the centre of her back, forcing her into a subtle arch that he released her from immediately. He came before her again, tilting the lead up so that it lifted her gaze, but he wasn't trying to make her meet his eyes. He was too busy ... examining her. Watching to see that she was responding the way he intended. After a few minutes of this, it became instinct to watch the rope instead of him, to respond to the pressure or lack of pressure around her neck.

Just when she felt like she had the game figured out, he removed the collar, reaching above him for a thicker rope that hung from wooden beams above them. He threaded the pale rope through the darker one before lifting her arms above her head, her wrists pressed together. He tied off her wrists, his movements rapid and distracted, like he was just trying to temporarily get her arms out of the way, and then he tipped up her face, forcing her to look at the ceiling. She let out a small breath, focussing on the little star-like lights as she felt rope cross over the top of her chest. Kalen was close enough that his scent soaked into her, his breath occasionally brushing her cheek or shoulder or the top of her head as he reached around her, passing the ropes from her back to her front. She could feel it crisscrossing, pulling tight over her chest, forming a cross between her breasts that hugged each soft swell, lifting them up as he circled her, beginning a much more complicated twist of patterns down her spine, pulling the harness along her front tighter and tighter until the rope was all she could focus on.

After a while, she began to drift off a little.

Maybe it was a combination of the soft music and Kalen's sultry scent, but she lost focus, forgetting about their audience, her arms sagging. He didn't reprimand or correct her. He merely reached up with one hand and released the bind on her wrists as rapidly as he had tied them, though he didn't allow her arms to fall, holding onto her wrists with his other hand. He lowered them slowly, laying them back into her lap before cupping the back of her head and drawing it forward until she could rest it on his chest. He went back to work almost immediately, but whatever he was creating, it wasn't attached to her as he spun something behind her back. She turned her face up, brushing her nose against his warm skin, and felt the slightest vibration in his chest.

He reached above her for a few moments, and then captured one of her wrists, pulling her upright again as he slipped her wrist into a thick, woven cuff of rope, which he tightened before straightening out her other arm. He dragged down a rope, and her arms pulled taut, stretching out her spine. He loosened it a fraction before tying off the end to one of the wooden posts above him.

Now that her arms were securely suspended, he returned to the pattern he had been creating down her spine, which crisscrossed up to her biceps, twisting and weaving to bind her arms together. At some point, she must have closed her eyes, lost in the sensations, every nerve ending focussed on Kalen's fingers because he made sure to touch her. *Often*.

She was always straining toward the expected brush of his fingers as they passed over her skin. Eventually, the touches evolved from casual to insistent. He gripped her with the full span of his hands, tracing his designs, playing with the contrast of soft, pinched flesh and braided rope. When his hands dragged down over her breasts, it felt like he had struck a match and shoved it down her throat. Her eyelids were so heavy, her body felt like it weighed a tonne, but she couldn't have possibly described the sensation as *sleepy*.

Not with her body on fire.

She didn't remember lowering her walls, but at some point, she must have, and she wasn't the only one. Kalen became a steady presence inside her head, his unguarded feelings twisting with her own. She could feel the calmness in him, the steady sway of power like a soft breeze rustling through an immovable tree. And she could feel the need in him, the shiver of an almost violent urge to claim her that wavered beneath the surface of his skin, held back by that wash of calm he seemed to wear so well.

She could feel his awe, and how it filled him with pride that she had given him her trust, and that she had *meant it*, because he could feel that she had given up all control, happy to let him do whatever he wanted with her.

She melted into their shared bond just like she was melting into his hands, allowing him to loosen and retie her, to arrange her and position her at will, her body becoming pliant as water, and yet somehow also taut as a bowstring.

The sudden sound of applause threatened to burst her bubble, and she blinked bleary eyes open to watch as Kalen began the slow and complicated process of untying her.

"We're done?" she whispered huskily, forgetting that people could hear her.

He nodded, his gaze sinking into hers, warm and gold. He still didn't speak, and she hissed in pain as all the blood rushed back into her unbound limbs. He left the ropes unspooled on the table, picking her up and carrying her into the changing room.

There was a couch in the room, and he sank into it, tucking her into his lap. He removed the clip from her hair and teased out the strands, spending a few minutes softly massaging her scalp.

She didn't even know how long they had been in there. It seemed to pass in a bleary blink, and yet it also seemed to last an eternity. She was a little confused, still. It was like her mind had disengaged.

"You were stunning," he whispered, running his hands gently down her arms like he knew they were starting to prickle with pins and needles.

She tipped her head back to rest on the soft arm of the couch, blinking up at him. "Do you always cuddle after?"

He smirked. "After a performance? No. I give them this couch, with pillows and blankets. There are snacks and drinks in the fridge if you want anything. Usually, they nap for a while or eat something. Shibari outside of a performance is ... a little different. For me, anyway. But for a performance? The come-down isn't so bad."

She wanted to take the edge off her thrumming body, but Mikel had already put a stop to that.

"What do you usually do after a performance while they're napping?" she slurred—*why was she slurring*?

"Because you're still coming down," he murmured, answering her inner thought and reminding her that he was still inside her head. "And after, I stick around until they feel better. That's my chair." He pointed to an armchair nearby, a book resting on it. "Subspace is just a mixture of adrenaline and endorphins, but it can put people into a vulnerable state. I won't leave them alone and unguarded. Sometimes, people need their arms or legs massaged to help with their blood circulation."

"M'kay." She wiggled, trying to get more comfortable, seeking some sort of relief.

Kalen's hand flattened to her ribcage, drifting down as she unfurled and stretched out her arms and legs, arching like a cat. His fingers drifted over her stomach, drawing absent, distracted patterns as he slowly extracted himself from her mind, putting the usual distance between them within the bond.

She winced at the sudden, cold, empty feeling.

He lowered his voice, roughening it with a subtle purr. "I'm still here, princess."

"Mikel has to obey you," she muttered, her eyelids too heavy to keep open as Kalen's fingers continued driving her insane with those absent patterns drawn over the satin covering her stomach. "Make me come."

He chuckled, the sound darkly amused. “You’re gonna regret saying that once you come back to yourself.”

“Can’t you lie down?” she whined, wriggling on his lap, and kicking her legs slightly. “This is so uncomfortable.”

Her legs didn’t feel good, almost like there were bugs itching beneath her skin.

He obliged her, stretching out and settling her on top of him, but the itching in her legs only grew worse, and after she began rubbing them together to try and ease the uncomfortable sensation, he finally sat her up over his hips, pulling her legs either side of his body. He began massaging them, rhythmically kneading the muscles, and she groaned, tilting sideways and relaxing into the back of the couch. He worked his way from her ankles to her calves, and then up her thighs until she forgot all about how relaxing it was and began to squirm again, painfully aware of how close his thumbs were to the heat between her legs.

“Isobel ...” His rough voice dragged her eyes open again to focus on him. “Stop moving, baby.”

She was beginning to *love* when the Alphas started to purr and call her baby. She especially loved it at that moment because it was usually accompanied by an erection, which would be exceedingly welcome in her current situation. She shifted backward, immediately coming into contact with something hot and hard and *huge.* Something that throbbed as she ground down on it. A whimper hiccupped from her chest before rough hands stilled her movements and the big body beneath hers rose, tipping her back, and back ... until she spooled onto the couch, her hair twisting into a chaotic cloud around her head.

Kalen loomed over her for a moment, his gold eyes darkened to a burnt amber, his heavy brows low, a muscle ticking in his squared jaw ... but then quickly stood, shoving his hands through his short hair.

"Stay," he warned, pointing at her. "I'm hanging on by a thread, Carter."

She was slowly sinking back to earth, a heavy pout tugging at her lips as she realised how she had acted.

"No, no," he said, returning to her, kneeling on the couch before her.

She was tearing up, she realised, as drops fell onto the backs of his hands. He kissed her forehead and then brushed several more kisses along her brow. "You didn't do anything wrong, princess. You're okay." He kissed her cheeks, and then the side of her mouth, and then a groan caught in the base of his throat, and he eased back.

"Lie down," he instructed. "I'll grab a blanket. We can rest for a bit before we go home. How does that sound?"

"Fine," she grumbled.

"Sir." His soft tone almost tumbled into a growl.

"Fine, Sir." She was pathetic. She was *crying*. Her lip

was wobbling. *What the hell was wrong with her?* And why did Kalen look like her trembling lip was about to be his undoing?

He closed his eyes, resting his forehead against hers, his chest expanding with a deep breath. His exhale dragged over gravel. “Okay,” he said, as though reminding himself of what he was supposed to be doing. “Okay ... we’ll rest for a bit.”

16
I Really Hate You

Isobel stepped out of the shower, wrapping herself in a towel and sinking into a chair in her dressing room, gnawing on her lower lip as she considered her predicament.

Her skin felt overheated and overstimulated. Even the brush of her towel against her thighs was too much, and the Ben Wa balls inside her were beginning to feel truly uncomfortable.

She had fallen asleep on the couch in Kalen's dressing room, and when she had woken up, she had been too embarrassed to say *anything* to him, let alone ask him for his assistance with the Ben Wa balls. She had fled his presence the second they returned to the dorm.

She fiddled with her phone before sighing and bringing up the group chat, since the dorm had seemed empty before she jumped into the shower and she didn't know where anyone was.

Isobel: I need help.

The thumbs-up icon popped up below her message and she clicked on it to reveal the name.

Mikel Easton.

She wrinkled her nose, shaking her head. "You're the literal devil," she said to her phone.

Kilian: Everything okay?

Isobel: There's something inside me that needs to be removed and I'm not allowed to remove it myself.

Niko: What the fuck, Carter?

Cian: Simmer down, Niko. She obviously wasn't asking you.

Theodore: This feels like a trap.

The little thumbs-up icon appeared below Theodore's message, and she clicked on it to reveal Mikel's name again.

Isobel: I need someone to remove it platonically.

Theodore: There it is.

Moses: I haven't laughed so hard in weeks. Thanks, Carter.

Cian: Is the platonic part negotiable?

Isobel: No. I don't feel like being spanked tonight.

Another thumbs-up.

Mikel Easton *was* the devil.

Elijah: Okay, for once, I'm at a loss. What the actual fuck is happening?

Gabriel: There's absolutely no way Kalen put something inside you during the performance.

Kalen (admin): Mikel punished her for disobeying the rules of the hunt.

Moses: Remind me never to disobey Mikki.

Cian: Pretty sure he would just beat you up, Moses.

Moses: I'm not willing to take the chance.

Mikel (admin): Shut up, Moses.

Moses: Don't come after my orifices!

Mikel gave Moses's message a thumbs-up, and Isobel snorted, shaking her head.

Kilian: Can you be a little more specific about what the object is and where it is?

Niko: Could you not?

Oscar: Don't pretend you don't want to know.

Niko: You're all insane.

Oscar: We'll be back soon, Carter. I can help you then.

Isobel sat up straighter, her fingers flying across the screen.

Isobel: Where are you all?

Theodore: Necklace hunting.

Kilian: Niko pretended to move his shit into the human accommodations for his week of sleepovers. They don't have cameras in there, so he searched their rooms. He found five of them—one in each of their rooms.

Moses: We're still looking for the rest.

Isobel frowned at her screen, before clicking on Niko's name to open a private message.

Isobel: I thought you didn't believe me?

His response was instant.

Niko: Open up.

Her head snapped up at the faint sound of a knock in the next room. She tossed her phone aside and hurried into the bedroom. Niko was standing on the other side of her bedroom door, his hands shoved into the pockets of a sports jacket, his hazel eyes guarded, his hair—bleached into a pale silver through the mid-lengths and ends, but still an inky black at the roots—framed his handsome face in a fretful, two-toned mess. He had a sports bag slung over his arm, but he wasn't in exercise clothes. He was in a pair of slim-fit jeans, artfully distressed and faded in all the right places, though she assumed it was from wear rather than a deliberate design. He wore a faded tee with *Ironside Academy* scrawled across the front, the material soft enough to hint at the sculpted torso beneath.

His attention slipped from her face, dropping to her towel, and she quickly stood aside.

"I was just getting dressed," she snipped, ignoring the blush creeping over her cheeks as she spun on her heel and stalked back to the bathroom. "Can you make it quick?"

He followed her silently, closing the bathroom door behind him. She collapsed back into her chair in the dressing room, and he dragged a footstool over to face her, sitting and crossing his ankle over his knee, his sneaker jiggling in agitation. He let his bag slip off his shoulder, falling to the ground. He had left it unzipped to fit his tennis racquet, and she peered into it now, spotting a change of clothes.

"Was it really an act?" she asked, nodding to his bag. "Were you just pretending you were going to stay with her?"

He glanced at his bag, fidgety and distracted. "I always carry around a change of gym clothes." He dug into the pockets of his jacket, producing several lengths of thin, braided rope, which he dipped forward to drop into her lap, before leaning back again, gripping the edge of the stool behind him.

"There." His voice was harsh. "Your little soul pieces."

NIKO WANTED TO PICK UP HIS BAG AND FLEE THE ROOM. He wanted it with every fibre of his being because even sitting this close to her was making him feel insane.

He couldn't think straight when he could see her, or even when the others talked about her. He struggled to remember what it was like before he was pulled from the river. There was nothing but deep, endless darkness inside him, twisting with ugly, grotesque shadows, the unsteady floor beneath him doused in gasoline and set on fire so that he was always screaming in his mind, crying out from the agony.

There wasn't any room for logic, or memory.

There was only pain, and deformity.

Except ... sometimes, if he tried hard enough or *looked* hard enough, he felt other things. It was easier to look at her now because it was easier to be around the necklaces. They calmed the screams and blanketed the fire—not entirely, but enough for him to breathe again. That was why he had stepped forward for Mei.

Isobel had said that the necklaces were their bond. Hers and his. And he remembered bonding with her, for the most part.

He could watch it like a movie, but all he felt was pain and anger and something ugly and poisonous. It was like his mind was broken.

He remembered the bond shattering more than anything else. He had tried to take it all, to keep it away from her, but he had damaged himself in the process.

Severely.

He knew it more surely than he knew anything. It may have been the *only* thing he knew with any degree of certainty.

Isobel stared down at the necklaces, fear and hope warring across her features. It was strange, to be able to look at her. To know, objectively, that he had found her beautiful. To see that beauty clear as day ... and to wish nothing more than to hurt it.

He felt that he would infect her if he stayed with her for too long. He would make her ugly. He would spread his deformity to her, somehow. But he couldn't drag himself away.

She's lying to you.

She wants to trick you.

The poison in his mind refused to listen to logic, to his best friends, to her. So he stayed to see what she would do with the necklaces. To force her to prove what she was claiming.

Without even looking at him, she placed one of the necklaces along her forearm, plucking at the string securing the ends until they began to unravel. She held her breath, her chest rising and falling above the towel, drawing his unwilling focus to where the end of the covering was tucked in.

He wondered what it felt like before, his lust for her. Had it felt as violent? As furious? As disgusting? As possessive?

The strands of hair began to glow, to burn, to hiss and steam as they melted through her flesh. He leaned forward, frowning as she clenched her jaw and bore the pain without a word.

This means nothing.

"Thought it would be prettier," he said, the rotten malevolence inside him refusing to stay quiet for long. "This is hardly a glorious reuniting of the soul."

"Bond magic demands blood at the best of times," she gritted.

He hated everything about her *except* the way she

braced herself against the pain, laying a second necklace over her other forearm. Her eyes burned as her skin burned, her jaw set, her muscles tight, every inch of her stubborn. Every sound that she swallowed made his cock lengthen ... until she sagged back against the chair, the final necklace singed back into her skin, and he found himself all the way hard.

Which he hated, of course.

She was so *painfully* inconvenient.

She regarded him with that fire still in her eyes as she panted. "You look pissed," she noted, suddenly ducking forward and dragging his gym bag toward herself. She dug around for a tennis ball, which she threw at him. "Here. Squeeze this."

His grip flexed around the ball on instinct before he scoffed and tossed it aside. It wasn't what he wanted to be squeezing. He much preferred the idea of wrapping his hands around her infuriatingly pretty little neck. So he stood to leave, because as pissed as he was, he knew that the others would *kill* him if he touched her, if he spread his ugly into her, if he made her catch his disease.

She jumped up before he could escape, closing the door and tossing her arms out to guard it.

"Just wait—" she rasped.

"Get the fuck out of my way, Carter." That felt wrong. He had always called her Isobel. Even her last name tasted like ash.

"Just *wait,*" she repeated, more insistently this time.

"I just ... I need to know why you're so angry at me. Is it true, what Elijah said? You took all the mental damage of the soul infraction?"

He flinched, rage boiling hot and fierce, clouding his vision.

How dare she.

He didn't know what, exactly, she had done wrong. He could barely remember what she had said, or why he was there.

The necklaces—that's right.

He closed his eyes for a fraction of a second, repeating the facts Gabriel had taught him.

We are a group.

We keep the bond a secret.

The group is safe.

Red means stop.

He opened his eyes again, his rage curdling when he heard the faint knock in the other room. He had locked the door behind him, but he wasn't sure why. He *had* locked it, hadn't he?

"Tell the others to back off and leave us alone," he grated out.

"Okay." She flipped her hands up this time, placating him, her tone soft and soothing.

He wondered what it would sound like if he squeezed enough to damage her vocal cords.

No.

That was against the rules.

We are a group.

We keep the bond a secret.

The group is safe.

Red means stop.

Isobel was part of the group, which meant she was safe.

She leaned over to grab her phone off the chair, sending a message and turning the screen to show him.

Isobel: Niko is with me. My body accepted the light without a problem. We need a minute.

He grabbed her phone and tossed it behind him. "That was stupid."

She sighed like she was sick of his attitude.

Well ... fuck her?

"You're the one who wanted me to stay," he reminded her, taking a step closer.

She backed up. Maybe she wasn't so stupid after all. He advanced another step, and her shoulders bumped the door. She groaned, a hand slipping over her towel-covered stomach.

"Fucking hell I hope that man gets the karma he deserves," she grumbled.

"What?" Niko recalled something about Mikel in the group chat, but he couldn't think clearly even with the most simple of tasks, so he had given up trying to unravel that particular mystery almost as soon as they began talking about it.

"Mikel put some metal balls inside me and told me

I'm not allowed to remove them on my own. That's what I was texting the group for. He obviously meant one of you guys, unless everyone is fine with me texting Silva to come over and put his creepy fingers in me."

What the actual fuck?

He surged forward in a dizzying rush of possession and fury, gripping her shoulders as he pinned her to the door.

"Just because I don't want you doesn't mean you get to throw yourself at fucking *Silva*," he snarled.

She shoved against his chest. "It was a joke, asshole!"

Mine.

He ripped her towel away and grabbed her chin, forcing her face to the side, glaring at the line of tiny black hearts stepping down her neck. The explosion inside him didn't cool until he had her bare and exposed, revealing their bonded mark.

Mine.

Now there was a chorus rioting alongside the furious chaos inside him, chanting that infernal word over and over and over.

"Yellow," she whispered.

He didn't lift his hands from her, but he stilled, and so did she.

Red means stop.

But yellow didn't mean red.

She waited, pulling in one breath after another, her skin growing hot beneath his grip.

. . .

ISOBEL RELEASED THE BRIEF SPARK OF FEAR THAT HAD FLARED TO life inside her. Niko was still immobile, still waiting. Fighting something inside his mind. She wasn't sure that he would stop, but now that she knew, she couldn't help the well of hope that rose inside her chest. She had tested him, and he had stopped.

She dragged his hand down from her neck until it was pressing over her frantically beating heart. "Nothing has changed for me," she told him.

He stared at the back of his hand ... and then seemed to realise she was naked. His eyes trailed down over her breasts, her stomach, her legs. His brow furrowed, and his lips twisted into a scowl.

"Yellow isn't red," he said, dragging his hand lower, over her breast, her stomach, following the path his eyes had taken.

He slipped it between her legs, finding her wet. His eyes darkened, a low, rumbling growl vibrating through his torso.

"Stop trying to fucking fix me," he demanded, shoving his fingers inside her without warning.

She yelped, soaking him further, because as much as he had *tried* to take all of the fucked-up darkness of their damaged bond, some of it remained in her. And it was viciously pleased that he was staking a claim, even though he was doing it with a look in his eye that bordered on disgust.

He seemed to have found the nylon loop because she felt the pull of the balls being slowly dragged downward.

Her breath turned ragged, her hands grabbing fistfuls of his jacket. She feared he would pull the thread out with a brutal yank, but his frown was one of extreme concentration.

Group is safe, he mouthed the words, staring at her neck.

She hiccupped on a sob, seeing the broken chaos in his eyes, and he seemed to shake off his trance, his hand freezing.

"Does it hurt?" he demanded.

He thought she was crying from Mikel's toy.

She shook her head, and his frown burrowed deeper. He pulled the thread free, releasing one ball, and then the second, from the fatigued clutches of her body.

He dropped the toy without even glancing at it, two fingers immediately tunnelling back into her.

"You're so swollen," he said, voice like gravel, searching her neck, temper flashing back into his eyes.

"I c-can't," she gasped, clutching his wrist.

"Can't isn't red." He dragged his fingers out before pressing them in again, his thumb brushing over her clit.

She shuddered, a jolt of pleasure making her almost dizzy with relief.

"No, I mean ... I ... really can't," she begged, gripping

his wrist. "Mikel said I'm not allowed to come until tomorrow."

"Do I look like I give a fuck what you or Mikel want?" Niko snarled, pulling his fingers out and dropping to his knees, his tongue laving at her heated flesh.

He groaned, the sound animalistic, his hands gripping her thighs, and the second he looked up at her, hazel eyes burning, she knew she was lost. The tension of Gabriel, and then Mikel, and then Kalen teasing her all night crashed through her body, and trying to stop it was like trying to hold back a sudden release of water. It poured through her hands and washed all over her body, a broken sound torn out of her mouth. The orgasm lasted too long, Niko tasting every moment of it.

He bit her stomach, her rib, the side of her breast, sucking the flesh into his mouth until it throbbed and ached. And then he took her mouth. He kissed her like she was anchoring him to sanity, before dropping to her breasts again. He bit and licked and sucked until her chest was littered with his marks, drawn like a magnet back to her mouth, his kiss rough as he shoved off his jacket. He eased away from her far enough to rip his shirt over his head, and then he was coming back down on her with the full force of his strength, lifting her against the door and pinning her there with his chest and hips as he pulled her legs around his waist and tugged down his zipper.

It didn't even occur to her to stop him, to say the

word that would end what was happening, or even the word that would make him pause. She was well aware that she was about to have her first time against the door in her closet with an Alpha who glared at her with disdain ... and she had never been more desperate for anything in her life.

She *needed* him.

She felt like she would die if he dropped her and left her unclaimed. Something slow and hesitant was trying to build between them, subtle and soft beneath the rough, feral battle between their bodies, something she wasn't even sure he noticed.

This thing between them was awful and messy and *right*.

"Fuck, I *hate* you," he groaned, notching the head of his cock into her entrance.

She licked her lips, her eyes glazing over as he surveyed her face. It was only a moment before he captured her lips again, his hands tightening on her thighs as he eased deeper into her. He rocked there for a moment, that tiny little thread of softness between them flickering in the dark of her consciousness.

His hands flexed on her skin, and she knew she would have bruises there to match the ones on her chest.

"Tell me how you feel, mate." It was a rough demand, full of mistrust and confusion. He didn't seem to realise he had called her *mate*.

"I care about you," she whispered, her breath

catching on a whimper as he seated himself fully inside her.

She was already sore, already swollen, but it was a strange relief to be filled again, to be filled until she was truly *full.* His breaths were choppy, his eyes unfocused. He ducked to taste her lips, the kiss exploratory. "I don't believe you," he whispered back.

He pulled back and shoved into her in a single, brutal stab, vaulting her toward a ledge she wasn't sure she wanted to jump off. There were tears in her eyes, and he pulled out halfway, rocking again, only a few inches back and forth until her tears slipped free and a whine was pulled from her body.

"Tell me the truth," he growled, thrusting deep, fucking her into the door in long, unrelenting strokes until she was clinging to his shoulders, hiding her head in his neck, her throat raw from the sobs she fought to swallow down.

It was too much emotion.

Too much pleasure and fear.

She was staring at it right in the monstrous eyes, acknowledging that she might have lost the Niko she had known and that she ...

"I ..." she whispered, the words failing her.

He released one of her legs, gripping her hair and pulling her back from his neck. He wanted to see her. He knew the words on her tongue, and he wanted to taste them.

She could *feel* his want.

Inside her head.

She could feel him.

He was connected to her again.

His lips hovered over hers, waiting. "Tell me the truth," he ordered, so quiet, his thrusts becoming slow and languorous.

His mind was chaos. Scattered thoughts, sensations, memories. Everything swirling around in an ugly vortex he struggled to stand upright inside of. But he was managing to ignore all of it, his focus on *cherries*. On softness. On the brush of her hair tickling his fingers where he gripped her thigh. On the rippling, squeezing muscles around his dick. On the words he wanted to hear.

Tell me.

This time, he spoke inside her head.

Her reply was easier, this way.

I was falling for y—

His lips crashed down on hers, cutting her off, and his groan was gravel. He lifted her, turning away from the door and ripping several articles of clothing from the nearest rack, tossing them to the ground before he deposited her on top of them. He was inside her again faster than she could reach for him, his fingers teasing her clit as his mouth latched onto her breast. It meant he could only circle the head of his dick inside her, because of their height difference, but he let out a rough, bestial sound against her nipple when she tried to tug him back up her body.

He wrung another orgasm out of her, and when she tried to wiggle away, her flesh overly sensitised, he ducked down to bite her thigh. He sucked her skin roughly, marking her over and over on each of her thighs until she was dripping and desperate for him again, and then he laved her with his tongue until she was on the edge of another release.

He rose, shoving into her, his body shaking.

"Won't last, mate."

Mine.

He repeated the word as he buried himself inside her and growled into her neck, licking over the little heart he had tattooed into her skin as he pulsed and throbbed, releasing into her.

He licked her neck again before rolling to the side so that he wouldn't crush her, his grip tight on her thigh as he hooked it over his hip, refusing to let her pull away.

They were both breathing in soft rasps, sweat misting their skin, his cock still hard and persistent inside her as the aftershocks of her orgasm continued to shiver through her body.

"Something changed." His voice was guttural and strained, misting the skin of her neck. He had turned her so that his mark was still accessible. "I can almost think straight ... like it's there but ... just out of reach."

It was *worse* before?

Her chest squeezed painfully.

"And I can hear you." He pulsed inside her. "I can feel you in my head, separate to all the chaos. Will you stay?"

"I'll stay," she promised quietly, hugging herself tightly against him. "I'm sorry, Niko."

He nuzzled his mark. "I'm sorry, mate."

Her heart melted, but her despair only swelled, because she could feel his darkness closing in again, whipping about his mind now that he wasn't so focussed on fucking her. He gently pulled out of her and rolled up to a sitting position before bundling her into his arms and carrying her to the shower.

She winced as the maelstrom inside his head swirled faster and faster.

"Out," he demanded, seeing her face as he set her onto the bench in the shower. "Don't stay. Get out." He shoved at her presence in his mind, constructing a clumsy wall to ward her off, and she was glad that he had cut her off in that moment, so that he couldn't feel how much she hurt for him.

"Part of the group," he said, some of the focus leaking from his eyes. "Red is stop."

He kicked off his jeans and turned on the shower, growing silent as he washed her with so much care and meticulous attention she could have been made of glass. She didn't dare push his hands away or offer to do it herself, but she monitored him, searching his eyes for any sign of the hatred he had possessed earlier.

It was gone, but somehow ... this was worse.

Without the fire, it was so clear that Niko was *broken.*

He dried himself and tugged his pants back on before he towel-dried her just as softly and carefully as he had washed her. He wrapped her into a fresh towel, carried her back to the dressing room, and sat her in the same chair as earlier, backing away with his hands raised like he was putting everything back exactly the way he had found it.

Pretending it never happened.

His distraction and confusion increased as he gathered his things, putting on his shirt, his jacket, and his shoes. He looped his gym bag over his shoulder and shifted from foot to foot as he stared at her.

"It didn't fix me," he said, staring at her forearms before his eyes crawled back up to hers. "As much as I would love to, I can't be fucking you every hour of the fucking day. I need ..."

"We'll fix it," she promised. "I promise, Niko."

He sucked in a heavy breath, licking his lips. "We'll see," he allowed, like he didn't believe her.

He opened the door, the distance between them already growing, but there was light between them again. A connection that *lived*. His wall slipped, just for a moment, his urge to stay with her warring with the persistent thought that he *didn't deserve it.*

She opened her mouth to ask him to stay, but he spoke before she could.

"You're safe?"

"Yes—"

"You're hurt?"

"No, Niko—"

He nodded and disappeared in a blink, slamming the door behind him.

17
A COLLAR FOR EVERY OCCASION

Isobel surveyed the chaos of her dressing room, slowly bringing her inner turmoil under control before she began to clean. She was tucked into bed by the time the rest of the group returned home. They used the group chat to check back in with each other, revealing that they had been split up, searching different areas, and that nobody had found anything.

The disappointment and fear she felt was muted, her body and mind exhausted.

She still didn't know who had knocked on her door, but she had a feeling they were discussing her in a separate group, because Kilian messaged to check that she was okay and to ask if she needed anything, and when she replied that she was fine and just wanted to sleep, the others left her suspiciously alone.

She had also received a few messages from her father—the first since she had been taken to the hospital.

Call me.

We need to talk.

It's important.

Go to the family centre, where it's private.

She ignored the messages and turned off her notifications, placing her phone face down.

Her body was relaxed, muscles aching in the best way, her core feeling battered and bruised, her arms tender from the ropes Kalen had used—and she *loved* it. But her mind wasn't so settled.

Her thoughts were so twisted up that she didn't even jump when her mother appeared beside her bed. She only grew still, maintaining eye contact with the older woman like she was scared the apparition would disappear if she glanced away.

She stayed still. She didn't speak. She waited.

For Crowe. For anyone. For wraiths and demons and ghosts.

But it was just her mother. Dressed in silk and a soft smile.

Isobel released a tense breath, getting up to pull the canopy around her bed. She grabbed her dorm tablet and turned on the white noise, glancing up as it spilled from the speakers above, a soft wash of noise that dispersed the sound of her rustling sheets as she turned to her side and settled her eyes onto the apparition again.

"Please don't go," she whispered, barely giving sound to the words.

"I'm here." Caran Carter knelt by her bed, a hand hovering over Isobel's cheek. There was no heat, no pressure. Nothing. "You're doing so well, Illy."

"Why did you stop coming?" Isobel asked quietly.

"There are forbidden topics," her mother replied. "To protect our souls. You can't ask about what happened to me."

"Okay." Isobel breathed, her chest constricting. She grappled with the question that had been playing on her mind since the year before. "Why didn't you visit me after you dropped me off? Why wouldn't you reply to my messages? It's like you forgot I existed at all."

"It is," Caran agreed, smiling sadly. There was a vacant look in her eyes. Something detached. It was as though she was there but not really *listening*.

"Are there other forbidden topics?" Isobel asked, and her mother's attention sharpened again, a spark of approval in that honey-brown gaze.

"If the living who can see us seek to upset or hurt us, we will not be permitted to stay."

Her mother had disassociated from the question Isobel had asked, so it was likely an upsetting one. Isobel chewed on the inside of her cheek.

"Can you see me all the time?"

"I'm not like this all the time." Caran spread out her

arms, glancing down at the silk dressing gown she wore. "Sometimes I'm just light, just floating."

"Where do you ... live? Where are you when you're not here?"

"The river of souls," Caran answered happily. "That's where we float. But sometimes I feel that you're scared, and I climb out, and when I do, I can see you. I've visited your father a few times. You're the only one who can see me."

Isobel struggled to word her next question, not wanting to drive her mother away. "He wasn't your true mate, was he?"

Caran smiled sadly. "He wasn't, was he?"

"What ... what was your real mate like?"

Caran wavered, her eyes flashing. "He had a demon," she said, her voice cracking. "Just like your—"

And she was gone, just like that. Like the flame of a candle extinguished by a powerful, icy breath.

Isobel pulled the duvet up to her mouth, muffling a frustrated sound before flopping onto her back to stare at the top of her canopy.

Just like her ... what?

She frowned, recalling Luis mentioning demons as well.

Just like ... her mates?

Snatching her phone up again, she sent a message to Sophia.

Isobel: Got your phone back?

The response came after a few minutes.

Sophia: Sure do! And before you ask, the answer is no. I will not help you kill yourself. You made your very wide bed and now you have to sleep with everyone inside it.

Isobel: Hilarious.

Sophia: Right?

Isobel: Have the officials left you guys alone?

Sophia: They dismissed us quicker than you dismissed the concept of a traditional nuclear household.

Isobel: Wow. You're on a roll.

Isobel: Heading downhill, by the way.

Sophia: I'll let you know when I hit bottom.

Sophia: Or will you already know, since your poor vagina is already there?

Isobel: I actually texted you for a reason.

Sophia: You need an ice pack?

Isobel snorted, a laugh breaking out before she shook her head, texting back.

Isobel: I might. But what was Luis talking about yesterday? He said something about demons.

Sophia: Ugh, you heard that. He says Moses and Theodore Kane have demons. He says, "Kane and his demon." He's been saying it for so long, I thought he was calling Moses the demon.

Sophia: He wasn't trying to insult them.

Sophia: Theodore seems nice.

Sophia: I'm sure Moses could be nice if he wanted to. Or if he wasn't Moses.

Isobel frowned at the screen, her mind turning over.

Could it be a coincidence?

Her father had owned a book on ferality. It was how she knew the signs when she first came across Theodore in the library.

Could it be possible ...

Could her mother's true mate have had ferality? And if Theodore and Moses both had it ...

Did that mean it passed to all siblings?

THE NEXT MORNING, COOPER ATTEMPTED TO CORNER HER ON the way out of the dorm, but Kilian intervened.

"Your father is insisting you contact him!" Cooper called after her as Kilian ushered her to the door, making excuses about how they were late for practice.

He joined in her dance practice in the morning with Gabriel and Elijah, his skills almost matching the other two Alphas. She was impressed and slightly star struck when she watched him, happy when he said he would join them again in the afternoon.

Kalen announced that her sixth period with him was being replaced by another group intensive with both him and Mikel, and she realised they were moving forward with their plan. That intensive would be filmed every week, showcasing the slow forming of their group.

During the first session, they sat around in a circle as

Mikel and Kalen explained their first "task." A challenge for each of them to perform the same set of lyrics to one of eight varied backing tracks.

Mikel piled coloured balls—each representing a different backing track—into the middle of the circle, and Isobel grumbled something about his obsession with balls that earned her a terrifying look from the scarred Alpha.

That look told her everything she needed to know.

He knew everything.

He knew she hadn't obeyed him. She hadn't obeyed him *hard*. Several times.

She decided to ignore him and pretend she didn't know that he knew. She sat back with Kilian, sharing an eye roll with the calm Alpha as the rest of them dove forward and wrestled for their favourite coloured ball.

Niko wasn't snapping and snarling like he had been the day before, but he also wasn't speaking much. He was withdrawn, his frown lines etched deep, his eyes sometimes soft when he looked at her, and sometimes hard.

But he was *always* looking at her.

When she tried to speak to him, he grunted in answer and walked away, planting himself somewhere else to stare at her from a distance. If she couldn't feel the hints and brushes of his inner chaos at all times, she would have been insulted. Instead, she just yearned to hug him.

Since he looked like he might stab anyone who came at him with open arms, she grabbed a tennis ball from his bag and shoved it into his hand. Moses thought it was hilarious, but Niko didn't react at all, other than to squeeze the ball like it was Isobel's neck.

For four days, that was how they proceeded. With a very deliberate, curated, light-hearted air. They trained hard, at all hours of the day, and they stuck together in the classes they shared, at mealtimes, and during their practices. She trained with Elijah, Gabriel, and Kilian in the mornings and evenings, while Theodore, Cian, and Niko preferred to train in the gym. Moses and Oscar—to her surprise—were spending most of their practice time in one of the studios, producing possible demo tracks for the group.

She looked out for Eve during mealtimes in the dining hall, but the Omega seemed to have disappeared completely. It should have eased Isobel's fear, but it only increased it.

On Friday morning, half of the Alphas were missing from their group intensive with Mikel. It was just her, Oscar, Elijah, and Gabriel. When Kalen walked in twenty minutes after the session was supposed to start, with all the missing Alphas behind him, Isobel knew something was wrong. They were shielding their emotions from her, but the hairs along her arms raised, and an uneasy feeling churned in the pit of her stomach. As soon as the door closed behind him, Kalen pointed to the stretching mats.

"Everyone gather up."

They fell about in a circle, faces tense, Mikel and Kalen closing the circle and sitting down. The professors were still in workout clothes.

Usually, they were showered and suited before everyone else, making use of the gym and other facilities before the students were awake.

"The Track Team has made their move on the rest of Dorm A," Kalen announced, a look of distaste pinching his features. "Cian received pictures of his brother, Logan, this morning. Pictures of him walking alone, playing with his friends, and sleeping. There was also a handwritten list of prices and codewords. We think it's a trafficking ... menu. The threat was clear."

Isobel swallowed, her eyes running over Cian, whose expression was pale. He was shielding himself from her Sigma ability, and she was shielding her mind from the bond, but she didn't need to read his mind to know how he was feeling—it was there in his face.

He was torn between murderous rage and stone-cold fear.

"Kilian received a video," Kalen continued, "of someone loading powder into a pill press machine. They tipped the powder out of a hazard-labelled container with *As* on the side, the abbreviation for arsenic. They coated the pills and then emptied another pill container, replacing the contents with the arsenic pills they had created, which had been made to look the same. The label on the pill bottle they used was for Kilian's adoptive mother, Sao-Yeong. Kilian sends home money every month so that she can afford medication for her advanced osteoporosis—it costs three times as much to have it sent into the settlement."

Kilian looked violently angry—an expression she wasn't used to, from him. Her heart was lodged in her throat, but before she could ask any questions, Kalen was speaking again.

"Niko got an email from his dad saying that the officials have doubled the rent he has to pay at their health clinic in the Rock River Valley settlement. A lot of people rely on that clinic, and since Taichi isn't allowed to charge for his services—because he isn't a registered doctor—Niko's Ironside stipend and some of our Stone Dahlia income is the only thing keeping them afloat. They used to scrape by when people had enough to trade food and other services for treatment, but since the commissary prices went up last year, people haven't had anything to offer the Harts."

Niko was staring at the mat, his jaw twitching, his eyes dark. Isobel hesitantly cracked her wall, reaching out to latch onto the emotion they were all shielding from her. She tried to be subtle, but Mikel felt it, his mottled blue-black eyes cutting to her in a warning look. She closed herself off from the toxic flow of emotion, sitting with the new darkness bubbling inside her stomach.

She gave him a brief, defiant look, but when he raised a brow at her, her eyes dropped quickly back to her knees.

"Theo and Moses got the same email …" Kalen stalled, considering his words, the first sign of unease rippling over his broad, impassive face. "It was a room with a line of threaded necklaces hanging on a stone wall—the same type of stone they have in the Stone Dahlia. The Track Team aren't just baiting them into the club—they're baiting them into a specific room. This isn't something we've encountered before, and we don't know what to make of them using you as their collateral." He settled his attention on Isobel. "Any way we look at it, it doesn't look good."

She nodded, and the others grumbled sounds of agreement.

Elijah sucked in a fortifying breath. "Gabriel and I are fully fledged members, and floaters, now. We can split up sponsorship of everyone."

"You may not be able to claim Moses and Theo," Mikel warned. "Not if they're hoping to assign them to a particular room."

"I guess we'll find out tonight," Moses drawled.

"They didn't actually poison your stepmom, did they?" Isobel asked Kilian.

He shook his head. "No, she's fine. She'd already be

dead if she had taken one of those pills. Kalen has people looking into testing her pills, though."

"What if they haven't given her the pills yet?" she asked nervously.

"She can test them herself," Gabriel murmured thoughtfully. "If she grinds down one of her pills, separates a small amount into a dish, and adds a few drops of white vinegar, the presence of a carbonate compound in arsenic will react with the acid in the vinegar. It's not foolproof, but the powder should bubble and fizz if it's dangerous."

Kalen was already texting Gabriel's words to someone.

"Thanks." Kilian gave Gabriel a tight smile, gratitude and relief colouring his ethereal features.

"How do you even know that?" Moses asked Gabriel, looking surprised.

"Because I read?" Gabriel shot back, rolling his eyes.

"Yeah, I read too," Moses grumbled, looking put-out.

"And your brother?" Isobel asked Cian.

"Just a threat," he sighed out. "But they're more than capable of following through on all of these threats. They own us, and they didn't even have to try very hard to prove it."

"But they don't know about the bond," Elijah said. "That's something we can hang onto. If they did, they wouldn't have bothered going to all the effort of threatening everyone individually. We already remotely disabled the failsafe Eve Indie had set up on her phone to trigger an email about our bond to the officials if anything 'happened to her', but we won't make any more moves against her until we can be sure that's the only failsafe she had."

"The officials don't know *for now*," Mikel corrected. "We need to stay obsessively on top of things to keep it that way. I don't like that they know that threatening Isobel is enough to bring in Theo and Moses."

"I have a bad feeling," Theodore admitted.

Moses nodded his agreement, and Isobel tried to shake off the awful feeling of expectation and premonition settling over her shoulders.

"Right." Kalen nodded at everyone. "I need to reach out to my settlement contacts to get eyes on Cian, Kilian, and Niko's families. Keep your heads down today. I'll see everyone tonight." He paused after pushing to his feet, his eyes finding Isobel. "We may have additional spectators. Oscar and Mikel's fights happen later than my show, and floaters are allowed to visit the rooms as spectators. If you don't want the group to watch tonight, you should say so now."

Isobel glanced around the room, but nobody seemed surprised by Kalen's announcement.

They wanted to watch her?

She felt a little spark of pleasure, accompanied by a wash of nerves.

"I don't mind," she said.

Kalen surveyed her a moment more, before sucking a hiss of air between bared teeth. The expression was … expectant. He shot Mikel a quick glare.

"No punishments before the session. The smell drove me fucking insane."

Mikel chuckled, and Kalen yanked the door open, leaving the room.

The rest of them fell into their usual routine for Mikel's morning sessions, dividing up into two groups to start warming up. Mikel drove them doubly as hard, foregoing everything but the physical aspect of their training, making up for losing the first half of his session. Isobel was dripping in sweat by the time they finished, and she was forced to stop by the dorm to change before first period.

During the week, there had been a subtle battle for dominance between the human group and the Alpha group. On one hand, the humans were popular with the rest of the students, most of whom already thought of them as celebrities and had already been following them on social media—or were at least aware of them. On the other hand, the Alphas were terrifying and had only grown more so.

They were bigger than last year, and Cian and Kilian had retreated from their sociable personalities. The incident with Eve and Aron, and what the officials had done to Kilian, seemed to have changed him. He had withdrawn into himself, his smiles to anyone outside the group growing cooler, harder. He now looked entirely unapproachable with his small frowns and guarded, pale eyes.

Cian had simply stopped flirting with everyone, though videos were circulating of him speaking to Isobel, where his aquamarine eyes smouldered and he licked his ruby lips, those delectable dimples furrowing as he grinned at her. The new tattoos that crawled up his neck, his new piercings, and his suddenly closed-off personality had shifted the public discourse about him from the man whore of Ironside to some sort of scary, unattainable trophy.

The Alphas had claimed the right wing of the auditorium for Icon Matters, and for their fifth-period class, Influencer Intensive, which was in the same auditorium. They were the only two classes that brought together all of the Alphas and all of the humans, so naturally, most of the talk online was gossip generated inside that auditorium. Since the new season of the *Ironside Show* wouldn't premiere until Friday night, all the public had to go on were the chat rooms and the photos all the students had been uploading.

The public was obsessed with the third-year group, the Alphas, and the humans ... but the officials had the power to turn the tide and set the tone in their premiere, so all of that could change.

Their only option to keep the momentum going for

Eleven was to create enough drama that the officials had no choice but to air it.

"Hey, Mei," Cian called out as the humans settled into their seats in the front row of the middle section. "I heard you did an episode on your podcast about educational inadequacies in lower socio-economic areas."

"I did," Mei exclaimed, sitting up in her seat, her entire face lighting up. She flicked Niko a quick look—she did that often, confused about the change in him and how he had cut her out of his acquaintance in the blink of an eye without explanation. Niko ignored her, uninterested. "Did you—"

"Maybe you shouldn't be sitting in the front row, then," Cian cut across her. "Since some of the people behind you came from the remote Gifted settlements and have pre-secondary literacy skills at best. It's hard enough to read that screen without trying to see it over all your blowouts. Nice cut, by the way. I heard you go down to the glow-up bar every morning. Expensive, but worth it." Cian winked at her, and it was somehow both smug and cold all at once.

Mei stared at him, her mouth dropping open, her face flaming red as she dropped back into her seat, now visibly uncomfortable. Some of the students behind her were snickering, some peering over at Cian like he was offering to be their new Gifted spokesperson. He turned away from them, leaning over Isobel to speak to Theodore.

In fifth period, the humans had relocated to the second row, and most of the class whipped out their phones to snap pictures of the change, as though a war had been declared and the Alphas were claiming their first victory.

During lunch, the humans chose to sit by themselves instead of pushing several tables together to chat with their fans as a group. They had their heads bent together and seemed to be furiously discussing something, a few of them gesturing angrily at the Alpha booth. Just before lunch finished, Kahn and Kostas walked over to the booth arm in arm, Kostas flicking her long blonde hair over her shoulder. She walked like the model she was, and Isobel had absolutely no idea how a chocolate sculptor was supposed to walk, but Kahn matched her friend well, the two women a striking pair.

"We just wanted to formally introduce ourselves." Kostas preened, batting her lashes at Theodore, who sat on the outside of the booth.

"Great to meet you." Moses didn't even look up from his phone. "See you later."

Cian rolled his eyes at Moses. Nobody else spoke.

The Alphas just stared—except for Moses, and Niko, who was pushing his food around on his plate with a frown, as he did every mealtime.

Kahn eased back a step and Kostas paled. Neither of them seemed to know where to look.

"Ah, hello," Isobel quickly spoke up. "Nice to meet you."

This time, it was the girls' turn to stare. They appeared uncomfortable.

Because they hadn't come to meet her, Isobel realised.

She slumped back down.

I tried, she spoke through the bond.

Commendable effort, Elijah returned dryly, before speaking aloud, his attention drifting between their two visitors. "Is that all?"

"We were hoping to collaborate," Kahn squeaked with renewed enthusiasm.

"We aren't available for collaboration," Gabriel said calmly.

"You're collaborating with the Sigma!" Kahn declared, pointing at Isobel. "We all know the whole 'Alphas and the Sigma' thing is a bit—we're just saying, we think you could reach a wider audience if you work with us, instead."

Oscar stood, and both girls scrambled backwards.

"S-stop being rude," Kostas admonished her friend, dragging her back by the arm. She avoided looking at Oscar. "Um ... think about it? Nice to meet you all."

"Move," Oscar grunted. "I lost my appetite."

Their group spilled from the booth without a word, but Isobel grabbed a protein bar on the way out, slipping it into Niko's hand. He flipped his grip, snatching her wrist in the blink of an eye, his pupils dilated.

It was like he thought she had been about to attack him.

His eyes returned to normal, surveying the protein bar now on the ground, and his hand, still gripping her wrist tightly. He lifted it off, finger by finger, his voice an echo in her mind.

Sorry, mate.

Her stomach flipped.

Niko picked up the protein bar and tried to hand it back to her, but she shook her head. "Eat something," she suggested.

He nodded absently, slipping the bar into his pocket, and decidedly *not* eating anything. He gestured for her to keep walking, and when she did, he fell back, following several steps behind her. She could feel his eyes boring into the back of her neck.

They all separated as soon as they got to the studio Kalen and Mikel were running their group intensive out of, squirrelling away in their own corners to pour over the lyrics they had been given and the track they had been assigned. Isobel's was a dragging, haunting instrumental—a little slower than she would have picked for the lyrics, but since Mikel had said they could sing in their own style, she assumed that meant she could manipulate the lyrics a little. She considered what she would do with the song for the rest of the day, but finally put it out of her head when it was time to head to the Stone Dahlia.

This time, they walked there as a group, but the woman in the foyer ushered her, Kalen, Mikel, and Oscar down the stairs instead of allowing them to wait with the rest of the Alphas.

Elijah and Gabriel were permitted to stay.

Kalen claimed a booth in the hall for them to wait in, waving off the waiter who shimmied out of the crowd and approached, half of his enthusiastic greeting stalling as he realised he wasn't needed. Isobel twisted her fingers together nervously, glancing back to the door they had entered through every few minutes.

"There's a lot of paperwork to sign," Mikel said calmly, crossing one of his ankles over his knee and running his scarred hands down over his vest.

Oscar, who had claimed her other side, slipped his hand onto her thigh, squeezing firmly. "You'll be floating soon, rabbit. Don't worry about the others."

"Floating?" she asked, ignoring the tingle that shot through her body. "Am I going in the air this time?" She looked from Oscar to Kalen.

Kalen was drumming his fingers on the table impatiently, but he stopped at her question, regarding her with a measured look. "He didn't mean that kind of floating."

She blinked, whipping her head back to Oscar. *He*

knew about the floating feeling? "Have you been tied up too?"

Oscar laughed, the sound husky, as though he didn't do it often enough. And he really didn't, because he was *beautiful* when he laughed, those dark curls tickling his neck as he tilted his head back, his sharp incisors flashing.

Even Kalen chuckled.

"No," Oscar finally said, his hand slipping further up her thigh. "I don't have that kind of patience."

Oscar was calmer than she had ever seen him, a kind of anticipatory focus simmering in his dark eyes. It was likely the promise of immediate violence in his future. He had been sneaking off to the Stone Dahlia more often than not since their bond was formed, and he usually returned to the dorm with several fresh bruises or cuts. On Wednesday, he came back so late that she caught him as she slipped out of her room in the morning. There had been a limp in his step, his teeth bloody as he flashed her an almost manic grin before disappearing into his room. Mikel also seemed to be indulging in violence within the Stone Dahlia with an alarming regularity, though he returned with fewer injuries.

Isobel's response died before she could even begin to formulate it. Her attention snagged by a familiar figure flashing in her periphery across the busy hall. She narrowed in on the brunette, her breath catching at the two patches covering Eve's eyes. She was being led by a chain around her neck.

Isobel couldn't breathe, her head pinging in panic and alarm, even as her chest constricted ... because what she was seeing wasn't right.

Eve had a golden collar locked around her thin neck, a slender gold chain attached to the collar. A man in a black face mask was *leading* her, walking ahead, uncaring of how Eve stumbled and hurried to stick close to his back. Isobel jerked to her feet, but Oscar tugged her back down again.

"She tried her best to kill you," he snarled, his dark eyes snagging on the Omega. "Don't fucking feel sorry for her."

"They're treating her like a *dog*," Isobel hissed back.

"I'm failing to see the problem." Oscar turned away from Eve, dismissing her. "She made her choices. She was warned."

"Nobody makes *choices* down here though, do they?" Isobel couldn't tear her attention away. Not from the collar, or the chain ... or the patches.

Her throat felt tight, her eyes hot.

"You're just as stuck down here as she is," Mikel warned, gazing across the hall as Eve was tugged into a passageway, out of sight. "I wouldn't feel too sorry for her. She was the one who made sure you were brought in. She's the one who collected your collateral. She's the one who threatened you into compliance. Whatever happens to her down here—just remember she's the reason it might happen to you too."

18

Mate Bonds and Big Wands

Isobel paced back and forth from the lockers in Kalen's dressing room to the small kitchenette and back again. It was a strange dressing room, now that she thought about it. There was also no remnant of Kalen in there, other than the book on his armchair. She was sure none of the furniture had been chosen by him. It was a stark contrast to the performance room, which he seemed to have curated entirely, from the lighting to the wooden suspension structure, and the collection of props.

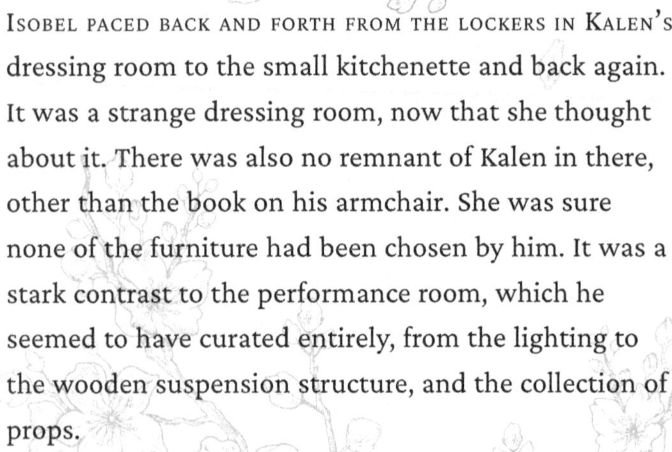

His dressing room seemed like a much more transitory space, less personal.

She glanced at her phone—*still nothing*—before tossing it onto the small benchtop beside the kitchenette sink.

Kalen was tense, checking the time. "We need to go

in—" He cut himself off, still staring at his phone. "They messaged."

She almost tripped over herself diving for her phone, and her heart was pounding as she clicked into the group message.

Elijah: All clear. I'll be sponsoring Moses and Cian. Gabe has Kilian, Theo, and Niko. They didn't even try to keep Theo and Moses together.

"Thank fuck for that," Kalen groaned, slipping his phone back into his pocket. "Time to go in, Sigma."

He strode toward her, stopping a few inches away, close enough that she could feel the heat from his body, despite the three-piece designer suit he wore. If she didn't know any better, she would think he belonged in the club with the rest of the billionaires. But Kalen only had four suits. He cycled through three of them during the week, saving the last one for his appearances at the Stone Dahlia. He was wearing that one on Monday night, and he was wearing it again now.

His jacket, vest, and pants were the same deep, rich burgundy colour, with a matching burgundy silk pocket square. The ensemble contrasted with his crisp white shirt and vintage-patterned tie, fitting him so perfectly it must have been tailored. He was wearing the same black leather oxfords he usually wore, but they were impeccably kept, polished to a sheen. The suit was slim fitting, the lapels a narrow, severe cut, the fabric stretching deliciously over his big frame.

It had been four days since he had last touched her, and he eyed her like he wasn't sure if it was a good idea to start again. Finally, he lifted a finger to trace the edge of her fluttery silk sleeve.

"What's under this?" he asked.

"A playsuit."

He arched a brow. "Show me."

She reached for the zipper at her spine, tugging it down and letting the dress fall to her heels—black, like the dress. Her playsuit was a plain grey, ribbed cotton, but it wasn't thick. It was designed to be worn by fitness models on social media—not to be truly lived in.

"I thought the cotton would feel nice with the ropes," she said as he shoved his hands into his pockets, rocking back on his heels, yellow-gold eyes dropping to her thighs.

"Nothing to do with the bruises Niko gave you?"

She flushed, smoothing her hands down over her hips. The playsuit *did* cover much more than her satin bodysuit had. The shorts were very short, only just covering her ass, and the sleeves were only thin straps. Still ... Kalen was right. She had been trying to find something that covered some of the fading marks Niko had left on her body.

"Shoes off," Kalen ordered before she could answer—or question how he even knew about the bruises in the first place.

She quickly bent to dispose of the heels, and he held

out his hand for her. “Anything you’d like to do differently?”

“Can you stay in my head?” she asked hesitantly. “It helps to relax me.”

He rumbled out a sound that seemed like an affirmative as she placed her hand in his. His palm was rough and hot, his grip engulfing her pale fingers.

“Anything else?” he asked, not yet moving to the door.

“What’s your favourite thing to do?” she asked.

His sharp grin appeared again, brief and vicious. “Nothing I can do in there.”

“Then …” She felt her breath shudder, her gaze falling to his hand. “I just want to float again. I don’t want to think about anyone else or anything else for a while.”

He nodded, his eyes softening. “My rules are the same, but especially tonight. I want your attention on me at all times.”

He led the way into the performance room, bringing her to the centre of the small, raised platform. She could have sworn she heard a few hushed whispers like the crowd was excited for something. She didn’t dare look, but she could feel more eyes on her than the last time. She even felt like she could hear their breathing.

Kalen moved to his prop area, selecting a song and filling the room with music, which had a subtle, relieved breath slipping from her lips. It wasn’t a soft instrumental track this time, but something a little more modern, with a subtly seductive tone and a slightly eerie melody.

The low, drawled voice of the singer managed to electrify the air in the room, creating a space full of tension. Kalen returned with the small table slung under one arm, several different colours and lengths of rope and some sort of material hooked over his other arm. He set the table where he wanted it, laying the rope down before flicking the material over the top of the table. It looked thin and rubbery, with some sort of silky coating.

He picked her up beneath the arms and sat her on the edge of the table, the material absorbing her weight slightly, making the table far more comfortable than it would have been otherwise.

He lifted her again, readjusting her to sit further back on the table, and then he picked up one of her legs, notching it against the edge of the table, his fingers a rough scrape against her sensitised skin. She felt like her nerves were on fire, and it was making her jumpy. She jolted when his touch drifted down the arch of her foot, and the shadow of a smile briefly crossed his face. He picked up a black rope and a pale lilac rope, forming a cuff around her ankle before laddering the rope up her shin half a handspan at a time, bridging each span with a pretty twist along her calf. When he reached her knee, he left the ropes hanging and switched to her other leg, repeating the same pattern, both of her legs now notched up against the edge of the table.

It was almost hypnotic to watch him work, the patterns furling over her skin in a way that would please even Gabriel's pedantic brain. When her legs were patterned, he grabbed her beneath her knees and dragged her to the edge of the table again, and then he gripped her hips and lifted her.

Knees, he spoke inside her head, making her jolt again.

She tucked her legs beneath her, kneeling, but he didn't guide her hips back down, so she remained kneeling upright, grateful for the mat covering the table. He picked up another pair of black and pale lilac ropes, twisting them around her spine and sawing them gently down her back until they rested just over her ass, and then he began to create some sort of harness for her hips.

He walked behind her, cinching the ropes into the crease of her ass as it met her thigh before tying a knot and feeding the ropes back through her legs. He returned to her front, pulling the ropes up and crossing them over her pelvis before looping his arms around her and leaning forward to look over her shoulder as he tied the ropes off behind her. The knot he had created between her legs was positioned perfectly, so that when he tugged, it brushed up against her core, making her body shiver.

He pulled in a deep, rough breath, as though he could smell how damp she was getting from the rubbing of that knot. He eased back, his hands brushing down over her hips, down to the taut, cotton-covered flesh of her ass, each cheek now circled perfectly by rope, some sort of pattern created at the lowest point of her spine. He didn't exactly grip her, but his hands were so big, it had a similar effect.

She felt the tension in her body ratchet up a notch, desperation for him to *grip* and *squeeze* making her frustrated. He began to slip into her mind, dismantling her wall while she was distracted by the placement of his hands. He didn't twist her hair out of the way, this time, but shifted and gathered it from one shoulder to the other as he worked, always dragging his fingertips across her scalp.

As he bound her chest and slowly brought her under his spell, he settled himself fully inside her mind. She knew he was there, but she was too preoccupied to push him out or attempt to salvage her mental barriers, which she might have done, even though she had specifically asked him to be there. It was just a knee-jerk reaction. She could feel his need to be there, despite how he had managed to separate *his* emotions from *her*, creating a one-way link.

He wanted to know how comfortable she was.

Where the ropes were too tight.

Where they rubbed and where they slackened.

He routinely shifted the rope between her legs, brushing against the growing damp spot, making it seem casual or accidental, though he observed her inner emotions just as carefully as her outer reactions. He liked when she shivered, because he quickly figured out how to make her do that, and then he did it often.

He brushed her nipples with innocuous touches, using every pass or twist of the rope across her chest to scrape her flesh until the little buds were standing on end and poking through the cotton of her playsuit, and a permanent tremble had taken up residence in her limbs. His eyes were a dark, smoky gold when he surveyed his completed chest harness, a flash of something else peeking out in his expression, disappearing before she could make sense of it.

Pain?

He was staring at her nipples, his thumbs brushing along the undersides of her breasts as he gripped her ribcage. He looped his fingers into the harness, using it to pull her forward, forcing her to knee-walk toward him with small movements, until she was at the edge of the table again. He pulled her arms out before her and looped rope into the side of her chest harness to crisscross in a wide, diamond pattern down to her elbows, where it became a thick and intricate bind, sticking her arms together and tying off at the wrist. The ends left a long lead that he looped into a black carabiner hanging above them, creating a pulley system with his ropes. He slowly put pressure on the loose end of the rope, drawing her bound arms up above her head before fixing them there.

The carabiner was attached to a wooden post above them, allowing him to reach up to the rope that secured it to the post and yank it further along, away from him. This immediately pulled the top half of Isobel's body backward, but before she could attempt to adjust to the new position, he had grabbed her hips and spun her around. He pushed her knees wide, and it took every ounce of her core strength to not wobble or swing to the side as he stepped away. She could hear the crowd gasping, even over the music, like they were doing something impressive.

Maybe they were. She had no idea.

Kalen stayed out of her sight, but she could feel the pull of the rope he had tied off beneath her left knee. His hands brushed down her calf, the rope weaving in and out of the pattern he had created earlier before he wrapped her foot in his grip and bent her leg back until her heel was below her ass, threatening to upset her balance further. He secured her leg in that position, attaching the rope to her hip harness before repeating the process with her other leg.

Suddenly, she was only balancing on the points of her knees, her body arched forward, her arms suspended above her. He ran his hand down the centre of her spine, weaving ropes into the back of her chest and hip harness. He didn't warn her before he lifted her, and the sudden pressure around her body as it slowly raised into the air was disorientating. He didn't raise her far, but far enough to slip the table out from beneath her. The seconds he left her on the stage alone while he returned the table to his prop area were starkly terrifying compared to the immense relief she felt when he returned and gently swung her side to side. He adjusted the height of her suspension and shifted some of his ropes, his touches soothing and explorative.

She wasn't sure when she drifted into that floating space that had her head lolling to the side and her every remaining thought narrowed to the subtle pressure of Kalen's fingers, but just like the last time, she was jolted out of it by applause.

Kalen had finished with her. She had no idea how long it had taken.

He untied one of her legs, helping her to set her foot on the ground. She balanced there on tiptoes until he released her hips, and then the other leg, and then her chest, and her arms. She was barely aware of how she stood or whether he had held her up the entire time, but then she was in his arms, and he was carrying her back to the dressing room. He took her to the sofa, sitting her in his lap as another door opened.

Mates, she thought sleepily, their scents creating a heady perfume as she sagged against Kalen's chest, her head falling into his neck. For some reason, they didn't speak, but she could feel them all draw closer, settling around the room.

Kalen had left most of the ropes still attached to her,

except the arm wraps, and he went to work on removing them quietly, starting with her chest harness. He brushed her nipples again, absently this time, almost like he had done it by habit. She shivered, a husky sound catching in her throat, and he continued like he didn't notice, though his unravelling lost its soothing motion, growing a shaky, jerky edge.

The energy between them seemed to change as soon as they passed back into the private room. It was less restrained, heavier and hotter—but still a controlled burn. She wondered what it would feel like if he tied her up in the same position in private, without the crowd of strangers. She didn't realise it earlier, but picturing it now, he could have easily stepped between her bent and bound and parted legs. She had spotted a large pair of scissors in his prop area—likely for safety, if someone needed to be freed quickly from their restraints—but those scissors also could have fit into the seam of her playsuit ...

A growl built up in his chest *and* inside her mind.

I'm still here, Carter, he chastised through the bond.

It was hard to remember that Kalen was out of bounds when he had just spent so long stamping ownership all over her body with the twist of his rope and the possessive grip of his hands, and the floaty feeling in her head wasn't helping.

She snuggled in deeper against his chest as he managed to rip off the rope tangled about her hips without hurting her or upsetting her position. He unwound the ties from her legs and then immediately started massaging them.

"She okay?" Moses asked quietly.

"Her legs itch after," Kalen grunted. "She's fine. Isobel, stop it."

She stilled at the command in his tone, wondering what she had done wrong. She had been brushing her nose against his throat, hadn't she? Had she licked him? She couldn't remember.

"You're so mean." She pouted against his skin.

"I know," he soothed, brushing his hands up and down her spine gently.

She melted further into him, closing her eyes as her body grew heavy. Whatever this feeling was, she wanted it to last forever. It was like she had just danced for hours on end, her body spent, her skin tight with fatigue, but her mind was floating, softly coming back to reality one deep, vanilla-filled breath at a time.

Her reality wasn't a living nightmare; it was happier than she could have hoped it would be and many people had it much worse, but it was still nice to forget for an hour or two. To release all the worries and expectations and pressures of her life at Ironside. She never really just *stopped* and enjoyed herself, so she was grateful Kalen was giving her the experience.

Thank you, she said, through the bond. *It's really special, what you do.* She could easily understand why all these rich and important people wanted to come and watch his show. He made something incredibly complex and difficult look as easy as breathing. As soon as he led her onto that stage, she was exposed and vulnerable, like a stripped-bare doll, and then he slowly covered her, slowly raised her, slowly sculpted her into a beautiful bird in flight without ever truly covering her up. It was a process of exposing and shielding, of stark exploitation and careful protection.

It was a stunning metaphor for Kalen's presence in the club. They had tried to misuse and abuse him, dragging him in as an Alpha commodity that they knew people would want to see in a sexual light—because he was a *beautiful* man. He had taken their use of him and flipped it onto its head, making his entire act about *control*, about *power*. He gave it all back to himself and offered to make the humans in his crowd powerless in return.

Except now ... she had replaced his usual targets.

She could tell from the occasional murmurings and rustlings of the audience that the way he touched her was not his normal way. He was adjusting his method so that she could make this cage her own, just as he had.

He was flooding her senses and sending her flying, giving her freedom when every true freedom had been signed away the minute she walked through the door.

"We've gotta get back out there," Kilian said, and she could feel him moving closer. "Do you mind?"

She was lifted into Kilian's arms. She wrapped herself around him as his hands held her up by her thighs.

You looked so soft, he whispered into her mind.

There was a hand against her back before she could formulate a response, her legs falling as she was passed to Oscar. He lifted her onto what felt like the cool tile of the kitchenette bench, his hands on her cheeks, pulling her face from his neck. He kissed her lips with an aching gentleness, treating her so tenderly that the action didn't break apart her lazy, satiated haze. She could feel shock pitter-pattering through her bond, little droplets that rained down as Oscar pulled back.

"I've gotta get to my fight," he said, squeezing her thighs before striding to the door.

He seemed distracted, like he was tunnelling all of his usual violence and aggression into the fight that lay ahead of him.

She felt sorry for whoever he was about to face.

Gabriel took his place before she could watch Oscar walk out of the door.

"You were perfect," he said, pressing close, his hands sliding up her thighs to her hips. *That* was when she realised something was off.

"Everything okay?" she asked, catching his russet eyes.

"Just a little rattled." Gabriel stared at her mouth like he wanted to kiss her as well, his brow furrowed. "It's not comfortable to have fifty strangers staring at your mate half-naked and obviously turned on." He gave her a tight grin and stepped back, his hands flexing.

Elijah took his place without speaking. He simply rested his forehead against hers, closing his eyes, his hands pushing up her thighs, his fingers slipping beneath the hem of her playsuit. He pushed his hands in further, stretching the cotton, until he could grip her bare ass. He dragged her to the edge of the countertop, eyes hard and narrow as they dropped over her face. "I never get tired of seeing all the beautiful ways you can arrange your body," he said, fingers flexing. "But forgive me if I can't watch that again. Not with a crowd."

"O-okay," she managed.

He squeezed her, roughly enough to draw a squeak from her throat before he ducked to kiss the side of her mouth. "Well done, today."

He forced his hands out of her playsuit and stalked for the door, much like Oscar had. "Cian, Moses—we need to get back out there."

Moses stopped by Isobel, pinching her chin, and tugging her mouth to his. She was shocked enough to part her lips, and another spattering of astonishment flowed through her bond, stronger this time. Moses' kiss was gentle, as it had been before summer break when he kissed her against Theodore's door. It was a slow, sensual coaxing, enough to leave her breath catching. He pulled back, his hand trailing from her jaw to her neck, brushing against her chest as he stepped away, not a word passed between them as he caught up with Elijah.

Cian was tugging her into his arms before she had recovered, inhaling deeply against the exposed skin at the base of her neck, jostling her body to pull her up higher.

"See you soon," he gravelled out against her ear, before sliding her back down again.

She tossed out a hand to steady herself against the bench, her bond wriggling around in joy. Kilian and Gabriel had gathered by the door, glancing back at Theodore and Niko. She didn't need to look at the two Alphas to know that they were torn. She could feel Theodore's jealousy pushing up against her chest ... and Niko's rage. She moved to Theodore at the same time as he stepped toward her, jumping up as he bent to hug her. He chuckled lightly, a breath of relief swelling his chest against hers, his hand tunnelling into her hair and gripping the back of her head to pull it back. He held her like that as his lips crashed to hers, the kiss brief but firm. It felt like a stamp against her mouth.

He set her down, and she faced Niko, unsure what to do. She didn't want to scare him again, but it wasn't just the Alphas who needed the reassurance, anymore. Something inside her was propelling her to check in with each of her mates, to re-establish their connection and soothe the rough, agitated threads tethering them together.

Niko loosened a rough breath. "It's okay. You don't have to."

It reminded her of his words under the tree a week ago, before they bonded for the first time.

Could you ever want more from me?

She needed this man to stop squeezing her heart so tightly; it was already bleeding so much for him.

She quickly slipped her arms around his waist, resting her head on his chest. A ripple of something chased over his body as soon as she made contact, and she worried that she had moved too fast for him, but his arms banded tightly around her, not allowing her to pull away.

His scent was a keen reminder of the last time they had been alone together, and he seemed to be thinking about the same thing, because she could feel the swell of him growing against her stomach. He ripped himself away, showing his hands like he had to prove he hadn't hurt her or something, before he spun to join Theodore, Kilian, and Gabriel by the door. Gabriel slapped him on the back, muttering something as they left the room.

Leaving her alone with Kalen and Mikel.

"Well," Mikel said, leaning up against one of the lockers with his muscled arms crossed. "Things have certainly developed."

She glanced between them, trying to figure out how they were feeling, since their faces were closed off and their emotions were hidden.

"Is ... did I do something wrong?" she asked nervously.

Kalen shifted his posture, crossing one ankle over his knee, his arms stretching out across the back of the couch, one of his brows quirking at her. He seemed ... amused?

Mikel looked at him, and his brow arched higher, answering some sort of unspoken question that passed between them.

"I think it's safe to say a few lines have been crossed." Mikel returned his attention to her. "Sex is no longer a matter of morality, but more a matter of *when*. You're attracted to us, and we're attracted to you and the bond demands we claim you *thoroughly* whenever you look at us like you want to be claimed because you're our fucking mate." He sucked in a breath, calming himself as Isobel came to the too-slow realisation that he was talking about *them*—as in, himself and Kalen, instead of the other Alphas. "So one day, one of us or both of us are going to break, and you are going to be taken so thoroughly, you won't even remember a time your insides weren't coated in our claim. This is a warning, Isobel. Nod for me."

She jerked her chin down in a shaky nod.

"Is that something you want, pet?"

"Am I allowed to want that?" She cut a quick glance to Kalen, who was staring at her impassively.

"You're allowed to want anything the fuck you like,"

Mikel said. "It's your body, Sigma. Your heart. Who you share it with is your concern."

"Within the group," Kalen amended. "For safety reasons."

"To prevent murder," Mikel further specified.

"Then ... yes." She swallowed. "N-not sex. Not right now," she quickly tacked on, her insides clenching hungrily at the thought. "But ... in general."

Mikel smiled at her, the lopsided one that made her breath catch. "Good," he said. "We were planning to stay well out of this space with you, but then the bond was damaged, and then the bond was *completed*, and now everything has changed. But if at any point you don't want this, things will go back to how they were before, completely without repercussion, okay? The bond might be pushing us together, but we don't fuck with unwilling. Not now, not ever." He paused, eyeing her, his smile slipping away, replaced by a stern expression. "Unwilling is saying red. Everything else is willing, even if you're screaming and crying. Just to specify."

She chewed on her lip, nerves flipping over in her stomach. "I understand."

"Good. That'll make this next part a little easier. Go stand in front of Kalen."

Kalen was still reclining lazily, his hard eyes surveying the two of them. She was already shaking again as she walked over to him, stopping between his spread thighs. They were both too unpredictable, and she was aware that her "no sex" comment still left plenty of room for other things. Like little metal balls, and whatever other insane ideas occurred to Mikel.

She could feel the heat of Mikel's body behind her, but she still jumped when his hands settled on her waist, dragging up over the sides of her breasts and then to her shoulders, his thumbs hooking into the straps of her playsuit.

"Not like that," Kalen muttered. "Use my rope scissors; they're in the other room."

Mikel eased back, the sound of a door opening and closing an eerie echo in the remaining silence. Kalen tipped forward, his gold eyes locked onto her, his hands creeping behind her knees.

"Did you think you would get away with teasing me, princess?"

His rumble vibrated all the way through her body as she realised exactly what he was saying, and when Mikel reappeared, the word *yellow* almost burst from her lips.

Because she *knew*.

She knew that asshole was about to punish her again.

"Start at the bottom," Kalen said.

She felt the cold metal of the blade slip beneath the hem on the outside of her thigh, cutting up along the seam, the cotton parting along her hip. And then he surprised her by hooking his finger into the crotch of her playsuit and pulling it away from her body. She felt the scissors against her inner thigh and heard the sound of them slicing through the material. Mikel tossed them to the couch and then gripped either side of the slit he had created up her hip, tearing her playsuit all the way up to her armpit. Kalen's hand flashed up to her neck, holding her in place, his eyes calm on hers as Mikel reached around to her front, gripping and ripping the playsuit again, tearing it open along the chest. Her breasts spilled out, and Kalen's eyes slid down. He licked his lips, his chest expanding as his eyes crawled slowly back to her face.

Mikel didn't remove her tattered clothing, choosing to leave it tangled and torn around her waist as he flattened his hand high on her back, between her shoulder blades, pressing her forward, lower and lower until she was forced to brace her hands on Kalen's hard thighs.

She felt vulnerable and exposed—more so than in the ropes. Mikel had taken several steps back, and she could feel his eyes caressing her heated flesh, examining the dampness glittering on her thighs.

"Kalen has a kink not many people know about," Mikel told her calmly, his hands suddenly on her ass, his grip punishing, his rough fingers digging in. "Would you like to know?"

"I think s-so?" Her hesitant words caught on a stutter when Mikel's hand suddenly lifted and slammed down on her right ass cheek, jolting her forward.

"Sir," he reminded her. "Ask him if you can take his cock out—he might tell you what it is."

She gaped at Kalen, since he was all she could see, but he only stared back at her, impassive and immovable as a statue.

"Can I ..." She swallowed, her flesh burning with colour. "Can I please take out your cock, Sir?"

"You might as well," Kalen drawled, still with his arms stretched out along the back of the couch. He wasn't going to lift a finger to help her, that seemed clear.

With shaking fingers, she reached for the zip on his fancy dark burgundy suit pants. His bulge was already hard beneath, already straining to be freed, and despite the terrifying size it hinted at, she felt a rush of pleasure that she could affect him so much. She lowered the zipper slowly and felt another hard smack, this time on her left cheek.

"Are you being a fucking tease, Carter?" Mikel asked.

"No," she yelped, shooting him a dark look over her shoulder.

His laugh was full of menace, his eyes growing shaded with desire. "Brace yourself."

It was the only warning she got before he reared back and smacked her five times in quick succession, alternating sides until her skin was smarting and a loud cry had burst from her mouth.

"I'm sorry, Sir!"

He soothed his hand over her stinging skin immediately. "Did I tell you to stop?"

"No, Sir." She quickly tugged Kalen's zipper the rest of the way down and then lowered the hem of his boxers, pulling out his long length. He hissed as soon as her fingers wrapped around him, his hips tilting up from the couch slightly. His dick was almost purpled, thick along the shaft, leading to a circumcised head that flared out, adopting an almost rosy hue. It was damp at the tip, and she was suddenly overpowered by a wave of rich, heady vanilla. It was almost woodsy, earthy, with an aftertaste so strong she could have believed someone had just poured vanilla liquor down her throat.

"Fuck ..." Kalen groaned. "I've been this hard all night. I think maybe you *are* a fucking tease, Sigma."

Mikel was softly stroking what she assumed to be big red marks now blossoming over her pale flesh. The tenderness felt like a threat, a precursor, a warning. Kalen's hand closed around hers, dragging it up his length. He didn't spring free of his pants and point upright. He seemed too heavy for that.

"Can you guess what my secret is?" he rumbled, squeezing her hand as they reached the end of his length. His skin throbbed beneath her fingers, velvety smooth and scorching hot. "Can you guess what I like?"

"If it's refusing to let innocent Sigmas come, then I don't want to know," she grumbled, adding quickly, "Sir."

Mikel chuckled. “Too late.” His hand whipped to either side, landing two stinging blows.

She jolted forward with the force, gasping, her pussy clenching. She prayed to every Gifted god she could think of that Mikel didn’t touch her between her legs because the spanking was making her uncomfortably wet. And then she added on a prayer that those same Gifted gods were busy watching something else.

“I like to stretch innocent Sigmas.” Kalen’s hand lifted from hers as he cupped her face, bringing it up to his. “If you kiss me sweetly enough, I’ll tell Mikki to go easy with your punishment.”

“It ... hasn’t started yet?” she asked, fear trembling her voice.

Mikel let out another low, dark laugh. “It hasn’t,” he confirmed. “So make sure you do a good job.”

She was going to kiss Kalen.

Kalen.

He was letting her kiss him.

While his dick was in her hand, and Mikel’s hands were on her ass.

While her ass was red and stinging from slaps.

Kalen pulled her head up higher, forcing her hands from his lap. She quickly gripped his shoulders to keep her balance and then settled her attention on his mouth.

“I won’t bite,” he promised, a quirk at the corner of his lips.

"Shouldn't we have kissed before I touched your ... before I touched you?"

"According to whose rules?" Kalen asked, before adding, "Are you stalling, Isobel?"

"Yes, Sir."

"Do you need me to do it for you?"

"Yes, Sir," she whispered.

His eyes darkened, a pleased sound travelling through his chest, but then he seemed to dispel his own reaction, relaxing further back into the couch.

"Too bad, princess." His thumb passed beneath her lip in a tender touch before he released her face, folding his arms across his chest.

She curled her fingers into the thick muscles along his shoulders and quickly ducked forward before she could second-guess herself, pressing her lips to his. As soon as she made contact, Mikel's touch slid between her legs, trailing through her honey before sinking two fingers deep into her channel. She gasped, and Kalen gripped the back of her neck, forcing his tongue past her open lips. She was supposed to be kissing him, but he took control of it immediately, encouraging her to respond or yield with firm licks and the pressure of his hand cupping her skull. She groaned into his mouth, and he backed off, nipping her lip hard enough to make it throb.

His breathing was ragged, control wavering in his eyes, his dick weeping. She drank him in as she pulled back, desire rushing through her body as she realised she was the one who had done that to him.

And then his words from earlier finally kicked their way to the forefront of her mind.

"Stretching?" she asked, confused.

"He likes to make girls scream with his dick and not necessarily in a good way," Mikel said, sounding amused. His fingers slipped from her channel, and he pressed her down again, forcing her hands back to Kalen's thighs. "Now, are you ready for your punishment?"

"What is it?" she asked nervously.

"I'm going to spank you twenty times," Mikel answered, tone gritty.

Twenty?

She blanched, but Mikel was already speaking again. "I'll start off light, don't worry. But there's a catch. As long as your mouth is full, I'll leave your perfect little ass alone. If your mouth isn't full, you're going to take my hand instead. Understood?"

Realisation settled in her bones with a horrible, heated weight. Her eyes fell to the *monster* still weeping in Kalen's lap, her head beginning to shake. That was *not* going to fit in her mouth. Mikel gave her a light slap, the shock of it making her yelp more than anything. She blinked up at Kalen, but his eyes only burned hotter as Mikel slapped her again, and again. Kalen gripped the base of his cock and dragged it up along the line of her throat, leaving behind a thin trail of pre-cum.

He bumped her lips, and she stared at him like he was *insane*, because she was going to break her jaw. Alphas were large in general, but Kalen seemed to be even bigger than normal. He looked like he needed to duck his head to fit through normal doorways.

He looked like he might dislocate her face.

Mikel delivered a slap that seemed sharper than the others, and she groaned, opening her mouth and ... hovering it over the angry-looking flesh before her. She stuck out her tongue, and Kalen slapped himself against it. Once, twice ... he growled, and Mikel hit her hard enough to jolt her forward again. She fit her mouth around Kalen, but it wasn't easy. Her lips stretched tight as he pushed into her mouth, pulling her head down at the same time. Mikel eased up on her abused flesh, his fingers pushing into her soaked depths again.

She heard him swear roughly behind her, his stormy cedar scent washing along her back, heavy and urgent.

Kalen guided her mouth down until he brushed the back of her throat, and she tried her best to breathe out of her nose, forgetting all about the spanking that awaited her if she lifted her head away and choosing to focus more on the fact that Mikel's other hand was cupping her from the front, teasing her clit as he pumped his fingers into her.

Her body and mind narrowed to a singular purpose, to chase the release he teased at all costs—before he took it away from her. She moaned around Kalen's hard flesh, his hands on her head directing shallow thrusts against the back of her throat, only an inch back and forth, grinding as deep into her mouth as he could fit himself.

She was beginning to drool around him, but he didn't let up, and she could feel herself drawing closer and closer. When her orgasm threatened to crash through her, she chased it with every inch of her trapped body, terrified that Mikel would deny her. But he didn't, he let her ride it out, and Kalen let her come off his cock as she gasped for air.

She was so relieved, she immediately started sobbing, her body still spasming, her skin overly sensitised. Neither man acted surprised, or like her sudden breakdown was strange. Mikel pulled her up and turned her around, but he didn't need to pick her up, because she was already climbing onto him, wrapping herself around him. He hummed in approval, falling onto the couch beside Kalen, who seemed to be tucking himself away—she couldn't see him, but she heard his slight hiss and the sound of his zipper.

She thought about how hard and ruby-red the tip of his engorged erection had been ... and felt bad for that.

"It wasn't about us," Kalen rumbled, his fingers trailing across her hairline. She wasn't sure if she had accidentally said something out loud, or if he was still inside her head. She turned her face on Mikel's shoulder instinctually, leaning into the soft touch of Kalen's hand as he cupped her cheek. "It's always about you, Isobel."

She closed her eyes, breathing in the scent of his skin and revelling in the feeling of Mikel's body digging into her front, his hands soothing down her spine. Her bond felt fully satiated, utterly and thoroughly claimed ... and they had managed to do it without having sex with her —though she had no idea if settling the bond had been their aim.

She was glad she hadn't stopped them, despite her fear and anxiety over not knowing where they would drive the interaction. They had pushed her hard enough to give her one of the most intense orgasms of her life, and then eased off at her breaking point without her ever having to tell them she had reached it.

"Do you always do ... stuff like that?" she mumbled, keeping her eyes closed, her tears drying up as something settled inside her.

"Not always," Mikel soothed, his tone soft, his hands massaging her shoulders. "Just when the mood strikes. We can be normal, you know."

She giggled, and his hands dropped to her battered ass, cutting her giggle off on a broken moan, but he only patted her consolingly, and then gently stroked the heated skin, soothing it in soft, appreciative strokes. She sighed and snuggled further into him.

"When you play like that." She paused to yawn. "Do you not want to come?"

"That wasn't the focus this time," Kalen rumbled, moving his fingers back to her hair.

"Doesn't that hurt?" she murmured.

Kalen chuckled. "Like a bitch. Do you think you can walk, Illy? Mikel needs to go and get ready, and I should get you back to the dorm."

"Just a minute more," she sighed, letting her body go limp against Mikel's.

"Just one," Kalen warned, but she was too busy smiling, because he had called her *Illy* and because Mikel had tightened his hold of her like he wasn't going to let her go anyway.

19
A Vicious Reclaiming

The Alphas went back to the Stone Dahlia every night for the next week, entering as many performance rooms as they could in search of the necklaces, but every night, they came home empty-handed.

Being left behind every night was making her skin itch, but they had decided as a group that it would be for the best after Elijah overheard a group of guests talking about requesting a private meeting with her and whether or not her sponsor could be bribed to leave her alone with them. At least Cian stayed with her, so she wasn't the only person who wasn't assisting with the search.

On Thursday night, they were sprawled out on the floor of the common room, taking selfies to send to Gabriel, who had recruited Kilian to help him edit photos and footage before he posted it all. Isobel and Cian had taken to creating as much content as they could as they floated around the dorm every night.

"Dance challenge time," Isobel declared, rolling over and springing to her feet.

Cian groaned, lumbering to stand beside her. "You're relentless with the dance challenges."

"Relentless at winning them, you mean."

He hauled her over his shoulder, her phone tumbling to the ground. "You clearly have too much energy, so let's go work out."

"You're just going to drag me to the spa again!" She laughed, slapping his back.

"Guilty. You can run on the spot while I relax like a normal person."

He swept up her phone, jostling her on his shoulder and swatting her on the butt when she tried to wiggle off. It was meant as a playful gesture, but it had only been six days since Mikel had thoroughly spanked her, and she now seemed to react to anything resembling what he had done to her with a gush of excitement and a full-body shudder.

If Cian noticed, he pretended not to, tightening his hold of her and striding for the front door.

"Isobel!" a voice called out before they were halfway across the foyer.

Cian spun around, blocking her view of Cooper, who she could hear stepping from his little hidey-hole beside the stairs. He had been trying to catch her alone all week.

"I really must insist that we discuss your father." His tone brooked no argument.

"Mine?" Cian played dumb. "Uh, hate to break it to you, Coops, but Hanale is a little old for Ironside. I can hook you guys up, though, if you're looking for a konane partner."

"Konane?" Cooper sounded annoyed. "Never mind, I wasn't talking—"

"It's like Hawaiian checkers," Cian cut across him. "Sometimes I forget that Hollywood still has a bit of catching up to do when it comes to diversity ... at least we're excelling in something here, right?" Cian laughed, the husky sound drowning out Cooper's attempt to speak again. "Tell you what, Coops. When I can no longer count the number of native Polynesian academy award winners on these hands—" He lifted his hand off her thigh and she imagined he was wiggling his fingers at Cooper. "—then I'll teach you how to play konane myself. Sound good?"

"Inside my office, Isobel," Cooper snapped, ignoring Cian's attempts to distract and derail him. "*Now*."

Cian clucked his tongue. "Rude," he said, adjusting her on his shoulder before striding forward.

She just sighed.

"I need to speak to Isobel in *private*," Cooper specified, his patience running thin.

"No can do." Cian swung her to her feet, looming behind her when she turned to face Cooper, his arms folding possessively over her chest and jostling her back against him. "Carter's bond is playing up and I'm on official surrogate duty. I swear if I remove my hands from her body, she's going straight back to Arizona."

He stepped forward, forcing her to step with him. She gave Cooper her best blank stare.

"I feel a teleport coming on," she said, deadpan. "Oh no. Hold me, Cian."

Cooper rolled his eyes, punching in the code for his keypad before shoving open the door and stepping inside. As soon as they entered, the door whooshed to a close behind them, blending back in with the wall. Cooper's office was small, with several monitors on the wall showing different rooms inside Dorm A. One of them was Isobel's bedroom. There were no more doors leading to other rooms, so she suspected he lived in the human accommodations in the official area.

He strode to his desk, spun his laptop around to face them, and smashed his finger down on a button.

"Go ahead," he said, stepping out of the way and revealing his screen.

Where her father sat, waiting, on a video call.

"Don't leave," Braun snapped. "We need to talk. It's important."

She folded her arms, and Cian set his hands on her shoulders, squeezing her lightly.

"What is it?" she asked, frowning at his familiar face, features pinched in aggravation.

"The officials are trying to edge you out," he said. "You and the Alphas. They have been ever since you got there—that's why they added the humans in. They're challenging the Alpha's popularity and influence."

She frowned. Even though the premiere wasn't for another day yet, there had of course been pictures circulating for the past two weeks showing the new human students, and people were going live from the privacy of their rooms to talk about their days. Her father didn't necessarily have inside information. He could have simply pieced together the situation from social media and was now trying to use it to bring her back under his control.

"So?" she finally said. "What do you want?"

"You're hitching your wagon entirely to the Alphas. You need to separate from them and start building up your *own* fanbase that doesn't rely on them. Ironside is going to sink them."

"Ironside can't sink them," she bit out. "Everyone loves them."

"For now." Her father was shaking his head. "This isn't a suggestion, Isobel. Ditch the fucking Alphas. Stop planning all your projects with them—I've seen the videos you're posting. I've seen the pictures. There's an Alpha in *every single fucking one*. At this rate, you're going to go down with them and all my hard work will be for nothing."

"I don't have to do what you say, anymore," she

stated calmly. "You're not allowed to live on campus this time."

"Don't push this, Isobel. I'll get my way. You know I will."

And he could, too.

He could pull her from Ironside for the fall break. She was still under his control, even if Teak had managed to intervene during the summer break.

"I've got this handled," she said. "My social media is doing well—better than when you were managing it. And we're going to make sure the officials have to use our footage."

"The officials are *pissed*," he growled. "The Alphas aren't playing the game the way it's supposed to be played, and everyone can see it. And what the fuck is with the *eleven* hashtag? What's that supposed to mean?"

"Nice talking with you," she said, spinning for the door.

She wanted to panic, wanted to think that her father could *see* too much, was watching far too closely, but she no longer had even a thread of trust in his motivations. He would say anything to bring her back under his control.

"I didn't realise how desperate Cooper was for nose reconstruction surgery," Cian fumed as he pushed into her room later that night, two shadows slipping in after him.

"Do you think Braun is still paying him a salary?" Theodore asked as the three of them pulled back the canopy around her bed and fell onto the mattress.

Cian had been looping the cameras and sleeping with her every night, watching over her while the dorm was empty and sneaking out around the same time as the others came home, just a few hours before sunrise.

This was new.

She pulled herself up, leaning over a body that smelled like Kilian and ... *champagne?* She dragged the dorm tablet into her lap and turned on the fireplace light, since it wasn't as bright as the overhead lights, and her head was still groggy with sleep.

Theodore, Cian, and Kilian were lounging around her bed, looking pissed.

"What happened?" she rasped.

"Just some fucking lady plying us with enough alcohol to get a damn elephant drunk," Kilian groaned, falling back with his arm thrown over his eyes. "Practically asked Theo if she could drag him into the bathroom and suck his dick."

"What?" she croaked, suddenly finding it hard to breathe.

She hadn't once felt even the slightest insecurity that

they were staying out all night, possibly drinking and entertaining clients of the Stone Dahlia. She knew they would never do anything to hurt the bond ...

But it wasn't the bond she was worried about.

At the end of the day, she was still just a girl with the world's biggest crush on Theodore Kane, and imagining some women getting him drunk and putting her hands on him made her sick to her stomach. She rubbed her eyes, blinking at the dark-haired Alpha as he leaned back against the carved post at the base of her bed, his eyes closed, long lashes fanning his sharp cheekbones. She thought he was drunk—maybe even already halfway asleep, but his voice was smooth and even when he spoke.

"You're the only person who gets to drag me into the bathroom and suck my dick, Illy."

She coloured, glad he didn't have his eyes open. "I ..." She had been about to say that she wasn't jealous, but the lie wouldn't do her any good. "Do they touch you?"

"We try to limit it," he answered, peeling one of his eyes open. "Do you want us to shower?"

She was nauseous, an insane urge welling up inside her, demanding she go from room to room and reclaim every one of them.

"No, it's okay." She kicked back the duvet and knee-walked over to him, slipping into his lap. His other eye opened, his hands automatically gripping her hips, but there was a subtle tremor in his fingers, and his scent was muddled by alcohol.

She knew that if she had been an Alpha, she would have been able to smell other people on him, and that thought alone had hot, possessive anger bubbling in her blood. She slipped off his lap and stood next to the bed, glaring at them.

"You both smell."

"Shower it is," Kilian quipped, rolling off the bed.

"No," Isobel said, before he could leave. "Just ... take off your clothes."

They all stared at her.

"What?" she huffed, colour high in her cheeks. "You've all seen me ... in various stages of being naked."

"You've got a point there," Theodore said, standing and unbuttoning his shirt. He shrugged it off, revealing the perfect, familiar ridges of his chest and stomach before he unzipped his pants and shoved them down his legs. "Good enough?" he asked her, standing there in nothing but cotton boxers that clung to his muscled thighs, his hands spread out in question.

She stared at him a little too long, her brain turning over until Cian began to laugh. It was a low, husky sound, full of expectation and genuine amusement.

"Why do I have a feeling we're all about to be very, very naked, doll?"

"No idea." She sniffed, wondering if he had slipped past her barrier to read her mind.

Kilian was evaluating her with a cool composure that had her nervously switching her weight between her feet. "The boxers are fine," she mumbled, flicking her eyes to Kilian again quickly. "You don't have to."

He removed his clothes silently, revealing boxers much the same as Theodore's, but blue. She nodded at them both without making eye contact and slipped back into her bed, climbing over Cian to settle into her previous spot. Cian shuffled down, lowering onto his side to tilt up her chin, forcing her to look at him.

"If you need to claim them, claim them. I remember how it felt watching you and Kalen perform. I needed to ... be close to you after."

"Okay," she murmured.

"Say no more." Theodore pounced on her, crawling up her body and nuzzling her stomach in a way that had her giggling at the ticklish feeling. He lifted his head, his perfect smile stretching wide. "Where do you need me? Here?" He dragged up her sleep shirt and nuzzled her hip, his fingers lightly tickling over her stomach.

"Stop it!" she squealed, trying to wiggle away from him.

"Never," he fake-growled, "you must be reclaimed!" He began gnawing her skin with fake bites, tickling up and down her sides.

Cian was chuckling beside her, and she felt Kilian settle into the bed on her other side. She tried to twist away from Theodore, but he only dragged her back, pretending to gnaw on her side.

"The Sigma is minneeee," he declared, pressing her to her back again and climbing further up her body.

As soon as his face appeared over hers, he became serious, ducking down to softly brush his cheek against hers.

"Do I smell like you, yet?"

She sniffed him, scenting only summer cherries and sweet amber. "Not yet."

"Lie," he accused, wrapping his arms around her, and switching their positions, sitting her up on his hips. He was hard beneath her, but his playfulness made it easy to ignore.

He tickled the tops of her thighs, and a laugh slipped out of her, but it was cut off as a hand wrapped around the back of her head, drawing her to face Kilian. His mouth descended on hers before she could even get a proper look at him. Her reaction was instant, and it seemed to cause a chain reaction in the Alphas in the bed with her. She moaned into the sudden kiss, sinking into Kilian's soft lips, swaying toward him as her legs tightened around Theodore's hips, her pelvis grinding down onto his erection.

All of the playfulness sank right out of Theodore's touch, and he palmed her ass, squeezing in a silent demand as he dragged her over his length. Her hand had flown out, gripping Cian's knee with the shock of Kilian's sudden kiss. Cian tugged on her hand, threading his fingers through hers, making a beautiful warmth blossom through her body to accompany the heat singeing her skin.

"I think you should move," Kilian whispered, pulling back from her mouth. "Rub the pretty little pussy we've all been thinking about all over the dick you've been thinking about."

"I don't just think about Theo, you know." She pouted.

He kissed her lips again like he couldn't help himself. "Mm?" he teased quietly. "Do you think about me too?"

Even though he was teasing her, she nervously eyed him and nodded. Theodore dragged her over his erection again, making her breath stutter.

Kilian gently lifted her shirt off her, revealing that she was wearing nothing but thin, black cotton shorts beneath, her breasts flushed, nipples hard and begging for attention. Cian groaned, and she felt Theodore's hard length flex beneath her.

"Do you want to know how often I lie in bed at night wondering what you'd feel like wrapped around me?" Kilian whispered against her lips. "How wet you'd be if I dipped inside you? How many times I could make you come before I made you take mine?" His words had begun soft but had ended on a groan.

She was soaking her shorts, leaving a damp patch on Theodore's boxers, and he was shifting her hips faster.

She wanted to feel good, wanted it desperately, and wanted them to feel good. But she wasn't sure if she was ready to have sex with three people, or how that would even work being with them all at the same time.

"It's every night," Kilian whispered, his grip slipping from the back of her head to her chest, where he palmed one of her breasts, his palm rubbing over her nipple. "I think about it every fucking night. That's what I'm thinking about when these desperate billionaires are plying me with champagne and asking how much I cost to get into bed."

Now rage was mixing with her desire, and it was a strange combination. It somehow made her hotter, her throat burning as she resisted the urge to scream, or swear, or beg for something more substantial than the friction she was getting.

She shoved at Kilian's chest, but he didn't even shift an inch. He hovered close, his mouth crooking up, daring her to try harder.

"You only get to fuck *me*," she said, temper rising in her voice.

"Glad we settled that," he murmured, nibbling on her swollen lower lip, his fingers pinching her nipple. "Want to come now, baby?"

"Y-yes," she breathed.

"How?" Kilian asked softly. "You want to be filled? You want one of us to lick you? Or you want to keep grinding?"

She groaned, the options making her head spin. "In ..." She cut herself off, re-evaluating if she was ready for what she was about to ask for. Her core clenched in anticipation. "Inside ... but one at a time."

Kilian and Cian both groaned, Cian squeezing her hand.

"You want us all, doll?" he asked.

She nodded, and Theodore lifted her up, Cian releasing her hands to tug her shorts down her legs. Theodore flipped her over, pressing between her legs, blocking the others out as his stunning face filled her vision. His tangle of dark hair fell to brush her forehead, his amber scent a warm balm of earthy sweetness, the ache between her thighs welcome as he stretched her legs wide to accommodate his hips.

He shoved down his boxers and locked his eyes on hers as he entered her, the movement a swift claiming. She was so wet that he was able to drive himself all the way in, forcing her channel to stretch around his girth. He paused once he was seated, his growl dispersed over her collarbone as her insides recovered from the shock of his sudden entry. Theodore licked up her neck, pulsing inside her, finding the tattooed marks on her skin. He seemed to know exactly which one was his, because he kissed it softly, pausing there to breathe her in until the tension in her body began to ease, and then he was fucking her in deep, possessive strokes, which gradually grew more frenzied.

"I need you so much," he groaned into her lips, causing her heart to pinch in longing even as her body edged closer to ecstasy.

Being with Theodore, Kilian, and Cian inspired an irresistible mix of adoration, happiness, and lust within her. It was a beautiful combination, so full of light and bliss. It was the exact opposite of what she had always associated with having a mate, let alone an Alpha mate.

She wanted to feel this way forever.

Theodore sat up, his body trembling on the edge, sweat dusting his beautiful muscles, both of their eyes falling to where he was holding himself inside her. He thumbed her clit, staring at her like she was a wellspring in a desert. Her orgasm seemed to set him off as he snatched up her hips and locked her to him, grinding into her as a low whine fell from her lips, her eyes fluttering closed as she fell.

Theodore was coming. She could feel it. The swelling and pulsing inside her made the spasms of her release last even longer.

She still had her eyes closed when Theodore pulled out of her, so it was a shock when she was suddenly pulled into the air, her back hitting the carved headboard of her bed. Cian thrust into her before her legs had even finished wrapping around his waist, and all she could do was fling out her arms and hold onto the top of the headboard as he worked her over his cock, forcing her to take his entire length just as Theodore had.

Small, desperate sounds caught in the back of her throat with each thrust, her body pushed past the point of being overly stimulated. It was a strange mix of pleasure and discomfort, which began to build to an even bigger peak. When Cian suddenly changed the direction of his hips, hitting somewhere new inside her, her groan was husky and broken and full of pleasure. He drilled into her incessantly, hitting that spot over and over again until she felt a scream building up.

Luckily, he surged forward, crushing her to the headboard at the last second, his hand covering her mouth as they catapulted off that peak together. Her scream was dashed against his palm, his groan deep, muffled by the other side of his hand. He filled her until she felt like she would burst, and then gently lowered her back to the bed.

She rolled onto her side with a heavy sigh, coming face to face with Kilian.

"How are you doing, baby?" He brushed his nose against hers.

"Almost full," she said.

His eyes flashed, his chest rumbling. "Almost?"

She held out her arms, pleading him with heavy-lidded eyes. "I'm tired, though."

He chuckled, rolling onto her, kissing her jaw, the side of her mouth, her tender lips. "You want me to do the work, lazy girl?"

"Yes." She grinned at him, loving his playfulness.

He freed himself from his boxers, and she stared at the beautiful, pale, silky-looking cock. She had seen a few penises now—definitely more than she thought she would see at Ironside—and *this one* was by far the most beautiful. He fed it into her inch by inch, grunting at the sensation. He wasn't as thick as Theodore or Cian, but he was longer and smoother.

Her sigh was contented. "You can live inside me if you like."

Someone slapped her right on the breast. "We're still here, doll."

She cracked one of her eyes open, surveying the stunning Alphas kneeling on the bed either side of her, looking like they already wanted to have another round as their eyes drank in the way she arched for Kilian.

She reached out to them without thinking and found her hands captured, fingers laced with theirs.

"If only Kalen could see you now," Kilian teased her, pale eyes almost swallowed by his pupils. "What a little princess."

She stuck out her tongue at him and he fell forward, capturing it between his lips and sucking it into his mouth, and then he was fucking her in earnest, driving her into the bed until she felt like she would scream again. He swallowed her sounds as she came, and then pulled up so that he could watch himself release inside her.

It was exhausting and perfect, and as Kilian held

himself slightly off her body, trying not to crush her, she wasn't sure if she had ever felt happier. Her mates felt so close, so warm, so safe.

Kilian blinked, pulling back, his eyes tracing over her hair. She flung up a hand, panic already in her throat, the sound of Eve sawing through her strands crashing back into her mind, but Cian caught her wrist, shaking his head.

"Nothing bad," he whispered.

Kilian was touching something in her hair, wonder and delight flashing over his angelic features.

Suddenly, he laughed, pulling back further, drinking her in. "Just when I thought you couldn't get any more fucking beautiful."

"What is it?" she asked, terrified.

Eve wasn't there, but she couldn't help her reaction.

"I'll show you." Kilian pointed at her phone on the bedside table and Cian released her wrist to hand Kilian the device.

He raised it to take a photo of her, and Isobel quickly wrapped an arm around her breasts.

When he turned the screen around to show her, all the breath dropped out of her lungs. Soft, pale gold roses were woven into her curls. Almost a dozen of them. She lifted a hand again, and this time, Cian didn't stop her. Her fingers brushed a velvety petal, the softness encouraging a wobbly smile to spread over her lips.

They began to carefully unravel the roses from her

hair, delicately untangling the thorns from her strands. They handed each one to her, and she sat up with the bunch of roses nestled into her lap, touching the petals with reverence, careful of the sharp thorns.

"Should we ... put them in water?" she asked nervously. "There are vases in the bathroom."

Kilian bundled her into his arms, carrying her into the shower, the others piling in after them. Theodore added the roses to the crystal vases on either side of the vanity mirror, arranging them around the crystal flowers already in there.

There were multiple sets of hands on her as Cian started the shower, her feet never touching the ground as she was passed from one of them to another, her body lathered and cleaned—theirs somewhat cleaned, because their focus was unwilling to waver from her.

She was worried they would have to leave when they got out of the shower, but they all piled into her bed, Cian and Theodore claiming either side of her and leaving a disgruntled Kilian to elbow in next to Theodore.

Her body sank into the mattress, a small groan slipping from her lips as a pained throb between her legs reminded her that she had gone a little overboard for her second time having sex.

"Icepack," she grumbled, flinging out an arm to catch Cian in the chest.

He rose immediately, sneaking out of the room, and

she fumbled with her phone, realising she had to let the rest of the group know about the new soul artefact.

She attached the photo Kilian had taken because she was too tired and sore to walk back into the bathroom and take new photos. She tried to crop out the part where her arm was flung over her bare breasts, but that ended up cutting out half of the roses, so she just winced and hit Send.

Isobel: There's a new soul artefact. The roses are in my bathroom right now. I wasn't sure what to do with them.

She began to put her phone back, but Theodore grunted behind her, lifting up his smart watch. "Was that you?" he asked groggily.

She winced again. *Shit.* She forgot about everyone's watches.

"Just telling everyone about the artefact," she whispered.

He chuckled huskily, dragging her back into the warmth of his body. "Good luck with that."

Her phone vibrated.

Elijah: I see you chose chaos, tonight.

Isobel: Sorry, I didn't mean to wake you up.

Elijah: My room is beside yours. I've been awake for a while.

Isobel buried her face in her pillow, humiliation crashing through her.

On the other side of the bed, she heard Kilian grumble something before feeling around on the floor for his pants, which he dropped again a moment later. She rolled away from her pillow and saw the light from his phone.

Kilian: Can this wait until tomorrow?

Elijah: Why? Is it time for round 4?

Moses: Wow.

Theodore: Thank you.

Isobel rolled her eyes, glancing at Theodore's smirking face, now lit up by his phone screen.

"You're awful," she said before her phone vibrated again.

Moses: I meant the fucking photo, you gloaty fuck.

Cian returned with an icepack wrapped in a soft cloth, which he fit gently between her legs, nuzzling it up into the juncture of her thighs.

"What's the drama?" he asked, eyeing them on their phones.

Kilian explained, "Illy sent the picture of the soul artefact."

"Ah." Cian smirked. "I ran into Oscar coming back from a run. He took one look at me and went straight back outside and started running again."

Oscar's was the other room that neighboured hers.

She buried her face in her pillow again.

"It's okay," Cian soothed, drawing her out and extracting her phone from her death grip. He slipped it onto her bedside table, catching her chin. "They're just jealous they weren't smart enough to stumble in here drunk and smelling like other people. Put your phones away," he scolded the others. "We only have an hour until the camera alarm. Try and get some sleep."

The room was thrown back into darkness, and Theodore curved around her body again.

Cian kissed her so delicately that she felt the inexplicable urge to cry, but then he kissed her again, and again until the urge dropped away, and sleep rolled over her.

20
THE GOLDEN TICKET

"ANYONE GET SNACKS?" MOSES ASKED AS SHE FELL INTO THE seat beside him, checking her phone.

13 missed calls from Braun Carter.

She turned off her screen, glancing around. "I think Kili."

It was time to watch the first episode of the new *Ironside Show* season, and selected people from all of the year groups had been invited to Ironside Row to react to the premiere. They entered the building labelled *The Den* and were ushered into one of several cinema rooms. The entire front row had their names on the seats, which had Isobel frowning. Her father had said that Ironside was trying to take the spotlight off them, but this very much looked like centre stage.

The humans in the third year sat right behind them, several other recognisable faces in the row behind that.

Bellamy, Silva, Wallis, Ellis, James ... Isobel winced, catching sight of a girl in the back with eyepatches covering her eyes.

Her heart was racing when she turned back to the front, and Moses must have been able to feel it, because he set his hand on her thigh, squeezing lightly. Oscar fell into the seat on her other side, passing her a cardboard sleeve filled with caramel chocolates.

"This is from Kiljoy," he said, before lifting his hips and digging into his pocket. "And this is from me."

He dropped a carrot into her lap.

She rolled her eyes. "Very funny."

He stared back at her, deadpan. "You don't like my gift?"

"Have you given it to me yet?" she shot back.

"Not yet." He ran his tongue over his sharp incisor. "Soon."

"Could you maybe stop threatening her?" Moses grumbled. "People are going to think you're hard for her."

"Who says I'm not?" Oscar stole one of her caramel chocolates.

It was obvious, over-the-top acting.

Throwing it right in the camera's face and giving the fans easy clips to throw into their compilation videos. She was saved from a witty response as the others all found their seats, and the episode began.

The first twenty minutes followed the humans as

they all opened their acceptance letters, packed their suitcases, and toured the new Ironside location wide-eyed and full of wonder. There was some footage of Niko with Mei, but even more footage of Bellamy and Kahn.

She turned and caught Bellamy's eyes. His brows shot up, showing her that he was just as surprised as she was, and she slowly faced the front again, realisation settling in. They weren't in the front row because Ironside planned to highlight them.

They were in the front row so that Ironside could *humiliate* them.

There wasn't a single piece of footage with her in it, or any of the other Alphas other than Niko.

Just before the premiere ended, Elijah's voice echoed through the bond, pulling everyone into her mind.

Post your reactions live.

But this is a planned event, Isobel answered. *Isn't that against the rules? Shouldn't it be photos only?*

Trust me, he returned.

I agree, Gabriel chimed in. *A little rule-breaking is in order, but maybe just one of us should post. Who would have the most impact?*

Theo? Elijah mused. *I would have said Niko, but ...*

But I'm a moody fuck, now? Niko snarled in their minds.

Kinda proving my point there, bud, Elijah said calmly.

Call me bud one more fucking time and I'll force-feed you your own goddamn teeth.

Fuck's sake, Niko, Moses groaned. *All this just because we wouldn't let you sit beside Isobel?*

I told you I'm not good at sitting still for so long, and she calms me down! Niko was like a snarling, snapping animal inside her head, unsettling their bond.

I'll do the live, she declared, standing up. The episode wasn't even over, yet, but it was drawing to a close. She crossed over to Niko and sat on the arm of his chair, pulling out her phone. She leaned back, resting her head backwards on his shoulder and angling her phone to capture the entire line of Alphas as they leaned forward in their seats, staring into her camera.

"Which one of these big idiots do I have to kiss to get some screen time?" she asked cheekily, forcing a carefree grin.

Niko, to his credit, was managing a calm, amused expression, even though his connection to her was still vibrating with tension. She winked at the camera, blew it a kiss, and ended the live, but instead of returning to her own seat, she remained on the arm of Niko's chair, kicking her legs up into his lap.

"Seriously?" one of the Russian twins leaned forward in his seat, glaring at her, his voice heavily accented. "That's your angle? Slutting yourself out for views?"

She tossed her head back, her laughter loud and genuine. "I'm sorry, aren't you famous for chopping wood half naked in the snow?"

His lip lifted into a snarl, but he fell back into his seat, choosing silence.

Cian leaned over Niko and patted her thigh. “Let’s go, then, before you get into a fight with the woodchopper.”

“Grandmaster,” the twin—she thought this one was Alexi, because he had longer hair—corrected angrily.

“Grandmaster of ... what?” Bellamy asked from the third row. “You mean like Dungeons and Dragons or something?”

“Of *chess*,” Anatoly snapped, jumping in for his twin. “The entire reason we’re *here*, freak.”

“Oh, *chess*,” Isobel drawled, fighting back her rage. Bellamy was her friend now, and she didn’t like that word being directed at him. “I thought it was *chest*, because you’ve literally never worn a shirt in any of your videos.”

“You really wanna go there?” Mei snapped, jumping to her feet. “People *only* like you because you’re pretty. Get your head out of your ass, Carter. Your pretty privilege is suffocating us.”

“Oh my god, *thank you*.” Isobel pressed a hand to her chest. “I thought they only liked me for my Alphas.”

Several of those Alphas were now laughing, and it looked like Mei was winding up to say something truly hurtful, but Isobel’s mates all rose, unfurling lazily, their expressions amused. Maybe it was the sheer size of them, or the cold personas they had adopted since the summer break, but the simple movement of them standing up seemed to silence the entire room before any further barbs could be thrown.

They made their way back to the dorm and into swimsuits, meeting again at the terrace. Since the premiere had cut into their normal practice time and they only had an hour free before they had to start getting ready for their Friday night at the Stone Dahlia, she had suggested that they spend some time in the water.

She didn't want to admit it, but Niko's plunge into the river had shaken her in more ways than one. She didn't like that the Alphas all had such an obvious, glaring weakness. They had begun teaching themselves to swim the year before, but she needed them to get to a point where they could be shoved into a river without the danger of *immediate drowning*. Being a big, strong Alpha meant nothing if they couldn't use Alpha Voice on a tide.

She considered attempting to find a length of rope to tie across the pool, but the Alphas descended into immediate chaos, throwing each other into the shallow end of the pool, most of their fear over the water worked off by their antics in Alpha Lake the previous year.

So instead, she just laid out her towel beside the pool and sat on it in her plain black swimsuit, worriedly watching them get closer and closer to the deeper waters.

They stayed longer than they were supposed to, and

her hair was still damp when she stepped into Room 43 with Kalen two hours later, but she was *happy*.

They had made Niko laugh.

Not a fake laugh for the cameras, but a genuine one, flashing his wide, bright smile and crinkling his beautiful hazel eyes as he tossed his head back, his silky hair sending droplets of water everywhere.

Four Alphas had to violently wrestle a snarling and kicking Oscar into the pool to drag that beautiful smile into existence, but it was worth it.

When she and Kalen returned home that night, she felt a little less uneasy about the others staying back at the club and continuing their search for the necklaces. She didn't generally spend much time with Kalen outside of their shibari performances or their recorded group sessions, but he didn't even bat an eyelid when she trailed him to his office that night.

He held the door open for her without a word, and then led her through another door to a small studio apartment on the ground floor. His bed was neatly made, both bedside tables stacked with books. He seemed to have an attached bathroom and dressing room like she did, but his sitting area was larger, with a small kitchenette and a little dining space, the luxurious furnishings matching the rest of Dorm A.

He opened his small freezer. "Chocolate fudge or strawberries and cream?" he asked, acknowledging her for the first time.

“Strawberries and cream,” she said, still hovering by the door.

He pulled out a small tub of ice cream, retrieved two spoons from the drawer of his kitchenette, and then lowered himself to the velvet chaise, turning on the flickering fake flames of his fireplace as he lowered a projection screen down to turn on a news station. They were talking about the Ironside premiere.

Even in the few minutes of an evening that Kalen had to relax, he was still working, researching, plotting.

She padded over to the chaise, folding onto the seat beside him and accepting the ice cream tub he handed to her before he stood again and retrieved a thick woollen blanket from a cupboard. The blanket seemed brand new. He draped it over her lap and sat again, an inch closer this time, his long arm winding across the back of the couch behind her. He had spoken a total of three words to her, but it wasn’t awkward.

It was dangerously comfortable, and she locked away the feeling of soft wool and warm vanilla, the heat of his arm so close to her shoulders as sweet strawberries and cream melted against her tongue. She only stayed for a little while, making herself stand and leave before he was forced to kick her out, but that sensation of warmth and sweetness was something she basked in as she curled up alone in her bed.

~

THE FALLOUT FROM THE PREMIERE WAS HARSH.

The fans were *rioting*, flooding the Ironside websites, fan pages, and social media pages with questions and disparaging remarks about the choice to leave Dorm A out of the first episode entirely. Isobel's live seemed to have worked, because it was the most trending video on several different sites the next morning, and people were praising her tongue-in-cheek calling out of the *Ironside Show*.

She received an email from the officials saying that as a penalty for breaking their recording rules, she would be fined the same amount of popularity points as she would have otherwise earned if her trending video had followed their rules. In addition, she was banned from the Friday night Ironside Row competitions for the rest of the month.

She also received a fresh barrage of messages from her father, all of which she ignored.

There was a new message from Sophia, the notification almost buried beneath her father's explosion of temper. She clicked on it, a smile breaking out over her face.

Sophia: Bitch, don't make me a fan of Ironside just to see their reaction to that shit.

As she was reading, another message came through.

Sophia: Ugh I'm going to watch the show tonight, aren't I?

Isobel: Only if you want to see Anatoly and Alexei's

nipples again. I swear they only spend every morning swimming laps to prove they can do something the Gifted can't.

Sophia: Luis hates them. He calls Anatoly Butthead and Alexei Buttface. Together, they're the Butttwins.

Isobel: Luis has taste.

Sophia: Want to skip the fancy food bar and come visit us for lunch? Mama made chile rellenos.

Isobel: How many overlarge men can I bring?

Sophia: One.

Isobel: Five?

Sophia: Two!

Isobel: Six?

Sophia: Oh my god. Fine. Three, but only if one of them is Cian. Luis put up a poster of him in his room and I think he wants it signed.

Isobel: One Cian coming up.

Sophia: Is that what your bond says when you get randy?

Isobel: Want me to switch Cian out for Oscar?

Sophia: You're so mean. Has anyone ever told you that?

Isobel: Bellamy, like every time he sees me.

Sophia: Oooh, bring Bellamy!

Isobel: ...

Isobel: Why?

Sophia: What? It was a joke. See you soon!

She was halfway out of the dining hall with Cian, Theodore, and Kilian when she suddenly paused, causing Cian to crash into her back. He looped an arm around her, catching her before he could bowl her over.

"Sorry!" A laugh bubbled out of her, realisation sinking in.

Was Sophia a fan *of Bellamy?*

There was only one way to find out.

She wove through the crowd of students, stopping at Bellamy's table and leaning up against it, tapping him on the shoulder.

"Hey nutte—" he started, before catching sight of Theodore over her shoulder. He cleared his throat, sitting up a little straighter. "Nut ... nutritious person," he amended, floundering for a moment. "What's up?"

"Come for a walk with us?" she asked, grinning at him. "I know someone who's a *huge* fan and would really like to meet you."

"Nope." He was already shaking his head. "No way." He waved his fork at Theodore, Cian, and Kilian. "That's three against one. My face is too pretty to be broken."

"Nobody is going to break your face," Kilian said, rolling his eyes. He frowned, glancing at Isobel. "Right?"

She bit back her laugh, tugging Bellamy's arm. "Just come on! She's your *biggest* fan!"

Theodore pulled her hand away from Bellamy as soon as he lifted from his seat, but he didn't glower at the Beta, instead flashing him a signature, superstar smile. Bellamy winced, muttering something about broken ribs, and followed behind them as they left the hall.

"What privileges did you get from trending in the premiere?" she asked him, forcing him to quicken his steps and fall in beside her.

He ran a hand through his hair, casting another wary glance at Theodore before answering. "They gave me a fucking date card to use with Kahn. I cannot *stand* that girl, but my dad is going to make me use it."

"What's a date card?" she asked.

"Some new thing they made up, I guess. It means they'll arrange us a fancy-as-fuck date and film the whole thing."

Cian scoffed. "How romantic."

"Where are we going?" Bellamy lowered his voice, pitching his head toward Isobel.

"The daughter of the Guardian who works at the chapel asked to meet you," Isobel returned, unable to contain her grin. "Listen, just ... I don't know. Say hi or something."

Bellamy rolled his eyes. "Fine, but only because you'll bully me into it either way."

They reached the cottage and Isobel knocked on the door. Sophia pulled it open, already stepping back to wave them in, her mouth opening to say something.

Before she halted, catching sight of Bellamy.

"Hey," she said, appearing at a loss for words.

"Sophia doesn't really watch the show," Isobel explained in a stage whisper, "so she doesn't know about how you've been a total dick since the beginning."

Bellamy grimaced. "How can she be my biggest fan if she hasn't even seen the show?"

"Please," Sophia scoffed, recovering from her shock and gesturing them into the house. "I don't *do* fangirling, but you can stay for lunch if you need a break from croissants and macarons."

"Actually, the theme today was global barbeque. I have a plate of perfectly good churrasco and bulgogi waiting for me."

"Go back to your precious Ironside meat, then." Sophia waved him off, looping her arm through Isobel's and dragging her into the kitchen, with only minimal pointed glaring from Theodore and Cian.

Kilian was busy introducing himself properly to Luis, who was sitting at their small dining table clutching a deck of tarot cards and staring at the pale Alpha with wide, wonder-filled brown eyes.

Bellamy peered around the kitchen, choosing to ignore Sophia and invite himself inside. "Where's the Guardian?" he asked.

"Just left to volunteer at the medical centre," Sophia answered. "Everyone, help yourselves."

There wasn't enough room to sit around the table, so they gathered in the small lounge instead, Luis ignoring his food in favour of having Cian guess which tarot card he was holding behind his back.

He was giggling so hard his glasses had fallen off twice, and he kept nudging them back into place with his shoulder.

Sophia and Bellamy were the last to squeeze into the room, eyeing each other warily as they sat stiffly beside each other on the couch.

"You shouldn't *only* eat the fried stuff," Sophia lectured Bellamy as soon as she saw his plate. "There was salad in there."

"Do I really look like I need a salad?" Bellamy drawled, popping a fried pepper into his mouth.

Sophia blushed, glancing away from him, and grumbling something beneath her breath.

"So you guys aren't allowed to eat in the dining hall?" he asked, peering around their lounge room.

"No, Mama has to put in a grocery order every week with the staff office. It comes out of her salary."

Bellamy frowned. "That's stupid. There's no way we finish all the food in the hall every day."

Sophia shrugged. "The food is for the show."

They stayed until it was time for their filmed group intensive, and Bellamy was silent as they walked back toward the rest of the academy, a thoughtful expression on his face.

"Do you think—" he began, just before they parted ways.

"Probably," Isobel answered immediately.

He frowned harder. "You don't even know what I was going to say."

"You were going to ask me to send you Sophia's number. The answer is probably."

He rolled his eyes. "You owe me, remember? So ..."

"So you're collecting?" she teased. "You sure you want to spend it on this?"

"I'm becoming less sure by the second," he grumbled, stalking off.

"You're *welcome*!" Isobel called after him, causing Theodore to chuckle.

They hurried to the studio, and Isobel nervously fiddled with her headphones as they waited for the others to arrive. Today would be the day they performed their songs, and it would be the first time any of them—other than Theodore—had sung for the cameras. Kalen and Mikel entered with armfuls of camera equipment, which they began to set up without a word.

It seemed overkill, but maybe that was the point.

Are we going live? Theodore asked through the bond, and Isobel could feel that he had addressed everyone, inviting them all into her head.

No, Mikel answered. *We're just recording. It's a message—that if they don't give the fans what they want ... then we will.*

As soon as the cameras were set up, Kalen and Mikel stepped up to the rest of them.

"It'll be Elijah's birthday in a couple of weeks," Mikel announced, "and one of your biggest tasks this semester will be to perform as a group at his party. If the performance gets over a million views in the first twenty-four hours, we will consider it a success. If not, you will have all failed the task."

He paused, letting that information sink in before he continued.

"This first task was to decide our main vocalists for the performance, and our singular vocal lead."

Isobel's palms were sweating. She should have known there wouldn't be any innocent, innocuous tasks. She was glad that she had spent so much time on her song, but she suddenly doubted if it had been enough.

"First up," Kalen announced, making her panic snowball as she realised they wouldn't even get one last practice in, "is Kilian. The booth is yours."

Kilian jumped up and disappeared into the recording booth next door, and they all gathered around the three wide, glass walls. The studio was a large one, with three sitting areas and two banks of recording equipment, speakers lining the roof.

They could clearly hear Kilian as he set his printed lyrics—which she could see he had scrawled notes all over—onto the stand and leaned into the microphone.

"Ready whenever you are."

He was so confident, so calm.

Mikel hit a button and started Kilian's backing track,

which was upbeat and poppy with a strong, driving melody and light, synthesized flourishes. Kilian's take on the song was almost unrecognisable from her version. His voice had a sweetness and a warmth that enveloped the entire room, making the song oddly comforting. He belted the chorus in a soaring countertenor range that had her mouth dropping right open. It was something she struggled with herself, but Kilian held his high range with almost perfect clarity and strength.

When he finished, everyone clapped, and he walked back into the room like what he had done was no big deal at all.

"Next," Kalen said, checking his notes like he *agreed* that it was no big deal, like he heard incredibly unique and powerful voices every day of his damn life. "We have Cian."

Isobel tried to edge closer to the glass, her heart skipping a beat as she came to terms with the possibility that they could all be that good.

Cian's backing track had a more sophisticated melody that had her palms sweating with nerves for him. It was a blend of piano, upright bass, and drums, the rhythm deceptively laid back, but he didn't look worried. He didn't pull out his lyrics, but simply began to sing. His voice was deep and resonant, with a sense of ruggedness. It had a raw, emotional edge, and he had a knack for adding texture with subtle nuances and embellishments, elongating the words or supplementing them with beautiful adlibs. His singing was layer after layer of depth, with a surprising range for someone so comfortable in his baritone. He was ... just as impressive as Kilian, though the two of them were very different singers. Everyone clapped again when Cian was done, and he returned looking almost sheepish.

"Could have done that better, sorry."

"I didn't hear any mistakes." Mikel brushed him off like this was something Cian did often, though his tone wasn't unkind.

"Isobel," Kalen said, "you're next."

She was shaking her head emphatically. "Please let me go last," she begged, too worried to be scared of saying no to Kalen. "I won't be able to listen to the others if you make me go now. I'll just be panicking about how bad I messed up."

Kalen considered her. "All right. Elijah, your turn."

Elijah stalked into the booth, producing a notebook, which he must have copied the lyrics into. He nodded at the window, and Mikel started his track. It was faster, with a repetitive bassline and a smooth rhythm layered in melodic loops and sharp drumming, creating more of a modern, urban sound. And ... Elijah didn't sing.

He rapped the first verse, his delivery smooth and impeccable, effortlessly riding the beat, his entire body as loose and relaxed as it was when he danced. He rapped the first verse and pre-chorus, and then seamlessly transitioned into singing the chorus, his voice steady and smooth—not quite as unique as Kilian's and Cian's singing voices, but she assumed that wasn't Elijah's focus. When he slid back to rapping in the second verse, his tempo suddenly increased, the words flowing twice as fast, every other word altered or added to turn the verses on their heads, making them suddenly clever and shocking.

An astounded laugh burst out of her throat, and beside her, Theodore chuckled like he was enjoying her surprise.

Elijah was *fast* and very, very clever.

But still, when he finished, everyone clapped like it was just another day in the studio. And maybe for them, it was.

"Gabriel," Kalen said, nodding toward the booth.

Gabriel slapped Elijah's hand as they passed each other in the doorway. "Could have been faster," he said.

"Didn't want to make you look *too* bad," Elijah shot back with a smile.

Gabriel also had a notebook, and he gazed at it with as much calm, relaxed composure as Elijah. His backing track had an upbeat rhythm with a pop feel, but it was fused with a more soulful melody, a bouncy bassline, and crisp chord progressions, making it more of a dynamic track. He started off singing, a slightly raspy quality to his otherwise smooth timbre, but then he switched up the cadence, and then the rhythm, and then the vocal tone, effortlessly shifting between rap and singing segments, adding in words and verses to bend the lyrics to his style. He displayed an impressive vocal range. Just like Elijah, his singing didn't quite match up to Kilian and Cian, but the shifting of his vocal inflections and the beautiful texture of his softer, slower rapping was hypnotising. Isobel wasn't very knowledgeable when it came to rappers, but she was certain that she was standing in the same building as two of the most impressive rappers Ironside had ever seen.

She gazed at Kalen, realising that all the talent she was seeing had, essentially, come from him. He had told her when she teleported into his house in the Mojave Settlement that his grandmother had perfect pitch and an eidetic memory, and that she had taught him everything he knew. Of course, *everyone* knew who Silla Carpenter was. She had been a born superstar, a musical genius. She had won her season of the *Ironside Show* and then refused to live in the outside world, choosing to return to her settlement instead. Kalen had said that Theodore had more talent in his little finger than most people had in their wildest dreams, but that Elijah was the real prodigy. With Kalen and Silla's knowledge, Theodore's talent, and Elijah's brains, they had somehow created and curated this little group of the most talented performers of their generation.

And they were just ... *sitting on it.*

Waiting for their moment to strike.

And she was somehow supposed to match them. As much as she had loved singing, it had never been where her natural talent rested. Her father had seen that and had forced her to drop the subject. Her talent was with dance. Even with Gabriel and Elijah in the group, she was sure that she still had something to offer, because if she wasn't as good a dancer as Cian and Kilian were singers, or Gabriel and Elijah were rappers—then she was going to train until she *was*. She was sure that she could. She just needed to try harder.

She needed to train longer.

"Niko, you're up," Kalen said, noting something down.

Isobel finally pulled her attention from the glass long enough to realise that Kalen had been taking notes on all the performances.

What could there possibly be to say, other than *perfect, perfect, perfect, ten thousand out of ten*?

Niko pushed into the booth, swathed in a hoodie, his features tight. "I didn't really practise," he said into the microphone. "Can someone send me the lyrics?"

Of course he hadn't. He could barely think straight.

"Sending." Elijah was tapping away at his phone.

"Ready when you are," Kalen added. He didn't sound pissed that Niko hadn't practised. If anything, there was a note of understanding in his deep voice.

Niko propped his phone onto the podium and

nodded, scanning the words quickly. He was quiet for a little while as his backing track played. It seemed like he had never heard it before, and she thought back to all their time in the studio over the past week. Niko had spent most of his time alone, either sitting in the corner or leaning against the exit, waiting for the session to end. Everyone had left him alone, and he brushed off any attempts at conversation. He spent most of the time watching her—she had grown so used to his eyes on her that she had stopped noticing.

He couldn't go on like this.

When he began singing, he had a rich, velvety tone and a smooth, stable delivery. His voice was so warm and inviting, it felt like she was staring at the old Niko, and she never wanted him to stop.

Just like the others, his range was impressive, and he played around in it with seeming ease, but it was his unique, rich tone that set him apart. He coloured the words he had barely bothered to read with so much raw sincerity and emotion that it took her breath away. Everyone clapped for him, but he walked out of the booth looking pissed off, rubbing his temples.

"You did great," Elijah told him.

"I read the words wrong," Niko snapped back.

"It's not a reading comprehension exercise," Gabriel said. "You were fine, Niko."

Niko sighed, giving him a nod, and moving back to the glass. Isobel edged toward him experimentally—it was always a gamble whether he would welcome comfort from anyone—as Kalen directed Oscar into the booth. Gabriel shifted, allowing her to stand beside Niko, and she hesitantly brushed her pinkie over the back of his hand, waiting for him to jerk in surprise.

He took her hand immediately, squeezing tight, a low breath rushing from his lips. He didn't look at her, or say a word, but she could feel something settle inside him, so she edged closer. He threaded his fingers through hers, looping his arm over her shoulders so that their joined hands crossed over her chest and he could tug her into the side of his body.

The cameras were watching, but he didn't care, and the action was so like what Niko had done in Kalen's office the day she was reunited with him that nobody could have pried her away from him in that moment. She sank into the side of his body, pretending that nothing inside him had changed.

Oscar started singing without preamble, playing with the softer, slower instrumentals of his track with a confident mastery. His singing voice, much like his speaking voice, had a raw, gritty quality, but he was able to manipulate it beautifully. The powerful delivery of his raspy timbre within his comfortable lower range lent him a unique edge that the others didn't have, giving him a deep and resonant tone that almost seemed to vibrate through the room. She felt the hairs along her arms rise as he finished, and everyone did their furiously polite, unimpressed clap again.

She should have gone third.

She should have gotten it over and done with before she realised how utterly *unimpressed* they were with the exceptional talent on display—though it was possible they were just too familiar with each other's voices. Moses was next, and her throat threatened to close up as soon as she heard his velvety smoothness. It was like honey pouring out of the speakers. It had a distinctly haunting quality, delicate and powerful at the same time, with the occasional growled edge that gave him a dark, distinctive sound. She was astounded that they had all received the same training—presumably from the same people—and yet they were all so *unique*. Though perhaps that made more sense than she realised. If they had all trained together, they would have deliberately tried to find ways to differentiate themselves.

Theodore was last, and even though she had heard him sing before, she still held her breath, waiting to see what he would do. It wasn't until Niko squeezed her hand that she realised she was still holding her breath, and it escaped her in a rush as she stared at the man inside the booth. Theodore effortlessly demonstrated, once again, that he was the most extraordinary voice she had ever heard. He had impeccable control over his breath, his modulation, and his vocal dynamics, easily navigating through complex vocal runs in a voice thick with raw power and magnetism. He easily danced between an incredible five octaves, from smooth bass notes to the most impeccably delivered high notes. Everything was a dance, an interaction with the lyrics and the music that commanded attention and refused to release it. He played with a vibrating vocal fry and a raw falsetto without a single hint of effort showing in his face or body.

He could have been talking about the weather if they had turned the sound off.

It was like he wasn't even *trying*, but he was. She had heard him sing without trying when he recorded the track for her first Ironside dance. She didn't realise it at the time, but now, the difference was obvious. This was him very much trying, his control was simply so extraordinary that none of the effort showed.

When he came out of the booth, several of the Alphas clapped him on the back, and she finally realised what she had been seeing for the past two years. She understood why they always shoved Theodore into the spotlight, why they always pulled back at the last moment and let him win everything, why they treated him like he was special.

He was their secret weapon.

Their golden ticket.

She did *not* want to go into the booth after Theodore, but she swallowed her pride and tucked her head down, approaching the podium and unfolding the lyrics from her pocket. She nodded shakily to let them know she was ready, and then she closed her eyes. She had the lyrics memorised, anyway.

She sank into the slow backing track, keeping her breath light, with the sweetness and purity that Mikel had said was her natural tone. It was the most comfortable pitch for her, allowing her more control when she slipped into her soprano range, allowing her to hit her high notes with more clarity and agility. She was still learning control over her whistle register, but Elijah had been training her all week during her sixth period, and she was able to pull it off this time without her voice breaking or wobbling. When she reached the chorus, she was able to belt it out just like Theodore had, her vocal runs sounding powerful and intricate, that sweet tone she maintained the whole way through infusing everything with a rawness and a vulnerability that she leaned into, right until the last note.

She didn't open her eyes again until the song was finished, and then she folded up her lyrics again and slipped them back into her pocket with shaking fingers. She pushed open the door, and there it was.

The polite clap.

Though this one was accompanied by a few shocked looks and Elijah's proud smile. She grinned back at him, wobbly and uncertain.

"Fuck yes, Illy-stone!" Theodore scooped her up,

spinning her around. "You're going to be our secret weapon!"

She stared at him as he set her down and then jumped onto Moses, his excitement contagious as he shook his brother.

Was he insane?

The way he didn't even realise he was easily the best singer any of them had ever heard absolutely floored her.

21
THEODORE FUCKING KANE

THAT NIGHT, THE *IRONSIDE SHOW* SHOCKED EVERYONE BY airing a surprise "part two" to the premiere. It focussed mainly on the Alphas and Isobel, and as they sprawled around the common room watching it, it was a struggle not to laugh outright at the officials' attempt to appease their angry fans.

The episode still heavily featured the humans, building up a narrative that Dorm A and the humans were at war, and they tried to show Isobel with as many different Alphas as they could, playing into the most popular topics online about which of them she might be secretly dating.

They showed Kilian holding her hand, and Niko glowering at her from a distance. They showed Cian leaning toward her over the breakfast table with a devious twinkle in his eye, his tongue poking at his lip piercing ... and Niko staring at her from the other end of the table. They showed Oscar glaring at her and Silva like he was planning on tearing off Silva's arms and using them to slap him all the way back to Dorm B, and they showed Niko turned around in his seat with narrowed eyes, staring at her like Silva—or anyone else for that matter—didn't even exist. They showed Elijah and Gabriel talking to her during dance practice, grins on their faces and warmth in their eyes, and Niko staring at the back of her head as they walked to dinner. They showed her playfulness with Theodore during the group intensive with Kalen and Mikel ... and Niko leaning against the wall on the other side of the room.

Staring at her.

They laughed the whole way through the episode. Even Niko cracked a tired grin, rolling his eyes at the screen.

The fans settled down after the episode aired, most of them deciding that it had been the plan all along to rile people up before dropping the surprise Part Two.

The next day, Kalen announced that Theodore had won the position of lead singer, with Isobel, Kilian, and Cian as the main singing group, and then he introduced their next challenge: to choreograph a dance to Theodore's version of the song they had been given. Once again, he would be awarding a singular lead dance position and several positions for the main dance group.

Isobel dove head-first into the task, her competitive

nature rearing its head as she worked tirelessly on different combinations for the next two weeks. During her vocal sessions with Elijah, she idly danced on the spot until he grabbed her wrists to keep her still. During breakfast, lunch, and dinner, she poured over different sequences inside her head.

The only time she wasn't thinking about the choreography challenge was when Kalen wrapped her body in rope and lifted her into the air, or the few times Kilian, Cian, or Theodore snuck into her bed.

It wasn't every night, and she had no idea how the others knew to stay away when one of them had crept into her room, but she would occasionally wake to Kilian hugging her from behind or Theodore climbing over her body in the dark.

One night, Theodore parted her thighs and tasted her until she was dripping enough for him to fuck the screams into her throat. He barely managed to muffle them before he was growling with his own release, his fingers slipping away from her lips.

Kilian was always touching her, and she was always searching for his soft lips, kissing and licking them until his entire body was vibrating and a desperate, gravelled whine was emanating from his body. When he slipped inside her, his rhythm was slower and softer than the first time, and he kissed over every inch of her body until she was just as shaky and desperate as he was, before he spun her suddenly around and drove into her unrelentingly, forcing her to shatter with him.

Cian liked to look at her. He would strip her clothes and shove down the sheets until she was laid out for him and he could trace his tattooed fingers over her body. The first few nights he did it, he wouldn't let her touch him back. He was too focussed on touching and tasting every inch of skin he could uncover like he was mapping it all out in his head. He quickly learned how to make her gasp, and what made her blush. He always ended up with his head between her thighs and her hands tangling in his golden hair, rasping out his name as he dug his hips into the bed for relief.

The third night he slipped into her bed, she could tell that he had reached his limit, and that was when she found out about the *other* piercing he had gotten over the summer break. After kissing her hungrily, his fingers shaking as he squeezed her breasts, thrusting against her stomach, he pulled off her and kicked off his boxers, falling to sit against the headboard. He dragged her into his lap, his golden cock stuck between them, a black piercing nestled beneath the flared crown. The two black metal balls glinted at her, pressed perfectly into his skin so that she couldn't see anything of the bar that connected them.

"You didn't have that last year," she said, shocked.

"No," he said, stroking her face, brushing the hair from her neck. After a moment, his cock twitched and his hand wrapped around her neck, which he had been so gently caressing. "I swear to god, Carter, if my dick isn't inside you in the next—"

She quickly pulled up her hips, and he gripped the base of his shaft, lining it up with her entrance as she lowered onto him, both of them groaning in relief. He allowed her to set her own pace for a little while as his hands travelled her body, showing that he had learnt her well ... but then his self-control broke, and he tipped her onto her back. He pressed her legs up, weighing them against her chest as his velvety length dipped into her in deep, indulgent strokes, his pace quickening, growing almost brutal until he suddenly released her legs, ducking his head to her nipple and shoving her hand between her legs, encouraging her to touch herself. He bit and licked her breasts until she was flying, a hoarse cry on her lips, and then he followed her over, a low growl torn out of his chest.

Despite the fact that it had proven to clear his head and help their bond, Niko didn't try to approach her in a sexual manner again, and she was too nervous from his jumpy reactions to make the first move. The others seemed to be giving her space, though she was beginning to feel like a doe being tracked through the woods whenever Oscar turned his eyes on her.

He seemed to be biding his time, waiting for something, wary of something.

Thankfully, she was too absorbed in the task of finalising her dance to worry about Oscar's plans for her.

When it was finally time for Kalen and Mikel to score their choreography, she felt a little more prepared than she had for the singing task. She was perhaps over-prepared, this time, though it didn't lessen the pressure on her. The stakes were higher than they had been a few weeks ago, because now the public was invested.

Their first evaluation had aired, with the entire world praising each of them, though especially Theodore. The Ironside fans seemed to agree with Kalen and Mikel's picks, reasoning that while Moses, Oscar, and Niko all had great all-rounder voices with incredibly unique qualities, they didn't quite have the control or stability of Theodore, Cian, Kilian, or Isobel.

Isobel didn't know what to say to that, because she was sure they all had more control and stability than her.

Despite being content with everyone else's ranking, the fans were quickly and loudly outraged that Elijah and Gabriel were scored on their singing abilities despite clearly being rappers. They demanded Kalen and Mikel give them special roles as rappers, which of course, Kalen and Mikel immediately arranged. It seemed like a strategic move, showing the fans that they had control, that they could influence the show.

It made them feel like they were involved, that they had a stake in the game, that they were almost as much a part of the group as the members of Dorm A themselves.

Kalen and Mikel gave them no time to warm up for the second assessment, but that didn't bother Isobel. She had skipped lunch to run through her routine one more time while Oscar and Moses fought over the takeaway containers of food they had brought over from the dining hall.

The order of the performances remained the same as their last assessment, with Kilian first, then Cian, Elijah, Gabriel, Niko, Oscar, Moses, Theodore, and Isobel.

The natural dancers in the group became quickly apparent. Elijah, Gabriel, and Kilian danced like it was what they were born to do, every movement in perfect synchronisation with the music, their motions smooth, strong, and powerful. Cian, Oscar, and Moses were less natural. They still managed to create commanding and beautiful choreography, but where the others make it look easy, Cian, Oscar, and Moses put visible effort into their movements. If they had been competing with *anyone* else, they would have looked perfect.

But they weren't competing with just anyone.

Niko's ability was surprising. He just stood there for the first few bars, until he seemed to remember the song—this time, it was layered with Theodore's vocals from their first assessment. After he recognised it, he began to move, his sequences fluid, expressive, seamless, and graceful. For someone who clearly hadn't prepared a second of choreography, he barely even needed to think about it. There was a sense of continuity in his choreography, in the subtle nuances and gestures of his body, giving everything a depth and a dialogue that had her leaning forward to examine him closer.

His expressions were subtle, his movements poignant, somehow sultry and smooth while also giving a haunting sense of emotion. He was easily as good as Elijah, who she had decided was the best dancer there ...

Until Theodore.

Theodore *Fucking* Kane stepped up with a carefree grin, tugging at his loose pants as he waited for the music to start, and then he blew her mind all over again. His movements were *sharp*, remarkably quick and precise, executed with a precision that had taken her years of practise to finesse.

And she had *never* seen him practise.

Him *or* Niko.

Theodore's footwork was intricate, but he made it look easier than walking. He had a very clear natural athleticism—just like Niko—infusing strength into his flow, but he was showing more than just his skill. He was proving that he was an *entertainer*.

He didn't analyse his moves in the mirror like he was at practice, as the others had. He stared at the mirror like it was his audience, his natural charisma falling over his body like a cloak. He was the only one who matched the obviously sensual lyrics of the track with a performance that had her cheeks heating. The others had danced like it was an assignment, and Theodore danced like it was a show.

And it worked.

She glared at him when he moved off the stage, and he broke into a devilish grin, swiping his hand through his hair as he tugged at his sweaty shirt.

It was so *boyish*. So utterly opposite to the raw magnetism he had just been channelling into the mirror.

Why didn't you tell me you could dance like that? she asked inside his head.

We can all dance, silly. You knew that.

He was completely missing the point, but as she took up her position and watched the Alphas clapping him on the back, she realised that maybe ... he didn't *understand* the point. He seemed to sing and dance for fun. Perhaps he truly didn't realise how incredible he was.

She surveyed the Alphas as the track started again, realising the scope of what she was dealing with. They were highly trained, highly focussed—with the exception of Niko, currently—and *exceedingly* skilled. Even without Theodore, they had a very good chance of succeeding at the game they were playing against the Ironside officials ... but *with* Theodore, they were a sure thing.

Still ...

There was always room for improvement, even for these men.

She smiled, and a few brows arched in response.

Except Mikel. His lips stretched out in that crooked smile like he knew exactly what she was thinking.

The track had been playing for almost ten seconds, and she still hadn't moved. She had missed her mark for the choreography she had slaved over for two weeks, but that was okay. She had designed the choreography to make it accessible so that everyone would be able to do it. She now realised she had been wrong, and this wasn't about trying to make the group work. The group already worked.

This was about making the group impossibly *better*.

She began to dance without warning, ditching the style she had practised and diving into her own style, which was a blend of acrobatic strength and lyrical, contemporary moves. The slim window between strength and beauty was where she *thrived*. It allowed her to be fearless and to still show vulnerability and delicacy. She wasn't just a dancer because she loved it. She was a dancer because it was all she had ever loved. Before coming to Ironside, dance was the only friend she had. Dance and her mother. And then, for a while, it was dance *without* her mother.

She had danced her entire life. To forget the pain her father caused, and to escape her small, lonely world. When she danced, she wasn't a vessel for everyone's emotions, or a puppet for their manipulations, or a face on a banner, hung in the settlements like an advertisement for the sale of her soul. She was a bird freed from a cage, falling and flying by her own design, creating a story with her body, her face, her eyes, her hands.

She could manipulate *them*. Whoever they were.

It didn't matter who they were. Because when she was moving like this, she was in control, she was in charge, and they would sit and wait and watch until she had poured out everything inside her and they felt every inch the vessel they had made her feel.

She danced to the very edge of her ability, forcing her body to appear light as a feather, untouchable by gravity, by them, by her past, by whoever tried to grope away at her future.

And then she finished, and they clapped.

It took her a few moments to realise it wasn't polite clapping.

They were cheering, whistling, and yelling things out, causing a smile to break out over her face.

She did it.

She *fucking* did it.

After Kalen announced that Isobel would be taking the lead dancer position, with Theodore, Niko, and Elijah as the main dance group, it was all on her to choreograph the entire group performance for Elijah's birthday.

She had a fairly good idea of their skill levels, and it

helped when Theodore and Niko joined their dance practises in the early mornings and late evenings. As pissed as she had been that they hadn't told her how well they could dance, she did understand why they had hidden it from the show.

It would be a fantastic reveal, especially for anyone doubting what kind of performance their group would be able to pull off. But still ... she was nervous about their screen time. Since she had been banned from the Ironside Row games every Friday and the Alphas refused to go without her, they were falling behind in popularity points while the humans raked in awards from the games and challenges.

Gabriel was trying to combat it by having someone go live from their bedroom every night. It was something they didn't have time for, but they didn't have a choice. When it was Isobel's turn, she was already running late for her performance at the Stone Dahlia, so she set her phone onto a stand in her bathroom and spoke to her fans while she got ready.

At first, it was awkward. *What was she supposed to say?* But the comments weren't being pushy, rude, or invasive. They joked, they chatted, they *played*, drawing out the mischief that lingered somewhere inside her.

When she tied up her hair, they commented that her new tattoos must represent one heart for every psychopath who had come forward in the media claiming to be her mate, making her laugh out loud.

When she tossed back that they got their wish after all, with a mating mark on her body, but they would have to share with nine other psychopaths, the comment section filled with laughter.

She squinted at the screen when she noticed a familiar username.

LilySquirt: Hi! Carter! It's me!!

She grinned, notching her elbow onto the countertop and leaning into the camera with a soft smile. "Hi, Lily."

Lily's response was almost lost in the flood of comments.

Sato_Stans: Who is Lily???

IronsideInsider: There's 27,000 people watching, how are we supposed to find Lily?!

The-moses-mafia: I now identify as Lily.

TheRealLily: Hi, it's me.

Lily92: Me too.

Lily-Confirmed243: It's meeee.

LilySquirt: Hehehe.

Isobel grinned, pulling away from the camera as the comments rolled on.

SHE WORKED ON THE GROUP CHOREOGRAPHY FOR THREE DAYS and then introduced it to everyone during their unfilmed intensive with Mikel in the morning, while Theodore introduced them to their individual singing and rapping parts. He had recorded base tracks for all of them, proving, infuriatingly, that he could also rap the sequences Elijah and Gabriel had come up with.

It was a long and gruelling day of trying to learn all of their parts, but they paused their intense schedules that night to celebrate Elijah's birthday, sprawling around the lounge room to have a movie night. It was the first normal moment they had enjoyed in a little while.

Isobel cuddled up with Kilian, who was having a hard time keeping his hands to himself, now that their relationship had changed. Eventually, he huffed out a frustrated sound and slid onto the floor by her legs, pretending like he just wanted to stretch out flat with Moses.

"The weaker surrogate not cutting it?" Oscar asked, sounding bored. He got up and crossed over the bodies strewn across the floor to plop down beside Isobel. He pulled her over his thighs and tugged a fluffy blanket around them, his hand wrapping up her ponytail, using it as a handle to pull her head back and to the side so that he could meet her eyes.

"Better?" he grunted.

He had that look in his eyes again.

A prickle of something predatory, shadowing behind a wall of control as he waited, and waited.

Silently, she nodded, and he released her, sinking back and leaning over the suede arm of the couch to get comfortable, his hips tilting up into her ass as he adjusted himself.

His hand traced up and down her spine as they finished their final movie, and she could still smell his smoking oleander all over her skin when she climbed into bed that night. Her heart was in her throat as she looped the cameras and padded to his room, raising her fist to knock on his door ... before lowering it again.

Anxiety swirled inside her stomach.

Approaching Oscar was like approaching a damaged Niko.

She turned on her heel and hurried back to her room, diving onto her bed and resisting the urge to hide under her covers, choosing to drag her tablet into her lap, instead. She snapped up her electronic pencil and tapped into a sketching program, wondering what kind of flowers she could draw Elijah for his birthday.

Finally, she began with a bunch of pristine white roses, the petals shimmering like freshly fallen snow in bright moonlight. She wove delicate little sprigs through the thorny stems in a lattice of tiny, suspended snowflakes, and then threaded through the stems of pale blue hydrangeas. The petals of the hydrangeas were a delicate cluster of points, like ice crystals forming on a winter's day. To finish off the bouquet, she added in a lush backdrop of pale green eucalyptus stems, the edges of the flat leaves crystallised with a frosted silver.

When it was done, she began to send it to Elijah

before pausing and sucking in a fortifying breath. She had already been a coward once that night.

She slipped out of bed and stopped at the room next to her own, raising her fist to knock.

You can do it, she lectured herself. It's just—

Elijah yanked open the door, his cool eyes settling on her face. "Came to wish me happy birthday, Isobel?"

She nodded, and he stepped aside, checking his watch as she stepped into his room.

Noticing that she had looped the cameras.

He closed the door and leaned up against it, crossing his arms. "I doubt I'm the reason the cameras are on a loop right now, but his loss is my gain."

She laughed nervously. "Why are you acting like I just walked into your trap or something?"

His eyes flashed, and he pushed off the door, plucking the tablet out of her hands. "What's th—" He paused as the screen came to life, showing him the picture with the name she had scrawled at the top.

Elijah.

He raised his eyes slowly. "You drew this for me?"

She nodded. "Happy birthday."

His smile was slow and sharp, his voice a soft drawl. "Happy birthday indeed."

His attention dropped back to her tablet as he sent the drawing to his phone, and then he was walking to his bed, setting the tablet on his bedside table. He tilted his head, cool eyes dropping to her sleep shirt.

“Staying or leaving?”

She hesitated, eyeing him the same way he was eyeing her. “To sleep?”

He chuckled, sitting on his bed. He pulled off his shirt, tossing it to an armchair on the other side of his bedside table. “Just to sleep,” he said, unzipping his pants. He lifted his hips, tugged them off, and discarded them to the armchair before sliding back and stretching out on his bed. His tight muscles bunched, his black boxers almost indecently low on his hips as he let out an exhausted groan, his arms folding behind his head.

He looked deliciously dishevelled all of a sudden, and she approached the bed nervously, sitting lightly on the edge of the mattress.

“Lie down,” he crooned, a teasing note in his voice.

She stretched out beside him, her body stiff, her hands folded onto her stomach. He twisted onto his side, and she could feel his gaze on her face, a rumbling laugh threatening the air between them.

“Face me,” he ordered, still in that same soft, teasing tone.

She rolled to her side, freezing when it brought their noses inches apart. He leaned over her, the pale gold skin of his chest in her face as he grabbed his dorm tablet, turning off the lights.

When he settled again, he seemed closer, his breath misting her lips.

"Now wish me a proper happy birthday," he whispered, gravel in his tone.

Her core pulsed at the rough demand, her thighs pressing tightly together, but her mind spun into a panic. The idea of becoming intimate with Elijah truly terrified her, for some reason.

She just had a feeling that he would break her.

Worse than Kalen, worse than Mikel.

Elijah would shatter her into a million pieces and then grind those shards into the ground with the heel of his boot. While he laughed.

"Just a kiss, sweet girl," he whispered over her mouth. "I won't be breaking you tonight."

She immediately checked her mental wall. It was still in place. He hadn't read her mind.

Her exhale was a shaky breath, her mind calming.

A kiss she could do.

A kiss was more than she could have hoped Elijah would want from her, in truth. She lifted a hand to his face, softly tracing his sharp, aristocratic cheekbone, his strong nose, his winged brow ... his hard lips.

Her breathing sped up, his clove and woodsmoke scent warming and thickening until she was dizzy from it. She pressed her lips to his, kissing him softly. They both breathed in deeply, his chest rattling as she pushed closer, kissing him again, his top lip and then his bottom lip, which she pulled into her mouth, tugging lightly.

He gripped her wrist calmly, pulling it from his face and twisting it behind her back, using that hold to drag her lower body into his. He forced his thigh between hers, notching it right up against her core, and then he took over the kiss, dominating her mouth in slow, drugging strokes of his tongue. He gripped her wrist harder, pressing where he held it against her lower back to force her hips down on his thigh. He sawed his thigh between her legs subtly, only the smallest movement as his kiss slowly hypnotised her. Back and forth, teasing her damp and throbbing flesh through her sleep shorts.

It surprised her to feel the tension building up inside her body, coiling her tighter and tighter, making her desperate for what promised to be a hard and drugging climax. She had never orgasmed from a *kiss* before.

"Just a kiss," Elijah whispered against her swollen lips, making it seem like he was reading her mind again, "because when I fuck you, it'll be because you're crawling on your knees and *begging* to be dismantled, head to toe." He pressed his thigh up tighter to her core, nipping her lips. "Ruined." He released her wrist and suddenly spun her to face the other way, his hand pushing into her shorts, his erection curving hard and hot against her spine. He shoved two fingers inside her, sending her hurtling over the edge she was hovering over.

"Shattered," he whispered, nuzzling into the back of

her neck, his cock grinding against her through their clothing.

When she blinked herself back to sanity, it was with a soft, surprised cry.

"Go to sleep," Elijah instructed her, his fingers still hooked deep inside her.

"A-are you ..." She closed her eyes, pulling in a shuddering breath as she tightened around his fingers, the aftershocks of her orgasm still rippling through her. "Are you going to k-keep them in there?"

"Yes." The word was a gravelled purr that travelled all the way through her body, making her ripple and clench around him again.

She thought there was no way she could possibly sleep like that, but when Elijah began to nuzzle her neck again, planting soft, soothing kisses along the line of her bond marks, she found her eyelids growing heavy, her breath beginning to match the measured, deep rise and fall of his chest.

It seemed that so many students and crew had piled onto Alpha Terrace that they simply wouldn't fit. They were spilling out onto the driveway and landing above, gathering wherever they could find room. Cooper had decided that the theme of the first Dorm A party for the year would be "the last day of summer," so everyone had turned up in swimwear and coverups, flip-flops, sunglasses, and large, floppy hats. The sun was beginning to set, so some of the hats and sunglasses were coming off, and people were pulling their legs out of the pool.

Cian and Kilian had worked on the outfits they wanted everyone to wear for the first performance, ordering clothes from Market Street during the week. The guys were all wearing tight black jeans and black combat boots, which they had already shown they would be able to dance in during their last practice. They had on black shirts and puffy jackets with a camouflage pattern. Isobel also wore combat boots, her high-waisted parachute pants in a matching camouflage print. Her tight white tank was cinched by a black chest harness, her hair in two long braids over her shoulders.

The military theme was deliberate, of course.

In a way, this was their first official declaration of war, their first true, public act of rebellion.

Mikel and Kalen stepped up to the stage first, and the crowd, who had been busy partying around the pool and the gardens, gradually fell silent.

"Good evening, everyone." Kalen held a microphone, his calm attention scanning the gathered people. "As you all saw on the *Ironside Show*, we've been putting our Dorm A Alphas and Sigma through a series of tasks, challenging them to bring you a special performance tonight, and I believe we have succeeded in that goal, though, of course ... their success is dependent on you, so I'll let you decide." He passed the microphone to Mikel, whose deep voice projected over the crowd.

"This song is called Trance. It was written by Moses Kane and Oscar Sato, and was produced by Kalen West and myself. Please welcome to the stage: Eleven."

Isobel felt her stomach flip as they stepped onto the stage that had been constructed along the back of Alpha Terrace, ignoring the whispers threading through the crowd below. They all had headset microphones strapped to their heads to free up their arms, so none of them spoke as they positioned themselves on the stage, waiting for the music to begin.

The crowd was deadly silent, but the heavy pressure of their silence was shattered by Elijah's slight chuckle before he kicked off the start of the song, his rapid delivery of the first verse electrifying the air immediately. The backing track had evolved over the past few weeks. It began with a grungy tone, gradually becoming loud, boisterous, and commanding, Elijah's raspy, fast-paced lines stirring everyone to attention.

Theodore took over the melody, and they fell into their dance routine. Their movements precisely synchronised—it was the one thing Isobel had pushed them for, above all else. She wanted them flawlessly in line, in flow together, despite their varying level of skill.

For the pre-chorus, Cian and Kilian layered their voices over Theodore's, bringing a haunting and sultry—but somehow still energetic—tone to the lyrics that Moses and Oscar had written. It was a sensual song, even with Elijah's twisting of the lyrics in the first verse, and Gabriel's manipulation of them in the bridge. The words they had written were still full of longing, mysterious and eerie at times, persistent and vigorous at other times, the entire song enforced with a stubborn, almost angry backbone that endured through every verse.

Isobel took the chorus, Oscar and Moses texturizing her voice with their lower tones as the routine gained energy, becoming more complex as they switched up their formations, falling back or twisting forward to highlight different members. Theodore and Isobel stayed mostly at the front, as Mikel had decided they had the most endurance to support the rest of the group. They were both able to maintain a steadier control over their voices while they danced through the more complex parts of the choreography, but without the unique timbres, tones, and vocal styles of the other Alphas, it wouldn't have been as special as it was.

And she knew, as they took a bow, dusted in sweat and panting into the microphones, that it had been special.

She knew, as they stumbled off the stage and the noise from the gathered crowd swelled and rumbled loud enough to make it feel like the ground was shaking, that they had *done* something.

As they tried to push through the mob of people who were clamouring over each other to get close to the Alphas, Isobel saw that even the crew members who had gathered to record the performance seemed shocked. They were huddled together, protecting their equipment, talking in panicked tones like they didn't know what to do. As soon as they caught sight of the Alphas and Isobel pushing toward the dorm, they started shouting their names and trying to make their way over.

Once they were inside the dorm, they stood around, shocked by the noise outside, before gradually breaking into nervous, exhausted smiles.

"I swear to all the meanest Gifted gods," Isobel warned, glancing between their faces, "if you all do another polite clap right now, I'm going to—"

Niko laughed, cutting her off and drawing a few surprised glances. He seemed ... more at ease. Spent, in the best way. He had given it everything, channelling his confusion and torment into energy and that was something she could understand. She grinned at him, and for a moment more, his beautiful hazel eyes were clear as he smiled back.

"Time to review the performance," Kalen said, arching a brow at them. "Or do you think you've made it now?"

Oscar rolled his eyes. "Can we eat first?"

"I'll order food and drinks from the dining hall," Mikel offered. "It's too chaotic to go outside. Everyone shower and meet up in the lounge."

As Isobel skipped up the stairs, she noticed Cooper slipping into his office, his phone to his ear, speaking hurriedly.

It was nice to see him thrown for a loop.

22

DORM A DADDIES

ISOBEL HURRIED THROUGH A SHOWER AND TOSSED ON A LOOSE, cropped shirt with a dark green camouflage pattern—in keeping with the theme of their performance—to pair with her high-waisted, stretchy exercise shorts. She downed a bottle of water, her body still trying to produce sweat even after a cold shower, and met everyone else in the lounge.

Kalen and Mikel had dragged a dining table to sit behind the couch opposite the TV, and it was filled to overflowing with junk food.

"Just this once," Mikel lectured the Alphas descending on the table, though Isobel knew he didn't police their eating too badly.

He sent them meal plans—and her, too, since the start of the term—and checked in once a week to see if they needed adjusting. But he wasn't overbearing about it.

Isobel picked up a container of fries drowning in melted cheese and salty seasoning, tucked a can of Coke under her arm, and settled on the floor. The Alphas always gave her a spot on the couch; it was beginning to feel unfair. Theodore, Moses, and Oscar sat behind her, and she leaned back against Moses and Theodore's legs as Kilian fell to one side of her and Gabriel dropped to the other.

Gabriel had found the only salad on the table, it seemed, but he had paired it with a bottle of sparkling water so maybe he was celebrating after all.

Mikel had managed to transfer the footage he had captured over to the TV screen already, and he began to play it without preamble, handing the remote to Elijah.

Isobel tried to analyse the dancing. She really did. But she kept getting distracted by the sheer athletic magnetism of the Alphas on the stage. The way they jumped, kicked, even the way they *grinned* at the cameras. Their muscles twitched and bulged, their breaths coming harder and harder, sweat dusting their skin, their eyes intense.

She started fanning herself, her body growing hot.

Theodore squeezed her shoulder in sympathy, the talented, irresistible, *condescending asshole*.

"Oscar and Moses need to be tighter," Elijah said, pausing the footage. "Their movements aren't as sharp."

"Dude, we wrote the song," Moses complained. "What else do you want?" He didn't seem to be genuinely complaining, more like backtalking for the sake of it.

Elijah apparently agreed, because he played the video again without responding.

"Here." He paused once more, on a shot where Isobel and Theodore had moved to the front of the formation again, breaking from the dance to sing the high note of the song together. "Almost fucking perfect," Elijah praised. "But Theo is overpowering Isobel. You need to work on your projection." He flicked her a look, and she nodded quickly.

"I was too scared to give the note full power because sometimes I wobble."

"We'll keep working on it," he promised her, playing the recording again.

He paused as Moses pushed to the front, his tone taking on the growly edge that was so unique to him.

"Vocal transition was good," Elijah said, but he paused for a moment longer, considering something. "I have a suspicion quite a few people are about to turn that into a clip."

Isobel pulled out her phone as they reached their fifth play-through of the recording, deciding they had picked it apart enough for one night. She navigated to one of her social media apps, where pictures of the performance began to flood her screen. There were no videos yet, per the Ironside policy, but the pictures were enough to tell a story. She clicked into a thread that seemed to have almost eighty pictures in it and scrolled through the comments.

@DormADaddies: Did Elijah Reed just dance, or did he just fuck me through my TV screen?

@who_is_lily98: Before I saw Oscar Sato dance, I thought he might break my legs. Now I think he might break my back. PLEASE BREAK MY BACK.

@jessleeXYZ: Carter is mother.

@filmfrenzy: I'm having daddy issues, because I don't know who's daddy anymore. Is it Theodore or is it Moses?

@lonely-hart: I don't even have a uterus and I think Gabriel Spade just impregnated me.

@sjohno21: Isobel Carter can bite off my head and eat me like a praying mantis.

@TheRealLily: Theodore is KING.

@KaneClub32: That entire performance made me question my sexuality.

@IronsideIsAlpha: RE: @KaneClub32: That entire performance just became my sexuality.

@HartHQ: Niko really just said 'ha, tricked you' and pulled out a whole-ass persona out of his tennis bag.

@The_Reel_Ironside: How have they been hiding this much talent all this time???

@hollywoodhighlights: Carter's mate should just stay hidden. He has no chance.

As she was reading the comments, a group message flashed across the top of her phone.

Kalen: 30 minutes until we're due at the Dahlia.

She immediately got up to change, but Kalen shook his head, touching her arm and bending to mutter low by her ear. "Keep the top. I want that and matching panties."

Her stomach flipped, but he was walking away from her before she could respond. It was the first time he had ever interfered in her costume choices, and she had to wonder why.

Was it because their patrons would have seen the photos by the time he led her onto that platform, or was it possible ...

She shook her head, colour flooding her face.

No, that wasn't right.

Kalen wouldn't have gotten excited watching her the same way she had gotten excited watching the other Alphas. Kalen didn't *get* excited.

Still ... the thought plagued her as they walked to the boathouse, and remained even as Kalen began to twist the ropes around her limbs, but he didn't touch her more than usual. He didn't grab her harder, and his eyes didn't burn any hotter. If anything, he seemed to have grown *more* in control of himself with every passing week, while she was the one always unravelling, wishing he would touch her more, desperate for him to ease the ache building between her legs as he carried her into his dressing room after the performance.

It was her favourite part, being cuddled into his lap, his fingers soothing through her hair and massaging her legs.

But it was torture.

Since the night with Mikel, he hadn't stepped over that boundary again, content to slowly but surely drive her insane.

"Can we go and watch one of the fights?" she asked, as she quickly pulled off the camouflage top—now wrinkled and wet with tears, because sometimes she cried, either from the release after being let down from the ropes, or with desperation for Kalen to touch her. She couldn't quite remember which it had been tonight. It was a bit of a blur. She shrugged a silk dress over her head and stepped into the silver heels she had worn on the way in.

"I suppose I can't keep saying no." Kalen seemed uneasy as he gathered his things. "My sponsorship of you is about to end. If anyone wants to request a private meeting with you, I'd prefer they do it while I can still insist on being in the room." He checked his phone. "Oscar's fight is just about to start. We might make it."

He led her out of the room, but they had barely even passed into the next hall before three suited men stepped into their path. They wore headsets and had human eyes.

"A guest has requested to meet Isobel Carter," one of them said.

Well ... that was quick.

Kalen sighed, rubbing his jaw. "Fine. Lead the way."

They followed the three men through the hall and down a passageway—the same passageway Eve had been led down a few weeks ago. They paused before a door, one of them stepping closer to her and Kalen.

"She will go in without you," the man said, holding out a hand to press against Kalen's chest, even though Kalen towered over him and looked like he could scoop him up into a bear hug and crush his bones.

But Kalen wasn't human.

He was powerless.

Pissed, but powerless.

"I'm her sponsor," Kalen began to growl, but the human cut him off.

"These two officials have been chosen to chaperone her in place of her sponsor." He nodded at the men standing behind him. "Do we have a problem here, West?"

Kalen barged into her mind, knocking down her wall like it was made of LEGO and seating himself with a furious huff right in the centre of her mind, his words a snarl that swirled around her head.

You stay connected to me.

Okay, she returned.

"No problem at all." Kalen held up his hands, stepping back. "I'll wait right here."

They opened the door and ushered her inside, the two men immediately leaving through a door opposite the one they had come through, leaving Isobel alone ...

With her father.

"You could have just called another twelve times," she drawled, fighting down panic.

It's my father, she said to Kalen.

Call out if you need my help, he demanded.

"Very fucking funny," Braun Carter snapped. He was furious, clutching the back of a fabric armchair like he might be able to tear into the velvety material and play with its innards in lieu of whatever violent urge he was feeling towards her.

"I guess you heard about the show?" she asked, examining her fingernails. "I told you I had it under control."

"*Stupid* girl!" He picked up the chair and slammed it back down on the ground again.

Kalen's insistent presence inside her mind grew alarmed, and she sent him a distracted plea to let her deal with Braun.

"You don't challenge the officials," her father snarled. "You don't declare *war* against the entire fucking network. This isn't just a stupid little reality show you fucking idiot. This is *Ironside*. This is *capitalism*. This is the economy of the world's superpower, and you are an *asset*. If you prove to be a sunk cost, they will *sell you off* before you can do them any damage."

"But I'm not a sunk cost, am I?" she asked calmly, examining the red flush of rage creeping over him, and the poisonous swell of his emotion crashing up against her chest like a storm battering the walls of a lighthouse with incessant, heavy waves.

How did he live like that?

Her father was no longer the standard against which she judged all Alphas. He was now the outsider, and for the first time in her life, she truly wondered what was wrong with him.

He continued to breathe heavily, clutching the chair like he might toss it against the wall next, waiting for her to explain herself.

"I'm pretty sure I just made Ironside history." She shrugged. "Or at least I will by the time they air that episode—which they will have to air because we've filmed it. If they don't air it, we will."

Braun shook his head, some of the rage easing out of his complexion. Maybe it was hearing her talk as though she were truly invested in winning, for once.

"You don't understand, Isobel. They'll break you down one way or another. You need to play their game *their* way, or they will end you."

"I really don't," she said, wondering if they had tried to break him. *Was that why he was so certain?* "Why do you care?" she added. "Why not just see me as a sunk cost and sell me off? Why do you keep interfering?"

"Is that what you want?" He released the chair, a strange, eerie sort of calm taking hold of his face and body. "You want to forget where you came from? Forget everything I've done for you? Everything I've sacrificed?"

He approached her, and she promised herself she would stand firm, but she still flinched when he raised his hand to rest on the top of her head.

"You're my daughter," he said. "That's why I care."

And then she felt it.

She felt him *push into her mind.*

It wasn't the same as when Bellamy tried to speak inside her head, or when Kalen barged into her consciousness, or when one of the guys pulled everyone into her mind to address the whole group, like it was a big echoey room with lots of doors.

When her father entered, it was with a ghostly hand that plucked and picked and sorted through the images inside her memory. He gathered up a little moment where Kilian had held her hand, and Braun's ghostly grip closed around the image, squeezing until it was ash, filtered through his shadowed fingers, and she couldn't quite remember what the moment was.

He plucked another, and she was simply too stunned to react, her body frozen with confusion and shock as a memory of Theodore's stunning smile nestled into Braun's ghostly palm and once again, was crushed. She watched the ashes float away and wondered why she had felt sadness a moment ago.

She couldn't remember.

And then she realised what he was doing, her body kicking into motion, her hands darting up to tear his grip from her head.

"Don't move," he growled in Alpha voice. "If you won't do the sensible thing, then I'll make you forget them, just like I made your mother forget you."

Just like I made your mother forget you.

That was why her mother hadn't come to visit.

Because her father had an Alpha ability after all, and it wasn't ferality.

The overwhelming fury inside her exploded outward, burning hot in her blood and making her hands twitch, her grip on his wrist tighten.

"Don't move," he snapped again, his Alpha voice compounding the need to *obey* inside her.

But he didn't feel so strong as he once did.

And she was too angry to obey.

She dug her nails into his skin, tunnelling them deep and scouring his arm as he jerked his hand away with a feral hiss.

"I said don't—"

"I don't give a fuck what you said," she yelled at him. "Touch me again and it'll be the last time you see me."

He seemed too shocked to speak, the anger still vibrating through his body.

“Are you even my real father?” she demanded. “Or was my mother’s *true* mate my father? I don’t see how I could possibly come from you. There’s something putrid inside you, just rotting you away. I don’t understand how *that* can give birth to life.”

He fell back a step, shock arresting his features. “It can’t,” he said. “But you were ... before.” He swallowed. “You happened before I got sick.”

Suddenly, all of his anger was gone, and it was like he was seeing a ghost. Blood dripped down his arm, and he didn’t even seem to notice. He stared straight through her.

“You don’t know what it feels like.” He moved back a few steps like he needed to get away from her. “I lost her.”

“You killed her,” Isobel countered, her tone uncertain. She wasn’t familiar with this empty, broken man.

It was like she had unlocked a part of him that he never visited, a part he was just as unfamiliar with as she was.

“Not your mother.” He waved her off. “My mate.”

Isobel swallowed tightly. “What?”

He sighed, and she could see him leaning into his anger again. He was about to dive back into the fury and violence to escape their conversation and whatever he was feeling, so she tacked on quickly, “Tell me about her.”

He slumped into the same chair he had almost torn apart a few minutes ago, wiping a hand down his face.

"You think I'm bad?" He laughed hollowly. "My father used to put out his cigarette butts on my legs. He used to mix cough syrups, mouthwash, cleaning products—anything he could get his hands on—into his coffee just to chase a high. He *taught* us this rage I feel, me and my brother. He beat it into us. But ..."

"But your brother was worse," Isobel realised out loud.

He had a demon.

"Caran was in love with *me*." Braun's voice was rough and uneven. "She waited for me while I was at Ironside, but she got sick before I graduated and guess who was by her fucking side?"

Isobel didn't know what to say. Quietly, she fell into the seat opposite him, staring at the stranger who had become her father. He stumbled over his words like he had never said them out loud before.

"My brother was her mate," he said. "But she still loved me. When she got pregnant ... well ... she was too scared to tell him the truth. He would ... he had a fucking *demon* inside him. It would make his eyes black, make him attack anyone near him. He almost killed me a few times, almost killed her once. She had to keep him calm all the time. Then one night—you were only a few years old—he found out. He commanded her to tell him, and she did. She told him you were mine, and he lost control."

His eyes clouded over, becoming unfocussed, his face creasing in pain. "I've tried to remove the memories, but I can't. It won't work on my own head." He stared down at his hands. "I was supposed to be meeting them in the house I was building for them with my Ironside stipend. I had just graduated three days before, and I wanted to make sure you and her were taken care of while I was gone. I was going to cut ties. With her, you, him, my father.

"I couldn't take the pain anymore. But that night, when I walked through the door, he was raging, ripping the whole place apart, threatening to kill everyone, and I could see his eyes were turning black. I pulled you and Caran into a room and locked the door, and the neighbour ..." His breath shuddered. "She ... came to investigate all the noise."

His hands curled into fists in his lap, the slow, poisonous rage beginning to filter back into his body like smoke, curling up against her chest with a familiar, haunting pressure. "He killed her," Braun stated plainly. "He ripped her to pieces and then tried to toss her body through the floor in the back room that was still under construction, but he tripped and hit his head. Caran locked you in my car and dragged me out of the house. There was something desperate inside me that demanded I go back into the house ... I didn't understand it. Caran was screaming at me, you were crying and trying to get out of the car ... I just ... I ignored my instincts. We found the officials and woke up the family who ran the settlement clinic. And then we hid you and Caran in the back of my car, and I drove you both out of the settlement."

He cracked his knuckles, agony etched into his face. "When I got to my hotel, I saw it. My eye had changed." He looked up at her, with two eyes very much the same honey-gold shade. "I watched in the mirror as the dark brown faded back to this, and the darkness has been with me ever since." He touched his chest. "She was my mate. She was right there. I didn't even get to *see* her before he tore her apart. She needed me and Caran pulled me away. All because you *are* my daughter." His eyes narrowed, examining the look of horror on her face. "You don't have the darkness, do you, Isobel? You don't know this poison, which means your mate isn't fucking missing at all. You know exactly who they are."

"I don't," she croaked.

She could never forget the sensation of the ground opening up beneath her like a set of wide, sharp maws, sucking her into a chasm of pain and sorrow for her to fall through, and fall through, without even the kindness of death waiting below.

Her father had been falling for a long time.

"Is it one of the Alphas?" he asked her, and she

thought this might be the calmest, most adult conversation she had ever had with him.

"No," she lied. "I don't know who it is."

"I won't try to tear you away from them." He gritted his teeth, that echo of pain racing across his eyes again. "Not if one of them is your mate, but I need to know why you're hiding it."

"You lost the right to know anything about me." She stood to leave but found herself filled with grief and regret as she looked back at him, realising that this tortured, warped man ... could have been Niko.

And maybe still could be.

"I'm sorry you have to live with that darkness inside you," she said, "but you don't get to use it as an excuse anymore, not to yourself or anyone else. I meant what I said earlier. If you lay your hands on me or my mind again, I'll make sure you die bitter and alone, tumbling down that dark, dark hole with nobody at your side and not even the barest flicker of light to ease the endless torment inside you."

"And if I don't?" he asked stiffly, as though the words were an admission of guilt and it pained him to utter them. "If I don't ever lay a hand on you again?"

"Then you might finally realise you have a daughter," she said. "And you've had her all along. Someone who wasn't paid to be by your side. Someone who didn't need to stay with you to survive. Someone who would have loved you purely and unselfishly if you hadn't hurt her and scared her and bullied her. You might find that you were never truly alone in the darkness."

He didn't answer her, his jaw tight, his agony and anger swirling into a spiral that threatened to sweep her up ... except ... he pulled it back. He struggled, unsure how to control himself, wincing as his torment sank back into his skin, likely sitting with the same sickening heaviness with which it always sat inside her.

He stared at her for a long time, before finally looking down at the floor. "Who are you?" he asked, unable to meet her eyes. "Three years ago, I dropped off a scared little girl, but I don't see her anymore. I don't know who you are."

"I'm a little bit of you," she admitted, drawing his familiar eyes back up. There were tears in them that stubbornly refused to fall. "And a little bit of her. But mostly, I'm still just that scared little girl."

"I think you could win this game, Isobel." It wasn't a forceful statement. It was an almost curious observation. "With or without my help."

"I *will* win this game," she told him. "With or without your help."

To be continued ...

BONUS SCENE
THE WHISTLEBLOWER

ANNALISE TEAK STEPPED INTO THE CONFERENCE ROOM, clicking the door softly closed behind her. Everyone else had already gathered, and when Callum saw her enter, he motioned for everyone to be quiet. She hurried to an empty chair, nodding quietly at Tilda, the creative director.

Callum cleared his throat and pressed a button, bringing up an image on the projector screen. It was a paused frame of a surveillance video. A room somewhere in the Stone Dahlia, if the rough stone wall was anything to go by, though the strange threaded necklaces nailed to the stone didn't really suit the decor of the Dahlia.

This was bad.

If she had been called, then it was about Carter ... and if Callum Rowe was there, heading the table no less, then ... perhaps Carter's mate had finally been found.

Found by the *officials*. Carter obviously already knew who it was.

Olivia Frisk—Callum's executive assistant—was also there, as well as Ed Jones, Jack Ransom, and several other officials.

"As you all know," Callum began, his small eyes crawling across the table as a meaty hand fell onto the shoulder of the official beside him, "Yulia has been sponsoring several students into the Stone Dahlia under the new permanent program. She suspected that one of them might have information on Isobel Carter's mate, and ... well, you can see for yourselves."

He started the video, stepping back so they could all see the screen clearly, and Annalise watched as a girl was led into the room by a gold chain attached to a thick metal collar. Bile spilled across her tongue, but she kept her expression unbothered. Unlike Ed and Jack, who both visibly winced.

The presenters of the *Ironside Show* partook thoroughly of the benefits the Dahlia had to offer, but they didn't have a taste for the darker side of the club.

The girl was directed into a seat, and it took a few moments of frowning at the patches over her eyes for Annalise to realise who she was looking at.

Eve Indie.

"What happened to her eyes?" Jack asked, frowning at the projection.

"That's the reason she was brought in," Yulia

responded, as several masked men entered the room on the screen, carrying large, heavy bags with them. "When I found her in the hospital, she was high on painkillers and laughing about how mad she had made them. I had a feeling she was talking about Carter's mate, among other people, so I had her followed. But ... nobody approached her, so last night, I decided to bring her in for questioning."

"We're going to try this the easy way," a female voice crooned over the video. *Yulia*. She stepped into the frame, also wearing a mask. "Tell me who Isobel Carter's mate is."

The masked officials pulled Eve's arms behind her back, tying them together, and then they tied her ankles to the legs of the chair.

"I don't know," Eve said, her tone flat, like she was bored of answering the same question.

One of the officials grabbed her ponytail and yanked her head back, another one pinching her jaw into a tight and unyielding grip. A third pulled a sloshing bucket out of one of the bags they had dragged into the room, and Yulia bent over it, prying off the lid. She leaned in and extracted a heavy, sodden cloth, which she folded and laid over Eve's face.

Immediately, Eve's body jerked, the cloth concaving as her mouth opened and she tried to pull in a panicked breath. Yulia reached into another bag, uncapping a large bottle of water. She poured it over Eve's face, soaking the cloth further as the girl tried to desperately jerk and wiggle free. When the bottle was empty, Yulia peeled off the cloth, and Eve coughed and spluttered in broken, raspy sounds.

"Please," she begged. "I don't know. I don't—"

Yulia slapped the cloth back over her face, and the wet sounds of Eve frantically trying to suck in air through the cloth had Annalise's stomach souring, turning over and over.

She was going to be sick.

Yulia emptied another bottle of water, and this time, when she removed the cloth, Eve vomited all over herself. "All of them," she sobbed. "Carter ... bonded ... all of them."

"All of who?" Yulia asked, stepping closer.

"The Alphas," Eve coughed. "She has ten mates. All the ... all the Alphas in Dorm A."

Yulia surveyed the girl. "You're not very good at keeping secrets, are you, Miss Indie?"

"Please." Eve sobbed harder, water dribbling from her mouth. "P-please, I won't tell them you know. I won't warn them or anything—"

Yulia had put the cloth back over her face. "No," she said, picking up another bottle. "You won't."

Annalise let her eyes fall to a spot just below the projection screen, wishing she could also cover her ears as the sloshing, kicking, and grunting continued. She could still hear the rasped, water-logged sound of the cloth pulling into Indie's mouth.

Even when the video ended, she could still hear it.

She looked up, seeing the paused image of the girl's lifeless, slumped body, and her vision turned blurry. She hid her trembling hands beneath the table, looking up with unseeing eyes as Callum said her name.

"Is it possible?" he was asking.

Don't lie. They're testing you.

"Anything is possible when it comes to the mate bonds," she replied, the slightest tremor in her voice. "I've never seen or heard about a Tether latching on to so many Anchors, but no ... it's not impossible."

"As we suspected." Callum nodded. "We need to put a stop to this. If any one of them wins the *Ironside Show*, we're contractually obliged to give freedom to their mates. We would have to award eleven winners. It has to be stopped."

"They're proving too difficult to control," Tilda said with a frown. "They have enough support that if we don't give them screen time, they'll start posting their own videos and people will turn to them instead of the *Ironside Show*."

"That is precisely why we aren't going to attempt to control them," Callum responded. "No, that won't work. We're going to eliminate Dorm A and everyone inside it. A gas explosion—can it be done?" he asked Yulia.

"I'll need a month to make sure it's a clean job," she responded.

"A month it is." Callum nodded. "Make sure Theodore Kane isn't in the building when it happens. He brings in the most viewers, and it'll boost our audience scores if they get to watch him mourn his Ironside family. We won't let him win, of course. But let's keep him around for the numbers."

"Understood," Yulia said, pulling out her phone as she stood. "I'll get right to work."

"I'll need your expertise to keep Kane alive without his mate," Callum said to Annalise as the rest of the people around the table rose from their seats, shuffling toward the door. "Just until he graduates."

Annalise nodded. *Keep it together, just a few minutes more.* "Consider it done," she said.

"Good stuff." He clapped her on the back. A little too low on her spine for comfort. "Give my love to that mate of yours, hm? I hope you're both comfortable in the accommodations we provided?"

It sounded like a threat.

"Very comfortable, thank you."

"Excellent, excellent." His hand slid a little lower, brushing against her ass as she hurried to the doorway.

She avoided the other officials talking quietly just outside the conference room—just another day in the office, for them, discussing the *people* in their show like they weren't even living, breathing cognizant beings, but puppets in a play.

A very expensive play.

She walked quickly past Ed and Jack, who were ashen-faced and a little wobbly on their feet. They spent more time with the Gifted than any of the other officials. She hurried to her office, her breaths swelling fast and hard inside her chest.

She closed her door and sat down at her desk, her fingers trembling as she pulled out her phone. She wasn't supposed to have Carter's number. As far as the officials knew, she saw and spoke to Carter when she was ordered to, and she reported back on every word Carter said.

They didn't know Annalise had been lying to them.

They couldn't ever know.

She tapped on Isobel's number, and, heart-racing, typed a message.

Eve Indie is dead. She told the officials who your mates are. You need to announce your bond to the world before they kill you all. Announce the bond to the world, and it will be too suspicious if an accident takes you all out. Do it now. Delete this message. Do not respond.

She deleted the message as soon as she sent it, and dropped her phone to her desk, running shaky fingers through her hair.

All cards were on the table, now.

The *Ironside Show* was about to go up in flames, and she had lit the match, knowing full well that she might burn down with the rest of them.

I HOPE YOU ENJOYED RELEVER!

If you want to chat about this book or catch all the teasers for my next book, scan the code below to check out my reader's group!

If you enjoyed this book, please consider leaving a review. Indie authors rely on the support of our incredible readers, and without you guys, we wouldn't be able to continue publishing. Thank you for everything you do for the indie community!

Thank you!!
Jane xx

CONNECT WITH JANE WASHINGTON

Scan the code to view Jane's website, social media, release announcements and giveaways.

Made in the USA
Coppell, TX
18 September 2024

37455146R00329